SAFE AS HOUSES

Safe as Houses

a novel by
Alex Jeffers

ff

Faber and Faber
Boston · London

First published in the United States in 1995
by Faber and Faber, Inc., 50 Cross Street,
Winchester, MA 01890.

Copyright © 1995 by Alex Jeffers

Cataloging-in-Publication Data for this book
is available from the Library of Congress.

ISBN 0 571 19860 0

Jacket design by Adrian Morgan at Red Letter Design
Jacket photograph by Catherine Hopkins

Printed in the United States of America

to Ilene Stern Procida and Tino Procida and Hannah
to Dawn Brooks-Rapp and Mark Rapp and Carver

esto de jugar a la vida, es algo, que a veces duele
this playing at life, it's a thing that sometimes aches
—Enrique Ballesté

to the family:
Lee Jeffers
Lindsay and Myoung Ja Jeffers
Una and H-D Honscheid
Robin Jeffers
Aengus Jeffers

Providence, Carmel, Santa Cruz,
San Francisco, Boston
September 1987 . . . November 1993

Acknowledgments

MY THANKS to Meredith Steinbach, Edmund White, and the late George Stambolian; for rather different reasons, to Neal Kane, Nancy Faris, Richard Dickinson, James Lord, Mitchell Duneier; for reasons equally distinct, to David Greenside, Stéphane Jacobus and Kent Brenneck, Betty and Alden Harrington, Blair Griffith, Jackie Tai; as well, to Tim Carlson and to Betsy Cullen; for reasons he will know, to Reginald Shepherd; for many of the same reasons and some others, to my agent, Robert Drake, gentleman and gentle man, and to my editor, Betsy Uhrig, and the other good, thoughtful, stern people at Faber. Dyke Garrison may not fully realize either his importance to the work or my affection and regard. My debts to Ilene Stern Procida cannot adequately be pronounced.

A novel, a work of fiction, has no business professing a bibliography. Nevertheless, it seems dishonest not to acknowledge this novel's indebtedness to *The Other Side of Silence* by Arden Neisser (Knopf, 1983) and *When the Mind Hears* by Harlan Lane (Random House, 1984), among others.

But old Christmas smiled as he laid this cruel-seeming spell on the out-door world, for he meant to light up home with new brightness, to deepen all the richness of indoor colour, and give a keener edge of delight to the warm fragrance of food: he meant to prepare a sweet imprisonment that would strengthen the primitive fellowship of kindred, and make the sunshine of familiar human faces as welcome as the hidden daystar.

—GEORGE ELIOT: *The Mill on the Floss*

You live with someone for how many years—you make a life with him, a home, with his son too and your own nephew: it happens. They don't tell you the stories you wish to hear, nor the stories they wish to tell, but it all works out. By now, likely as not, he'll know more about my childhood and my parents than I do.

At night you dream, a story or a scrap of taped narration, in the morning transcribe your dreams; you're sick in bed, the delirium of a bad summer cold when the air in the bedroom feels as dense and as penetrable as your own flesh, or in the hospital with what your doctor bravely calls an episode—the clear astringent aerosol flavor of pure oxygen or the bile-in-the-back-of-the-throat taste of potent medications suffusing your wheezing lungs. . . . And you recall stories, relive memories —stories and memories not your own except by right of your claiming them. Because you weary of novels and the biographies of people you don't know—because you're not strong enough to hold a book in your hands or a paragraph in your mind—because if you don't know the principals of memory better than they do themselves, who will—and because if you don't why bother? Imagine that Jeremy kept a diary, why not, that your father indulged in memoir, or Toby and Kit appre-hended the histories of their own conceptions, gestations, and births: or that you did. How otherwise can you comprehend your own?

Ill, I feared my illness would become the central fact of my existence: the heavy gravity that pinned down event and particular. If your life were only your own you could survive the knowledge, could find a begin-ning and predict an end, envision a closed system, but a closed system had no entry or exit, nothing within or without, so that a beginning would be both arbitrary and imaginary, and an ending inconceivable. I knew I would die, not later but sooner. When nights ran through me like fever and mornings crested in a wake of sweat; when, peering into the mirror to shave, I felt the muscles of my face pull at skin like damp paper that would tear if I opened my mouth too wide or poked my tongue into the cheek with too much pressure; when, soaping my limbs in the

1

*shower, I saw the naked bones cobbled together with cartilage and found
my heart thumping in a nest of ribs and tried to draw breath into lungs
like saturated sponges that could contain no more; when, crouched over
to dry my feet, drawing the fabric of the towel between the toes, I seemed
to detect a scent like violets and saw the innocuous blue spots on the left
ankle that might have been tiny flowers tattooed into the white skin
above the bone, soft and blooming as the petals of a violet.*

*Dressed and alive, I drove Toby and Kit and myself to school—
leaving Jeremy at home, hard at work imagining childhoods neither
of us ever lived. I parked my car in the staff lot and told the boys to have
a good day; then, after they sauntered off to their first classes, waving,
I climbed to the office on the second floor of the administration building
where an engraved metal plaque mounted on the wall beside the door
revealed my identity to all who bothered to read it:* ALLEN K. PASZTORY,
DIRECTOR OF ADMISSIONS. *Looking up from the newspaper spread
across her desk, Annie glanced at the Dictaphone beside her keyboard as
if to indicate she'd get busy any minute now—not that I begrudged her
the morning nor would do anything much with it myself for an hour or
more. She told me I looked well and asked what was in store for the day.
In the inner office I loosened my tie, took off the suit jacket and hung
it up. Sitting at my own desk, I prized the plastic lid off a paper cup of
French roast from the coffee shop on Thayer Street where I stopped every
morning, and unwrapped a cranberry-orange muffin.*

*My desk faces the door. Before it stands a pair of upholstered side
chairs with a small table between them, the table holding a crystal bowl
filled with redolent potpourri. There are two more chairs against the
wall, beside the door. As in every administrative office in the school,
framed photographs of grounds and buildings ornament the walls. My
predecessor had also pinned up staged genre scenes of students at work
and play, but I preferred that my surroundings not look so much like
a page from the catalogue and took them down. In their stead I hung a
quartet of Jeremy's pen-and-ink drawings, portraits of houses he has
lived in. More recently, I came home one day and discovered Kit in the
backyard with a fistful of colored pencils, drawing a portrait of Toby with
the cat in his lap. My nephew is only precocious, not a prodigy,
so the perspective of the Adirondack chair on the lawn is slightly wonky,
the foreshortening of Toby's limbs faulty, but the cat's head, peering
over Toby's knee, bears the eerie, wide-eyed expression of Providence*

when she stares into an empty corner of the kitchen and sees a ghost, and Toby's face is meticulously, lovingly observed. Kit gave me the completed drawing with a nonchalant grace, as if he had planned the gift rather than being asked for it; I had the drawing matted and framed, and hung it where I could look up from my work and find it. The parents who visit my office never ask about it, and if ever they did I don't know what I would say.

When I moved into the office I was asked if I wanted a bigger desk. I said yes, knowing how much paper would pass through my hands, but in fact when I am evaluating application packages the desk isn't large enough and Annie and I use the table in her office. I placed the computer terminal and keyboard on the pull-out extension to the right and the Dictaphone in a drawer to the left, all plugged in so that I need only draw out the long cord of the microphone with its start/stop and rewind/fast-forward toggles on either side of the grille into which I recite. The telephone I couldn't hide or disguise, but it is the only permanent object on the main surface of the desk, aside from a grouping of photographs in Lucite frames on the opposite corner. Everyone whose employer provides a desk has one of these iconic displays. Office supply stores sell frames for just this purpose, and each executive's desk in the furniture section of the store will have a three-fold frame on one corner with pictures provided by the manufacturer's marketing department: my lovely wife, my attractive children, my golden retriever, my new house in the suburbs, my vacation in the Caribbean. . . .

- Janos and Marit: my loving parents
- Jeremy: my indulgent lover
- Toby: his clever son
- Kit: my sweet nephew

Your life is never only your own story, and what you don't know for sure you must invent, using all the clues you can gather. Although the workstation in my office can be networked into the school's systems, it's a stand-alone machine, compatible with the computer we have at home. When I find myself with nothing else to do—an occupational hazard at certain times of the year—I'll boot up the system, and then insert the disk I carry in my briefcase, never leaving it around where Jeremy or the boys might pick it up, and then I scan the directory. Abbreviated by necessity and design, each cryptic entry conceals a document that is, in itself, an abbreviation, an approximation, a lie or a half-truth or a fantasy that would tell anyone more about me than I wish to know myself, and yet, cobbled together somehow in a scheme I cannot visualize, they must tell a comprehensive truth that hardly concerns me at all.

For everything wants to be remembered, chronicled, documented: everything—*all of this and all the rest, because your life is neither a finite length that can be measured out to a certain point and severed, nor is it only your own.*

FOUNDATION

An Enchanted Family

I: My Father Holds His Voice in His Hands

THESE ARE STORIES my father never told me.

HE HAD NEVER heard his name. He wrote his name in all his books, on the flyleaf: Janos Kossuth Pasztory. First or given or Christian name; middle name; family or last name, or surname. Why did they need three terms for the same idea? He had no family. Why did they need three names for him. One turn of the hand, one elegant gesture, that was enough, surely.

ABOUT HIS YEARS at the Pennsylvania School for the Deaf my father says only, They tried to make me speak — they tried to stop me from talking. Once, when I mentioned the chimpanzees and gorillas that were supposed to have acquired a vocabulary of signs, he said, I pity the apes—that's what I went through. I'm not put together to speak, they're not put together to sign. My father is the least self-pitying of men, but I knew he was setting me up. Did I know who liked the signing monkeys, he asked, and this is a poor translation of the sarcasm in his hands— *The National Geographic.*

My father's laugh is a harsh, loud, grating noise, awkward to an ear accustomed to the polite cultured laughter of the hearing, yet I love to hear it and have been told that my own is similar; together we are like a chorus of ravens. Later, though, I found I had to explain the joke, and no-one, no hearing person, sees the humor.

BILL WAS HIS best friend. Bill wasn't his name, his name was William Colby Smith—first, middle, last. Bill was short for William. Sometimes Billy. Conundrums like this made my father glad he didn't speak English. Whatever relationship existed between Billy and William couldn't be one of shortening, both were two syllables, while *B* and *W* were distinctly different letters whether written on paper or spelled in the air. He knew that their articulation required entirely different manipulations of lip and tongue. My father could never remember from one lesson to the next which started with the lips pursed, which with lips together. He didn't want to. Bill's real name was an abbreviation of the gesture for white, after his paler-than-straw hair, just as my father's refers to black eyes tilted at an angle by high Magyar cheekbones. If my father knew that Janos (properly János) is the Hungarian equivalent of John, and if I listed for him only the permutations I know—Jan, Johann, Jean, Juan, João, Giovanni, Sean, Ivan come to mind—his hands would close up in perfect silence and stillness.

Bill slept in the bed next to my father's in the long dormitory. There were tall windows between the beds, and radiators under the windows. Thick flakes of paint peeled off the coils of the radiators, collected in their crevices and angles and on the floor, where they lay for long periods before being swept up. Nor was the dust that gathered under the beds often swept, and the panes of the windows were thick with grime, inside and out, so that if Bill or my father rubbed out a circle to look at the grounds the view was still obscured. The janitor, whom they called Old Hairy, was one of the few signing adults associated with the school. Eager to talk to anyone, the students left Old Hairy little time to clean.

WHAT DID THEY talk about?

THEIR BEDS WERE narrow, iron-framed, the iron painted the same dingy white as the radiators, with thin lumpy mattresses and frayed moss green blankets. The beds stood in a file like tin soldiers down the long narrow room, each accompanied by its pasteboard footlocker in which the boys stored their belongings. Cold gummy linoleum covered the floor, unpleasant under bare feet when my father stumbled out of bed in the morning to join the rushing tumble of boys toward the row of six basins at the end of the room, hoping to get there before the hot water ran out. If someone didn't wake up someone else would bang hard on the foot of his bed and the vibration would shiver through the hollow iron frame. Occasionally, a master might complain about the unholy racket the students made in the morning. Weren't deafies supposed to be quiet and well-mannered? Then another would say, "They can't hear themselves, stupid." Four harsh electric lamps hung from the ceiling. The switch was the responsibility of the senior boy, a youth of eighteen called Lips for his especially inapt lipreading; some of the staff called him feebleminded, but they could trust him so far.

I am aware that I'm describing an Edwardian British public school, but this is the material I have to work with. I have never seen the Pennsylvania School for the Deaf, inside or out; I'm not even sure where it's located or whether it is still in operation. I have done some research, but graduates of the state deaf schools are understandably reluctant to write about them, those who can write, and I do not trust the reports of the hearing.

This is what I know. They were residential schools; coeducational, although naturally the boys and girls were kept apart so far as possible; publicly funded and funded by wealthy families, often those that had been struck by the scourge of deafness—a lovely little daughter or handsome son, the parents' hopes silenced. They couldn't understand, the parents, for how could the munificent God Who had granted them their railroad fortunes, their iron and steel fortunes, mercantile or banking fortunes, how could He visit upon them such disaster? The sins of the fathers, they muttered, and made large gifts to the deaf schools. Their children would be educated. Their children (if they believed the claims of the administrators, and they dared not disbelieve), their children would become perfect counterfeits of normal youths, able to speak intelligibly and to divine others' speech through lipreading and trained intuition. You'd never know they were deaf.

But most of the students, my father included, did not come from such privileged backgrounds. Their parents were laborers or middle-class shopkeepers; often the children were orphans. My father was an orphan. A child of the Depression, he was housed and fed. I suppose that I, son of postwar prosperity, am more appalled by the deprivation of his youth than he. Perhaps he is grateful for what he had. Or perhaps I have it all wrong—perhaps he was never happier after he left the school and had to deal with the hearing world, its indifference more intolerant than the conspiracies and rivalries within the iron gates and high granite walls surrounding the Pennsylvania School for the Deaf.

HE CAME TO the school relatively early, a scrawny child of four, but his first memory must be of the orphanage where his deafness was discovered. Having no language, no means of ordering his perceptions, much less any access to metaphor or figure, my father's only recourse was brute passivity or mute hysteria. What can it have been like for him? The two-year-old baby who was brought to the merciful sisters seemed a bright child, at first. Too thin, but he showed no sign of malnutrition and seemed healthy overall, with good coordination and appetite. Even as a baby my father was handsome, with his alert black eyes and thick black hair, and Sister Paula, a girl of nineteen, was delighted with him. The sisters had been told his name, but Sister Paula called him Johnny, her little man, petted and spoiled him. When she sang lullabies he watched her with grave eyes, clutching a sordid rag doll, until he fell asleep.

Mother Superior tolerated Sister Paula's infatuation, so long as all her duties were performed. Paula often carried Johnny with her on her rounds, or encouraged him to toddle after her, trailing the doll by one leg, its yarn hair dragging on the floor. He watched her carefully, with an intentness she had seen in no other child and which she mistook for the hunger of affection—and indulged. Rather than striding down the corridors, the hems of her habit billowing, she slowed her gait to match his and let one hand swing in anticipation of his grasping it. He knew the expression on her face when she spoke his name, and reacted appropriately; she had no occasion to suspect his disability although he never made an intelligible noise. Some of the children called her Mama, something that made her happy and uneasy at the same time, even as she corrected them. "Sister," she murmured, bending over them, pushing the black veils of her coif back from her face, "Sister," changing their diapers or checking temperatures with small, cool, white hands. Although she had been assigned to the orphanage while a novice, she still knew little about children and often found herself wrestling with a nearly physical dislike for them, a pallid nausea like a knot in the throat. But not for her little Johnny, who clutched at the coarse fabric of her habit or the crucifix on her scapular as she rocked him in her arms, and watched her lips with the fascination of devotion. She would have liked to have him sleep in a cradle by her bed.

Mostly, my father played by himself. He liked to arrange blocks in careful ranks and orders. If another child sat down with him, my father cooed with amiable distraction, pushed a painted wooden block into the other's hand, went on with his own chosen task. My father communicated through a concrete shorthand of nods, gestures, grimaces—not terribly effective, I imagine, choppy and forced—that the other orphans accepted as an alternate discourse. It was not a language yet, but I have read that the human impetus toward language is imperative, as strong as that toward the satisfaction of hunger or desire, and that deaf children deprived of contact with their peers invariably develop their own idiosyncratic syntax and vocabulary of gestures. I have no doubt that my father was on the way toward his own system of home sign before Sister Paula discovered his secret.

He was drawing contentedly in the big playroom, crouching over his tablet in a lozenge of warm sunlight from one of the windows. The cheap paper glowed like parchment; the colors of his wax crayons gleamed as brightly as stained glass, although they weren't as various or subtle as the box of sixty-four colors of my own childhood, many years later. My father didn't scrawl one color randomly atop another in swirls and muddy scribbles but would place each coherent patch of pure pigment next to another, building up an abstract mosaic of waxen tesserae. As he worked he bent stiffly over the tablet, chewing his lips and the insides of his cheeks, going cross-eyed in the effort to ensure grass green didn't overlap sun yellow. He looked, I imagine, like his grandson Kit, when Kit was little, leaning over his coloring book at his mother's kitchen table, crayon held fiercely and clumsily, pointed pink tongue, furrowed brow.

In another part of the room an orphan had begun to squall—a stuffed toy snatched from him, or a dispute over a smashed citadel of blocks. Sister Paula must have been slow in going to his aid, or impatient in comforting him, for his voice expanded and was joined by another. All of the babies should have been put down for their naps by now, but benefactors were visiting the orphanage and Paula had been requested to keep her charges awake. None older than four, the little boys were cranky with sleepiness. The discontent of one, then two, spread through the room. Soon enough twenty children wept, howled, sniveled, croaked, wailed, an unnerving, hopeless cacophony that made Paula feel dizzy and wild and drove one of the novices who assisted her to tears of her own. Paula sent this novice off for aid and to warn Mother Superior away from the nursery.

For a moment, standing in the center of the room and clasping the crucifix of her scapular so that its crossbars dug into the flesh of her palms, Sister Paula wrestled with impulses she rejected as unchristian. Her assistant, an edge of panic coloring her eyes, knelt holding a child to her breast where he snuffled and hiccuped, staining her shoulder with snot and tears. If he was calming and relatively quiet, ready to be laid on a pallet for his delayed nap, there were still nineteen more to be comforted. Paula's anger was helpless, a slick gummy obstruction in her throat, as she gathered another boy into her arms, stuttered to him, bounced him against her chest, pacing a circle within the stream of bright winter light below a window. As she glanced about, once, twice, her gaze passed over the single quiet child, uncomprehending, and then she saw that it was my father, little Johnny, still calm, absorbed in his regular patchwork of vivid colors while passion rioted all around him. How cruel he was, she thought, the voice in her mind as harsh as when it condemned her own fury, how cruel to ignore his companions. Worse, how he ignored her. She wanted to slap him, kick him with the pointed toes of her tight boots. To make him cry out as loudly as the others.

Three more sisters, older, more experienced, less sentimental than Paula, swept into the nursery. Canny as generals in wartime, they set to comforting the orphans, a gentle wing of black serge, a starched white veil smelling of lavender, cool palm on hot forehead. One of them, babe in arms, stepping deftly past my father, muttered, "That one's good as gold, lambkin, why can't you be like him?"

She had stepped through his light, though, or he'd caught the flip of her hem in the corner of his eye. My father looked up, startled, his eyes drawing into focus and the irises big and black, Paula thought, as plums washed of their haze. He grunted, stumbled to his feet, tottered toward the sister before realizing she wasn't Paula. His legs gave way and he fell with a little chirp of dismay. Breathing through his mouth, eyes shocked and wide, he stared at the nun, waved clenched fists at her. "What's wrong, duckling?" she murmured, but, intent on the child she held, didn't understand my father's gestures, little hands chopping and flailing.

Paula bit down on her nausea—fear of and distaste for the other children, she knew suddenly, compounded with a startled comprehension so complete she couldn't manage it, encompass it. She approached my father. With a baby gulping against her shoulder she couldn't do more than nod at my father, waft her affection toward him on a small, exasperated breath. If anyone had asked she could not have explained why she didn't say his name. My father saw her, his hands calmed in expressive relief, and he grasped her skirt to haul himself back upright. While Paula and the three older sisters calmed the exhausted boys, helped them all to sleep on their pallets, my father followed her around, muffled himself in her skirts when she paused, as his suspicion changed to curiosity, then playfulness, until it was clear he was playing hide-and-seek in the folds of Paula's habit.

When all were quiet, sleeping or nearly sleeping, the calm, stuffy air thick with the souring-milk scent of babies breathing, Paula sank into a chair to watch them. My father clambered into her lap. The eldest of the other nuns nodded sternly, and the three left.

AFTER THIS, PAULA must have regarded my father with some suspicion, some unease, a feeling that he wasn't telling her everything he knew—or that she wasn't deciphering his clues. She saw that when he wanted her attention he gestured or made faces; that the sounds he uttered, be they laugh or cry, seemed unintended and extraneous, and that he might go through the motions of laughing or crying without making a sound beyond his slightly raspy breathing. When she spoke to him, sometimes, he mimicked the movements of her lips, blowing air with a *hoo-hoo* sound. Children younger than he spoke, muttered to themselves over their blocks or crayons, a ceaseless, lisping narration of their activities, "now my put thith one here, and thith one over here, oop, all fall down!"— but Johnny never spoke. He was slow, she told herself, he would never grow up. Realizing that this prediction pleased her made Paula light-headed, giddy with horror. She wouldn't tell anyone. She would continue to watch over Johnny, who needed all her care and protection.

MY MOTHER'S DEAFNESS is congenital but my sister and I are both hearing, so I conjecture that my father was born hearing also. This is how it must have been. Samaritans of the Red Cross or the Salvation Army enter a tenement in the poorest slum in the city, a rat warren of recently arrived immigrants, the dregs—so the missionaries would think—of Europe's barrel, Poles, Ukrainians, Ashkenazi Jews, Greeks. To my knowledge there was no significant Hungarian exodus to the promised land until much later when, soon before my own birth, refugees fled the Soviet troops who trampled Imre Nagy's brief, chilly spring. I imagine my grandparents even more isolated in their new life than any of their neighbors. Those neighbors were exiles themselves but shared tongue and custom with a handful of others, at least; were bound however loosely into the vast net, the spreading branches like an immense family tree of Indo-European languages. Knowing only one spoken language well, and that not Magyar, I cannot confirm my belief that my grandparents would have felt less alien among Finns, Lapps, Estonians, equally incomprehensible but their closest linguistic cousins, than in the babel of Slavic, Germanic, Semitic, Hellenic of the Philadelphia slums. They would have placed surname before Christian name, would call their son Pasztory János as if he were Chinese and his family history more crucial, more real, than his individual identity.

When the epidemic swept through the slums on foul air or tainted water or simply leaping from one weakened body to the next, cholera perhaps, scarlet fever, whooping cough, influenza, my grandfather—a young man of twenty-seven, say, good Magyar stock warped by malnutrition and exhaustion (he ran a power loom for twelve hours a day, smelted steel, guided some apparatus through one incomprehensible action one hundred twenty times in an hour midway down an assembly line)—my grandfather would succumb first, I think, unless my father had a little sister, a nursing infant who strangled on her mother's milk. Before emigrating, before the long journey—on foot, I imagine—up the Danube to Vienna, then by rail to Trieste or one of the Italian ports and stifling, rank steerage across the Atlantic, my unknown grandfather must have been as handsome as his son Janos would become, but taller, sturdier, raucous and cheerful, while his wife would have been a spirited, coltlike beauty of the Alföld when she was married, plump and rosy and with her lustrous black hair coiled in thick braids on her head.

Five or six years later, two or three children later, who would recognize the gaunt widow with her constant dry cough and greying hair. She speaks no English, of course, but she and her neighbor have developed a colloquy out of scraps of several languages and of gestures as fluid and knowing as sign. I picture this neighbor a Polish woman a few years older than my grandmother (perhaps her husband was my grandfather's overseer at the factory), and suppose that she has no children of her own. When my untimely-widowed grandmother knocks at her door, still-healthy children clutching her skirts, the childless Pole understands at once. Weeping with gratitude, she welcomes in the little ones; desolate, my grandmother turns away. And so I comfort myself with the thought of my prosperous uncle and aunt who despite unpronounceable Slavic names are children of the Danube and the Hungarian plain as much as I.

My father, though, little János, his mother's little hero, would be already ill, and she returned to him, returned to her sordid, frigid, dark little room, and bolted the door behind her. When the Red Cross men or the soldiers of the Salvation Army broke the lock a few days later they would find the filthy, sick, whimpering child beside his cold mother, and would discover his name among the talismanic official documents she grasped in one rigid hand.

Although if my grandparents were peasants of the Alföld, I suppose I should assume that she, at least, was illiterate, and I suppose I should wonder why my father's middle name is the surname of a hero of the revolution of 1848. I believe, also, that Pasztory is a name of the Magyar aristocracy.

SISTER PAULA WOULD have gone with Mother Superior to deliver my father to the School for the Deaf. The granite walls around the property would close little Johnny away forever, she thought, and she drew him closer against her side in the rear seat of the orphanage's car. In front, Mother Superior directed the driver through iron gates, up the tree-lined gravel drive to a massive stone building that could have been a prison or a convent, four stories, with tall, narrow windows, pointed gables, gothic crenellations. Paula shuddered on a small breath. My father, feeling her unease, looked up into her eyes.

When the driver had halted the car and engaged the parking brake, Mother Superior climbed out. Her boots crunched on the gravel. She stood, settling her habit like a bird's rumpled plumage, waiting for Sister Paula and the boy. Mother Superior was displeased, with nun and child both. Faced with her error, Sister Paula had shown no remorse. That she was being selfish seemed not to have occurred to her. Sister Paula must understand that her responsibilities did not allow for extraordinary attention to a single child, and that a child like my father would prove a disruptive influence in the orphanage. The boy would be better off among his own kind. The basic contradiction, though, was this: motherhood and sisterhood, maternity and vocation, these were mutually exclusive concepts. Mother Superior pressed her lips together, nudged a knuckle of gravel with her toe, and, rather than examine the building, which she found inexpressibly ugly, turned to oversee the school's grounds. A shabby meadow starred with dandelions and daisies sloped away into the lee of a rhododendron thicket; behind and above rose low, ragged trees, hardly screening the walls beyond. Born and raised in the country, Mother Superior had little patience for managed wildness. The grounds looked tired and untidy. A spring blooming of dogwood and, no doubt, naturalized daffodils was unlikely to improve matters. For herself, she disliked rhododendrons.

"I believe the boy can walk by himself," she observed, seeing that Sister Paula held him in her arms.

The younger nun flushed—small improvement, Mother Superior felt, weary of Sister Paula's pinched, unhappy aspect. My father kicked his legs once or twice as Sister Paula half-knelt to put him down. One of his dark socks was crumpled around the ankle. Paula pulled it up the thin white shin, settled the jacket straight on his narrow shoulders, adjusted the round collar of his shirt. She straightened up, reached for Johnny's hand.

"Are we quite ready?" There was a blankness about the boy's expression that disturbed Mother Superior—something other, she thought, than the isolation imposed by his deafness. An even-tempered, attractive child, she would admit, if too thin to look quite healthy. His good temper, too, seemed unhealthy, as if his responses were stunted. No child should be immune to fits of temper or caprice; she could understand his being mute but not so unnaturally quiet. No child should observe those around him so carefully, slyly, yet with so little involvement. My father's hands dipped and swooped as he gazed around, a halting calligraphy, but his expression did not change, and he did not accept Sister Paula's hand.

Paula may not have wept when she surrendered my father to the matron of the Pennsylvania School for the Deaf, but I don't imagine it would be because she understood how little her tears would mean to him. More likely, aware of Mother Superior's stern eye, she simply knelt before Johnny, took his hands in her own and gazed for a moment into his eyes, before striding from the dormitory and down the stairs without asking for someone to show her the way.

MY FATHER LEARNED to talk. *Talk* is how I transcribe a verb others might label *communicate*, pinning a Latinate profundity and difficulty —as though attaching genus and species name to a chloroformed moth —to a word as swift and easy in the hand as the Anglo-Saxon syllable in the mouth. *Sign* would be an appropriate translation, but to the English-speaker who finds training voice, breath, and memory to the measures of another tongue already insupportable *sign* implies an implausible effort. Humans were meant to speak with their voices, hear with their ears. There are still those—educators, philosophers, unhappy parents—who insist my father's native language is no language at all yet assert that it cannot be learned. Rather the way, I imagine, a non-Indo-European tongue, Hungarian say, sounds like so much undifferentiated verbal garbage to one who would have no trouble recognizing Italian or even Lettish as an authentic language; the same person will claim that Magyar is clearly too difficult even to attempt learning, its bases and assumptions alien, impossible.

My father learned to talk the same way any child learns to speak. Matron assigned him to a bed next to a boy the same age as he, a sturdy hellion with ruddy cheeks and hair paler than his skin, the color of thick cream. Friendly, the boy waited until Matron had left, then waved his hands in the air before his chest, staring at my father's face. One phrase, one gesture, was repeated several times with the same raising of the brows and widening of eyes like caramels. Finally he put his fingers to the corners of his eyes, pulled them up and out into tilted slits. He grinned, and expelled a puff of warm air.

The first lesson that stuck, after the sign for Bill's name and the childishly sarcastic gesture that my father adopted for his own, was the necessity of not talking in the sight of Matron or the other adults. In the sudden exhilaration of being able to hold meaning in his hands, grasp it, mold, shape, and share it, he might forget, but Bill wouldn't answer and if Matron saw she slapped him. Her mouth opened and closed, gulped and gobbled in a manner that was, in afterthought, ludicrous but, in the event, terrifying, her spittle spraying over his face as she shook him. She didn't want him to talk. If he'd had any memory of Sister Paula, if he'd been able this early to arrange his thoughts with coherent syntax and grammar, he might have wondered whether she would have disapproved so violently or not rather have encouraged him, attempted joining him in the adventure. A hidden adventure it must be, suppressed and persecuted, a language with the defensiveness and ragged edges of samizdat.

It was Bill, eventually, who explained what they wanted of him, although even he couldn't explain. Nevertheless, my father felt guilty, inadequate, that he couldn't interpret the pouts and grimaces of Matron or his teachers nor successfully imitate them. Often, even before he knew the words or conventions, he could grasp Bill's meaning on the expressive canvas of his face. How strange it was that his elders, who depended on tiny, subtle modulations of the lips, had faces so stiff and masklike, and never looked in each other's eyes. And it seemed especially odd (this was before he met Old Hairy) that adults' means of communicating should be so different from Bill's and his own and the other boys'. Weren't adults people just like him?

An older boy, ten or twelve, tailoring his gestures to my father's limited vocabulary, tried to make it clear. Adults, these adults anyway, weren't like the boys. They weren't talking with their lips but their breath. Did they listen with their noses then? my father wanted to know, wrinkling up his face in amused disgust. No, with their ears. My father had never seen this sign before, and the other boy showed him, cupped his hands over his own ears, then touched my father's. You know how you can feel someone running past you, feel it through the floor—they can feel like that through their ears. He touched my father's ears again. When they breathe through their mouths the air shakes the way the floor does.

Then why don't I feel it too?

Because you have *bad ears.* We all do. That's why they hate us.

MY FATHER IS five, a handsome boy with skin the color of mare's milk and a shock of black hair, a curious, articulate, intelligent child. Why is he still in bed, curled under the blanket, the sheet over his head? Bill knocks on the iron rail of the bed, six times, six o'clock, get up, Janos, Bill is saying, there's no hot water left and you'll miss breakfast too! Fingers flying, Bill repeats the phrases when my father rolls over to look at him. But why is Janos crying? A five-year-old boy, a little man, the flesh around his eyes bruised with violet shadow, the eyelids pink and raw. Tears well slowly in eyes like tarnished coins and roll across his cheeks; his nostrils are clotted with snot. What's wrong? Bill asks.

He can't tell you, Bill, he pulls his hands from under the blanket where he has kept them warm all night between his thighs, and Bill reaches for but does not touch them.

Can you see my hands, Bill, from so many years ago can you see the hands of Janos's son? I'll tell you why my father weeps.

Janos held the burning candle before his mouth. He watched his teacher, closely. The only sign Mr. Henderson knew was the verb *to articulate* so his students called him Mr. Articulation, but my father wasn't clear what one did when one articulated. He imitated the grimaces Mr. Articulation made, the exaggerated rictuses of lips and the flapping tongue. Lips and tongue, Janos, Father, were telling you to make the candle flame flutter, but how could you know? You hardly breathed at all, concentrating so hard, and the flame burned tall and straight. The teacher's face grew red and angry, and he kept saying to articulate, to articulate more and more broadly until the sign lost any sense it might have had, and then the hand struck my father's wrist. A gutter of hot wax flooded over his knuckles and splashed his legs. It hurts! my father cried, flinging the candle away, I don't know what you want, I'm doing the best I can, why did you hurt me, it's not fair! "None of that!" shouted Mr. Articulation, yelling at a child who couldn't hear him, so close that breath rotten with a decaying molar gusted over the face of a child who didn't understand that voice is formed of breath, "none of that. Only savages talk with their hands."

If you could see my speaking hands, Bill, they would tell you that Janos's articulation tutor, Mr. Henderson, beat the boy's hands with a ruler until the knuckles bled. My father holds his voice in his hands.

❧

II: My Mother Tells Her Children Stories

MY FATHER WRITES very slowly, a beautiful, lucid italic hand full of apt, unconventional abbreviations and oddly poetic figures. But he types faster and more accurately than any secretary who's ever worked for me—too fast sometimes, so that the paper tapes unreeling from the TDD might fill with stuttered garbage where he'd overloaded the line. Since we both acquired computers and subscribed to an electronic bulletin board this hasn't been so much a problem; once or twice a week I dial up the modem for messages and there they are, clear, characterless signs on the screen. The TDD sits idle most of the time, and I see my father's handwriting only on birthday and Christmas cards.

I seldom hear from my mother directly. Her grasp of written English is idiosyncratic and distrustful, too fragile to be entrusted to a keyboard. Occasionally I receive a letter, a slipshod, leaky basket barely containing her meaning, woven of strips of fiercely written illegible observations and phrases that read like transliterated clichés. She is a woman whose hands can hold the most inviolable concept, whose eloquence ties her husband's thumbs behind his back and long ago frightened her children into speech, out of their native language. She has three grandchildren to whom she cannot speak a word. Their father, a sensible man, is terrified of her, frightened of his wife's unreadable childhood; American for more generations than he can count and English before that, he wants his children to know only one language. I taught Toby some sign before we moved East, and he and my father get along like gangbusters, devising their own argot as they go along, resorting to pen and paper when they have to, vivid and ungrammatical as buccaneers. Often enough the messages on the bulletin board are for Toby. My mother ridiculed the clumsy shaping of his signs, his slowness—He talks like a baby, she told me deliberately, a slow baby. Toby, nine on that first visit, wasn't so slow that he didn't understand her. Now he says, Hello, Mrs. Pasztory, how are you? and goes off in a corner with my father. Even Jeremy has lost patience with her. He sees her, I think, unconsciously, as an illiterate, unassimilated peasant, an immigrant willfully blind to her new world, like the hunched, black-clad Sicilian beldam in a movie about the Mafia. He doesn't understand that my mother is a princess in disguise.

HER MEMORY IS less to be trusted than my imagination, I think. For instance, she claims to remember her family's palace in Budapest, an estate below the Carpathians whipped by that cold wind bending the beeches in the jardin anglais, a townhouse in Vienna. There was a history of deafness in her family, she says; she had an uncle, Ferenc, who studied at the famous Asylum in Paris and never came back to Hungary. But if this is so why wasn't she also sent as a child to Paris? Or to a school for the deaf in Budapest or Vienna or Prague—there must have been such, even in the chaotic years between the wars. Because she was a girl, I suppose. Instead, the ten-year-old Marit, daughter of refugees, was enrolled in the Pennsylvania School for the Deaf signing no real language but a sort of baby talk that only her family could interpret. The family then vanished, like the bad fairies in a children's story, and so I have two sets of imaginary forebears. My mother's I can imagine less clearly than my father's for, though knowing better, I see them as spoiled aristocrats of the Double Monarchy, the Habsburg courts of Vienna and Budapest, refined and overbred, dancing to Strauss waltzes across a vast polished ballroom gleaming and twinkling with wood and crystal, or drinking chocolate mit schlag and eating flaky pastries, or bowing and scraping in eighteenth-century satins and powdered perukes. This is my mother's fairy tale. In fact, the whole fabric crumbles to dust if you look at it too closely.

AFTER I WAS born my parents brought me back to a tenement apartment near the print shop where my father worked, but the house I remember growing up in stood on a quiet street on the edge of town. A strip of scraggly grass set the front off from sidewalk and street. You climbed four steps to the porch, enclosed by turned wood and metal screening. For a few weeks in early summer an old wisteria canopied the porch with drooping pendants of blossoms fashioned of equal parts blue tissue paper and perfume. Drifts of faded petals, a papery snow, piled up around the porch supports, and then the sweet peas my mother planted every spring began to bloom. The vines with their clinging, wiry tendrils climbed the wooden lattice enclosing the space under the porch, then continued up the balusters and pillars, cloaking the lower front of the house with pale greyish green foliage so that my father was never able to paint the porch. The original deep blue faded and blistered over the years to grey. Every year when the weather got trustworthy enough for the project he began to complain. Equally house-proud, he and my mother turned their pride on different axes. It looks trashy, he'd say. The supports will rot if they're not painted. Shaking her head over his obtuseness, my mother would indicate the vase on the kitchen table stuffed with every pastel shade of carmine, magenta, lilac, then take him out onto the porch where the hot, quiet, enclosed air shivered as thick with fragrance as if it were water, and finally led him down to the sidewalk to see the impressionist mound of foliage scattered thickly with blossoms like blots of clear oil paint from which rose the lines of the house.

My mother loved flowers but didn't trust plants the way a

gardener must. Toward the end of the blooming season every year she would notice mildew like fine face powder on the leaves of the sweet peas, and would avoid the porch and the front of the house, muttering angrily to herself with small, constricted movements of hands held close to her breast, until my father had a chance to pull the dying plants out and hose down the porch. My sister, who was seven when my parents bought the house, says she remembers tulips in the backyard the first two or three years, but they must have succumbed to a lack of proper care. Perhaps my father, misunderstanding their needs, removed the foliage as it began to yellow. There were three large rose bushes, left by a previous owner; untended, unpruned, each bush became an untidy thicket of deadwood and arching canes that, nevertheless, produced freights of stupefyingly perfumed peach or tawny blossoms in the summer. One spring when I was five or six, exploring, I discovered that the source of the feathery foliage that appeared like a green haze amid the canes of one of the rosebushes was a thrivingly neglected asparagus bed. Even as a child I loved asparagus and recognized the slender green spears, dragged my mother out to see them. She shrugged, as though disdaining a gift from a deity she mistrusted, and told me that even if it were my favorite vegetable she had no notion how to harvest it—she wasn't a farmer's wife—but that it was probably something else, something that only looked like asparagus, sure to be disagreeable. After all, we didn't harvest the fruit of the sweet peas, which appeared equally succulent.

The biggest house my father could afford, it was very small, a floor and a half smaller than the house Jeremy and I bought twenty-five years later in a city with a healthier economy—although, admittedly, we rent out the first story. We had two incomes between us, as well, and only one child. I slept in the same room with my sister until I was eight, cramped in a corner between kitchen and bathroom. My bed stood against the wall where I would wake up to hear my father run his bath before going to bed, nights he worked the late shift at the printers—all the private, personal noises he was unaware of making—and I would slip back into sleep comforted by the sloshes and sighs.

During the summer Steph and I slept on the porch, screened from the street outside by a hedge of sweet peas and their stifling, beneficent perfume that no breeze seemed to dispel. My parents would sit out with us, if my father was home in the evening, sitting in straight-backed kitchen chairs at the far end of the porch, a small shaded lamp between them to illuminate the small conversation of their hands. My father drank cold coffee, slow meditative sips at long intervals. My mother smoked. On her cot at right angles to mine Steph shifted and grumbled in her sleep. I tried to stay awake until my parents went in. With my eyes closed I listened to the night and tried to understand what it would mean not to hear.

Summer evenings when my father was at work, my mother would sit with us for an hour or two, usually on my cot because I was smaller. She might start out reading to us, to me really, bright picture books that Steph and I fetched from the library. Invariably, Steph became impatient and took the book from my mother's lap. My sister read well, transliterating the text into graceful periods without effort, where my mother hesitated, feeling out the shapes of the words with her hands and only then going back to string them together, and losing control if it were more than a simple present-tense declarative sentence. She knew the vocabulary and conventions, I believe the sentences made sense in her mind, but she had trouble focusing one syntax, one grammar, into another completely different. When Steph read, aloud and at the same time with her hands, there was no telling the two narratives apart, separate senses apprehended them but they mingled in the understanding, folded in and out of each other so I couldn't tell where one began and the other continued.

I remember a particular group of books, by a man who was identified as a mime, a modern dancer, and an interpreter for the deaf. The books were dissimilar—some of them stories, some concept books—and illustrated by different artists to varying degrees of abstraction or stylization; one or two were illustrated with photographs. In my memory they seem innocuous, not even very interesting—I tried one on Toby when I first met him; he didn't respond. My mother hated them. One was a story about rabbits, latest variation on a theme by Beatrix Potter, in which a man's hands, photographed in bright light, enacted the characters and their actions—shadow figures, essentially, without the shadows. I liked the shape and strength of the hands. The fingers were long without being fragile, blunt-tipped. Thick dark hair grew over the wrist, around its bony protrusions, and onto the back in a wave toward the outside of the hand. Bent, tendons like drawn strings formed a pattern like the ribbing of a paper fan. My mother, outraged, recognized a number of signs in the flexing and turning of the hands. Choppily, she said to us, When someone talks to you you should watch the face, never the hands. The hands are the least important part of it.

By this time I was reading for myself, at least was capable of reading so long as there were more pictures than text. My sister must have tired of the limitations of picture books, and began to bring home from the library stories for children older than I although still younger than she. (Years later, finding books for Toby, I learned that librarians call this group the middle-aged child.) She would sit cross-legged on her cot, leaning forward over the book open in her lap but with her back straight, a serious, intent girl in striped boy's pajamas. Her thick chestnut hair was drawn punishingly tight to the skull, braided into two plaits that fell forward over her shoulders. Lamplight illuminated her face, irradiated skin that took a tan easily, gracefully, and lit two tiny lamps in her eyes. Her hands moved, quick but legible, and she spoke aloud as well, pitching her voice to fill the enclosed porch but extend no farther.

The second cot was pushed against the fluted balusters of the porch railing. My mother reclined against the railing, feet tucked under. She smoked steadily, stubbing out butts stained with brilliant dark lipstick into a large ashtray beside her on the bed. Her hair, as thick and dark as her daughter's, hung loose on shoulders bared by a cotton sun dress, and her eyes fixed on her daughter's face, so unlike her own, with infrequent glances for her son sprawled on his belly, chin in hand, watching and listening. My feet generally lay in my mother's lap. She would close one hand over my calf, pushing the fabric of my pajamas up to the knee. Her palm would feel cool only because of the summer heat still imprisoning the evening air. If she noticed me closing my eyes, to listen with the ears only, she jabbed the filed nail of her index finger into the sole of my foot.

My sister might be reading *The Secret Garden* or *A Little Princess*—these were the kinds of stories we all liked, better than the fairy tales they resembled because the magic seemed more plausible, the happy endings more secure and deserved. When Sara Crewe woke to find her sordid little garret at Miss Minchin's transformed to a pavilion of Oriental comfort, when Mr. Carrisford the Indian Gentleman discovered her to be the lost daughter of his dead friend, our gratification made the air on the porch as thick as the dense humidity and the fragrance of sweet peas. My mother would squeeze my bare feet between her palms after we'd finished reading for the night, and tell Steph and me to go to sleep quickly. She took the book with her and went in the house. If I leaned up on my elbow, I could see her through the unshaded window, seated at the dining table with the book before her. As she read, her hands moved in small telegraphic signs.

Later, my father came home. A fellow plant worker lived a few blocks away and gave him a ride. The car would pull quietly up to the curb. Although he and his friend couldn't speak to each other—they wrote notes back and forth—my father believed it was polite to make some kind of noise. Climbing out of the car, he uttered a cheerful, hollow "Hoo-hoo," loud enough to be audible on the porch, and decisively slammed the door, then waited for his friend to drive away before turning to enter the house. Of course, he didn't know how much noise he made coming up the stairs, the screen door slapping shut behind him, but he never seemed surprised that Steph and I were awake to greet him. He gave us each a quick hug, a kiss on the crown of the head, went inside. He would smell of ink and grease, hot metal and new paper and sweat, and his cheeks and chin were bristly.

My mother never stood or sat with her back to a door. The slightest change in the light or, for all I know, the air pressure alerted her. Calm, she closed the book and looked up. My father shaped her name with his hands—not Marit, or the version of Mother that Steph and I used, abbreviated to the equivalent of Mama, nor the name-sign the few people she could talk to called her, but a small affectionate gesture I don't know how to translate. She looked across the table and the room at him, the same steady gaze as when she disciplined her son or daughter, and said she'd fix him something to eat while he cleaned up.

MY MOTHER HAD no contact with my or my sister's schools. She made sure we were up and dressed and breakfasted in time, had lunch and milk money to take with us; the rest was up to us or, if necessary, my father, who was expected to deal with teachers or principals if the occasion arose. Knowing my parents were deaf, our teachers never requested conferences but wrote polite notes to which my father replied equally politely. My parents never knew, therefore, how fervently the authorities disparaged Nancy Drew and Hardy Boys mysteries. Steph preferred the Hardy Boys—as did I, later—and brought a few home from every trip to the library. We went once a week, on Thursdays after school. More fortunate than other children, we could talk as much as we liked in the library without rousing the ire of the librarian, a woman we thought much resembled Miss Minchin. In the sunny children's room with its sixteen-foot ceilings, tall arched windows, and low ranges of shelves, the slightly moldy smell of much-handled books, the low murmur of children and their mothers, we floated like dust motes among the stacks, drugged by the sheer mass and presence of so many books, so much paper and ink. I asked my sister once if she thought our father might have printed some of them. I had no clear idea what printing a book involved; I knew about typewriters, and I suppose I thought my father and his coworkers typed each book front to back, and then began again. How they would reproduce the illustrations I had no idea. Steph said she was sure he had.

Once she found me kneeling before a rank of picture books. Look what I found, she said, showing me a sturdy volume called *The Good Master*. It's a story about Hungary, where Mama came from. We had read stories about children in many countries, there was no end to books about English or American children, nearly as many about French, Italian, Spanish, Dutch children, but never before had we encountered Hungarian children.

We—I should say I—knew nothing about the land of our ancestors. Like most white children, I imagine, I didn't think I was different from my playmates. The city where I grew up had a substantial black population; they, clearly, were different. But I thought the only thing separating me from the other children at school was that my parents were deaf. It didn't occur to me, for instance, that my last name was more peculiar than Johnson, O'Connor, or Witomski. I noticed that adults who first saw it written couldn't figure out what to do with the *sz*; some gave it a buzzing *z*-sound, others pronounced it like *sh*. I have always said "Pass-STORE-ee," with no idea whether I'm correct. (I only learned recently, looking through a guidebook to Budapest, that the Magyar *g* is soft: I had always mentally pronounced the word MAG-yahr when apparently it's closer to MAHJ-jahr.) I suppose that if a boy with a simple, two-syllable Anglo-Saxon name, Tom Smith, John Jones, had told me I had a funny last name, I might have begun to wonder why—not so much why Pasztory was funny as why it was my name, rather than Smith or Jones. In the event, my ethnicity—more self-created than inherited—my being Hungarian, isn't something I thought about much until nearly an adult, when I realized how easily my grandparents' surname might have been anglicized on Ellis Island, to Pastor, say, and then how we would never have known we weren't ultimately English.

I WENT TO the bookstore near my house recently, and found that they had *The Good Master* in paperback but not its sequel, *The Singing Tree*, which is out of print, and which I remember being a better book. The story of *The Good Master* is nothing much, traditional, sentimental, clichéd; patronizing, in a reassuring way, to both the American children, its intended audience, and the traditional culture it intends to celebrate. Nevertheless, it is the deep source, I'm sure, of any picture I have of my grandparents' lives. My paternal grandparents, I should say. When we brought the book home from the library, Steph and I, my mother said shortly, I read that book. That's not what it was like. Not for my family. We lived in the city. She wouldn't let Steph read it to her.

Steph read it to me, anyway; years later I read it to Toby; and now I have read it again. Often, these days, I prefer the gentle certainties of old children's books—run myself a warm bath with lavender-scented salts and recline in the tub with a thin paperback whose pulp-paper pages swell and curl in the humidity while the water cools around my shoulders and summer rain drums on the window screens. On the front porch of my parents' house, Steph and I pulled our cots away from the screens so the bedding wouldn't get wet and watched the rain thunder down until the street outside was awash, runoff nearly cresting the curbs. The sky broke open with lightning; a moment later the crackling peal of thunder rolled through the clouds, shook the house to its foundation. Bruised by the downpour, the sweet peas emitted more scent though, waterlogged, it seemed not to rise but to collect in a damp odorous fog along the floorboards, mixed in with the scent of rain and of damp earth. Inside, in the kitchen, my mother was preparing dinner. It is a peculiar feature of *The Good Master* that the mother is said to be as admirable a figure, as worthy of emulation, as the Good Master himself, her husband, yet she never does anything—is effaced within the narrative, a billow of starched white petticoats making sausages. The little girl from Budapest, sent out onto the Hungarian plain to live with her uncle and aunt, little Kate the tomboy hellion, the imp as she's called, worships her uncle and imitates her boy cousin Jancsi. *Jancsi* I believe to be a diminutive of my father's name.

We had built a bivouac of blankets, Steph and I, on a cot pushed against the wall of the house. Steph read to me aloud, not needing to translate. The rain fell, and outside the screens it was as dark as a winter afternoon, a creeping-up on dusk rather than a twilight of the kind we enjoy in New England in the summer when the evening lasts as long as the day preceding it and the sky is still light long after the backyard has gone dim, shrubs, fence, trees, house merged in an indistinct mass. The sauce simmering on the stove inside sent out savory hints and vapors. My legs stretched over the canvas sling of the cot, brown, skinny, scabbed about the knees. Jancsi was teaching Kate to ride, Jancsi mounted on his chestnut Bársony whose coat I imagined the color of my mother's hair, Kate perched unsteadily on a stolid mare she called Old Armchair. I don't believe I wondered what my father's childhood would have been like, had he grown up on the Good Master's estate, but I wondered about my own.

KAROLYI LAJOS, MY mother's elder brother, the handsome rake, his parents' pride, helped Marit pack. He knew best, knew what she would need. She had her own trunk, wood bound with metal straps over its barrel lid. Although Lajos could communicate with her better than anyone, he hadn't been able to explain to Marit why they were leaving. She didn't really understand that they were leaving, thought it was another of the games he invented to amuse her (to keep her from slipping entirely away into silence), enjoyed pulling out things he had just put in. He scolded her, and they packed underclothes fit for a little princess, foaming with Belgian lace, kid and patent-leather slippers and tiny boots, silk stockings, pinafores and frocks, warm woolen coats with satin linings and a rain cloak, gloves, hats with ribbons and artificial flowers. They packed her doll, the big one with porcelain head and hands, with real blonde hair and blue eyes that closed when the doll was tilted back, with a wardrobe as extensive and rich as Marit's own— but didn't pack the cloth doll, which Marit would prefer to carry herself. Then they filled a valise with clothes and necessities for the voyage.

On the morning they were to leave, Lajos came early to her room to wake her. He wore a chocolate brown suit and a yellow tie, had shaved carefully and slicked his hair down with scented pomade.

Sitting up against the pillows, for she was already awake, Marit watched her brother come through the door, and told him as best she could that he was beautiful. He smiled, but was distracted, tense. Marit's maid had gone away a week before, but Marit could wash and dress herself. Lajos sat in her small armchair by the hearth, smoking, his legs too long, while Marit put on the clothes laid out the night before, then he brushed her hair and tied it back with a pink velvet ribbon. Lajos carried her valise, she her doll and an ornamental handbag; they went downstairs to a hurried breakfast served in the drawing room with only the old butler in attendance. All the other servants had left, except Cook, who was going with them and who, in a plain traveling dress and cloth coat, didn't look like Cook at all but some other woman, a housewife one might see on the street when going to the dressmaker across the river in Pest. Mama and Papa were dressed for traveling, too; Mama wore her lush mink coat and looked cold.

This would have been in the late spring of 1939, as far as I can determine; that is, after the Munich Pact had dismembered Czechoslovakia, Hungary's neighbor to the north, but before the German invasion of Poland and the beginning of the war. I don't know why my grandparents emigrated, nor can my mother tell me. Were they Jewish and prescient? This seems unlikely, although perhaps, in the short-lived republic, it's not impossible that a member of the hereditary aristocracy might marry a beautiful Jew of wealthy family, for love or to prop up a sagging family fortune. Perhaps the family had lost major holdings in the Sudetenland. Maybe they had dangerous socialist connections. Or perhaps my grandparents simply saw the situation more clearly than my image of them would suggest. There are so many mysteries in my mother's past that this seems one of the less important.

With all their luggage, they boarded a train. My mother remembers eating in the dining car, the linen-draped table that rocked with the train's motion and the world rushing past outside the windows, stern dark waiters graceful as acrobats tiptoeing down the length of the car to or from the kitchen with great silver trays held at shoulder level. She remembers sleeping in a lower berth of the wagon-lit, rocking and rattling, and her brother climbing down from the upper berth in the morning, unshaven and mussed in royal blue silk pajamas and burgundy robe, reaching through the heavy drapes to wake her. She doesn't remember how long they were on the train, which great European port they finally reached—Trieste, Ostia, Livorno? Could they have gone through Austria, Switzerland, France, as far as Calais? One night in a hotel, and they embarked on a great ocean liner for New York.

MY MOTHER RETAINS two souvenirs of her European childhood. One is a small silver locket on a chain, chased and filigreed with an ornate engraved initial *K*. If you hold the locket in your palm and click its catch, it springs open. On one side, under a crystal lens, is a tiny lock of fine black hair, on the other an oval portrait photograph, black and white, a youth of nineteen or twenty. He is handsome, my uncle Lajos, with the depraved good looks of a thirties screen idol. My mother says I resemble him, but I don't see it. His hair gleams like patent leather, slick with oil. The planes and angles of his features are hard and refined, but his nose is a little too large, chin slightly too small. A small clipped mustache looks as if it had been drawn above his upper lip with an eyebrow pencil. His skin, matte, pale, is nearly the same hue as the stiff collar that grasps his neck and is not softened by the tight knot of his tie. His eyes seem pale, but there is no way to determine their true color.

I wish the photograph showed my uncle's hands. He could talk to my mother, she claims, almost as clearly as she to me, even though brother and sister had to invent their own code, which she no longer remembers. He was urbane and cultured, she says, well educated—before they left Budapest he had been planning to enter a school of law—had traveled throughout Europe. Did he visit Paris, meet his uncle Ferenc, pick up a little French Sign Language to take home to his sister? He spoke French, German, and English as well as Hungarian—how my mother knows this I don't understand. He loved his little sister.

Her other relic is a tiny bisque porcelain hand, broken at the wrist, the mute, stiff hand of the doll she brought with her from Budapest to the new world.

SHE WOULD LOSE patience with this mosaic of moments and fragments —my mother believes in narrative. The last time I visited my parents, not long ago, alone, I asked her to tell me a story. Here we are, the three of us, my mother, my father, and their grown son, sitting in straight kitchen chairs on the front porch. The floorboards, slightly warped, have recently been painted, as have the balusters and railings, the frames of the screens. The screens are heavy with the mass of sweet peas clinging to them, climbing to a height that would be above my head if I were to stand beside them on the strip of lawn below the porch. My mother claims their fragrance isn't as sweet, as penetrating, as years ago; she would trade the new brighter colors for stronger scent. My father rises to go in and fetch me another cup of herb tea, to freshen his and my mother's drinks. The floorboards creak beneath his feet. I ask my mother for a cigarette, as I do once or twice a year. She shakes her head first, then leans forward to offer the pack, and lights my cigarette with a wooden kitchen match.

Here she is, my mother, a slender woman approaching sixty, her hair, largely grey, clasped loosely at the neck and her lips, thin now, still brilliant with lipstick although she no longer paints her eyelids, rouges her cheeks, or powders her nose. The small garnet earrings I sent her for Christmas last year flash as she turns her head, the chain and locket glitter on the breast of the severe, high-necked cotton dress she made herself. She sits erect, silent, smoking, breathing through parted lips with a slight rasp, until my father returns, sits beside her. Then her hands, still long and slender, the nails perfectly shaped and lacquered, begin to speak.

They were sitting in the headmaster's reception room, my grandparents the count and countess, he stoic, for naturally he is impoverished now and in the new world his title means nothing, she tragic, ravaged, beautiful; their handsome son Lajos perfectly turned out but tense, nervous; their lovely little daughter Marit in a chair too large, poking at a scrap of embroidery. On the floor beside her, an old-fashioned doll with porcelain head and hands. Lajos the interpreter slipped from a formal, Frenchified English to French to Magyar, depending whether he spoke to headmaster, mother, or father. With his little sister he was brusque yet tender, he understood her best, watching her pantomimes closely and miming back with a natural flair that scandalized the headmaster.

Marit would learn to lip-read, the headmaster claimed, huffing behind his huge desk, English of course—here the countess sighed. Students of the Pennsylvania School for the Deaf, he said, were encouraged to view their handicap as an opportunity, to hone their natural powers of observation, that perceptiveness which deaf children possessed to such degree. Why, it did one's heart good to see a class of children, stone-deaf since birth, concentrating on their instructor's lecture with a quiet intentness one would never observe in normal boys and girls, to see them comprehend the teacher's most subtle points with ease. With dedication and sincere application, he continued, she would learn to speak. He could not promise miracles, they understood, his face reddening slightly as Lajos stared at him; her speech was unlikely to be as lovely as she, and it would be difficult for those not close to her to understand, yet it would suffice, would give her access to real language rather than the primitive gestures the poor child must now employ. Such a pity she wasn't younger—here he was stern, disapproving—a very young child learns more easily; it could be a lifelong project, they must understand, he couldn't promise miracles, but they had come to the right place. Only the most advanced techniques were employed at this school, not like those in Europe where, he believed, pupils were actually encouraged to use their hands—as if that didn't cut them off further from the world. As if a simple code of gestures such as savages from different tribes use for barter and trade—and that a code the deprived children themselves invented—could serve the necessary purposes of language. How, after all, could little children who knew nothing but the concrete and the visible comprehend such concepts as the Soul, Responsibility, or Democracy without the resources of language.

He had become carried away. He was eyeing the countess's diamonds, her furs, the pearl stickpin in the count's cravat, Lajos's beautifully tailored suit, and the ruffles of fine lace spilling out below the hem of Marit's skirt. They would like to see the facilities, of course, meet the instructors and the dormitory matrons.

No, the countess couldn't bear it, it was too tragic that they must abandon their darling.

The count, restrained, shrugged. It must be understood that they were strangers here, hardly more than guests of this great country, and it was difficult to know what to do. They only wanted what was best for their daughter.

Agitated, the countess had drifted to a window. Holding her furs tight at the throat with one hand, she pushed aside the curtain with the other and stared out on the play yard below. A number of boys dressed in drab blue serge kicked a ball back and forth, played with yo-yos or jacks. The countess's gasp was like a pistol shot. "That boy!" she cried, indicating a black-haired child, short, slim, pale—"my dear brother looked just like that as a child, he is Hungarian, he must be."

Lajos rushed to her side, called the headmaster over: "Who is that boy?"

He was my father, of course (my mother pats his hand absently), for this is a bedtime story, my mother's favorite, which she never tired of telling nor her children of watching.

~

III: The Princes in the Tower

MY FATHER TAUGHT me to read before I went to school. Understand the difficulty of this project. Remember first that the written alphabet is a congeries of arbitrary signs that purport to represent sequences of spoken sound, equally arbitrary, and recall that my father cannot hear. Remember that these signs are arranged in particular ways to form words, phrases, sentences according to the slipshod rules, with all their exceptions, of English orthography and syntax, and that English is not my father's first language—nor mine, for that matter. His second language is the clumsy pidgin called Signed English, a pedagogical synthesis that attempts to graft a vocal, linear, time-bound grammar onto a simplified gestural vocabulary. The syntax of my father's native language is spatial and global, not necessarily better or more efficient than that of English, but manifestly different. Bilingual, more or less, I arrange my thoughts in an entirely distinct manner depending whether I am speaking with hands or mouth. The processes of thought themselves are different, the plotted graph of an English speaker's cognition more similar to a Hungarian's or a blind person's than to a deaf man's— my father's, say.

I don't remember my father's reading lessons, but consider this, consider how difficult a task it is for hearing, speaking parents (Jeremy and me, for example) to teach a hearing, speaking child (Toby) to read when that is only a matter, really, of demonstrating the one-to-one correspondence of written characters to spoken sounds the child already knows. What I am trying to say is that although I was a hearing, speaking child myself (no less or more articulate than Toby, I'd say) and although I could print a good hand and had read some of the simpler R. L. Stevenson before ever encountering the fat cat on the mat, it wasn't until I encountered the cat on my wooden blocks in kindergarten that I found out speech and writing were different assays at the same language. So far as I knew, speech, writing, and sign were each unique and separable symbolic constructs. I could, for example, recognize the written configuration *Allen* or the spoken syllables "AL-lun," and knew that both referred to me, myself, but I didn't realize there was any correspondence between them closer or less arbitrary than that between either of them and the supple gesture of the left hand that is my real name. But keep in mind, also, that my father and his three-year-old son had a language in common, and that my father loved me.

When Janos Kossuth Pasztory left the Pennsylvania School for the Deaf, apprenticed to a Philadelphia print shop at sixteen, he could read at a fifth-grade level. This was considered exceptional.

OCCASIONALLY BILL'S FAMILY would visit their son, or, more often, might send a package with a warm sweater handed down from one of his elder brothers, a fruitcake, cookies. Twice a year, at Christmas and in the middle of the summer, they came and took him away for a week to the farm in western Pennsylvania. When he came back to school he would be exhausted by the effort of being with his family, his hands aching from disuse, his throat sore. They try, he told Janos, they try so hard.

In the meadow behind the main school building the two ten year olds sat in tall grass sharing a tin of cookies Bill had brought from home. They faced away from the school, toward the woods that backed the property. High summer, the grass thick and succulently green, the air still and liquid with humidity. Bill's hair was even paler than usual, bleached by a week working in the fields, his skin dark and supple. A mustache of sweat condensed on the down above his upper lip. Frowning in concentration, Bill shaped his lips and blew through them. My brother wants to talk to me, he said. Cupping one palm before his mouth, placing the other on his throat, he breathed out again. I can make noise, I can feel it *here*, he said, but I'm not speaking, I don't think I am, I can't tell. He closed one hand into a fist, dug the knuckles into the hollow of his throat until he gagged and coughed.

Bill's father and his eldest brother, Robert (Bob), had arrived for him mid-morning on Saturday. Tall, lanky, blond farmers, windburned, dusty from the long drive, they waited in the entrance hall, uncomfortable in their Sunday suits. When Bill came down from the dormitory, he went first to his father and made a harsh, forced sound that Mr. Smith tried to believe meant "Dad." He put his hands on his son's shoulders, said, "Bill," then, "You've grown since winter, son."

Head cocked, frowning so that his pale eyebrows met in a pair of furrows above his nose, Bill watched his father's mouth. He uttered the same guttural noise, then turned to his brother. Bob was holding a battered grey felt fedora; he clapped it on Bill's head. "Brother William," he said, taking the boy's right hand between both his own.

Bill pushed the hat back on his head. His voice was cracked, deeper than his twenty-two-year-old brother's, painful to hear as he croaked three syllables.

"Hear that, Dad? He said, Hello, Bob, clear as day. Good man!"

Bill sat in the back of the truck for the drive. Dust in fine chalky clouds billowed up from the tires. He felt bewildered, disappointed— he'd been sure he would understand his brother and father this time. In class he was one of the best lip-readers. But the teacher spoke slowly and shrewdly, exaggerated his enunciation. In any case, this teacher, whom his pupils called Mr. Mouth-and-Hands, was more progressive and sympathetic than most others, knew some Signed English and used it sometimes, although this was prohibited. Usually, too, he wrote what he planned to say on the chalkboard. Bill's brother's and his father's mouths worked too swiftly, with too little distinction. They were glad to see him, he understood that much, and thought they'd been pleased by his own speech, painfully practiced. He closed his hand over his throat to feel the vibrations of the vocal cords and said again, "XHA-lwo, BHAH, xha-lwo, BHAH." Fields green and growing with corn, yellow with wheat rolled past beyond the dust. "DAH!" Bill shouted. "PFAH-dhah! MAW. MOH-dhah! MOH-dhah, xha-lwo!"

For one long week Bill worked with his hands, his back, shoulders, thighs, hoisting, hauling, lifting, carrying, mowing, gathering. He knew all these tasks from early childhood, before he could talk, still remembered the code of hand signals that indicated each job. In fact those signals and perhaps a score more were all the language he had known before going to school; were, now, the only language available to him this week once it became clear his family's lips were unreadable. When he called his mother Ma the first time, with his voice, she wept, but the utility of his voice went no further—he could speak to them, after a fashion; they couldn't talk to him.

Bob wanted to learn. As the eldest, he had his own room. As the youngest, and an infrequent visitor, Bill shared his bed rather than being crammed in with the other three boys. By the light of a guttering candle, sitting at the foot of the bed facing his little brother, Bob tried to make his meaning visible. He had left school at fourteen to help his father on the farm, but he was intelligent, perceptive, seemed to have understood on his own something the entire hierarchy of deaf education denied: "Billy," he said, "they may be able to teach you to speak, but they can't teach you how to listen. What you've got is your hands, your hands and your eyes—that's what we've got to work with. Show me how to talk to you, Billy." He knew this was forbidden. Their father and mother wouldn't use even the tenuous pidgin of signals, afraid that any manual shortcut might sap their youngest child's will to learn. This lesson had been emphasized by the headmaster many times. Father would say, "Time to feed the chickens, Bill," and unless Bob were there to translate, surreptitiously, Bill never knew he was being asked. "Chickens," Father said, raising his voice hopefully, "Chick-ens, Bill. Feed. The. Chickens." Watching his father, Bill tried to distinguish the syllables. His teacher never spoke about poultry. Without looking away from his father's mouth, Bill caught the flutter of Bob's fingers like the shudder of dowdy plumage, the useless flap of a hen's wings, and the flick of Bob's wrist as though scattering grain. With a vigorous nod, rewarded by his father's smile, Bill would run out to the pen. Now, in their bedroom, he repeated Bob's gestures, and showed Bob how to say Feed the chickens.

JANOS THOUGHT ABOUT having a family. Would a mother be like Matron, a father like one of the teachers? Which one? He was better off without. If he had a brother, that sibling would surely be more like the new janitor than like Bill's Bob. Old Hairy had been caught talking with the boys and summarily dismissed; his replacement, a hearing man, had received different epithets from different segments of the student body. Older boys, sixteen, seventeen, eighteen, who admired his truculent masculinity, called him Strongman and visited him in the basement to be coached through sequences of calisthenics and in the use of his set of improvised barbells. Others, angered that their only adult confidant was gone and the massive, ham-handed twenty-four year old who was meant to take his place couldn't, or wouldn't, talk, called him No-hands and imagined that he couldn't speak, either, was undoubtedly an idiot. The little ones called him Bogey.

The cellars of the Pennsylvania School for the Deaf were divided among several different realms. Once you'd descended the stairs you passed the furnace room, where there was a lavatory and the area the janitor had set up for his exercises, then the dark, squalid room where he slept. Further down the corridor you came to two of the vocational classrooms, huge subterranean spaces lit by harsh electric lamps and small windows just below the ceiling, at the level of the ground outside. Here the boys learned printing and weaving—two professions to which deaf men ought to be especially suited since the clamor of vast presses and power looms was no handicap to those who couldn't hear.

Janos stepped away from the shuddering Linotype. He wrote *toilet* on a scrap of paper and took it to the teacher, who nodded impatiently and waved him away. To reach the lavatory Janos had to pass the hulking, labyrinthine coal furnace, idle in the summer heat. In a corner, a steel pipe had been suspended from the ceiling and here the janitor, stripped to his undershorts, was doing chin-ups. With his toes pointed and knees locked, a line straight as a piston transfixed him through the shoulders while his arms like oiled cranks lifted and dropped the rigid body on a strict, slow meter. Janos paused for a moment, struck by the mechanical rhythm of the man's actions, his torso streaked with sweat and coal dust, his face distorted by the effort of maintaining breath. The man seemed beyond noticing his surroundings, eyes squinted and peering deep into the center of the exercise.

When Janos came out of the lavatory the janitor was no longer there, no longer rising and falling like part of a machine, greased and filthy and efficient, but Janos sensed a presence near him. As he hesitated and turned he was enveloped in the rank, hot smell of the janitor, whose huge hands grasped him under the arms and lifted him off the floor. The boy kicked out, but was lifted helplessly as the man's arms extended to their full reach. The odor of sweat, the hot breath on the back of his neck made Janos wild, dizzy, nauseous. He was lifted, propelled through the air, until his chest collided with the suspended pipe. Pinned there, Janos guessed that the man wanted him to grasp the pipe. His hands had barely closed around the bar when he was released and fell, hard, but not hard enough to break his hold. His feet hung several feet above the floor.

The janitor came around to face him. Huge and dirty, still redfaced from his exertions, the man crossed his arms across his chest and stared at Janos, dangling, his shoulders beginning to burn. After a moment the man turned his head, hawked, spat into the corner, then stepped forward. His hands were oddly gentle as they closed on the boy's rib cage and urged him upward. Janos pulled his chin over the bar ten times before the janitor lifted him down, slapped him on the shoulder and sent him away. At the door, Janos looked back. Hanging from the bar again, the janitor pointed his toes and raised his legs in a slow, smooth arc until they stretched toward the ceiling. Through the whole interchange he had never moved his mouth in the abrupt manner of speech, nor made the simplest gesture.

DEAR BILL, my father wrote, *To you I am write letter because teacher say family and no family have I. You be my brother. Today I think about your old brother Bob want talk to you but we know not use the hands, I think him you should write your letter, you do not like I will write for you. You like do the work on the farm, give food to chickens and cut down plants with him. You are learning hard in school say words and hear and learn a trade so work you can do when you will be a man. Glad have family and a brother Bob you are. Today I read more in my book, hard but I enjoy. Today eat chocolate pudding. Glad you are my brother Bill. Your friend,* Janos.

HERE IS A story about my father and me.

When I won a scholarship to attend a prestigious prep school in New England, my father was so proud. Already, only twelve and a half, I had more real education than he ever did, despite the fancy certificate that said he had completed both academic and vocational programs of the Pennsylvania School for the Deaf, despite living his education year-round from four to sixteen, and he knew this. But Allen Pasztory —only son of Janos Kossuth Pasztory, best Linotype operator at the plant, gang foreman—his son Allen was going to go to the best school in the country, and then to university—there was no limit to what I could achieve. I was named after my father's supervisor, but Allen MacDonald's son Paul, my age, was only going to the public high school. My father took me to the biggest department store downtown and bought me a grey suit—my father who owned only one suit, the one he'd been married in. He bought me a footlocker, and together we read the school's recommendations as to how to fill it. He gave me two hundred dollars in ten-dollar bills. The night before I got on the train, to Washington, DC, first, then Boston via New York City, and from Boston a bus north, the night before, he came out onto the porch where I was trying to read because I was too excited to sleep.

My father was a slender man, taller than I am now but not tall, who walked strongly and stood straight. His hair was still thick and black, and his face—his face I would call noble, both for the fineness and strength of the features and for the clarity and distinction of those expressions that lent the same flexibility and color to his hands as the timbres and emphases of a good speaker can give a voice. He sat in the straight chair by my cot and smiled at me but didn't speak, and I stared at the silent hands on his knees.

A car rolled by on the street, its headlamps throwing a shaft of light across the screens, making them momentarily opaque. On a small breeze the sweet peas outside scraped against wire mesh with a sound like paper crumpling. Inside, I knew, my mother was furiously reading while my sister, nearly as angry if for different reasons, would be staring at the ceiling of her bedroom, trying to sleep so she could go to work in the morning. Putting my book down, I sat up. Daddy, I began.

Your mother doesn't want you to go, my father said. Oh, she knows what an opportunity this is, she wants you to do well, it's the going away she doesn't like. You understand that, Allen? He didn't call me Allen but used a cursive abbreviation of my real name, a little sign that might be translated Lefty. In a way I don't want you to go either, he said. I'll miss you. Who'll speak to the garbage man and the furnace man and all the other men for me? Have to go back to pad and pencil.

I'll miss you too, Daddy, I said. Friends of mine, hearing friends, are appalled by the responsibilities my father gave me when I was a child, his interpreter and translator, but they could never be as horrified as he was to have to do it, and this is why I was glad to accept, why I pictured him or my mother trying to explain something to the meter reader or the milkman and wanted not to leave; why, in a way that shames me, I wanted to leave.

I managed before, Allen, before you and your sister both. I can manage again. My father touched his forefinger briefly to the tip of my nose. You manage too, be careful—not just on the train. School can be the worst, and you're not a big boy.

I didn't know what he meant. I suppose I had never thought about what school would have been like for him—as a child you don't think about your parents' having been children. Although I was more or less constantly aware that coping was, for my father, harder than for most men, a more delicate proposition, comprehending and projecting this knowledge was something I hadn't had to do. Despite performing, often, as my father's interface with the hearing world, I was, I believe, a naïve and sheltered child. Perhaps, in fact, it was precisely *because*— because in so many ways our relationship as son and father was inverted, I the vocal, articulate figure of an adult to whom the mortgage officer spoke, unwilling to catch the eye of my father standing a little behind me, grubby in his printer's coverall, acting the mute child. A clever performing dog, a circus artiste's meal ticket, is treated with more care than a mutt from the pound.

My father brushed my hair back off my forehead and told me to go to sleep. He took my book from my hands, marked the place and closed it, turned out the light. Before he went in, he pressed his lips to my cheek.

When he took me to the train station in the morning, when he embraced me before I climbed aboard, he seemed so big. Other people on the platform waved to faces pressed against the glass as the train started to roll, but only my father, my father and his strong articulate hands, could say Good-bye Allen, good luck, I'm very proud of you, good-bye.

SOMETIMES AT NIGHT, cold winter nights in the long, high, stark room like the dormitory of a Dickensian orphanage, this room in my mind so unlike my own two-person boarding-school bedroom, sometimes my father would climb into Bill's bed and they'd sleep together for warmth, two hot little boys' bodies in coarse pajamas crowded together under thin blankets. Sometimes, then, in the mornings, older boys would leer at them, maybe say things with their hands that my father wouldn't understand.

MY FATHER WROTE to me every other week when I was away at school, and I wrote to him. Sometimes my mother would scrawl an oddly formal p.s., or my sister enclose a note. When I wrote that I had made a good friend, Stan, a boy older than I, and he had asked me to join his family for Thanksgiving, my father wrote a sentence that seemed to contradict itself: *You can take care of yourself, Allen, take care.* Many years later I made up this story, which I believe to be true.

Deep in the night, everyone asleep, someone climbed into Janos's bed. At first he thought it was Bill and that was nice, he was cold, but then he realized that someone was bigger than Bill, and Bill had never pushed his hands inside Janos's pajamas to stroke the bare flesh. The hands were gentle and calming, sliding here and there, until one of them found his privates and squeezed hard.

My father flailed out. One of the hands caught his wrist, the other struck him lightly across the face. Moonshine through the tall dirty windows made a little light. My father turned over and Lips placed one big hand on his eyes for a moment while the other kept petting him, caressing him. Lips was sixteen, the oldest, biggest boy in the dormitory, and my father had seen him washing, seen the hair under his arms and in his groin, but had never seen Lips's stiff twig. The older boy tickled the younger's privates to show him they weren't all that different after all.

In the dimness only the broadest phrases would have been visible, so Lips didn't attempt to explain what he was doing, only placed the boy's hand on his twig for a moment, then put his mouth on the boy's little shoot. That felt good, the moist warmth, the suction, the swirling tongue, and after a while something happened, at first it seemed that he was pissing in Lips's mouth but the sensation, the burning and the release, was stronger, and it spread throughout his body on a series of fast tremors, and when it was over he felt pleasantly weak.

When Lips pushed his head down my father thought it was only fair, but he couldn't get his lips around the hard twig, could only lick it, and didn't like the taste or the hair that caught in his teeth. Lips pulled him back up against his chest and petted him some more, kissed him, and turned him over. I'm sure that Lips was as gentle as any horny sixteen year old would be, but even for a grown man, an experienced homosexual who knows what's going on and wants it, the moment of penetration is painful.

My father was eleven when this happened. I was fifteen, and the other boy wasn't Stan, who had already graduated.

Didn't you know? said Bill.

My father shook his head. His eyes were still cold and staring, burning and raw, although it was daylight and he had slept two nights alone and safe. They sat in their usual hollow in the tall grass. The sky overhead stretched blue and serene forever. Bill touched Janos's shoulder lightly, not enough that the other boy should recoil.

He goes down to the cellar, you know, said Bill, to see No-hands.

No-hands showed him how, I bet. That's why the little kids call him Bogey.

My father, remembering the size and bulk of the janitor naked save for stained undershorts that clung to his haunches, damp with sweat, batted off the vision with small hands. But I don't know what he did!

It's what men do with women, to make babies.

I'm not a girl, my father said. Will I have a baby now? I don't want a baby. It hurt!

There aren't any girls, none Lips could do it with. Anyway, he doesn't want babies either. But—well, the first part, that felt good, didn't it?

I guess so.

When it gets hard you have to do something or it doesn't feel good. Especially for someone grown-up like Lips or No-hands. If there aren't any girls you have to do it with a boy. Or.

I won't. Even if it hurts bad. It can't hurt as much as he hurt me.

If he tries again, Bill said fiercely, we'll stop him. You and me.

Janos stared at the sky. Has anyone, he asked after a moment—to you?

Bill didn't answer. He looked into Janos's eyes, then ducked his chin. When it gets hard you don't have to put it in a girl or a boy. You can do it with your hand. Watch.

As a child I had no close, special friends—not until I went away to school. It seems important, though, that my father should have had a confidant during his years at the Pennsylvania School for the Deaf, a brother as it were, both protector and, on occasion, protected: Bill Smith. On the other hand, my father has not, to my knowledge, maintained contact with any of his schoolmates. Bill must have died, then. This would explain many things.

Visiting his family in the summer, Bill went swimming with his brother Bob in a flooded quarry or a swift-flowing river, and drowned.

One of the epidemics so common before the development of sulfa drugs and antibiotics swept through the school. Most of the victims recovered, but two or three, Bill among them, succumbed.

Working with one of the huge presses in the vocational training room, Bill miscalculated and slipped. His leg was crushed, gangrene set in, he died.

For weeks afterward Bill's best friend Janos saw the world around him through a numb, blood-tinged, glassy haze. He stopped speaking, which his teachers were sympathetic enough to excuse, and when he talked his hands faltered, broke into a digitolalia of bereavement. In any case, he could barely concentrate enough to focus on what people said to him. It was toward the end of this period, the age of grief, that he met the young woman called Lace in sign, although she owned no more lace by this time, who would become his wife and my mother.

~

IV: Within Walls Strong as Anyone's Hands

WHY I FELT I must reconcile the inconsistencies and lapses of logic in the fairy tale of my mother's childhood I no longer understand, since it is clear that anyone's life is equally a farrago of coincidence and miraculous opportunity, occasions mistaken, incidents misremembered, imaginary chronicles and made-up stories—lies and half-truths. I read through Jeremy's picture books—both those he's written himself and those more numerous, by other hands, whose stories he has made manifest—and I see our lives transformed, his and Toby's and mine, turned magical, glamorous, fantastical, true. Or I recall my nephew Kit, years ago, explaining to his little sister Jess that their grandfather couldn't speak because he had been bewitched. By his wife, no doubt. I think Kit no longer believes this, if he ever did, but perhaps he was right, as right as anyone can be about the past, which seems to me, now, far more uncertain than the future.

I watch Kit, and it seems no more remarkable that his parents should send him to live with us than that he should be twelve, nor less astonishing. I watch him in deep colloquy with Toby, catch snippets of family history, and wonder whether my nephew is making sense of them or if, more perceptive than I was, he isn't broadening the canvas, highlighting pigments with the kinds of glazes that change color over time, deepening, intensifying, so that the sketchily painted background looms forward, revealing forgotten or unrealized details, to surround and incorporate the figures in the foreground. Whose faces they wear. How many they are. How bright their shining eyes.

THE CHILD LAY on her narrow bed, staring at the ceiling far above, at the groined, scalloped arches of the Gothic Revival dormitory. She felt unwell, but like a sick dog did not know this, could not elucidate to herself the source of her discomfort, the fact of her discomfort. Had she possessed the skeletal and muscular flexibility of a dog or a cat she might have stroked her belly with her tongue. Instead she lay on her back with her arms rigid at her sides, fists clenched, and stared dry-eyed at the ceiling. From time to time, when a cramp struck, she made a little whimpering sound but did not hear herself, nor was there anyone else in the hall who could hear.

THEY CALLED HER Lace, for the fine Belgian lace on her petticoats and panties. Like Sara Crewe in *A Little Princess*, when my mother came to school she brought too varied and too fine a wardrobe, but she was not given her own little sitting room, nor did she have a French maid. Like Sara Crewe she was an oddly attractive rather than a pretty little girl. By the time she met my father she had grown into a striking young woman of fifteen who could not clearly recall how she had acquired her name. She no longer wore lacy Belgian linen, to be sure, but cheap cotton underpants that she washed herself because the harsh detergents and bleaches used in the school laundry gave her a rash, and a stiff, wired brassiere. She had no friends among the girls her own age. Her companions were little children, babies of seven, eight, nine whom she alternately mothered and bullied. She hated them, really, but there was no-one else to talk to. Nobody she could talk to.

They told her she was slow, teachers and peers alike. She was hopeless at lipreading, uttered only ugly, evil squawks when asked to speak. She did have lovely handwriting, holding the pen loosely in fingers to which it seemed a grafted extension so easily did it trace the elegant cursive loops and ligatures without blot or hesitation. (Her brother had taught her, she remembered that, she remembered sitting in his lap at a broad desk in the most beautiful, spacious room in the world, Lajos's large hand on her tiny one, drawing her through the alphabet and the graceful letters of her name, and his name—how lovely were the extravagant *K* and sweeping *L*, the twin looped tails of the *y* and the *j*, the little flip of the *s* of *Karolyi Lajos*.) But what was the use of a charming hand when all she did with it was create designs like black lace across the paper, or write phrases in foreign languages that she could not translate—homilies or truisms in French, German, Hungarian learned by rote at her brother's knee. (Lajos had apparently not found it necessary to include any English in his battery of penmanship exercises.) Children five years younger could read better than she.

These were the failings of Marit Karolyi, her teachers' pupil. Worse was the incapacity of Lace—she could hardly talk. I blame her family. They waited too long to place her with her own kind, waited until the drive to communicate was deformed within her, stunted. Especially I blame my uncle Lajos. I'm sure that his intention was to give her some kind of voice, some means of speaking and listening, but he made her dependent on him and on their private language so that she could talk to no-one else. It was a language largely without syntax and with the most limited vocabulary, a set of signals rather than a web of signs. For instance, their private code had no pronouns—Marit could not say *I*, only *Marit*, nor *you* but only *Lajos*. Marit hungry. Lajos tell Marit dress. It was as poor an excuse for a language as hearing educators are apt to accuse sign of being, practically useless in fostering the processes of cognition, so that my mother at nine or ten was little more capable of abstract thought than a preverbal infant, no more communicative than the trained acrobat dog in a circus act. Like the prized pet of a circus artiste, she became helpless in her master's absence, reduced to reflex and instinct.

Lajos was her god, she his vessel. When he left her she went into a decline.

OR THIS IS what I thought—these were my speculations, my stabs at understanding my mother's personality, before I realized their fundamental implausibility. A woman who signs with the fluency, the fiery grace, the venom and comprehensiveness of my mother could not have been dumb throughout her childhood. I had a romantic notion that my father had taught her to talk. Perhaps this is what she wished me to believe (wakened to life like Snow White by her prince's kiss), but she is more eloquent than he. In any case, they didn't meet until she was fifteen.

Interactions among girls and boys at the Pennsylvania School for the Deaf were discouraged, officially. The administration's claim that their charges would become normal, productive young Americans by graduation—ready and capable to enter the great hearing world beyond the gates—required that the students not form a community, most particularly not a community circumscribed by its own language, a ghetto. Passing for hearing would necessitate constant effort, constant vigilance, which might be undermined if the graduates associated with each other. There should be no need to do so, in any case. The school turned out fine, upstanding young men and women, good citizens, who would fit into society like tenon into mortise. Besides, as had been pointed out by the great pioneer of deaf education Alexander Graham Bell, intermarriage among the deaf must be avoided lest a permanent, self-perpetuating race of cripples result—crippled not only by their physical handicap but by their lack of true language. Bell himself had set the example by marrying a deaf woman, one of his students. Their children were hearing. Most telling, Mrs. Bell professed an aversion to the company of other deaf persons, those who talked with their hands, who would not fit in. They were defective. Thanks to her husband's tutelage, she was not.

In practice, however, the boys met the girls, the girls spent time with the boys, teachers and matrons ignored the meetings if they did not, perhaps, encourage them. Perhaps among the staff were some who knew that Mr. Bell had been inspired to teach the deaf by his deaf mother. Perhaps there were those who knew that the incidence of congenital deafness was low, that the majority of their students had acquired the disability through illness or accident and so would not pass it on. In any event, the girls met the boys, the boys spent time with the girls. My mother met my father.

FEELING UNWELL, THE girl lay flat on her back on the narrow bed, arms rigid at her sides, fists clenched. Dry-eyed, she stared at the ceiling. When a cramp struck, from time to time, she moved her lips and exhaled, unaware that her breath uttered forth with a high-pitched moan. If anyone tried to talk to her she would not reply, would close her fists more tightly until the knuckles showed white and the nails had dug crescents into her palms. But nobody would try to talk to her. Everyone was used to her, accustomed to her monthly incapacitation. Matron would no longer give her aspirin—it did no good, and in any case Matron suspected the girl of malingering. She was still cursed herself, thank the Lord, but you didn't catch her taking to her bed once a month. A fine mess the hall would be in if she did. Privately, Matron, who maintained friendly relations with one of the gentlemen on the teaching staff, felt that a man would cure the girl quickly enough—and didn't the girl think so herself, her with the sly eyes and pouty lips and a bosom that was a scandal on a child of fifteen. In her own fashion, Matron was a philosopher and a fatalist: she believed that her charges had so little they should take what they could get; and believed that no hearing man would have a deaf girl. Or if he would, he wasn't a man who should be trusted with a deaf girl, nor a man a deaf girl ought to want. Like calls to like, she said to herself—or, more aptly, *waves* to like.

Bustling down the central passageway of the dormitory between the ranks of iron-framed beds, Matron noted that the girl with the odd, foreign name and the bad attitude, the one with no friends, had retreated to her bed again, lay still save for an occasional voiceless groan and nearly invisible contraction of thighs and pelvis. Matron carried a load of freshly laundered towels. Having deposited them on the shelves beside the three basins at the end of the dormitory, she returned to Marit's bed. She stood above the prone girl. When she wished, Matron could make herself understood. It would be better for you to be moving around, the blood needs to flow if it is to flow.

Marit stared at her stonily.

"I'm not asking you, girl," she said aloud, restating a pantomime my mother must already have understood. How arrogant are the hearing. Nor do I excuse myself: inventing a past for my mother as if she weren't capable of doing so herself—heedlessly imagining the voice she could not hear. Matron placed her hand on the girl's shoulder, told her to get up, dress herself, and go down to the laundry in the basement. "Here, I'll write a note to Mrs. George. I want you to deliver towels to the boys' dormitories." Curse me for a bleeding Samaritan, she told herself: a pander.

When her trial came, every month before the blood that was itself a trial, Marit looked into memory in search of her crime. It wasn't that she linked the violent cramps, dizzy nausea, and headaches with being abandoned by her family but that, feeling physically miserable, she was reminded of a more authentic misery that was inescapable, the context of her existence, her life itself. But what could a child who could hardly talk have done that was so terrible as to merit such punishment? She could only remember Lajos, his kindness, his gentleness, the gift of his smile, his hands that, in her memory, spoke more clearly than anyone's, told her how much he loved his little sister—his arms and starched chest, which, carrying her to bed, told her the same thing.

The towels smelled of bleach, as Lajos's shirts had smelled of bleach, but Lajos's shirts had also carried the scent of lavender and his own special perfume, distilled of tobacco, starch, pomade, eau de Cologne; of the anise pastilles he sucked and gave to her sometimes, although she only liked them because they were his and crunched them between her teeth instead of allowing them to dissolve on her tongue; of masculine sweat. Entering the boys' dormitory, Marit was staggered by a surge of sick giddiness and leaned against the jamb of the door, gasping.

The towels were taken from her arms, and she was led with a brusque courtesy away from the doorway, settled on the edge of a bed as hard as her own in another wing of the school. Opening her eyes against the taste of bile in her throat, the quickening in her belly, she saw a pair of white hands that said, Are you all right? She focused on the motion of the hands, and then looked up.

Lajos! she said. Or it might have been Brother or Beloved or simply You!

I don't understand, the hands said, and now she saw that it wasn't her brother for Lajos would not wear a coarse white collarless shirt and short trousers—Lajos was not a child. Lajos would not have needed to ask if she was ill, he would have known.

Who are you? she asked, her hands clumsy.

My father told her his name, and because it was his name—had been his name as long as he could remember—he didn't understand why she started and crooked her lips. For him the gesture had lost its meaning except as it meant himself, a dead metaphor, an ideograph shorn of its original referent the way the Chinese character for *house* has become only a few strokes of the brush that little resemble the cottage with peaked roof of which it was once a sketch.

Tilt-eyes? the girl repeated, then shook her head. She made the same gesture as before, something that did not look like a word, that read as foreign, indecipherable. Then, reaching into the neckline of her blouse, she drew forth a fine silver chain. She snapped open the locket and gazed at it, compared the photograph against my father's face. The resemblance was there—not as close as she had believed, more difference between the two than age and clothing only, but there. Unhooking the chain's clasp, she handed the locket to the boy, and told him, again, his name.

DURING MY CHILDHOOD my mother was frequently ill, although I don't think I recognized the periodicity of her indisposition until after the fact. For a day or two she would be pale and fragile, would complain of headaches and less specific pains, and often retreated to the darkened bedroom whence she would emerge, finally, not cheerful but with a better color and most of her authority. One day in the fall when I was seven or eight, I think, I returned from school to find the house locked and, as far as I could tell, empty. This had never happened before. Even if my mother were inside it would have been useless to bang on the door or shout. Neither of these courses occurred to me anyway. I sat on the steps to the porch for a little while, and then I noticed that the hose spigot beside the steps had leaked and formed a puddle of irresistible mud.

I had been playing for some time when I heard a car door slam shut. Ordinarily, as if I were deaf myself, I simply don't hear quotidian neighborhood noises, cars, the shrieks of children or their parents calling them, but I looked up. The car belonged to the woman next door, a person I believed to be very old although I imagine, now, she was perhaps fifty. She came toward me, her heels clapping on the sidewalk. "Allen," she said, the first time in my memory she had ever addressed me, "Allen, you poor boy, you don't even know."

A polite child, I said, "Hello, Mrs. Phillips, how are you?"

She crouched, stiffly, a step or two away from me and my mud puddle. "Allen," she said, "listen to me. Your mother is very sick, she's in the hospital. Do you know what a hospital is?"

ONLY AN HOUR or so before, my mother had written in large, shaky letters on a piece of paper, *Sick Hospital Husband Janos*, and staggered out of the house. Luckily, Mrs. Phillips was outside as well, admiring her patch of front garden, as I think my mother would not have thought to knock on her door. "Mrs. Pasztory!" said Mrs. Phillips as my mother, white-faced, grunting and moaning in a way that in a hearing person would suggest dementia, tottered toward her. "You poor dear!" Mrs. Phillips cried after reading the note my mother thrust at her, "wait here," making ineffectual little patting and soothing motions, "I'll get my car."

Mrs. Phillips drove my mother to the hospital and explained her into the emergency room, had the admitting nurse call the print shop for my father. He arrived accompanied by his supervisor, Allen MacDonald. The two men understood each other almost as though they spoke the same language. "The children," Allen MacDonald said to Mrs. Phillips, "they'll be getting home from school."

Steph must have explained to me what had happened although I have no memory of her telling me—it's as though it were something I knew for myself. My mother was pregnant, had miscarried, hemorrhaged. The emergency room physician called in a gynecologist. This doctor, a man I hope never to meet, unable to understand my mother and assuming, I suppose, that she was mentally deficient or simply that he knew best, quite calmly performed a hysterectomy.

Allen MacDonald and others of my father's friends encouraged him to sue, but this was before medical malpractice suits became a public issue and a growth industry; and anyway, my father said, a deaf man, a blue-collar worker—what chance did he have against a respected physician? Any jury would agree it was best to prevent the propagation of cripples.

Janos held the locket in his cupped palm. He did not recognize the face in the photograph. He had seen the girl before, from a distance; someone had told him her name. He wondered why she was called Lace, there was nothing lacy or delicate about her. Certainly she didn't talk with the precision or patience required for lace-making. She would tear any lace she held. Her hands flared with explosive inflection, as if she were grabbing for her meaning, rending it, or fending it off. Some of her signs he did not recognize at all; some of her syntax was muddled, childish. She had looked so peculiar when he glanced up and saw her, leaning against the door frame. Girls never came into the boys' dormitories, yet there she was. Her chin propped atop the stack of towels so that it appeared for a moment to be part of the load, or as if the towels were cushion for this gift she brought him: her face, pale, pale as though drained of its animating blood, pinched and tight, the eyelashes fluttering and the thin lips parted, and all of it bundled in her extraordinary hair, a color he could not name, a hard brilliant color like copper or the polished wooden tables in the formal reception room, or the leaves of frost-struck rhododendrons, brassy, metallic, curled into tight quills. It was like none of those colors; none was more than a hint, a suggestion. Her hair was thick, tangled, vital—more alive than the face it surrounded. He wanted to touch it, to gather its energy in his hands as he pushed it back from her brow, and then to transfer the electricity of her hair to the pained, still features of her face. She leaned against the door frame, her torso hidden by the towels. The leg on which she placed no weight trembled violently.

When he took the towels from her arms, she opened her eyes wide for an instant, blind, then pressed both hands against her belly and bent forward, not, it seemed to Janos for a moment, on the pivot of her waist but as if her spine and shoulders were crumpling. He led her to the nearest bed and, when her eyes opened, asked if she was all right. The idiocy of the question: Are you all right? Of course she wasn't. She pressed her hands together, then looked up into his face with those thick, luminous eyes whose color he could not remember, and her hands like startled birds flew up and apart, then dove in toward each other and articulated a word or a phrase he had never seen before.

It was the name of the person in the photograph, he realized now. She thrust the locket into his hand, repeated the unknown name. Then her hands, articulate, arbitrary and autonomous as if she had borrowed them from someone else, darted to her face, the fingers pressed against cheeks flooded with color, and she leapt to her feet, shoving him aside, and ran out the door. She was strong. He thought she had been taller than he. He remembered the knob of her shoulder in his hand, through the stiff cambric of her blouse, remembered how his knuckle had grazed her breast as he helped her sit. He would need to return the locket to her. He gazed at the photograph a moment longer, then latched the locket and strung the chain around his own neck, tucked the locket into his shirt where it lay cold and hard against his breastbone, then warmed.

FRAMING

Roads, Signs

AT ABOUT THE same time in my own life, I loaded my suitcase into the belly of a bright steel bus and climbed aboard, heading south, heading home. There was a new driver's license in my wallet, first official portrait, my rucksack was filled with college catalogues and viewbooks, Matthew had promised to write, and it was the summer of 1974.

The train from Boston stopped at Penn Station in New York, two hours to wait, but I had nowhere to go in that time, no-one to see, and the terminal was crowded with so many hundreds of intent travelers who knew exactly what they were doing, where they were going, that I was scared. This happened every time I passed through New York City. I had grown up in a city but outside the center, on a quiet street where magnolia and dogwood bloomed in the spring, then catalpas with their racemes of white blossoms, where my parents in their small wood-frame house created an isolated silent world that anyone might take to be as stylized and formal as Japanese Noh theater. For the last three years I had spent fall, winter, and spring in a small New England town, divorced from the life of the town by the invisible barriers around the school, and from the school, to an extent, by being a scholarship student and having the family I did. I'm not proud of that boy, who wanted to be like everyone else in public but insisted on retaining his secrets and silences. There was a boy in my class, a Swiss from Ticino, who every year did a turn on growing up multilingual—English was his fourth language. I never talked about my background. Everyone knew, but I wouldn't let an issue be made of it. One of my English teachers asked me to read to the class an essay I'd written about my father. I said I'd rather not, and didn't write about my family again.

In the train station I sat on a bench, eating my hot dog, drinking my soda, paging through my catalogues, like any other prep-school boy going home for summer vacation. Glancing up once, I saw two men talking together in an eddy of the crowd: talking with their hands. For a moment I stared at them, then lowered my eyes to read another paragraph about Duke or Stanford or Yale, then looked up again. They were talking about a book one of them had read, an exhibit the other had seen, the best place to buy something whose name I didn't recognize— it wasn't an interesting conversation, yet I felt like a spy overseeing it because they were so intent. Because they must have assumed no-one around could eavesdrop. Young, in their mid-twenties I think, and handsome, they had nothing on their minds but this colloquy, and stood still, hands flaring and their faces passing through so many vivid changes that the most expressive speaking actor's face would seem a blank porcelain mask in comparison.

The crowd whirled around them, some startled by the obstruction, some annoyed, most not noticing at all, and I watched, until the one who seemed a little older glanced at his watch. He may not have been older—it could have been the suit, the trim beard, in contrast to his friend's blue jeans and leather jacket. Time to catch your train, he said. They shrugged at each other, looking momentarily sad, and embraced. Someone passing by muttered, "Goddamn queers." As if they had heard, the two deaf men kissed, and I checked my watch. I wanted to follow them to the platform, to get on the same train with the leather-jacketed one, to talk to him all the way to Baltimore. My train wasn't leaving for another forty-five minutes.

I got off the train again in Baltimore, early in the evening. Going straight home I would have stayed on to DC, changed there to another train, but the plan was for me to stay a few days with my sister, and then we'd drive down together. I intended to do most of the driving. Steph wasn't waiting for me on the platform, nor did I see her in the vast waiting room. She was often late; I wasn't worried. I set down my bags, got a cup of coffee from the snack bar, and sat down to wait. The Baltimore terminal didn't scare me the way the one in New York did, although there were very nearly as many people milling about.

Along with all the college catalogues, I carried a book, a hefty paperback novel. Matthew had given it to me for my birthday but I hadn't had time yet to do more than write my name on the inside front cover, above where Matthew had written *Sweet sixteen and getting sweeter, April 18, 1974, love from Matthew Sanremo.* There was a bookmark too, stuck into the thick of it, which I pulled out since I had no place to mark. Cut from heavy drawing paper, it had my name across the top in laborious calligraphy, below that an imitation-Beardsley pen-and-ink vignette of an androgynous medieval youth holding a sword and a mirror; and below that a short pseudo-Imagist stanza, which I am glad I can no longer quote—although it was important to me then, and I still recall its existence gratefully.

On the back Matthew had written in his usual choppy, forceful hand and with a candor that reinterpreted the fin-de-siècle aestheticism of the front, *Allen, this is not a very good book, it's all lies, but they're agreeable lies and you should treasure the book if only on account of the* look *the woman in the bookshop gave me when I picked it up—what's a clean-cut young man like you doing buying such degenerate trash, she was thinking, but I'd special-ordered and prepaid so she couldn't not give it to me. What was she doing looking at it, I wonder. Anyway, I felt marvelously sordid, and now you can too. Love, Matthew.*

"What are you reading, Allen?" my sister asked.

I looked up, and stood up. "Steph." I was taller than she—we both noticed this at the same time, I think, just before we hugged and she apologized for being late. The bookmark fluttered to the floor. As my sister stooped to retrieve it her hair drooped along the line of her jaw, six inches shorter than it had been at Christmas. "I like your new hair," I said.

Hooking it behind her ear with a gesture that looked invented, un-practiced, she peered sidelong at me. "It's not new, I did this months ago. I guess it's been a while, Allen." She started smiling in the way she had, acknowledging that we were friends. "And you've gone and grown on me—two inches? Three?" Hardly glancing at it, she handed me the bookmark. "Come on. I figured you'd be waiting so I parked illegally." She shouldered my rucksack. "What've you got in here?" she asked, wincing and staggering melodramatically. "It feels like rocks."

Steph's car was a tiny Japanese toy but we were both small. Pulling onto the street she said, "I feel like I'm trusting myself to an eggshell every time I take this machine into traffic." She was driving—she knew the way. "How've you been, little brother?"

One of those polite queries that ordinarily doesn't expect an an-swer—but between Steph and me it meant something, meant she had something to tell me. Close as children, as close as a little girl and her best doll, we were no longer close since the evening thirteen-year-old Stephanie told her parents that none of her friends shared their bed-room with a brother and eight-year-old Allen said he didn't want to sleep in the same room with a stupid old girl anyway. We made up, we had to, but there was still that distance, that strain—it was about then, I think, that we began speaking English, exclusively, with each other. Friends nevertheless, but Steph is always more eager to share her secrets with me than I with her. "I'm okay, I guess," I said. "Tired."

She wasn't looking at me, was staring at the street before us, the hill rising and hastening off into a future when the daughter of deaf-mute parents, pre-law at Johns Hopkins, would test her voice in the courts—toward Stanford, why not, Yale, Duke. "I don't have anything entertaining planned so you can go to bed early. Allen, I'm not living alone, did I tell you?"

"No. What's she like?"

"Who? Oh—she's six feet tall and has a beard. He's my boyfriend. I'd rather you didn't tell Mother and Daddy. Funny thing, he went to your school."

"Okay." I looked away from my sister, out the window, a cavalcade of dilapidated row houses. I suppose I was shocked, not imagining, the way one doesn't imagine one's parents having a sex life. "Is he nice?"

"Stupid. Of course he's nice. His name's Mickey."

My sister's apartment was small and mean. Bright art postcards made a shabby mosaic on one wall of the short entrance hall. Mickey, her boyfriend, surprised me—big and fair and bearish, he seemed to materialize from the brightness beyond an open door, and Steph moved into his aura without a word or a sign. The top of her head level with his chest, she looked as small as a child as she nuzzled into his side and he patted her head, then extended a huge hand to me. "Allen," he said, an amused bass rumble, "good to meet you."

I let him take my hand, half the size of his, and I coughed. I couldn't look at him, couldn't look away. Massive as a quarterback, wearing only a gold chain around his neck and clean white Jockey shorts, he was too much for me to take in, his erotic presence as powerful as a drug.

"You think maybe you should get dressed, Mickey?" Steph said, but fondly, no edge to her voice—her voice, I thought, I assumed, furred with desire.

"Aaw, Stephie," Mickey grumbled, "it's so hot and we're family." But he turned back into the thick golden light in the doorway and vanished again. Although he moved quietly, his feet less loud than my heart, the building seemed to move with him, lumbering side-to-side tremors.

Steph glanced at me, then hugged me quickly—coquettishly. "Sorry," she whispered. "Mickey doesn't like clothes. I'm surprised he remembered to put on his shorts, actually, even though I reminded him. Last winter he kept the heat way up so he wouldn't have to get dressed—good thing he pays the utilities." She drew me after her, into a small living room that seemed large because of the windows in the far wall.

Mickey came through another door. He had put on cut-off jeans and a t-shirt but didn't seem any less naked. "Like a beer, Allen?" he asked over his shoulder, veering into an alcove-kitchenette where he crouched to rummage in a small refrigerator.

Steph put her hand on my shoulder again. "Isn't there Coke or something?"

"I'd like a beer." My voice squeaked on the last syllable, then grated as I grappled it down to its new register. "It won't be my first, Steph."

"I shouldn't let you. But okay." She touched me again. All this touching and embracing was new. "C'mon, I'll show you the rest of the palace, Allen. You can leave your stuff here." She showed me the small dark bedroom—a mattress in the corner, block-and-board bookshelves, untidy piles of clothing—and a dank bathroom with a powerful odor of urine and mildew. "What can I say?" she said, leading me back. "The rent's cheap."

In the living room Mickey was standing at an open casement, looking out. Two green glass bottles, already frosted and puddling with condensation, stood on the floor in front of a twin-bed mattress covered with an Indian bedspread and piled with pillows. Picking up the beers, Steph handed one to me. "One for me, one for my little brother. Make yourself at home."

I sat on the edge of the mattress, stared at the lip of the bottle in my hands. It wavered. The glass was cold and slippery.

Mickey turned around, sat on the windowsill. "Cheers," he said, swigging his own beer, "and welcome, Allen." He flattened both syllables of my name, drawing it out, giving the name an odd, courtly, Southern formality.

Gathering up my courage, although I still couldn't look at him, I raised the bottle, muttered, "Cheers," and put it to my lips. I'd lied to Steph, it was my first. The glass lip knocked against my teeth, but the beer was cold, so cold I couldn't taste it and had to swallow. "Mickey," I said, trying for a similarly easy accentuation, "why don't you call me

Lefty." I wanted him to use a name as casual and friendly, as intimate as his own.

"Lefty?" he said, and Steph, "Do people really call you Lefty?"

"Well, it's sort of like what Dad calls me."

"I guess." When I glanced at her, not at her face, Steph's hand was tracing my father's nickname for me.

I drank my beer too quickly as Mickey and I talked about the school that had graduated him three years before, that I still attended—teachers we both knew, small change. It bothered me when I realized he was younger than Steph, but not as much as I was bothered every time I glanced up to see his sturdy torso, his broad shoulders outlined against the light in the window, or saw the small contractions in the muscles of upper arm, shoulder, chest when he raised his own bottle. He asked if I'd like another and got up to fetch it. I didn't know what it felt like to be drunk; I thought I might be drunk. My arms and legs seemed very far away. Heavy, my eyes slid in their sockets without my intervention, from the radiance of the windows to an overstuffed Salvation Army armchair, faded burgundy plush, and a stack of thick textbooks beside it, to a travel agency poster of Budapest and Beautiful Hungary taped to the wall near the kitchen alcove, and then on a long delirious swoop to my sister on the mattress beside me, leaning forward, over her shoulders molding the pink fabric of her shirt, the straight gleaming fall of chestnut hair and the pale curve of her cheek.

I pushed my shoulders back into the pile of cushions, closed my eyes for an instant. My stomach dropped away. "Your beer, Lefty," someone said, and my body lurched forward, very slowly it seemed, my left hand accepted the bottle offered to it, and I took a sip, held the palely bitter liquid on my tongue before swallowing.

"Shall I start dinner?" said someone else, and I glared across the room to the armchair where a person I knew was Mickey lounged back into the curve of the wing, one leg hooked over the opposite arm.

I knew he was Mickey yet he looked like Matthew, a head shorter, slight, wiry, gracile, bony. Matthew and I had been friends since freshman year, competing against each other as the liberal arts brains of our class and, in a way, as athletes, he on the soccer field, I in the pool. The competition wasn't real, though, if only because I was poor and from the South. In the invertedly snobbish atmosphere of prep school my prestige was automatically greater—the virtue of exoticism; while as a

privileged child of the metropolitan Northeast Matthew had a background that was more useful to him. Yet we managed to get along,
hilariously, conspiring as much as competing. Halfway through our
second year, fed up with roommates who seemed duller than necessary,
we asked to be reassigned.

On returning from winter break we found ourselves suddenly in
close quarters. Some eight feet separated our beds, on either side of an
imaginary funhouse mirror that reflected, on one hand, his down comforter and a poster of Venice's Grand Canal, on the other the blankets
on my bed and a bare wall. Matthew had a small electric kettle, strictly
illegal. He made instant coffee for us late at night when we were study-
ing in the stifling dry heat of the radiator under the window. Wearing
flannel pajamas, I pressed bare feet against the metal supports of the
desk to absorb their coolness. Behind me, Matthew leaned over his own
desk; he wore a white t-shirt and tartan or tattersall boxer shorts, and
mocked my pajamas. If I went to bed later than he, turning before I
switched off my desk lamp, I would see his bare shoulders half uncov-
ered by the comforter, hard and angular, the sweet color of coffee ice
cream; I would see the shorts and shirt discarded on the floor.
Imagining his naked body cocooned in downy warmth, I would find it
difficult to sleep.

I had seen Matthew nude on many occasions, when he got out of
bed in the morning, rumpled and surly, in the communal bathroom or
in the showers after his soccer practice. In fact his body didn't interest
me as much as did the beefy hirsute maturity of some of the older students or the raw sculpted masses of my coach's chest and back when he
stripped to his swimsuit after practice to join us roughhousing in the
pool. Yet the image of Matthew lying quiescent under the quilt, knees
pulled up, one arm crooked under the pillow and the other hand
tucked in his armpit—this was a very different picture. Asleep, he
breathed silently through his mouth and a thread of spittle hung from
the corner of his lips to the pillow. His thick dark eyelashes lay on his
cheek like a stroke of soft charcoal across newsprint. Ear, cheek, and the
rims of his nostrils were flushed a rose-tinted beige.

My fantasies about the men whose bodies I liked to look at were
amorphous, nonspecific. More athletic, really, than erotic, for lack of
knowledge and experience as much as for a kind of shame I could not
articulate—they involved vague narratives of racing or swimming or

wrestling, and I described to myself the other man, the movements and stresses of his muscles, the way skin clothed bone and flesh, more clearly than I could reconstruct his actions—inconclusive little stories that were sensual but not properly erotic, in which I wasn't really engaged or involved. But for Matthew, fragile and defenseless in slumber, I felt something tactile and tactical. Lying in bed, pajamas binding my joints like poorly wrapped bandages, I felt in a way that my limbs were the same as his, assuming the same posture and configuration the way our thoughts often merged so that one could complete the other's sentences. I would lie there shivering within my bones with an anticipation I couldn't distinguish from dread, worsened by the impression—which couldn't be pinned down—that he knew and understood more than I. That he enjoyed his superior insight, that in the occasional catch of his breath or quirk of his eyebrows Matthew acknowledged something, tossed me clues I couldn't read.

On a night when the swim team returned victorious from an away-match where I had bettered my freestyle personal best, a cool fall night, the windows open and the scent of freshly cut grass outside confiding with the heavy smell of chlorine on my skin, I plundered into the room and threw myself on the bed.

"You won," said Matthew from the other bed where he reclined in a nest of pillows, reading.

"We're going to the semifinals," I told him, and he looked across at me with an expression that contained a secret, a clear yet illegible statement.

"Go take a shower," he said, "and I'll make some coffee."

Because there was no way to keep milk, and sugar might attract ants, we drank our coffee black, a habit in which I have persisted although I no longer drink instant. When I returned, smelling of soap and the sweaty flannel of pajamas more than of chlorine, Matthew handed me a cup, said, "Congratulations," and smiled.

I draped towel and swimsuit over the windowsill to dry, recounting my triumph. When I turned around I saw that he sat on the foot of my bed instead of his own, balancing his mug on crossed ankles. He asked when the next home meet was so he could plan to come watch, and whether he could travel with the team next time to root for us. I pulled out my desk chair. Matthew said, "Shy?" so I giggled, sat on the edge of the bed, gulped the muddy, bitter coffee.

"Allen," Matthew said, then seemed to change his mind, said, "Congratulations," again and reached out to shake my hand. Bending forward I tipped my cup, slopped scalding coffee over my legs, leapt off the bed with a shout, sloshing the rest of the cup over the bed.

Before I understood what he was doing Matthew had pulled off my pajamas and was wiping my legs with them. "Clumsy," he kept saying, "clumsy." A pink blotch marred the flesh of my thigh; its heat, spreading in, felt cold. I started to shiver. "Get in my bed," Matthew ordered, "get under the quilt, you'll catch a chill."

From there I watched him strip my bed, throw blankets and sheets in a heap with the pajamas. "Clumsy," he muttered again. "You'll have a bunch of laundry to do tomorrow. Good thing it didn't go through to the mattress." Gazing down at me, he said, "You okay, Allen?" then grabbed my towel off the windowsill and sat down beside me, rubbed my damp hair with the towel.

"Matthew." I drew away from his concern, away from the soothing warmth of his bed and the comfort of his fingers digging into my scalp. "I can't sleep here tonight."

"Why not? Are you afraid I might kiss you?" he asked, kissing me. "That I might start something you wouldn't want to stop?"

"Yes." I was shivering, trembling from the bones outward, unable to stop, afraid of his knowing smile that just tipped the corners of his mouth but etched his eyes deep in their molasses brown centers and etched deep into my eyes. "Yes, I'm frightened."

"Don't be," he murmured.

I felt someone lift my feet, stretch me out on the narrow mattress. "A beer and a half and he's gone," someone said. Someone else, "He's just a kid. I bet he didn't eat lunch." I wanted to say I was there, to open my eyes, sit up, start talking, but it seemed I wasn't there, was there only enough to feel a distant sloshy nausea as they moved me. Someone was untying my shoelaces, as though I were a little child. "He'll be uncomfortable in all these clothes." "Come on, Mickey, not everyone has your nudist tendencies." Shoes and socks off, then the shirt being unbuttoned. "No, I mean it, they'll cut off his circulation. What does he sleep in—his shorts? PJ's?" I wanted to thank them for their concern, ask them to leave me alone. "In his clothes, right now. How should I know. For Christ's sake, he's sixteen." The hands undressing me were gentle, severe. "Look, Stephie, I know what it's like passing out and then waking up. You want to be comfortable. Go make dinner and I'll take care of the kid." By now the jeans were gone and I felt the careful hands on the waistband of my underpants, knuckling into the flesh. "Prep school boys," the voice muttered, "think they're grown-up 'cause they've got hair on their balls, but show 'em a beer." Swatting me lightly on the rump, he covered me with a sheet. "Sleep it off, Lefty. God willing, you won't have a hangover."

Marriage

THIS IS WHAT it was like. Buying the smallest chicken in the poultry display at the supermarket, shrouded in plastic shrinkwrap on its yellow Styrofoam tray. The apartment is only four blocks from Cala Foods, so you walk, uphill, and then trudge up two flights. Put the groceries away in the kitchen, toilet paper in the bathroom cupboard. Sean complains that you don't think to buy toilet paper. He won't be home but if he does return the chicken's big enough for two. You're still dressed for work, suit, tie, white shirt, loafers, briefcase. In the bedroom take it all off, put it all away and start over from the beginning, clean white Jockey shorts, button-fly blue jeans worn to the matter-of-fact softness of chamois, a t-shirt, extra large although you're small. This one is the color of weak tea and bears, silk-screened across the chest, the image of an old-fashioned, jointed teddy bear wearing a droopy red bow. Captions indicate the salient points of a teddy bear's anatomy— *Brain: teddy bear brains are remarkable for remembering only the good things. Heart: although it is invisible the heart encompasses the entire torso of the teddy.*

Barefoot, you return to the kitchen, a mean, small space without enough counters, Sean says, but with a window through which you can see a neon-lit fraction of the Castro Cinema marquee. Sean is a man who knows how to cook and therefore owns only specialized cookbooks, the kind that assume a working familiarity that you don't have, may never have, eight years of academic cafeterias broken by incursions of your mother's safe, clean, sturdy cooking. You bought a bulky paperback, the latest revision of *The Joy of Cooking*, and dream of Baked Alaska, Floating Island, Apple Pan Dowdy, Brownies Cockaigne.

Remove the chicken from the refrigerator. It looks smaller than when you purchased it, shriveled, wrinkled, with warty butter-yellow skin torn around the cavity to reveal milkily pale flesh. Unwrap it and discard the wrappings. Should you stuff it? You consult the index, the recipes, decide you won't, you've never much liked stuffing and anyway you forgot to buy celery or onions. In the cupboard under the

65

sink you find a metal pan that ought to fit. As you lift the fowl from its tray into the pan you notice an edge of bloody paper protruding from the cavity. Surprised, disgusted, reach in and pull out the wrapped neck and giblets. The liver—it must be the liver—slides through your fingers, slimy as gelatin. Gingerly, fastidious, toss the whole mess into the garbage and wash your hands.

Cut a large pat of butter into a saucepan, place it over a low flame as you set the oven to preheat at 325°. With Sean's pastry brush (he'll yell at you later), tenderly coat the bird with a mantle of melted butter, then sprinkle salt liberally over. Two or three grinds of pepper and a dusting of paprika from a red, white, and green tin, the only one on the spice shelf that's yours: Pride of SZEGED HUNGARIAN Exquisite 100% Sweet Delicacy PAPRIKA and a red, white, and green outline map of Magyarország. Check the recipe again. Twenty-eight minutes per pound for an unstuffed bird, an hour and a half more or less. Glazed with butter, russet with the gilding of paprika, the chicken still looks horrible. Slide it into the oven.

Nervous, you'll check it every fifteen minutes, brushing it with the unctuous juices and oils that puddle and bubble in the pan, spitting when they hit the hot metal sides. ("Have you never heard of a turkey-baster?" Sean will yell, waving the implement at you. —"I'll buy you a new brush, I'll buy two of them.") The skin takes on a rich red brown translucence like stained glass, crisp, and the kitchen fills with savory odors. The recipe advises you to poke a skewer into the thickest part of the drumstick when you think the chicken's ready. If the juices run clear it's done, but they're cloudy with blood the first three times.

And then it is done, cooked through, the leg moves easily in its socket, and you have forgotten to peel, boil, mash the potatoes, to steam the string beans. Staring at the chicken afloat in its lake of drippings—you were going to make gravy—its rich glazed crust, you'll find that you're no longer hungry, and shove it back into the oven with only the pilot light to keep it warm.

Then, later, much later—and what have you done in the meanwhile?—you'll return to the kitchen and pull the pan back out again, balance it across two burners on the top of the stove. The liquids have separated, a thin savory brown aspic, floating plaques of congealed fat. The chicken's skin seems also to have congealed, to have absorbed moisture and become thick and rich rather than crisp, a rind instead of a crust. Lift the fowl from its bed of jelly and fat to a platter. What to do with the drippings? Not gravy at this point. Scrape them into the garbage pail, set the pan in the sink with detergent and hot water.

Reclining in simple splendor on the white platter the chicken is either beautiful, succulent, toothsome, or revolting, you can't decide. You find that you're unwilling to take a knife to it, yet you're hungry, and less willing to discard the chicken after all your effort. In fact, it is some accomplishment to have prepared it in the first place, whether or not you can bring yourself to eat it. If Sean had been here to see the fowl brought out of the oven the first time, if he had praised it, you'd feel proud. If Sean had been here you would have remembered to prepare the side dishes. How does anyone cook for himself alone, how enjoy the result as well as the process? You'd like to know how to cook for other people. But Sean wouldn't praise roast chicken—he'd dismiss it as a tiresome banality. You'd rather go out to dinner, to a restaurant, or to someone's house where you could watch the chef as he works, admire his expertise and concentration, compliment the final meal. The chicken ought to sit on a bed of glossy watercress, there ought to be attractive serving plates mounded with fresh baby vegetables, barely cooked, a mountain of mashed potatoes scented with nutmeg or mace, a boat of rich gravy; there ought to be a table spread with white linen and heavy silver, a bowl of roses, silver candlesticks and beeswax candles, two bottles of good wine, crystal goblets. There ought to be someone to dine with you.

The drumstick comes loose easily, hardly a wrench, as if the cartilaginous joints had softened and dissolved in the oven's heat. In your hand it feels slick but with a wrinkled, seductive texture, and it fits your grasp well. A thin hard glaze of salt fractures under your teeth, a flavor that is no flavor yet which excites you, an intense breathless saltiness permeating the slippery, chewy skin under the crust. The skin slides off the flesh in one piece with only a little drag, a hesitation, and hangs over your lower lip, dabbing at your chin as teeth and tongue draw it into your mouth. Bent over the platter and the dismembered fowl, you're chewing now, gobbling it down, your free hand clutching the lip of the counter as you absorb the inextricably mingled flavors and odors of chicken skin, salt, paprika, pepper, butter, as you hear your teeth grate and slip, your breath hiss through your nostrils, hear yourself grunt and hum, biting into the tender flesh. Finished with the drumstick, discard the bones, lick greasy lips, rub the greasy tips of fingers together before digging them into the firm, yielding muscle at the side of the breastbone, tearing off strips of thinner skin and pale flesh to push between your lips, between the jaws that won't stop chewing for a moment because you cannot satisfy your hunger.

BUT IT WAS also like this. I half-woke every morning at five-thirty when the alarm rang and Sean rolled out of bed—easy enough with a bed that was no more than a mattress on the floor—pulled on shorts and shoes and went out running. By the time he returned forty-five minutes later I would be stumbling around the kitchen making coffee or sorting through the closet for something to wear or, depending how well prepared I was that week, ironing a dress shirt in the living room, the only room in the apartment with enough free floor space to set up the ironing board. Sean would come pounding up the stairs and throw open the front door. He didn't bother locking it for so short an outing, so early in the morning. It never seemed to be cool enough that he needed to put on a shirt for his morning run, although I knew it was vanity, his wanting to display his perfect chest, his admirable belly to anyone who might be about, other early runners, men who worked in the East Bay or Silicon Valley and queued up to catch their buses to the downtown BART station or CalTrain, other men who didn't work or who worked night shifts and staggered home at dawn from after-hours dance clubs or a trick's apartment. There was no point in wondering whether Sean himself never tricked on his morning runs—I was sure he did, a grope or a quick blow job once in a while, hidden away in the shade of a thicket in one of the parks he traversed. It was none of my affair, as he'd made clear. Why should I expect him to resist temptation? I couldn't resist him.

At first, when I first moved in with him, when I got up after he went out I'd put on a robe or undershorts or trousers to do whatever it was I did before he got home. The apartment had many windows and no curtains. It became evident, though, that he wanted me to be naked when he returned. He would say, "Modest?" He'd say, "What are you trying to hide?" He'd say, "This is a symptom of your hypocritical bourgeois upbringing. No-one cares if you wear clothes or don't, and if they do they need some shaking up. This is the new world. I like the way you look in the morning, all sleepy and rumpled." He might have liked me still to be in bed when he thundered into the apartment, but on the other hand he liked his coffee to be ready for him.

He would close the front door and yell, "Allen!" then find me wherever I happened to be, would stand in a doorway, posing really, leaning against the jamb, and watch me. I liked to look at him. He ran five miles a day every day; he pumped iron twice a week, maintaining a chest that needed no development, maintaining arms he wanted not to become densely muscular, bulging with muscle, but to be lankily graceful and strong; three times a week he swam, monotonous laps in an indoor pool where, the one time I went with him, I became simultaneously agoraphobic and claustrophobic under the low roof echoing with shadows and the sodden, repetitious slosh of swimmers. He sunbathed, in season, on a grassy slope of the nearest park, and when there was no sun he used a sunlamp, although he disliked the scalded tinge it gave to his skin.

Returning from his run he would be flushed and breathing hard through his mouth, licking his lips frequently; his belly rippled in and out as he breathed from the diaphragm, expanding his lungs to their fullest extent and expanding his chest. He would have stretched downstairs, after walking the last block, but now he pressed his hands against the door frame and pushed against it, bending the forward knee and drawing out the hamstring of the other leg with small, slow bounces, staring at me all the while. He was damp, glowing with sweat, his hair spiked and tousled, his mustache bristling; sweat dripped into his eyes and spilled down his spine; his filmy nylon shorts, sodden, clung to buttocks and hips. The shorts, his favorites, were patterned after the flag of the Irish Republic in panels of green, white, and orange. When he turned to face me, finally, placed his hands on his hips, the white central panel was revealed to be translucent with damp so that the shadow of his pubic hair bled through and I could distinguish the sturdy pink bulk of his penis caught in the sling of the shorts' nylon supporter, white, translucent, before he clutched it lewdly and stepped forward.

He stepped forward, saying, "Hey, Allen," shrewd, masterful, and light tangled like glass in the invisibly blond hair on chest and forearms, "Just who I was looking for," and I smelled the thick, dark, sweaty fragrance of him like a savory stew or the darkest rum, or like the distillate of a rank, musky cologne, the kind sold in drugstores—"Hey, Allen," he said, "wanna wrassle?"

Sean liked it if I sank to my knees, clasped my arms around his thighs, nuzzled and mouthed his genitals through the fabric of the shorts. He liked it when I dug my fingers into his ass and climbed upward, dragging myself by my teeth, clutching at the hair on his belly and then the hair on the breastbone until I reached the hollow where clavicles hooked into sternum and dabbled my tongue there, drinking his sweat, then ran my tongue up his neck, swirled it over the hard bud of the Adam's apple and into the fleshy depression under his jaw, prickly with stubble, and closed my lips over his chin. He liked it when I kissed him because he said nobody before had ever kissed him with such innocent, petrified passion, as if I were his creation, something he had made that feared to love the god but feared not to, as if I were scared that if I didn't adore him as he expected to be adored he might banish me back to nothingness. Cruel and tender, he said that he had had better sex any number of times but never such desperate, dangerous sex, as if one or the other of us could evaporate without a moment's notice and, greedy, we wanted everything. We took a shower together, and sometimes in the steamy slipperiness of hot water and soap he slyly asked to fuck me again, and I let him. I was twenty-two.

AND MATTHEW? But Matthew? Because he had moved to San Francisco, too, the same month I did. I was living with Sean, Matthew was involved with a cute boy named Sebastian. The first time you're unfaithful to the person you love is as memorable, as sweet and tart in memory, as a high-school romance. Matthew and I went roller-skating in Golden Gate Park, a brilliant June Sunday, breezy and warm, kites flying. We skidded and whooped among the crowds on the paths around the museums. Chasing each other, we fled to the white Conservatory where, removing our skates, we prowled barefoot the tropical jungle within the shabby Victorian pavilion. There was no-one there but ourselves and the attendants. As we came to the shallow pond beneath its dome of wrought-iron lace and a lace of hanging vines, I saw the sweat on his face and removed my shirt to wipe it off. "Do you remember—?" I said, but before I could continue I had pressed my palm against his chest where the heart beat in crazy exhilaration and I had kissed him. Oh, the surprise that warmed his eyes! "Of course I remember *that*," he said.

Stolen kisses, furtive embraces. Again, we went to the grand Beaux-Arts papier-mâché Palace of Fine Arts, where immense caryatids and atlantes clung to the capitals of massive, hollow columns, high in the air, and we necked in their muscular shadows. By the broad pool, the fountains, we ate sourdough bread and unctuous Camembert. We fed each other summer peaches and tossed the pits into the shrubbery, saying they would grow. Another time, we walked across the Golden Gate Bridge to Marin in the stiff wind off the Pacific, Alcatraz to our right and sailboats scattered across the bay like a litter of bright candy wrappers, and he said, "In Turkey, all the young men walk in pairs, together, hand in hand." He took my hand, there where we had paused halfway across the bridge, midway between strait and sky. Traffic roared past behind our backs. Taking my hand, Matthew squeezed it tight, saying, "Imagine we're in Istanbul. There—can't you see it?—there's Hagia Sophia. . . . Well, a minaret." It was the thin white needle of the Transamerica pyramid, far away on a different continent, and crossing the Bosporus to Asia we walked shoulder to shoulder, arm in arm. It couldn't last. Neither one of us would have wished it to last. The defining characteristic of an idyll is its fleetingness.

First romance is sweet: you never forget it, you're never so young and heedless again (we each had a lover to go home to, knew it, wouldn't have had it otherwise), fantastical, absurd. We were about to graduate from prep school, Matthew and I—this was four years before —and before my heart could break at the prospect of saying good-bye, Matthew invited me to go to Greece with him for the summer. "What's money for," he said, "if not to spend it on your friends?" and I understood that the offer made meant more than whether or not I accepted. I declined, went home with my family, driving south, and I could have wept except that I was driving. My father sat beside me, silent, proud, my mother and sister in the back seat.

I thought my heart would break, because I had realized I wasn't in love with Matthew. I longed for him that summer, to make love with him again, to hold him in my arms—to be held in *his* arms, smooth and strong as silk, to kiss his lips like tart raspberries and bland cream, to hear his silly giggle. . . . I wanted him to be my best friend for the rest of my life. I masturbated with romantic fervor thinking of him, but I wasn't in love with him. I couldn't separate desire from affection and was disheartened by the understanding, incomprehensible, that my love for Matthew and my lust for him, however conflated, did not equal out to *being in love*. The characters in novels were never so disturbed, not in the same way. There was a surety about falling in love, in novels. I read romantic novels all summer, searching for clues.

But even if I had gone with him to Europe, it wasn't in Matthew's family's plans for him to attend a university in California, and that was where my scholarship would take me. He was going to Yale. He sent me brilliant postcards from Athens, Crete, Thera, Mykonos, with notes whose affection was barely coded, barely hidden. And then came a sealed letter from Kos, enclosing photos. The most brilliant showed Matthew and another young man standing on a broad tawny beach, the glazed blue and gilt Aegean behind them, arms around each other's shoulders, both in swimsuits. I couldn't decide which was the more attractive. The back of the snapshot was inscribed *Mykonos, June 1975*, but the other man was not identified, nor did Matthew mention him in the letter. Then a postcard from Bodrum, a name I found in the atlas on the Turkish Aegean coast, scarcely an eighth of an inch across the blue paper sea from Kos. Turkey was orange, the neighboring islands yellow. The postcard showed the castle of the Knights of St. John, the red flag of Turkey fluttering from the battlements, and Matthew wrote only enough to state the obvious: *I'm in ASIA!*

Then nothing for three weeks. I wanted to write to him but I didn't know where he was. I gazed at the photos: there he was, my Matthew, whom I adored and lusted for but wasn't in love with, browner than I could have imagined, delectable, grinning, wearing a tiny black bikini so conspicuous that, if the snapshot were only enlarged to twice its size, one could have made sure that he was circumcised. His companion, I decided, on reflection, was even more handsome: dark and sturdy and sultry, with a thick black mustache that did nothing to disguise his brilliant smile and a growth of hair across his chest that traced the profile of a martini glass. His swimsuit was as small as Matthew's, Aegean blue.

And then a letter postmarked Istanbul, with more snapshots: the same young man in various picturesque settings, with or without Matthew, in the blue bikini or fully dressed—at the entrance of the Blue Mosque he wore trousers and a long-sleeved shirt, was sitting at a fountain washing his feet. His name was Mehmet, Matthew wrote, he was a Turk. *Isn't he lovely? I have a whole roll of pictures that I don't dare get developed here and I don't know whether I'll dare do it at home. Pretty steamy. He brought me to Istanbul to meet his family—can you stand it?*

Oh, not as his boyfriend, only his charming friend from America, but the apartment's quite small so I sleep in his room anyway. And outside— Turkish men are very affectionate with each other so it would look odd if we <u>didn't</u> hold hands as we walk around the city. His older brother, Mustafa, who's married with two little babies, is always coming with us and holding my hand too, it's very sweet, he likes to be in the middle. It's a good thing Mustafa's English isn't as good as Mehmet's, though. I don't want to leave (next week, damn), they don't want me to leave, Mehmet says he'll come visit me in the States, but it's no use, really—he's engaged. (His parents arranged the match!) "But I must have a wife to bear my sons," he says, bewildered, when I ask if he wants to get married. Do you like women— have you ever slept with one? "Oh, no!" (shocked) "That doesn't appeal to me at all. I will still see men after I marry. I will come to New York [he's convinced I live in Manhattan] to see you!" Poor dear—his poor fi- ancée! . . . Will <u>you</u> come to "New York" for a visit, sweetheart, pretty please, in August before you fly west? I've told my parents to expect you.

Mehmet and Mustafa had been teaching Matthew Turkish: he ended the letter with the words *seni seviyorum*, which meant, he said, *I love you*; then, in Greek (which Mehmet knew as well as he did English), because I would appreciate the irony, αγαπημενε φιλε μου— *my beloved friend.*

I FLEW WEST for college, to a landscape that seemed to have confused or misunderstood the seasons, greening up in winter when the rains came, browning off in late spring. The wide campus was studded with fake-Mexican-colonial buildings, adobe or concrete block, mellow plaster, terra-cotta roof tiles like split water pipes. There were trees I had never seen before, trees that wouldn't survive a New England or even a North Carolina winter. Allées of steepling eucalypts bore leaves as stiff as vellum, grey, blue-green, umber, which emitted a sinus-clearing medicinal fragrance, and their bark shredded off slender, muscular trunks in fibrous strips. There were rows of handsome olives whose foliage changed color when the wind blew, inverting the leaves from resinous, oily green to silver. Out in the fields, which reminded you that the university had started out as a railroad baron's ranch and private fief, stood live oaks whose spreading branches and brittle, prickly foliage formed lacy, insubstantial domes, miniature Hagia Sophias, shrines to which you could retreat to study for an exam, to read a turgid textbook, yellow highlighter, blue ballpoint, spiral-bound notebook at the ready, or to read *Tom Jones* or a history of the last days of the Ottoman Empire.

Or perhaps it was I who was confused. I looked around—I looked at men, at boys my own age. Their wardrobes seemed to contain nothing but vast selections of shorts and t-shirts, perhaps a pair of blue jeans for cool evenings, sneakers or sandals or beaten-down penny loafers. No-one owned a raincoat or an umbrella, except professors—adults—and I; everyone else walked around unencumbered in the rain, absorbing moisture from the air as if it were a special gift for skin burnished and dried by too much sun. I cut down khaki trousers into shorts, hemmed the cuffs of the first pair but not the rest, since no-one else did, and stopped ironing my shirts or polishing my oxblood loafers. I became tanned, neglected to shave every day, let my hair grow shaggy, accumulated a wardrobe of colorful t-shirts and twill gym shorts. And I met a few boys. It caused me little pain to say good-bye when summer came.

I went home the first two summers, to a small house that seemed smaller yet at the same time expansive after the cramped dorms, smaller and more silent in the absence of Steph, married now, newly distinct and, it seemed to me, a startlingly separate person, a grown woman who was also, but only by convention, by accident, my sister. She had left Mickey, the only boyfriend I'd met, a frivolous distraction while she prepared for the LSATs, and met Derek Sheridan during the hazy, uncertain period when she was waiting to learn which of the five law schools she'd applied to would accept her. He was a businessman who startled me, when I met him, by being brawny and blond—a sturdy tenth-century Viking berserker co-opted by British rectitude who looked incongruous in a suit but seemed always to wear one. Four of the five law schools extended invitations to Steph but she declined them all and instead sent out her own invitations, lacy engraved script on heavy cream-colored stock: *Mr. & Mrs. Janos K. Pasztory request the pleasure of your attendance at the wedding of their daughter Stephanie Marit to Mr. Derek Christopher Sheridan.*

The first summer, the summer after my freshman year, my father took two weeks' vacation in August and we drove north, first to Annapolis, to the bungalow Derek's parents had given the newlyweds, then to a cottage in Rehoboth Beach on Delaware's Atlantic shore.

Derek visited on weekends, arriving late Friday night, leaving before dawn on Monday. Those two weekends at the beach Derek seemed hardly to unbend. He gamely stripped down to madras swimming trunks and embellished an already luminous tan, organized a clambake, grilled steaks on a barbecue. He spoke to me with hearty, man-to-man fraternity although I could tell he found questionable my swim-team Speedo, snug, vibrant jewel-bright nylon (it was not as racy as Matthew's or Mehmet's). "Mother and Daddy make him nervous," Steph told me, as though I needed to be told, seeing how he raised his voice whenever he wished Steph or me to translate for him, turned the flattest statement into a question.

Steph herself seemed nervous sometimes. When she addressed our parents her gestures were clumsy and small, as if she were pronouncing words she had only ever read and feared making mistakes a child would ridicule, but I attributed this to her pregnancy. She was lovelier than I had ever seen her, a sleek personification of the ocean's warm fecundity. She wore loose, colorful shifts, baring arms and legs, and navigated the cottage, the streets of the town, the beach, with the calm, slow dignity of a schooner under full sail—until she had to talk to our mother, when her serenity foundered as though the ship, first command of an inexperienced lieutenant, had hit a squall. In a new white bikini that not only exposed but glorified her swollen belly, she lay out on the sand so that her unborn child would absorb the beneficence of the sun. That child I expected to be a daughter, blonde as her father, slender and fine as her mother, but when Derek called me in October, after I had returned to college, to tell me I was an uncle—his pride disguising the habitual distance of his voice—he told me I was uncle to a little boy, Christopher Stephen Sheridan. And the snapshots the new parents sent me later revealed a dark, wise-looking child who, so Steph wrote, looked just like me.

When I went home the following summer I expected that we would make a similar excursion to visit Steph and Derek and Christopher. My father suggested it; my mother refused, flatly, without the explanation I felt my father and I deserved but which he didn't appear to expect. I called Steph. She seemed unsurprised and not especially disappointed, although halfway through our conversation her voice, which had become husky and intimate with maternity, cracked on a small, swallowed sob. It was both of them, she told me, Derek and our mother both—they couldn't stand each other, wouldn't make any kind of effort. She didn't want to talk about it on the phone, she said, and suggested I come up for a week or two by myself, to see Kit—that was what they called Christopher. I'd probably want to get away from Mother and Daddy for a while anyway. It would do me good.

My daughter is ashamed of her parents, my mother said. She doesn't want us to know the child. We might infect him—as if we were sick!

Marit, said my father, spelling her name out carefully, slowly, as though that might hold her attention. Derek comes from a wealthy family. You have to expect him to be nervous around us, not just because we're deaf—I'm the sort of man who works in his family's factories. We're poor in his eyes. Give him time. The name my father had given Derek was a complicated pun on the sign for *money.*

It's your daughter, my mother said. Derek—he's nothing. She made him inconsequential with a movement of her hands, flicking him away like a mosquito.

MY MAJOR WAS modern European history, a discipline I understood to be as useless, unless as foundation for advanced degrees I didn't wish to pursue, as my work-study job in the university library, shelving books. In the spring of my junior year I applied for a summer internship with a San Francisco advertising agency. Selected for an interview, I had my hair cut, bought a new dress shirt and tie, polished my shoes, sent my suit to the dry cleaners. There were two interviewers, a woman from the personnel department whose name I forgot immediately I shut the door behind me, afterward, and the most beautiful man I had ever seen, whose name I have not forgotten. His name was Sean Forestal. He was an associate copywriter and the master to whom the successful candidate would be apprenticed. I remember nothing of the half-hour interview after the woman from personnel asked how I pronounced my last name, and Sean asked if they could call me Allen. Bewildered by his beauty—which seemed to me of a fineness, a splendor, a superlative genderless quality that the most stolidly heterosexual man, the most committed lesbian must be attracted to him—I must also have been inspired by it. A few weeks later I returned from a class to find a message scrawled by one of my roommates. I was to call Shawn Forest at a 415 area-code number, before four-thirty P.M.

It pains me now that I cannot any longer recall Sean properly, cannot call to mind his image. Beauty has that effect. He was blond. He was not tall, but so finely put together that you couldn't imagine his being any other size. His only standing there, at a bus stop, say, or by the desk where I worked, had a quality of decisiveness and withheld motion, as though he might spring into action at any moment, stand to battle at the head of his adoring troops, yet there was a quietness about him too, a gentleness that was unreachable, untouchable. And yet, too, he was someone you wanted to touch. His voice I remember clearly, engraved on my mind and reproducible as the laser-tracked pitting on the surface of a compact disc, but I cannot describe it except by metaphor, a translation from binary code: a thick, fluid, unfiltered honey, piney and resinous, struck to gold by afternoon sun and containing within it, one of its essential properties, the capacity to crystallize.

I gave the receptionist my name and she patched me through. "Allen, hello!" said Sean, his voice hardly distorted by the telephone. "Thanks for getting back to me. Sorry it's long distance—I should have said to call collect." A letter would be coming from the personnel department but Sean had wanted to let me know personally since, although agreement had been general, I was his choice and would be working with him.

"You're offering me the position," I said, appalled.

"Well," he said, "I wouldn't have called otherwise. Congratulations, Allen. You will accept, won't you? You aren't looking at another job? I'm looking forward to working with you."

The phone was in the common room of the suite. There was a couch near me. I sat down, feeling blinded. "Thank you," I said. "Yes, I'll accept."

"Good. That's great. I shouldn't say this—" Sean laughed, the shiver of light on a breeze-ruffled pond—"but the other candidates really weren't what I had in mind. No, I won't say more." This was typical of him, I learned, the advance and then the retreat. "Now, you'll have to be thinking about where you'll stay while you're here. Do you have any openings, any options?"

"I hadn't thought about it." Even without his golden, disarming presence, I felt, now, comfortable speaking to him. "I only applied on a lark, sort of, I didn't really expect to get the internship."

"That's entirely the wrong attitude." He laughed again. "Or maybe it's not. Anyway, it just so happens that a friend of mine here in the city is going to Europe for the summer and needs someone to look after his place. It's not palatial or anything, actually it's kind of a dump, but look, it's available, and all he wants is someone to water the plants and pay the utilities—no rent. After all, we won't be paying you much. What do you say?"

He suggested that I come up to the city that weekend. Had I spent any time in San Francisco? Not really, I said. "It's not as bad as some people say," he said, "and even better than others think." Why didn't I catch the train Friday afternoon; we'd go out for drinks, dinner, he'd show me around, on Saturday I could meet his friend and see the apartment. Unless I had a midterm to study for—or a hot date.

"Where would I stay?"

"There's a big, comfy couch in my living room just waiting for overnight guests." He had the CalTrain schedule right there, told me which station to go to, which train to take, he'd meet me at the San Francisco terminal. "Okay? Look, this *is* long distance, I'll let you go. See you Friday, Allen."

THE TRAIN LEFT from Palo Alto at the end of the business day, relatively uncrowded with men and women in business suits heading home, though it seemed odd there should be as many as there were. Didn't one live in the suburbs and commute to the city? Although the South Bay couldn't be called suburban anymore, in the flush of the silicon boom. I looked around from my perch on the upper deck, a mezzanine lined with single seats, over the railing to the opposite balcony and down into the lower part of the car. Many of the passengers, after all, if not most, were men in their twenties and thirties who draped their suit jackets over the luggage racks, loosened collars and ties, rolled up their sleeves. They wore severe sunglasses and read newspapers, smoothing their mustaches absently, or sat in pairs and talked. You didn't have to know San Francisco to know its reputation. I decided that these handsome young men with their strong wrists, their self-assurance, worked in Silicon Valley's computer industry but preferred, naturally, to live where they felt at home. Where they could go out at night and play. So far as I had thought about life after college, I assumed I wouldn't go back to my parents' home, would migrate to a big city, DC, Philadelphia, New York—despite being scared of New York—Boston. San Francisco, too, was an option.

The commuter train rattled up the peninsula, through Atherton, a suburb in fact, where the rails ran through a concourse of tall trees screening the prosperous backyards of houses I assumed to be less desirable than those that didn't abut the tracks, though they looked large enough; it paused at a quaint suburban station, then veered inland, toward the bay, where the landscape became industrial. An hour from Palo Alto, we pulled into the San Francisco terminal.

It was cooler here. I put on my jacket and went into the station building. "Over here, Allen!" called Sean, standing near the exits. From a distance he might have been any other blond man in a dark suit, but I noticed how people on the way out paused almost imperceptibly, turned their heads toward him, how there was a small circle of free space around him. Stepping into that circle felt like privilege enough, but then instead of shaking my hand Sean threw his arm around my shoulders and led me out the door. "First we'll go to my place so I can get out of this monkey suit," he said, "then we'll have some fun. Welcome to Baghdad-by-the-Bay, Allen, the city where dreams come true."

DOORS

Life's Work

"I CAN'T SEE you this weekend, Allen," said Jeremy. "Tonight, but you'll have to leave after breakfast." He balanced the tip of his index finger on top of the red and white plastic straw in his drink, moved it in a circle, clinking ice cubes.

I loosened my tie. "Have to?" I think I grasped my own glass too hard but I don't think he noticed.

"I'm sorry." The straw was still going around. It was his second drink, he'd arrived before me. "I meant . . . I'm asking."

"Okay, Jere." I tried to sound casual, easy. He liked me to call him Jere, I'd already found that out, as though a nickname were something new in his experience: *Zhair*, the diphthong extruded as though I still boasted a southern drawl. Six days, one full Sunday and a week of evenings and nights—what did I know about him, what did he know about me? "Long as it's just the weekend."

He picked up his glass without answering and I thought perhaps he hadn't heard me. The bar was clotted with men in suits carrying attaché cases and stylish gym bags, and more kept crowding in. Men in suits with their vivid ties loosened around starched collars, their gestures loosening up and their voices growing expansive, their conversations concrete—decompressing, as though the bar were a halfway point, a necessary breathing space between the Financial District and the Castro, between the pleasures of business and the business of pleasure. I wore a suit too, and carried a briefcase although my work wasn't important enough to take home. No gym bag, though; after a year of watching Sean tune his body, a machine for desire, I had given up swimming, tossed my school-color Speedos into the trash.

Jeremy wasn't wearing a suit. I suspected he didn't own one, a supposition I based on no evidence. He wore a burgundy leather jacket which he pulled off now and draped over the banquette where he sat, his back to a window that revealed another sortie of business suits piling up the stairs from the Metro station across the street. Jeremy's eyes passed over me as easily, as uncomprehendingly, as any of theirs might. More so. I put my hands in my lap before they started talking out loud, and then I pushed back my chair and said, "I'll be right back."

I went to the bar for change, then to the cigarette machine, then to the john. As I came out, a grey serge elbow deliberately knocked into my gut. "Who's your humpy friend?" said Sean. His teeth were ferociously white. "Is he why you haven't slept at home all week?"

"Hello, Sean." His beauty still clutched at me, still made my stomach shudder with the reflex of desire. "How are you?" I no longer even liked him.

"Lonely. Horny. Why do you think I'm here?" He groped me, discreet but unfriendly.

"Really, Sean. At this time of afternoon?" I pushed my shoulders against the wall of the narrow corridor, ducked my head, and slid past him. "Happy hunting."

When I got back to the table I slipped onto the banquette next to Jeremy. He glanced at me a little dizzily. I reached for my drink. "Are you okay?" I asked. I meant, Ask me if I'm okay.

He covered one eye with his hand. "I was trying to remember if I'd cleaned the bathroom."

I pulled out the pack of cigarettes I'd just bought. (Why did his bathroom need to be clean?) I couldn't get the cellophane off. After watching me struggle for a little bit, Jeremy took the pack from my hands, removed the cellophane, opened the foil at the top. He knocked one cigarette out, neatly, tamped it on the table, and placed the filter between my lips. "I didn't know you smoked," he said, lighting a match. He watched the sulfur flare and burn off before raising match to cigarette.

I wanted to say, There's a lot you don't know about me. "Once or twice a year—" I accepted the flame, drew in smoke—"when I'm feeling extremely tense I'll buy a pack but I never finish it."

"I remember in Mexico the little corner groceries used to sell single cigarettes for people like you." He remembered Mexico: he had a whole life. I had a week, if that. Blowing out the match, he tossed it into the ashtray. "Are you extremely tense? Right now?"

I coughed. I am not an effective smoker. "The very attractive blond at the corner of the bar, the one who's glaring at us."

Jeremy took hold of my free hand. "Friend of yours?" His face was blank, unreadable.

"My roommate—my boyfriend. Ex-boyfriend, really, only we haven't worked that out."

When Sean had made his point, and I mine by directing Jeremy's attention to him, he scowled. The proportions and balances in his face were so delicate, so precise, that little distortion was required to make him ugly.

Jeremy's hand left mine, rose to stroke my cheek. "Do you want to leave?" Eyes half-closed, his face had taken on an expression of concern I welcomed only because it was the first time that afternoon he'd really noticed me.

Suppose he had a lover who'd been out of town all week, a man who was due back tomorrow. Suppose I was just a temporary filling for the cavity in his bed. He would want his apartment clean, the bath scoured of my traces, the sheets disinfected. He'd go to the laundromat as soon as I left in the morning, and spend the afternoon in the kitchen. Jeremy and this other man (a man not as inconveniently young as I, as eager) would have had more than a week to demonstrate they had more in common than physical attraction. They would eat the dinner Jeremy had lovingly prepared; over coffee and dessert they would tell each other what they'd done while apart. Being civilized and sure of each other, neither would hesitate to talk about the other men they'd seen. Unless I wasn't important enough for more than a passing mention. "How was your day, Jeremy?" I asked him.

"Fairly quiet." He sipped his drink. I watched the way his Adam's apple rose and then fell in his throat. "I wasn't in much of a mood to work so I mostly just footled around. Cleaned house. Went shopping. Made a few calls. What about you?"

"Work is work." It hadn't been one of those days when I hated my job, few enough yet, I hadn't been working long, but what I did for a living wasn't interesting even to me. In any case, Jeremy knew all about Grace & Fenton. I glanced around the bar, and every second man looked like someone who might work in my office. "Jere, can we get out of here?"

"I did just ask you," he said. He tapped his index finger on the back of my hand, then lifted his glass, drained it to the ice cubes. "Let's go," he said.

Outside, at the intersection of Castro and Market, I took the last drag off my cigarette and threw the butt into the street. Jeremy touched my arm. "You left the pack on the table."

"I know," I said. "I meant to. Where are we going?"

"Back to my place. I'm making dinner for you." He smiled—a ridiculous smile, a meltingly tender smile unwarranted by the situation, by our relationship (whatever it was), a smile I should have welcomed but which made me feel mocked.

"You don't have to do that."

"I want to." The new smile was harder—funnier. "Okay?"

I stared at him. I couldn't work him out. "Okay." He was too tall, too old, not really handsome—you might look at him twice, but not three times. It didn't seem to mean anything to me that I knew so little about him. I knew this: the mysterious distance he enforced made me unhappy, so that when he gave signs of opening up I became annoyed. I knew that he made me so happy I became clumsy. I knew that I was willing to abide by his terms, and this made me rebellious. "Thanks, Jere. That'll be nice. I haven't eaten home-cooked in a while."

We had moved down the sidewalk a little to join the clump of people waiting for the next bus, but instead of standing at the curb Jeremy steered me to a wall plastered with flyers and placards. He put his arm over my shoulder and placed me so that I straddled his thigh and leaned back against his chest. He was so much taller than I. I held my briefcase in one hand but didn't know what to do with the other. With Jeremy this curbside intimacy made me nervous, where with Sean, at least at first, I had thought nothing of giving him a hug and a kiss on a downtown sidewalk when we met for lunch. With Jeremy it felt flagrant and forced, as though he were trying to demonstrate something—to me or to himself I couldn't guess. Blowing warm air on my neck, he said, "You one of those busy young professionals with no time to cook?" He tucked my shoulder into his armpit, swung his arm up around my throat. The smell of his leather sleeve rose into my nostrils, gaggingly rich. "Your boyfriend doesn't feed you?"

Was he deliberately unkind? Was he testing me? I nearly said, What about yours? "I'm looking for my own apartment, all right? Let's drop it."

"Hey, Allen," he said, "hey, Allen." Out of nowhere a bus pulled up to the curb. As I leaned forward he held me back. "Wrong one. That's a Market bus. We want the Divisadero bus. You are extremely tense, aren't you. Do you want to buy more cigarettes?" He pressed his lips to my nape. "Could get expensive."

The bus drew away, electric engine quieter than its clacking turn signals and the crackle of sparks when its poles crossed a snag in the overhead wires. It turned onto Market. I looked down the street but there were no further buses in sight. "I'm tense because I'm confused," I said tightly, quietly. "Confused and unhappy, Jeremy. Here you are mauling me, making love to me on a street corner, and ten minutes ago you didn't see me when I spoke to you and ten minutes before that you kicked me out of your flat before I even got there." He started to say something. "No, listen to me, Mr. Kent. The first time I saw you I de- cided I wanted to sleep with you. I've done that, all right? I don't know what you want from me. I don't know what I want from you."

"Are you hungry, Allen?" His voice was small. "This is a serious question. Because if not — let's walk around for a while."

He had loosened his arms. I stepped away from him, then turned back. I was breathing hard and felt dizzy. "That's not an answer."

Nodding sadly, he said, "I know. I'm just thinking maybe this con- versation wants to happen on neutral ground."

"Conversations don't want things, Jeremy. People want things." I started down the street, toward Sean's apartment. I had nowhere else to go.

IT WASN'T TRUE that the first time I saw him I wanted to sleep with Jeremy. The first time I saw Jeremy was a lunchtime at work when I stopped by my supervisor's office to let him know I was going out. Grace & Fenton's offices, two floors of a building a few blocks south of Market, were set up as a warren of cubicles and work spaces by movable partitions upholstered in industrial-grey fabric, assigned by position and seniority. An assistant copywriter, new, I was given a cubicle near the center of the maze, far from such amenities as rest room, coffee ma- chine, and windows; Michael Quillen had a real office on an outside wall, complete with window, freestanding desk, and, most luxurious of all, a door he could close — although he seldom did. I was late leaving; nearly everyone else had already gone. As I walked through a series of short, angled corridors on carpet that deadened my footfalls, the floor seemed deserted, nobody hunched over keyboard or telephone or story- board, as if in the wake of a general evacuation. The design people were on the other floor, video was contracted out, so there was no telling, walking around, without voices or bodies to place tasks in context, what happened in the office; it could have been a banking headquarters, a publishing house, one of the administrative departments of a university, or a moderately successful advertising agency. Approaching Michael's office, I shook my shoulders to settle my jacket, straightened the knot of my tie, and took one step through the door before I noticed he wasn't alone.

Michael saw me, waved his hand, said, "Allen." His visitor turned slightly.

"Excuse me, Michael. I didn't mean to interrupt."

"No problem." He glanced at the clock on his desk. "Lunchtime?" I nodded.

"Jeremy," Michael said, addressing his visitor, "this is our newest employee, Allen Pasztory. Allen, Jeremy Kent."

Jeremy Kent stood up, so tall that I saw nothing but his height, and extended his hand. "Pleased to meet you, Allen." His hand enveloped mine, large and warm. I noticed now that, unlike most visitors to the office, he was dressed casually, plaid shirt, no tie; but still it was his height that registered. "Interesting name," he said, "Pasztory," lingering over the syllables as if trying to place them.

"It's Hungarian." I wondered why Michael had bothered to introduce me. He gave no clue, staring across the cluttered surface of the desk with his usual expression of benign preoccupation. Nor did Jeremy Kent seem interested in my presence, after the formalities; he glanced back at the papers on the corner of the desk nearest his chair. "I'll be back in an hour, Michael," I said. "Good to meet you, Mr. Kent."

"Fine," Michael said. "Go."

I left, feeling I had probably committed a minor faux pas of business etiquette and that a black mark would go on the list of merits and demerits that, with the paranoia of the new hire, I was sure Michael Quillen kept on me. But, confident enough of my work and general subservience that I didn't expect it to rank high, I was ready for lunch within the sixty seconds it took to reach the reception area.

There were four Michaels at Grace & Fenton. Michael Fenton became Mike after the second time you called him Mr. Fenton, and anyway I hardly ever saw him. The young Dublin-born intern with the lovely brogue was called Mick, inevitably; he would be returning to college in September, lowering the confusion quotient. My supervisor and the receptionist wouldn't answer to any name but Michael, though, which I understood to have caused some friction at first, but by the time I joined the company they were known as Michael Q. and Michael D., respectively. Privately, I thought of Michael D. as Mikey, something I'd never tell him, lunch companion, source of gossip—company or outside—sounding board and confidant. He was waiting for me, not patiently. "This little shrub," he said, indicating the Ficus benjamina by his desk, taller than either of us, "although a conversationalist of limited range, was about to be taken to lunch."

"Sorry, Michael. I got caught up in something."

"The secret of survival in the business world, my child, is: not to get caught up." He swung his jacket over his shoulder and waved me toward the elevator. "Do I ever get *caught up in something?* In order to appear busy, you must always be somewhat behind."

Easy for you to say, I thought: you're a receptionist. "I'll make a note."

"Not on my lunch hour." The elevator arrived; by the time we reached the street I had been castigated for not noticing Michael's new tie, warned about an upcoming client presentation, and informed, in confidence, that Michael Q. had routed my latest little job of work upstairs—that is, to the corner offices—and both Fenton and Grace had approved. "Nice work, my boy," Michael said.

"Hey," I said, feeling buoyant, "lunch is on me, then."

"Don't be foolish." Michael looked up and down the street. "You can't afford me."

Compromising, we decided on a new restaurant, pricier than usual, farther than usual from the office, where Michael would allow me to buy him a glass of wine. On the way I received a progress report on the performance piece Michael was putting together. The month before, someone had published a novel with the same title—"a remarkably silly book"—which catastrophe had precipitated a radical re-envisioning of the work as he tried to come up with a new name for it. "I have decided to include a singer, a beautiful black boy. It will add an extra frisson." I promised, again, to attend the opening when it was produced.

In the restaurant, after Michael had told me what to order, he folded his hands in his lap and offered me a seraphic smile. "Okay, now for the real stuff. How's life in the war zone, Allen?"

I didn't want to talk about Sean. I scowled at Michael. "I was in a good mood."

"If you had bothered to ask me," Michael said, "I could have told you that Mr. Forestal was an appealing trick, an acceptable brief fling, but *not* someone to get involved with beyond that."

"I didn't know you then, Michael."

He lifted his glass of wine. "We must simply get you disinvolved."

"Michael, a lot of the time I don't want to be disinvolved."

"We must find you, one, your own pied-à-terre, and two, another man."

"I can't afford an apartment of my own."

"Or better, several. Serially, of course." He nodded wisely. "Or maybe not."

"Michael, let's talk about something else." I took a slice of bread from the basket, buttered it. I couldn't think of anything else. "Who was the guy talking to Michael Q.?"

"No!" Michael set his glass down sharply. "I won't speak of him." He glanced from side to side. "Quillen and I have been in competition for Jeremy Kent's attention for *two years*."

Michael Quillen was married, lived in the suburbs, had two teenage daughters. Michael Quillen was forty-five, scrawny, and bald. Michael Quillen brought his lunch to work in a brown paper bag from San Ramon. He was the least likely candidate, to my mind, to be subject to a secret homosexual infatuation, but I knew better than to protest. Michael D. would call me callow and naïve. "I didn't think he was so special."

"He's *six-four*!" Michael, six-two, had a weakness for men taller than he. "He has a simply luscious mustache, a not-bad chest, and the most beautiful eyes."

I tried to remember the eyes. "But who is he, Michael?"

"Who cares? He's gorgeous."

The waiter delivered our lunches. I indicated Michael's nearly empty glass. "No, he's not," I said to Michael. "He's tall. They're not the same."

"He's hot," Michael insisted. "He's a freelance artist. You've seen the Gateway Winery campaign—that's Jeremy Kent."

MID-MORNING, A WEEK or so later, I had come out for a cup of coffee and Michael asked me to sit in for him while he went to the rest room. I warned him that I didn't know how to handle his phone. "Put 'em all on hold," he said. Luckily no-one rang, but a tall man stepped out of the elevator, looked at me, and said, "Where's Michael?"

"He just went out for a moment." I had no idea how to be a receptionist. "May I help you?"

The man was carrying a large portfolio under his arm. "You're Allen—" he said, "the Hungarian surname. I'm afraid I don't remember it."

I stared at him. I don't remember names, but I had looked up the Gateway file, so I remembered his name. "It's Pasztory, Mr. Kent. Are you here to see Michael Quillen?" Knowing what I was to look for, I tried to see what Michael D. saw in him.

With a small, polite smile that barely warmed his eyes—a very pale grey, I noticed—but gave an engaging tilt to his mustache, he said, "You can't call me *Mr.*, I'm not wearing a tie. I'm Jeremy." He set his portfolio down on the couch opposite Michael's desk and looked at his watch. "Jim Grace is expecting me, but I'm early so don't announce me yet." He went over to the coffee machine, completely at home, completely at ease.

He was pleasant to look at, I decided, not spectacular the way Sean was spectacular, and not the type I would have expected Michael to go for. On the street, going to lunch, Michael always commented on the charms of handsome passersby. Jeremy Kent wasn't particularly in their league. Squatting to reach into the refrigerator for cream, he moved so gracefully that *squat* was an inappropriate verb—not like a tall man, I thought. And then he stood, and turned, holding his Styrofoam cup, and I saw what it was that Michael meant.

"I wouldn't have expected them to stick you out here, even temporarily." He wasn't looking at me, concentrating on sitting down without spilling his coffee. "Is the hierarchy crumbling? Maybe I should look for somewhere else to peddle my work." His notion of idle small talk struck me as eccentric.

"No, I just happened to be here when Michael had to go to the john." I looked down at my cup, on the desk next to the phone. My office mug, a gift from Sean when we worked together, it was tall and slender with a slightly flared lip, porcelain with a transfer print like a glazed chintz, chrysanthemums, peonies, less identifiable blossoms, on a ground of plummy blue. "I was just getting coffee myself."

Jeremy Kent smiled at me, then took a sip from his cup. "I'll say this for Grace & Fenton—the coffee's better than most places. Although not much. One of the major advantages of working at home is my own coffee in my own cup." It was an odd smile. I would have called it flirtatious except that he hardly seemed to see me. It made me feel very young. "So, you're a copywriter, Allen? How long have you been here? Maybe we'll work together sometime."

"I liked the pieces you did for Gateway Winery, Jeremy."

"Yes?" he said, and blinked mildly. "Thanks. I thought it a fairly silly idea, myself, but it seems to have worked."

Michael D. swept back in and took it all in in a glance. "Good morning, Jeremy," he said. "You're early, as usual." He darted a speculative look at me. "I hope Allen hasn't been boring you."

"Shut up, Michael," said Jeremy.

Flushing, I stood up. "No-one called, Michael. I'll get back to work. Nice talking to you, Jeremy."

Back in my cubicle I stared at the project I was supposed to be working on. I had wanted to slap Michael. It was Sean's fault, I told myself, I was jumpy and irritable and impressionable. I'd pick up a newspaper at lunchtime and look at apartment listings. There was, if it came to it, a roommate referral service in the Castro. With this decided, and feeling calmer, I opened the file of promotional material on a country inn near Mendocino for which I was trying to distill a snappy spot ad in twenty-five words or less.

"Hard to find you back here," said a friendly voice.

Startled, I turned in my chair. Jeremy Kent leaned against one of my partitions. "Oh, hello. What can I do for you?"

"You forgot your coffee." He held out my cup. "Nice mug. It's still warm."

For a moment I couldn't do more than stare at the hand holding the mug. "Thank you," I muttered, and took it.

"No problem," he said. "I'll see you around, Allen."

I NEVER WENT out at night, not by myself, but Sean had gone to a cocktail party and not returned by midnight. We had been fighting for weeks, I slept on the couch in the living room, I wanted to hurt him although I knew I couldn't. I might have called Matthew, but I called a taxi and had it take me to an after-hours dance club south of Market, a great bedizened ocean liner steaming through tropic waters eventually to collide with the reef of morning—to founder, to sink in a phospho-rescent wash of amyl nitrate and sweat. The vast cavernous space pumped like an oxygen-starved heart. Men asked me to dance and I danced. All around me whirled colors more brilliant than any paint box, scents more impulsive than the perfume counters at Macy's Union Square, battalions of noises more distinct, more alive than individual soldiers. A man danced in front of me—pivoted and swung and rocked his knees and hips, hurled his fists at the steel brackets upholding a ceil-ing miles over our heads, sweat flying from his hair to drench me with drops of warm mercury. I had never seen him before. He reached into the watch pocket of his jeans for the little brown glass bottle of pop-pers, handed it to me. Hardly slowing, I unscrewed the lid and lifted the vial to one nostril, then the other. An enormous incandescent pressure opened out my skull with a chorus of massive thuds harder than the backbeat of the track we were dancing to; my heart swelled like a he-lium balloon; my mouth opened so wide I could not see; and I gave the bottle back to him. He howled something and I staggered a little.

He howled again, reached out, drew splayed fingers from my throat down chest and belly to grasp the waistband of my trousers. He unhooked the top button, then danced back. I could still feel the ribbon-traces of his fingers on my flesh. There was a brief clumsy segue between tracks—confusion dulled his face before he shrugged, and be-fore I could surrender my autonomic nervous system to the thudding bass of the next mix he grabbed my hand, shouted, "Dehydration break!" and tugged me off the dance floor.

But that was enough. Not knowing why I was here, I knew it wasn't to find a quick fuck. I lost him in the crowd on the edge of the dance floor. I was ready to leave. Tucking my shirt back into my trousers, but-toning them, I headed toward the exit, the coat-check.

Approaching, I recognized the tall man handing his jacket over the counter. Reckless, amazing myself, I stepped into a shadowy alcove and said to myself: I can have him. I hadn't known I wanted him but it was clear now, I felt an urgent specific shrill desire within which, deep within, a pair of hands flexed and said, He's kind, he won't hurt me. Jeremy Kent stuck the claim check into his wallet and stalked past me. I followed. He looked focused, intent, in a way he hadn't when I'd seen him at the office. He moved like a salmon breasting rapids, slick, silver, muscular, and following him through the rocketing tumult, the barrage of hands and faces, I felt like a shambling circus bear sure of instinct but not of technique—I didn't know how to pick up a man, what words to say, what signals to display. His fine, thick hair was too short to lie flat but wasn't full enough to obscure the fragile vault of his skull. He climbed the stairs to the bar on the mezzanine and bought a mineral water.

I followed him back downstairs. He stood on the edge of the crowd, sipping from his bottle, observing the dancers on the floor. I thought, watching him, that he was seeing each man as an individual, the way each flower in the Dutch-master still lifes he had painted for Gateway was individual, individually observed, although together they made up a composition. In the crazily swirling lights I couldn't make out any of those men, save him, and him I was surely inventing—or re-creating: a tall broad-shouldered figure in vivid orange t-shirt and faded blue jeans whose Adam's apple jumped as he swallowed, who licked drops of water from his full mustache and turned his profile away from me. He was the tallest person in sight. I moved toward him. His shoulders had begun to sway, his head to roll a little on his neck. I sidled up to him. I brushed against him, shoulder against biceps.

Jeremy turned. He didn't recognize me. "You look like you need to move," I told him. He didn't hear me, smiled and shrugged and bent down. "You look like you need to move," I said again, louder, into his ear, and could hardly hear myself.

He didn't recognize me until we had been dancing for what seemed like hours, and then we took a break but didn't say much, necked like adolescents in resolute shadow as close as two men could stand together until I couldn't tell whose clothes I wore, whose tongue filled my mouth. Whose flesh filled whose hand. Whatever I might have been expecting, I had not expected him to be so passionate but perhaps it was a reflection of a heartless passion of my own, extreme, wild, dangerous.

His apartment (I'd paid for a taxi) was on the third floor but the stairs went straight up from the front door in one long stretch for what must have been most of the first two stories, only then turning on a small landing. Following him as he climbed the stairs I thought I understood how, though he was at least five years older, he'd been able to dance longer than I could, flat-out and at high speed, why his thighs had felt like marble when I knelt down in the middle of the dance floor (shocking him, I think), embraced them, and nuzzled his crotch. I had meant to shock him, to shock him into asking me home with him.

Reaching the turn at the landing, he slowed, took it too carefully, as though a surprise might wait around the corner. I followed him into the living room. There was a vast expanse of polished floorboards, un-interrupted but for an armchair in one bay window beginning to fill with dawn. His boots clattered as he crossed the room.

I looked at the small painting hung by the door. It was watercolor, an almost architectural view of this same room—or an interior de-signer's vision of its potential, because the painted room was furnished, a long slouchy colorless sofa, two chairs, a coffee table. They were placed at odd angles as though to frame the outstanding addition to the room, a huge, vibrant Oriental carpet, tendrils of dense blue and carmine on an almost obscured cream ground. The detail of the car-pet's pattern was excessive.

Jeremy had turned on the standard lamp by the chair. Now he came back to me and switched off the overhead light. He touched my arm. "I couldn't decide whether I really wanted the carpet." He shrugged and looked at the painting again, moved his face in small ad-justments and rearrangements. "Then, when I made up my mind and went back, it'd been sold."

He pushed his nose into my neck.

I looked at the real room and it was somehow colored by the vi-sion of the carpet, overlaid with brilliant, translucent dyes. I would have bought the carpet on immediate impulse.

He blew warm breath against my clavicle. "Let's take a shower."

I followed him again, out of the living room and down the corri-dor to the door of his bedroom. Here he stopped and I raised my hands to his shoulders and he lowered his face until I lost sight of his eyes and his lips touched mine. His lips were dry, chapped. I ran my tongue over them, moistened them with my saliva. His mustache brushed my tongue. It tickled and tasted salty. Slowly my hands slipped over his cupped shoulder blades and then they fell to his waist and I felt I was here, in his apartment, undercover and disguised, thinking he expected an easily forgotten one-nighter—and then I stepped back quickly. Breathless, looking at the floor, I said, "I want to watch you take off your clothes."

"MAY I CARRY your briefcase?"

I looked at him. He was walking with short, clumsy steps, matching his stride to mine, dodging pedestrians who dodged to avoid me.

"When I'm angry," he said, "I like to thrust my hands into my pockets."

"Jeremy," I said, and stopped for a moment. "Leave me alone."

On a warm, late summer Friday evening, Castro Street was thriving, bustling, busier than any block downtown at lunchtime. From cars lined up at the stoplight men waved and yelled at other men on the sidewalk or crossing the street, gaily honked their horns. Groups of two or three men chatted at the entrances of shops, All American Boy, the hardware store, the Hallmark franchise, The Obelisk, then split up, some going in, others continuing along their way. A man in a black suit with an armload of purple iris hailed another man, black leather trousers and boots, a white athletic shirt; they kissed fondly and continued arm in arm. A youth at the bus stop whooped crazily and dashed across the street and down Eighteenth. Disco music pounded out of the open doors of bars on the far side of the street, The Bear, Phoenix, Elephant Walk, different tracks that merged into the soundtrack for a documentary—*A Day in the Life of the Gay Ghetto*. I started walking again, crossed Eighteenth, started up the incline past the bank.

"Allen! Damn it, stop and listen to me!"

"Screw off, Jeremy."

"I won't." He grabbed my shoulder. "Allen, I can't."

I shook his hand off. "Why not?" Staring at his chest I said again, "Why not, Jeremy? You've done it before." It felt as though I was shouting, my voice and throat raw. "You've screwed me around from the beginning, Jeremy."

"You tell 'im, bay-bee," someone said, one of the grinning men watching us.

"Don't let that big ol' man give you no line."

"Smack him with your briefcase," urged a third, laughing.

Then another said, "Ah, no, man—kiss and make up."

Glaring at them but not seeing them, I walked on. I knew Jeremy was still beside me; I didn't care. Past Nineteenth, where the hill steepened, there were no more crowds.

"I'm not good at this, Allen."

"Causing scenes?" I kept walking, one foot after another. "I thought you did pretty well."

"You're the only man I've slept with for five years, Allen, that's what I meant, I'm not good at dealing with other people."

Something in his voice made me believe him. Stopping, I saw how hard I was breathing, the air rushing into my lungs and then out again before it could do any good. "Why in hell," I said, ragged on the edge of laughter or tears, "did you choose me to practice on?"

"I'm not practicing."

"Christ. One boyfriend who makes out with anything on two legs as long as it isn't a woman and another who's a born-again virgin. I don't need this." I raised my head and stared all around, at the neat houses climbing the hill in staggered ranks on either side of the street, at the thin blue sky overhead. I coughed harshly. It turned into a laugh. Setting my briefcase down, I sat on the step of the nearest house. "I do not need this. Jeremy—"

"Don't ask me what I've been doing for five years." Jeremy looked at his feet, kicked at the sidewalk. "Please." He sat down but left some space between us. "I'll tell you but not yet, okay? I'm not ready to tell you yet, Allen."

"Who says I want to know? Who says I want to know you anymore?"

We were silent, our breathing returning to normal. I said to myself: Mikey should be glad—, and laughed. I said to myself: Sean's *easy*—. I said to myself: Stand up. Walk away. I said, "Jeremy. Last Saturday you kicked me out in the morning without even a cup of coffee. After two hours of sleep I didn't even know which bus to catch to go home. I walked halfway across the city. And then you called me. Why?"

I turned to look at him. He stared into the street. After a moment, still silent, still not looking at me, he reached over and took my hand. "Fifteen sheets of paper, I couldn't draw your face." He turned his head. He was frowning. His big painter's hand squeezed mine to the edge of pain. "You were the only Pasztory directory assistance had ever heard of."

Words on Paper

WHEN THE ENVELOPE appeared in my in-box at Grace & Fenton I didn't recognize the handwriting—there was no return address—but because it was handwritten I didn't set it aside. Business correspondence would have been typed, and would have come in a standard envelope. The envelope was more square than oblong, heavy personal stationery with a blue border on the flap. ALLEN K. PASZTORY, the envelope said, in spiky capitals, the *A*'s like deltas, the *E* three horizontal strokes with no upright, and the *Z* crossed. An architect's hand, I thought, but I knew no architects. None who might write me a letter. I slit open the envelope with my paperknife.

The large sheet of paper inside had been folded into quarters around a small colored-pencil drawing. A single green apple sat on a saucer, beside it a dark blue cup that matched the saucer. I recognized Jeremy's coffee service and felt something I couldn't name, a feeling that caused my skin to prickle and a flavor like weak tea to settle for a moment on my tongue. The species of discretion or whatever it was that led Jeremy to mail his letter in care of my job upset me more than that it was the first I had heard from him in two weeks. He had not called me, I had not called him; I had told myself it was over and a good thing too. Finding an apartment of my own was the priority, I told myself. Time enough to score a boyfriend after that.

The way the paper was folded, both obverse and reverse were divided into four rectangles; except for the one with the drawing, each unit was filled with lines of neat capital letters, seven blocks of text oriented in different directions. I could not find a salutation, a date, a close—nowhere to start or to end.

98

WHAT DOES THE "K" STAND FOR? I WROTE YOUR NAME ON
THE ENVELOPE & IT MADE ME SMILE, THE PEN FELT VERY
COMFORTABLE WITH YOUR NAME AS IF THAT WAS ALL IT
WANTED TO WRITE ALLEN K. PASZTORY ALLEN PASZTORY
ALLEN ALLEN ALLEN ALLEN ALLEN ALLEN ALLEN ALLEN
ALLEN ALLEN ALLEN ALLEN ALLEN ALLEN ALLEN ALLEN
ALLEN ALLEN ALLEN ALLEN ALLEN ALLEN ALLEN ALLEN
ALLEN ALLEN ALLEN ALLEN ALLEN ALLEN ALLEN ALLEN
ALLEN ALLEN ALLEN ALLEN ALLEN ALLEN ALLEN ALLEN
ALLEN ALLEN ALLEN ALLEN ALLEN ALLEN ALLEN ALLEN
ALLEN ALLEN. MY MIDDLE NAME IS DAVID. I NEVER USE IT.

I CAN'T DRAW EXTERIORS OR LANDSCAPES ANYMORE, I
DON'T KNOW WHY, ONLY ARCHITECTURAL INTERIORS OR
STILL LIFES OR FIGURE STUDIES, & IF I LOOK AT SOME-
THING I CAN'T SEE IT PROPERLY, NOT TO DRAW IT. SOME-
THING IS WRONG. THERE'S SO MUCH WE DON'T KNOW
ABOUT EACH OTHER. WHY IS IT THAT I WANT TO KNOW
ABOUT YOU? BECAUSE IT IS CLEAR THAT I AM AFRAID TO
LET YOU INTO MY LIFE, TO LET YOU KNOW ANYTHING AT
ALL ABOUT ME. MY FAVORITE COLOR IS ORANGE, WHICH
IS NOT A COLOR I CAN OFTEN WORK INTO MY PAINTINGS
& THEREFORE THE SECRET, ALLOWING YOU IN ON IT,
IS MEANINGLESS. I WILL BE 29 YEARS OLD IN FEBRUARY.

YESTERDAY I CALLED SOMEONE WHO HAS BEEN DISAP-
POINTED IN ME FOR SEVERAL YEARS. I TOLD HER ABOUT
YOU. RATHER, NOT <u>ABOUT</u> YOU BUT THAT YOU <u>WERE</u>, <u>ARE</u>,
THAT I CAN'T STOP DWELLING ON YOU, THAT I DON'T
KNOW WHETHER I WANT OR DON'T WANT OR WHAT I WANT.
SHE SAID THE WORD WAS EITHER "WISH" OR "DESIRE."
THE TASK AT HAND IS TO DETERMINE WHICH. I WISH I
COULD ASK YOU. I DESIRE TO KNOW THE ANSWER. BUT
WOULDN'T THIS BE LIKE KNOWING THE LATIN NAME
FOR EVERY PLANT OR ANIMAL YOU SEE—NOT USEFUL
INFORMATION? NOT INFORMATION ONE ACTS UPON.

I CANNOT IMAGINE WHAT YOUR LIFE HAS BEEN LIKE. I
HAVE HEARD YOU SPEAK & I THINK ABOUT ENGLISH NOT
BEING YOUR FIRST LANGUAGE. I USED TO KNOW SPANISH
WELL ENOUGH THAT I DREAMED IN IT, BUT HOW DOES ONE
DREAM IN SIGN LANGUAGE? SOMETIMES I WOULD DIS-
COVER MYSELF THINKING IN ONE LANGUAGE BUT SPEAK-
ING THE OTHER, & MY ENGLISH, FOR EXAMPLE, SOUNDED
TRANSLATED — LIKE THE INSTRUCTION BOOKLET FOR A
JAPANESE TAPE RECORDER. ONE NIGHT I SAW YOU TALKING
IN YOUR SLEEP. I THOUGHT, IF I WAKE HIM UP HE WON'T
KNOW HOW TO SPEAK TO ME.

A PAINTER OUGHT TO KNOW THE NAMES OF COLORS BUT
THE COLOR OUTSIDE MY WINDOW RIGHT NOW, IN THE SKY,
IS NOT ONE I COULD NAME. I LIKE THE DANGER OF USING
WATERCOLOR WHETHER LIQUID, THE KIND IN TUBES, OR
THE SOLID BLOCKS IN CHILDREN'S PAINT BOXES, BECAUSE
YOU CAN'T COVER UP YOUR MISTAKES. WATERCOLOR IS AS
MUTABLE AS LIGHT, THOUGH, A DROP TOO MUCH OR TOO
LITTLE OF WATER, & THIS COLOR HAS A CERTAIN OPACITY
THAT WOULD DISAPPEAR INTO THE PAPER. GOUACHE &
TEMPERA HAVE THE RIGHT OPACITY BUT THE SAME
DISADVANTAGES. I DON'T USE OILS BECAUSE THE SMELL
OF TURPENTINE MAKES ME NAUSEOUS.

ONCE UPON A TIME IT WAS EASY, I SLEPT WITH ANYONE &
HAD LOTS OF GOOD SEX—THIS WAS LONG AGO. BUT THEN I
FELL IN LOVE WITH SOMEONE WITH WHOM I HAD SEX THAT
WAS INTERESTING RATHER THAN GOOD, PRECISELY, & THE
WHOLE QUESTION OF SEX GOT VERY CONFUSING. IF I HAD
MET YOU LONG AGO YOU WOULD HAVE BEEN TOO YOUNG,
FOR ONE THING. SOMEWHAT LATER I WOULDN'T HAVE PER-
MITTED MYSELF TO BE INTERESTED. I WAS IN LOVE, & THEN
I WAS IN LOVE AGAIN AT THE SAME TIME, & THEN THE
THIRD TIME I WAS IN LOVE WITHOUT QUALIFICATIONS.
MAKING LOVE WITH YOU IS SOMETHING I TREASURE, BUT
TREASURES YOU HIDE AWAY UNDER LOCK & KEY.

I WOULD TELL YOU NAMES BUT HOW CAN I TELL YOU WHAT
THEY MEAN, WHO THESE PEOPLE ARE, HOW THEY ARE
PARTS OF MY LIFE? I FEEL THAT WITH YOU I DON'T HAVE A
HISTORY, & THIS TERRIFIES ME. NO MATTER HOW MUCH I
TOLD YOU, NO MATTER HOW MUCH LATER HISTORY WE
MIGHT CREATE, NO MATTER HOW WELL WE KNOW EACH
OTHER. I AM AFRAID YOU WILL TRY TO INVENT ME. SEVERAL
YEARS AGO I WANTED TO TELL MY PARENTS TO STOP TRY-
ING TO WRITE THE STORY OF MY LIFE. THE UPSHOT WAS
THAT THEY WROTE ME OUT, OR I WROTE THEM OUT, I'M
NOT CLEAR ON THIS. YOU SPEAK ABOUT YOUR FAMILY AS IF
THEY WERE FRIENDS. HERE ARE TWO NAMES: TOBY. RUTH.

Bedrooms and Dining Rooms

"THIS IS ONE of our most popular models," the saleswoman said. "Six layers of cotton batting around a foam core. The frame is solid pine, pegged and glued, no nails. It comes in four sizes, twin, full, queen, king. What size are you looking for?"

"Queen, I guess." I had never in my life bought a bed—any furniture at all. My new apartment, a studio in a big, ugly white building behind the Mint, had nothing in it. One trip in Sean's small car had done to move everything I owned, and the night before I had tried to sleep in a nest of blankets and pillows on the uncarpeted floor.

"Well, try this one out. Just don't put your shoes on it." She smiled brightly. "If you need any help, just ask."

What did you look for when you were buying a bed? The frame appeared solid, sturdy and plain, sanded, varnished white pine. I sat down on the edge. Sean slept on a futon, but without a frame, spread flat on the floor. Since the summer after turning thirteen I had mostly slept on thin, hard dormitory mattresses atop metal cots. Jeremy had a massive mahogany bedstead, Victorian, its tall headboard heavily draped with carved wreaths of acanthus and oak leaves. It stood in solitary magnificence in an otherwise empty room. I kicked off my shoes and lay back in the center of the bed, staring up at the acoustical-tile ceiling, the flickering fluorescent fixtures. I would need at least one lamp. Under me the futon settled, firm, resilient, the polished cotton cover cool and smooth to my fingers. I was only a few minutes early. Jeremy would be here soon. I hadn't seen him in weeks, save an unsatisfying, dissociated lunch downtown on a day when he was delivering work to Grace & Fenton. We kept asking questions at cross-purposes without ever asking the right questions, or answering the wrong ones. He wouldn't call me at Sean's place or at work, and he didn't answer the phone during the day, so I'd only spoken to him twice, to tell him I'd found an apartment of my own and later to ask him to help me buy furniture. There were limits set every way I turned—in his flat, there were doors that were always closed; this had been going on for more than two months.

I pulled myself up and looked around. The other beds on the floor looked comparable to this one. Some of the frames were more elaborate, some folded up into ingenious couches or daybeds but I knew I couldn't be bothered to make the conversion on a regular basis so the bed might as well be permanently a bed. The futons themselves varied between pallet-thin—ascetics' mats—and those that resembled conventional innersprings in their thickness, every one covered in glazed cotton with prints like the embroidery on antique kimonos. The one I sat on had a design of butterflies and paper fans, a pattern so busy I felt I'd have trouble sleeping on it. Perhaps it was thick enough to accept a fitted sheet. That would mean buying bed linens too—my sheets from college were twin size.

Everywhere I looked I saw things I needed but didn't want. What I wanted was a new life, a new way of living, but I didn't know how to go about it. I had never been a grown-up before, never made choices, unless going to one college instead of another was a choice, unless moving in with Sean was a choice. At the same time I wished someone would make choices for me: tell me which bed to buy. I hardly knew how to cook. I would need to buy pots and pans, dishes, silverware. I could run all my new credit cards up to their limits and I still wouldn't have a life. The weekend before, after signing my half-year lease, I had gone to Emporium-Capwell and Macy's, bought a new suit—now I had four, a suitable number for an adult. Macy's was having a shirt sale, so I bought shirts; an underwear sale so I bought socks and undershorts.

Bookcases. Tables. In Jeremy's bedroom there was a nightstand by the bed with a lamp and, clustered around its base, a little shrine of objects. There was an abalone shell piled with tiny dried rosebuds and spikes of lavender. There was a small box of painted tin in the shape of a gaudy Queen Anne Victorian. An oval silver frame enclosed a photograph of a baby with sleepy blue eyes. Propped on a miniature bamboo easel stood a full-length portrait only four inches tall of a woman with heavy auburn hair, wearing a long white dress. She might have been an undiscovered Whistler or a Burne-Jones. High on the wall above the bed hung a vivid expressionist male torso, heavy impasto on unframed canvas, and across the room a large mirror that reflected both the brutal painting and the bed.

I looked at subtle, Shaker-style dining room tables and chairs, oak or maple. Salespeople asked me if I needed help; I told them I was just browsing. Surely it was unrealistic to expect to furnish a whole apartment, even a tiny studio, in one sweep. Young men were trying out chairs and sleek plastic-laminate tables—young men in pairs. A man sat on a futon, then reached up and pulled at the hand of a woman until she fell on the bed beside him. They both laughed. I glanced again toward the entrance, where the glare of a late afternoon on Market Street collided with the glare of the store's fluorescent lamps, and saw a black figure tall enough to be Jeremy, but it wasn't Jeremy. I went back to the first futon. It was still there. The pattern on the cover was so involved it inspired a sort of vertigo. I sat down again.

"Is that him?" a voice behind me asked. It was a child's voice, an enthusiastic treble. No, I replied. I remembered an old nursery rhyme, or a riddle, I wasn't sure—I'm nobody, who are you? I'm nobody, I said, no-one anyone's looking for. Jeremy wasn't coming. I'd have to buy the bed by myself. One was as good as another. I wanted to sleep in a bed that night. There were bars. There were men.

"Is that him," more insistently, "Daddy? Huh?"

"Allen." This was another voice—a man's. Daddy's. I knew three other ways to spell my name: Alan, Allan, Alun. The only Daddy I knew was my own.

"Allen. I didn't want to tell you, and then I didn't know how to tell you."

I turned around. The child was a little boy, perhaps three feet tall. He wore miniature blue jeans and a yellow t-shirt, tiny scuffed white sneakers. His skin was pale, his hair black. His eyes had changed color since the photograph on Jeremy's bedside table. Now they were the same grey as his father's. "I know your name," the child said. "You're Daddy's friend Allen."

"Jeremy." I couldn't look at him. "I didn't think you were going to show."

"This is Toby," Jeremy said, "my son."

Toby had lost interest. "I'm hungry, Daddy, I want a *ham*burger. Can we go to Hot'n'Hunky?"

"Your son." For an instant, still, I'd thought—hoped—he would say nephew. Anyone could have a nephew—I had two. And a niece. As much as a smallish child of five or six, as delicate as a little girl though clearly a boy, could resemble a man of twenty-eight, six-four, bushy mustache, Toby resembled Jeremy. "He's handsome." Many things were clear. More were not. "Like his daddy. Does he live with you?"

"Daddy!" Toby pulled on his father's hand, insistent.

Jeremy grabbed him around the middle and held him squirming and giggling against his hip. "Hush a minute, kid. I'm sorry, Allen, I should have told you." Toby was spanking him. "Look," Jeremy said, "this place is open late. Can I interest you in a burger at Hot'n'Hunky, and we'll come back here later?"

Without noticing, I'd stood up and come around the bed to face them. Now I sat down again. "Put the boy down, Jeremy. All the blood's going to his head. He'll get hysterical."

On his feet again, Toby shook his head, which involved shaking his whole body until he staggered against my knee. I steadied him. "You know what, Toby?" I asked.

He stared at me. His head was too big for his body. "What?"

"Your daddy's a naughty man."

"Is not!" He shook his chin again. "Is he?" He ran back to Jeremy and swatted him on the knee. "Are you? Are you a naughty man?"

Almost smiling, Jeremy was looking at me. "Does that mean you'll come?"

"I don't know, Jeremy. I don't know how to deal with you. Will he throw french fries at me?"

"Probably." He knelt down and put his hands on Toby's shoulders. "Yes, I am a naughty man, Toby," he said, "but you're a naughty boy. So there."

"Am not!" Toby rushed back to me. "I'm not a naughty boy, am I?"

His face was so serious that his eyes had crossed a little. He was panting. I wasn't worried that he'd start crying but I wanted to gather him into my arms anyway. "I really don't know, Toby, I haven't known you long enough." He closed his mouth so tight the lips disappeared— fierce or annoyed more than stricken. "Probably not, though," I added. "I'd say one bad apple in the family was enough. Do you want to go get that burger?"

"Hot'n'Hunky!" Toby yelled.

I looked up at Jeremy. "I'd say you owe me at least a hamburger."

Hot'n'Hunky, the burger joint for hot, hunky Castro clones, had two branches in the area, one down Market near the Mint, around the corner from my new building, the other on Eighteenth near the action.

I expected we'd go to the latter, closer, but after leaving the furniture store Jeremy turned left instead of right toward the crosswalk. "Less business down here," he said. "If the kid starts throwing french fries I don't want some leather queen getting hysterical. Or worse, sentimental." He was too studiously calm—everything in stride, everything, as they said, copacetic. This trick of talking over Toby's head as if the boy couldn't hear or wouldn't understand seemed uncharacteristic, and wasn't something I liked, although I imagined we'd both be doing more of it before we were through.

Not many months before, my sister had flown out to attend my graduation from college—our parents wouldn't fly, her husband wouldn't take time off from business. Steph brought her elder son with her, Kit, not the portly, somnolent, saint-like eight-month-old baby I remembered but almost four, thinner and less fragile, adventurous, giddy with language and a vocabulary that seemed to double every hour. We talked over his head, of course—we argued a lot that weekend —but I was surprised, not having any experience with children, how much he took in and repeated later, and wondered how much he understood. Sitting on the floor in the motel room he scolded his teddy bear: "Not coming home for the summer? Why not?" His rapid, lisping pronunciation was hard to follow, but not so difficult that I didn't catch him calling the bear a homosexual.

Sean had come down from the city for all the ceremonies, too, staying in my room—something that might have scandalized my suitemates the first time but after a year they were over that. We had entered dangerous territory already, Sean and I, but I had moved most of my belongings into his apartment in the city immediately after exams were finished, and putting on a front for my sister seemed to help. The point, though, was that he took to Kit as if he'd always been in training to be an uncle despite being an only child. He never talked over Kit's head; when Steph and I became obstreperous, throwing names at each other, words Sean thought the child shouldn't hear, he took Kit off into a corner or for a walk or to the motel swimming pool until we'd calmed down.

Walking down Market Street, I glanced over at Jeremy. I would not have expected to find him lacking in comparison to Sean. But then, I had expected a different species of surprise from him—a different variety of secret, the kind of secret Sean wouldn't bother hiding. "What about Toby's mother?" I asked. "Is that Ruth?"

He halted. Toby, a step ahead, kept going. "Toby! Wait up!" Jeremy's complacent half-smile had vanished. "How did you know her name?"

Toby turned around. "Daddy!" he shouted, impatient. He stamped his foot. I hadn't thought people really did that.

"Oh—I'd forgotten the letter." Pressing his lips together for a moment, Jeremy shook his head. "I can't ask you to forgive me, can I?"

"I don't know yet. I don't know what I'd be forgiving. Is she the woman in the portrait by your bed?"

Jeremy nodded, just as Toby, running back, grabbed him around the knees. "Daddy, I told you, I'm *hungry*. Very hungry." A foot taller, twenty-five pounds heavier, Toby might have knocked his father over. A trio of slight, elegantly butch men passing by stared at us with raised eyebrows. The one who had the expression down best—one eyebrow, only—muttered "Adult abuse" to his companions, who laughed, and they walked on. "Allen's hungry, too," Toby claimed. "Aren't you hungry too? Let's go!"

"Didn't you eat lunch today?" Jeremy asked. To me he said, "He goes to a private school. Good lunches."

"That was *hours* ago, and I didn't get anything else to eat before you came and got me, and it's dinnertime now, Daddy, I know it is." He was bouncing up and down. "Come on!"

"Okay, okay, we're coming."

"Toby," I said. I thought I liked him better, at this point, than his father. "Do you want to walk with me?" I put out my hand for him. "Your father can stay here if he wants, or dawdle along as slow as he pleases."

Suspicious for a moment, Toby glared at me, before smiling and taking my hand. His smile was sunny, cheerful, devastating. "You're not as big as Daddy," he said after a step or two, as if congratulating me. "I don't have to stretch so much." His hand was sticky, a melting lollipop in my palm. "Do you like ketchup on your hamburger?"

"Sometimes."

"I don't. It's icky. *I*—" he drew himself up tall, butch in embryo, and almost stumbled—"I like mustard. And bacon."

"His mother's Jewish. Blame me. Toby, do you want to hold my hand too?"

"No. I'm mad at you right now, Daddy."

"Oh. Well. Then can I hold your hand, Allen?"

"Jeremy, I'm relatively angry too. I don't think so."

"Okay." His voice was low. He walked half a pace behind his son, his legs too long for a shuffle, more a shamble. "Ruth's gay too," he said.

"Did you use a turkey-baster?"

"That's unkind, Allen."

"Springing this on me isn't unkind? Leading me on and holding me off for two and a half months isn't unkind? I thought you had a lover or something—I thought I was an illicit affair, your mistress. Is that what I am? Don't talk to me about unkind, Jeremy."

We walked on in silence. Holding onto my hand, Toby seemed content, his gait between stride and toddle. I pointed between buildings up at the Mint on its promontory. "See that big grey building, Toby?" I asked. "I live right behind it."

He glanced up at me, unimpressed. "I live at twenty-one seventy Sutter Street," he said. "In the Western Addition."

"I know." Apparently he did live with his father. "I've been to your house." I remembered something—the folding gate at the top of the stairs. The closed doors.

"You did?" This was a puzzle. "I never saw you there."

"It was when you were in Santa Cruz with Mommy and Candace," Jeremy said.

"Oh. Have you been to Mommy's house too, Allen?"

"No. I don't know your mother."

Jeremy placed his palm, flat, in the center of my back, between the shoulder blades, as though he were pushing me faster, farther, away. "Ruth and I met in art school. We were friends for so long we just sort of fell in love even though we're both gay. I—" His voice was low and fast, unhappy. "I got involved in some stuff that frightened me, lots of drugs and drinking, sleeping with almost anybody, doing anything, some really nasty, scary scenes, and I asked her to marry me. I wasn't trying to go straight or anything, if I was I guess I'd have asked a straight woman, I just thought—I wanted something to hold on to. Someone." He took a breath that sounded like a sob. "Toby was an accident. After he came along it was like it wasn't a game anymore, not the same way, we weren't playing at husband and wife—we were parents. If it's not a game, you can't stop it any time you like. You can't change the rules. Ruth didn't see it that way, and I, I sort of, I fell in love with my son, I guess. —That's what I said in the letter, isn't it? I mean, he needed me as much as I needed him. Ruth never needed me. She always sort of took care of me. Ruth—" this statement was very flat, almost hateful— "is an extremely wealthy woman. Then, after a while, she met Candace. We were kind of a menage à trois for a year or so, or à quatre with Toby, except Candace wasn't in love with me by any means and I only like her a little. Now. So Ruth moved in with Candace and we got divorced. I had to sell our house, Allen. I really loved that house. I felt safe there." Another painful gasp. "What I told you before, it was true, I hadn't screwed around with men at all since Toby was born. It almost didn't occur to me. When he was with me it never did. When he went to visit Ruth I'd—I went out drinking and dancing, but I never picked anyone up. You were the first. A year ago a guy I was in love with when Ruth and I lived in Mexico, Roddy, Roddy came to San Francisco on a visit and looked me up and I almost—but I didn't. Then, and then I met *you*, Allen. I saw you in Michael Quillen's office and I thought Oh, he's cute enough isn't he, but. That night at the club, I was drunk way before I got there but I was just going to dance up a storm and then go home and, and jerk off, but then you asked me to dance and I'd been thinking about you, I mean *really thinking* about you, and there you were and you wanted me, and I wanted you, so badly, Allen, so badly, so much, you were like . . . you reminded me of every man I was ever in love with, only, only better. Kinder. Stronger. Kinder and stronger and better than Ruth or anyone."

"We're here, Jere," I said. I hadn't looked back at him before. He was weeping, his eyes and his nostrils red, swollen. "I'm not kind, Jeremy, or very strong. Come on in. There's a rest room, you can wash your face."

"Why are you crying, Daddy?" Toby stared up at him, amazed, and held my hand tighter, until Jeremy knelt on the sidewalk before us. Toby threw his arms around his father's neck. "What's wrong, Daddy?" he cried.

Standing, his son bundled against his chest, Jeremy stared wide-eyed at me. "That's all, Allen. That's all there is." His voice thick, clotted, he coughed. "You've got to believe me."

I couldn't bear to look at him. "I believe you." I glanced around. People in the restaurant stared out at us, passersby on the street, a car backing into a parking space on the curb had stopped and the driver was staring at us. "I do believe you." I focused on my foot for an instant, and then I put my arms around them both.

"Will you forgive me?"

"I'll work on it." I was crying too. So was Toby, tiny gasping whimpers and sobs. "Let's get something to eat. Toby's hungry."

Adultery

SHE WAS WAITING to meet us at the Santa Cruz Greyhound terminal, this woman, this ex-wife, Ruth Goldman, a tall, slender, stylish woman—Toby Kent's mother she was, Jeremy Kent's former wife, the woman he loved. She waited at the gate, stood against a plate glass window between two concrete piers but did not lean back against it, calm, surely, far calmer than I could imagine being. I knew her before Toby rocked against me, rising to his knees, clambered more or less into my lap. "There's Mommy!" His hands reached for the window. My own hands automatically clasped him around the waist when he leaned; they were neither his father's nor his mother's but only the neutrally friendly hands of someone he knew who would—as anyone might—reach to support him if he appeared in danger of a tumble. In this way they felt to me like someone else's hands, although attached to my own wrists. Peculiarly clumsy, inarticulate hands they seemed, which might or might not know what to do with the strange, substantial bulk they held, because he wasn't just any child whom any adult would wish to protect. The cotton jersey of his striped t-shirt, blue and white, was cool under my palms because my hands were warm. From across the aisle, Jeremy materialized suddenly in Toby's seat. "That's Ruth," Jeremy confirmed.

She looked up as the bus completed its wide turn and pulled in. In shadow her hair appeared simply dark around a long, narrow, very pale face—a great deal of dark, wavy hair tumbling over her shoulders. I knew, though, that it was one of those colors called red for lack of an alternative, and I knew that she was taller than I. Seeing Toby wave, she raised one hand, a pale, slender hand extended from the sleeve of her bulky cardigan like a lily from its leaves. Smiling, she took one step forward. Her skirts ruffled around the calves of heavy leather boots, which, high-heeled, would make her even taller.

Jeremy had said, "You'll like her," but I had my doubts. Speaking of his mother, Toby said, "She's pretty," but doesn't every child believe his mother to be beautiful? And what use to me was the knowledge even if it were true.

We were sitting near the front of the bus. As passengers before and behind rose to their feet and reached into the overhead luggage racks, Jeremy leaned shyly against me. "Will you handle the kid? I'll take the bags." Before I could reply he had stood and retrieved the knapsack packed with his and Toby's things. He slung it over one shoulder, then grabbed my briefcase and the small bag that went back and forth from my apartment to his and, this weekend, contained two complete changes of clothes. I thought, first: What's she going to think when I'm tending her son? and second: I should have changed—I had left work early but still wore a suit, and had only loosened my tie because Toby kept trying to strangle me with it.

Yet, gazing at his crotch because it was on a level with my eyes, holding his son in my arms, I felt sure of Jeremy. He blocked the aisle so I could slide across the seats and stand. Without protest, Toby took my hand, but the aisle was too narrow for us to go abreast. I gave him a little shove ahead of me, steering him with my hands on his shoulders.

"You don't know my mommy, do you, Allen?" he asked. "I'll introduce you."

"Thank you, Toby."

We followed the other passengers to the front of the bus, down the three steep steps to the door. Here, Toby allowed me to grasp him under the arms and swing him to the pavement a foot and a half below. Jeremy had placed one hand on my shoulder to steady me. Ruth, off to the side, out of the way, came forward.

As I released him, Toby cried, "Mommy!" and rushed to her with the clumsy violence of little boys, threw his arms around her legs. She rested one hand on his head but was staring at me, or at Jeremy, above and behind. I stepped down from the bus. Ruth's expression was serene, benign. "You're Allen," she said, pitching her voice over the clamor of less ambiguous greetings and welcomes around us, a rich, amused, cultivated contralto.

I nodded and moved out of the way of all the others who wanted off the bus. Putting his hand on my shoulder again, shepherding me toward her, Jeremy said, "Ruth, I'd like you to meet Allen Pasztory. Allen, this is Ruth Goldman, Toby's mother." He pressed his arm along my back as if to say, It's okay.

"Daddy!" Toby, turning very fast, glared at his father. "I wanted to introduce them!"

She shifted her hand to Toby's shoulder. "Well, why not?" she said. "Let's start over." Pulling him into the folds of her wide skirt, she said, "Who's that man with your father, Toby?"

He shrugged her off. "You already know!" he shouted. "Don't be dumb, Mommy." You couldn't fool Toby, who had a voice like a siren when he wanted to let it loose. "He's Daddy's boyfriend."

I couldn't be certain that we were boyfriends yet. I had never been in Santa Cruz before and was suspicious of the town. I didn't want to know what kinds of reaction this proclamation would inspire in the people near us, but Jeremy tightened his grip on me and Ruth smiled, held out her hand. "Hello, Daddy's boyfriend," she said.

Her smile seemed to me a good one. I liked the uncomplicated authority and strength of her hand. A good head taller than I, she drew no attention to the discrepancy, did not bend or peer. When her hair blew across her face she brushed it away, smoothed it back around her neck. "Hello, Toby's mommy," I said. Her shawl-necked cardigan was knit of a tweedy golden brown wool, over a deep blue shirt and pine green skirt. She looked warm enough for a cooler afternoon. "I'm happy to meet you, at last."

"Likewise." Taking her hand back and stuffing both into the pockets of the cardigan, she said, "Jeremy, let's blow this joint. You should never have gotten rid of the car."

That Jeremy should once have owned a car was a surprise to me. Despite the thousands of cars that clogged the streets of San Francisco, jockeying for parking spaces, collecting tickets like windfalls, it seemed to me that no-one who lived there owned one. Everyone rode Muni's buses, electric trolleys, or the Metro—all those cars being a municipal charade to convince newcomers that the city was in fact a city, just as the cable cars were meant to persuade casual visitors it was nothing of the sort. I knew only one person with a car, Sean, and he never drove it except to go out of town. Jeremy urged me after Ruth and Toby, across the tarmac toward the parking lot. "We wouldn't all have fit in the MG anyway, Ruth," he said, "and you know I don't like to drive." An MG, yet—a sports car. Who was this man?

THE DIFFICULTY LAY in imagining Jeremy and Ruth together as anything other than old friends, affectionate friends who hugged and kissed on impulse: to imagine them without intermediaries. That Toby was Jeremy's son I had grown used to quickly enough, without noticing its happening. I had little more trouble recognizing Toby as Ruth's child, but couldn't understand him as *their* offspring, a joint project. I couldn't visualize their having been married, having been lovers. A characteristic failure of imagination, encouraged by the easy interplay between Ruth and Candace. There was a kind of pervasive eroticism there that had more to do with tones of voice and slight shifts of facial expression than any indiscreet actions, which, they clearly understood, would have embarrassed their houseguest, a naïve, squeamish, and very young man. In fact I was already embarrassed simply by an attempt to imagine what I needed to label *physical intimacy* between Jeremy, my boyfriend, and Ruth, his former wife, sufficient to have engendered a child—any child, but more particularly Toby, their son. He seemed less a link between them than a division, a separation, a factor in that distance which allowed Jeremy to explain that I had been at work all day, probably wanted a shower, different clothes, perhaps a nap. Candace kindly suggested she and Ruth take Toby to the beach for the half hour or so left before sunset. The Boardwalk could wait for tomorrow.

IT WAS A rattletrap, slapped-together little house. Jeremy had told me Ruth's family was wealthy—I had expected something very different from this rose pink stucco weekend-at-the-beach cottage, its front blazing with bougainvillea the rusty color of garnets, Mexican poppy with broad crinkled petals the white of a wedding gown centered by pure gold bobbles, orange and scarlet hibiscus. Inside, the floors were terracotta quarry tile spread with straw mats and worn Turkish rugs, the plastered walls cluttered with bits of ethnic handicraft, posters and postcards, Ruth's vivid, disorienting paintings. It seemed to me the kind of bright, junk-strewn household a commune-cum-rock band of the late sixties would have set up, and that there ought to be a palpable haze of marijuana smoke in the air, an ineradicable reek of patchouli oil, the droning whine of sitars. In fact Candace, when we arrived, had been practicing sere Satie piano pieces on the old honky-tonk upright in the living room, and the air smelled of the sea and of Ruth's all-day chili, Toby's favorite. Nevertheless, there were, after all, two handsome pot plants beneath the morning glory–crowned pergola in the backyard.

The backyard was actually on the order of an inner court, because a second building stood behind it, the wall facing the garden an unbroken expanse of wooden-sashed windows—Candace's ceramics studio, Ruth's painting studio, the guest room. Ordinarily, Jeremy said, leading me through the house and the yard, he would sleep in the living room or in Toby's room, but ordinarily he didn't bring someone with him. He stopped me under the pergola, and kissed me, and said, "Are you regretting this already?"

Ordinarily, I understood, meant that he had never before brought a guest. I closed my hands around his wrists and said, "No."

Inside, Jeremy let down the rice-paper blinds, making of the light in the guest room a pale, corrosive dusk that, by lowering the contrast between shadow and substance, made it easier to see but harder to distinguish. Beside the low, wide bed with its Navajo blanket, on the nightstand, stood a tall slender ceramic vase with a large arrangement of white and purple iris. It was the second week of February—still attuned to the seasons of my native land even after five years in California, flowers in February astonished me. It was the second week of February, the week of Jeremy's birthday, his twenty-ninth. He was twenty-nine and I would not turn twenty-three for another two months. He was twenty-nine and had a seven-year-old son, the same span of years as that separating Jeremy and me; he was twenty-nine, four years divorced, on good terms with his ex-wife, where I had not spoken to my ex-lover for five months and didn't expect to; he owned—*owned*—a plump, handsome Victorian building in San Francisco, wedding-cake pink, with two apartments besides the one he and Toby lived in: he was a landlord, who repaired his tenants' doorknobs, cleared their plugged drains. He was turning twenty-nine, and on the table beside the irises was a flat package wrapped in Italian marbled paper. I ignored it.

Jeremy didn't notice the package or, perhaps, on my account, ignored it as well. Setting down the bags and my briefcase, he took off his jacket, slung it onto the bed. "A shower?" he asked, and approached me. Fingering the knot of my tie, he said, "Many years ago, when I was a boy, I used to trick with men in suits. I'd forgotten what a turn-on all these layers of respectability are." He undid the tie and unbuttoned the second button of my shirt, then removed my jacket and tossed it beside his. "And then underneath it all," he said, unclasping my belt, unbuttoning my trousers, and drawing down the zipper, "there's a boy," he said, allowing the trousers to crumple down over my shoes, and pushed his big hands under the elastic of my underpants to hold my buttocks, "a boy in white Jockey shorts. You know," he said, running the fingers of one hand up my spine, "I read somewhere that briefs keep your testicles too warm and impede the production of sperm. You're threatening your fertility, boy."

"I'm not worried." He had started calling me *boy* only recently, as he became sure of himself, confident enough for irony. Confident enough to take charge. The endearment was as soothing—*endearing*— as it was alarming. And yet I meant to hold him to it. "One kid's enough in my family."

"He's a handful." Jeremy was unfastening the rest of the buttons of my shirt. The cleaners' heavy starch made the process a delicate one. "So are you." Spreading the panels of my shirtfront, he flattened his palms on my chest. "Quite," he said, a low, slurred mumble at odds with the precise consonants of the words, "a handful," as he pushed one hand beneath the fabric and under my arm, drew me into a flannel-shirted embrace.

AFTER JEREMY OPENED the package and saw what it contained he set it aside. "Not kind of Ruth," he said, looking away from me.

I sat down beside him on the bed, leaned my damp head against his shoulder. "What is it?" What is it about the past that it eternally impinges on the present and the future. Already, even at twenty-two, as self-absorbed as any infatuated young man, I knew this about the past. I knew this because the chronicle of my own family was a well-thumbed, much-revised volume, and because I was working (prematurely, I often thought, irresponsibly) on the Book of Jeremy.

"She ought to have kept it, or given it back to her parents." He stood up and away from me, walked across the room. He looked back. "I thought you were tired?" About Jeremy I had discovered this, a little late: that he was a father first, even stark naked and eager for me. Even, as now, fresh and damp from the shower, standing against the dim, diffuse radiance of the paper blinds, barefoot on the tiled floor and wearing pale, patterned boxer shorts whose waistband, pleated by the elastic, rode high on his hips, creasing his belly, illuminating, by contrast, the dark furze of hair on stomach and thighs. He was a father first, whose priority was to take care. "Aren't you tired, Allen?" Wrapping his arms around his chest, he turned in profile to the light. A big man—not simply tall but large, substantial, with the peculiar, slow yet inexorable vitality of big men who, though their movements are fastidious, thought-out, maintain a dangerous speed confined, as it were, within their flesh, waiting to be let loose and giving an edge to their caution. You never knew what to expect. Before he grew a beard, several years later, Jeremy often shaved twice a day; his hair grew so quickly he had to cut it every four weeks or look shaggy, disreputable; after every shower the drain was clogged with his fine black body hair although there was always sufficient left over to please me. Despite my being—so my mother said, disapproving—an adult (I held down a job, yes, lived away from my parents, owned four suits, but if this made me a grown-up I wanted none of it), I felt it was Jeremy who was a real man, and felt that he had been already a man at my age and younger. I imagined Jeremy at twenty-one, already a father a year before his son was born, taking care. "Let's lie down for a little while," he said. Taking care, he would have been, of Ruth.

"What did Ruth give you?" I asked as he came across the room.

For a moment he stood before me, arms crossed on his chest, and for an instant shut his eyes. His brows, which in any case were thick, nearly meeting on the bridge of his nose, met. "Too many things," he muttered. "A child, a home—memories." He opened his eyes and placed his hands on his hips. "Pictures from our wedding." He smiled, though it was nearly not a smile. "I'll show you."

"You don't have to, if you don't want, Jere." Leaning against the headboard, making room for him, I was afraid he wouldn't want. I wanted to know everything about him, everything about his past: he meant this much to me. I wanted to know how he had come to be married to a woman, and what that was like; how many men there had been before me and why it was I rather than somebody else who sat on this bed in his ex-wife's house asking him to show me his secret history. I was trying to discover, essentially, I think, why it was that my falling in love with Jeremy seemed to have so little to do with his being enormously attractive to me, with the fineness of the sex we had together—with our bodies, after all, or what we did with them. It was hard enough to admit it—the fact of it, the fact that I was in love—to myself. I did not know how to tell Jeremy I loved him.

What I said instead, when he had settled down at my side with a pillow in the small of his back and one arm in the small of mine, was, "Show me?" I leaned forward for the album and laid it across his knees.

By NOW I knew, or thought I knew, Jeremy and his son; I tried, there-fore, to learn his ex-wife and her lover—to learn them by heart, as though they were the lesson for the week. I hardly knew any women, beyond my elder sister, confidante of my youth. More particularly I knew no gay women. Ruth liked to be called a gay woman whereas Candace's preference was for the term lesbian.

WE SAT IN the kitchen—it was too early in the year to eat on the patio outside—over substantial bowls of chili, which was hot, hotter than I would have expected a boy of seven to tolerate. Picante, Ruth called it, although hardly Mexican. The first year of their marriage Ruth and Jeremy had lived in Mexico, this much I knew—Toby had been con-ceived there. They had lived in a town on a lake in the mountains northwest of Mexico City, which was to say not in any landscape I would recognize as Mexican—not, that is, desert and cactus, not shanties up against the walls of colonial palaces, nor palm trees above white sand beach and a warm sea the same blue as Candace's eyes. Between spoonfuls of beans and shredded beef in a thick red sauce with crisp slivers of red and green chiles, between crumbling bites of corn bread, Toby chattered to nobody in particular—playing, it oc-curred to me, Daddy's boy. He had seen a pelican at the beach, the water was too cold for his toes, were there sea otters in the harbor, had we seen this pebble of blue glass he'd found, could he have a Coke with his dinner?

"No Coke," said Jeremy.

"There's apple juice." Candace began to stand. "Would you like some apple juice, Toby?"

Toby stared at her down the table, as if she had spoken before her cue, thrown him off. It was an oddly adult look: Where did *you* come from? I knew what he was like when he was angry, when he was tired and cranky—this, for an instant, was a different child. Ruth's son? Then he smiled, back in character. "Yes, please, Candace," he said. As if con-scious of my expectations, he turned toward his mother. "The chili is extra good, Mommy."

"Thanks."

Getting up, Candace went to the refrigerator and in passing stroked Ruth's neck. My eyes tracked her, a target in my sights, from refrigerator to cupboard for a glass. Smaller than Ruth and more beautiful, she wore her hair very short and wore blue jeans and an embroidered Mexican blouse with the assurance and insouciance, I thought, of a man. She smiled at me.

"Right to bed after dinner," said Jeremy. "It's late."

"I know it's late, Daddy, I know how to tell time." Sitting on a telephone directory Toby was tall enough to reach his bowl and not make much mess, but still there was a stain of orange like a clown's ineptly painted lips around his mouth. "'Course it's late, you and Allen were fooling around when I came to get you or we could've eaten earlier." He smiled wisely.

Candace set the glass of apple juice down by Toby's place. "Is that what you were doing?" she asked, sly, conspiratorial.

Jeremy glanced at Ruth. Candace sat at the head of the table, Toby at the foot, Jeremy and I on one side, Ruth across from us. Ruth widened her eyes. I moved my free hand to Jeremy's thigh, squeezed. His voice clear, Jeremy said, "We were looking at the photo album Ruth left me. Thank you, Ruth, I guess."

"Well, happy birthday after all, Jeremy." She glanced over at Candace, then back to Jeremy.

Clinking and scraping, Toby pushed his spoon around the bowl. "They were on the bed," he told his mother, "and Allen didn't have any clothes on."

"He was just out of the shower. He hadn't gotten dressed yet. May I have another piece of corn bread?"

Ruth's expression was wry, amused—her chin wrinkled by a frown on the verge of a smile, her eyes slightly tilted. "Are you trying to justify something, Jeremy?"

"Daddy had his underpants on," said Toby, an honest child.

One weekend morning a few weeks before, Toby had pushed open the door of the bathroom in Jeremy's flat where I lay in the tub (my own apartment had only a shower), and strode to the toilet. He was in his pajamas—it was Sunday, still early. "I have to pee," he announced, reaching into his fly. He unleashed a healthy stream, then tucked himself together and washed his hands, on tiptoe to reach the faucets. I had sat up. He hadn't seen me naked before. Drying his hands on his own towel, he came over to the bathtub. "Daddy has hair on his chest." His tone was matter-of-fact as he inspected me. "You've only got a tiny bit on your tummy. Some men have hair on their chests, some men have mustaches, some men have beards." Chanting this refrain as if it were a nursery rhyme every child should know, he touched my shoulder, testing. "Daddy says I'll be hairy like a monkey when I'm grown up, like him." He grinned, relishing the prospect, then turned serious. "But my penis is just little." First he leaned over the tub to look at mine, then pulled down his pajama bottoms to show me his. "See. You have hair there, like Daddy, and he says I will too, but will my penis get big like yours?" Staring at him, I had said, "I expect so."

"What's for dessert, Mommy?" Toby asked, pushing his bowl away.

Jeremy covered my hand in his lap with his own, a kind of comforting gesture, I guessed, worried that I might feel overwhelmed. "Wipe your mouth, kid. You're a mess."

In fact I knew about families, and although the configuration here would likely shock my sister and brother-in-law, the dynamic was similar. I was closest to Toby, so I leaned over and dabbed my napkin at the corners of his mouth. He didn't pull away. Thinking about it, with a little more experience, I imagine most boys his age would have. "A napkin's not going to do much good. You'd better wash, Toby."

"Okay," he said, confident and cheerful. "Help me down, Allen."

"Please," said his mother.

"*Please* help me down, Allen, I'm so *high up* up here—" he was waving his arms around, but carefully, widening his eyes—"it's so *scary*. I might fall!"

Toby was small for his age and sometimes fooled me into thinking he was younger than he was, but this was sheer good-humored caricature. I stood and pulled out his chair, then grabbed him under the arms and lifted him to the floor. "Thank you, Allen," he said, bumping companionably against me before he left.

"Ice cream when you get back." Ruth began to clear the table. "Who's going to put him to bed?" she asked, carrying the stack of bowls to the sink. I followed her with the platter of corn bread crumbs. "Sit down, Allen, you're a guest."

"I think you should," said Jeremy.

"Oh, no." Turning to face us, she leaned back against the counter. "He's tired, he'll be cranky, he'll need a story. You're the nurturing one, remember, boyface." *Boyface,* she called him—they had a history, they had their own language. I had called him *sweetheart* once or twice. "I'm just the person who gave birth to him. You're Daddy. Besides, I want to talk to Allen."

"What color ice cream?" Toby said color when he meant flavor, standing in the kitchen doorway, knowing exactly what was going on and what he was saying.

"White," his mother told him, "but there's gooey brown stuff to go on top if you can wait while I warm it up."

"Dark brown? Not caramel?"

"Chocolate. I'm making coffee for the grown-ups too. Go into the living room, all you people, leave me alone."

"Can I have hot chocolate, Mommy?"

"Brown milk, heated up? Ick. I guess so."

Toby came over to stand by me. "Allen knows how to make it best," he announced, "the way I like it."

"Is that so?" She frowned at us. "Your father always liked the way I make cocoa, but okay. Allen, would you mind mixing up some hot brown milk for the child?"

"I'd be happy to."

"Now, shoo, the rest of you. Allen and I have work to do."

They left, noisily. Ruth fetched me a saucepan, showed me where to find what I needed. She worked smoothly, without wasted effort, detouring around me as easily as if we had been cooking in the same kitchen together for years. I still felt shy of her, a feeling a little like fear, a kind of emptiness or hollow in the pit of my stomach, a kind of light-headedness, and didn't speak. After a while, after she had the coffee put together, waiting for the water to boil, after she had decanted the chocolate sauce into a double boiler to heat, she said, "It's good that Toby likes you."

"I like him."

"I like him too, so does Candace, but we don't wish to live with him." She stirred the sauce. "Jeremy says you're going to move in with him when your lease is up."

I wanted her approval. "Is that all right?"

"I'm not married to him anymore, Allen, it's not my concern."

"Toby's still your son." I hadn't meant to say it, but it was true. I turned the whisk in the saucepan, setting a whirlpool revolving in the liquid, unwilling to look at her.

"As far as it goes." Stepping back from the stove, she pushed her hair off her face and regarded me. "Toby's a very small part of my life, something Jeremy doesn't understand at all. I didn't particularly want a child, Allen, any more than I particularly wanted to be married to

Jeremy. I love them both but our lives are on different trajectories." She lifted her chin with a faint smile; I had to look up, making me feel even younger, naïve, inexperienced. "I don't understand it myself, you see," she said, "but I like the situation just as it stands. From my side, mine and Candace's. Except that I've thought for a long time that Toby was too big a part of Jeremy's life—it's like he hasn't had any life at all outside of being Toby's dad. The habit of caring for the man carries on, you know, and it's bothered me to see his happiness so limited. And I don't know how good it is for the kid, either. I'm very glad you came along." Here she blinked for a moment, as if confused by her own sentiment, amused by it, appalled, then she placed her hands on my shoulders and pressed her lips to my cheek.

"Thank you, Ruth." Distraught, I glanced down at Toby's cocoa and lifted it off the burner before it boiled over.

"I just hope it works," Ruth muttered. Turning away, she said, "Don't let him take you over, Allen, don't let him make you take care of him. I'll get you a cup for that." She laughed. "He's insidious that way, he needs taking care of and he's *so* appreciative."

I poured the hot chocolate into the cup she handed me, then held it, warming my hands. "What can I do now?"

"Go on out. I'll be done in a few minutes."

"Ruth?" I asked, "why did you marry Jeremy?"

"Hey!" Tossing her head, she laughed again, a full-throated laugh on three distinct notes. "That's a real story. I'll tell you later, when he puts the kid to bed. Thanks for coming down this weekend, Allen. I'm enjoying this."

IN THE END she didn't tell me, although she may have thought she did. We sat in the living room over the dregs of our coffee, Ruth and Candace and I, while Jeremy took care of Toby, and Ruth told us stories, stories I couldn't reconcile with the Jeremy I knew—making him out to be a helplessly dependent bumbler, a lovable dolt, an idiot savant of a kind, a terminally confused mess of a human being who, rationally, ought not be trusted with a tank of goldfish let alone the upbringing of a child. They were amusing, these stories, in a cruel way (Candace certainly enjoyed them), but I recognized neither the buffoon called Jeremy nor, on an afternoon's acquaintance, the incisive, corrosive dyke-bitch-goddess named Ruth. She was a wily raconteuse, I thought, untroubled by plausibility or psychology, and although I thought I liked her I was afraid to trust her.

"How ARE YOU, boy?" Jeremy asked, "how're you doing? Coping okay with the girls?"

This was when I came in to say good night to Toby. The room that Ruth and Candace maintained for him was narrow, at the side of the house, with one tall window looking into the passage between house and fence, and another, wider, that showed the back garden. Toby's bed was under this window, against the wall, so that Jeremy, sitting near his feet, was silhouetted against the glass. Toby said, "Why do you call Allen a boy, Daddy? I'm a boy. He's a man."

"I'm not calling him *a* boy, kid, I'm calling him *the* boy. The boy for me." Jeremy moved one hand to rub his eyes and leaned back against the window—his profile vanished into the obscurity of a darkened room and his head stood black against illumined glass. "Your mother calls me boyface."

"Is it a nickname?" Toby asked. "Like Toby for Tobias?" His face I could almost discern against the white pillow he'd pushed up against the headboard. Above his head hung a mobile, intricate shapes cut out of clay, fired and glazed, catching brief glints from the window and the open door behind me as it circled in the breeze.

"Your name isn't really Tobias. Just Toby—that's the name on your birth certificate, Toby Goldman Kent."

Toby sat up. "You used to call me Tobykins, when I was real little. Is that a nickname?"

"You're still real little," Jeremy said, his voice clear, almost angry. "How can you remember so far back?"

"When your father calls me boy," I said, "when he calls you kid, that's called an endearment."

"Like when you call him sweetheart?"

I nodded, although the motion would be difficult to make out.

"That means you love each other."

I nodded again, hopeful, leaning against the jamb.

"You never call me anything special, just Toby." Pulling his legs up to form a peak under the blankets, he leaned forward. His small white face gleamed, surrounded by heavy dark hair, the eyes dark pits. "Don't you love me too?"

Jeremy grunted. "Tyrant. We'll call you tyrant."

"What's that mean?"

My lungs felt as though they could not contain the air I breathed. "What would you like me to call you, Toby?" Shaky on feet that seemed a hundred miles away, I approached the bed, staggered, knelt down beside him. "Toby, hey, yes, of course I love you, I thought you knew that." I managed not to glance up at his father. At first, it was true, I had been afraid of Toby, and after loved him as a reflection of Jeremy, a part of Jeremy's life. Close to the boy, I smelled his hair, fine, clean, fresh, a scent as ineffable and indistinguishable as the fragrance of sliced cucumber. Close to him, I could make out the shape and contour of his face.

"My friend Sacha," Toby said, cunning as a weasel, "calls her daddy's boyfriend Papa and she calls her stepfather Pops, but she calls her mommy and daddy Joan and Andrew. I like it when you call me Toby, Allen. You say it sort of funny, like it was a special name."

Sitting forward, Jeremy peered into his son's face, not seeing much of anything, I imagined, a pale oval like a drawing in white chalk on dark grey paper. "It's late. Are you ready to go to sleep?" Toby nodded vigorously, then yawned and, a moment late, covered his mouth. "I would prefer it if you didn't call me Jeremy, kid. I like being Daddy."

"Okay, *Daddy.*" Toby put such emphasis on the word, stretching it out to three syllables, that it sounded sillier than usual. When I called my own father Daddy it was, in his native language, more an abbreviation than an endearment or a nickname, although it carried the same weight, but when I was speaking English with my sister *Daddy* sounded forced. We seldom referred to my mother as anything but Mother. Toby shrugged. "You didn't finish my story but it was pretty dumb anyway."

"Well! Maybe Allen would like to tell you a story."

"That's all right." With a kind of hop that involved his entire body, Toby shifted his position to lie flat on his side, knees crooked, and his head facing me. "Can you fix my pillow, Allen?" he asked.

I flattened it out for him.

He sighed. "Thanks. G'night. Give me a kiss?"

His cheek, soft and silken as a rose petal, smelled of his mother's lavender soap.

WINDOWS

The Measure of His Days

As if Jeremy had told me all his stories

San Jose, California: July 1968

Andy was sixteen when Jerry was sixteen, the two of them giddy with the freedom of new driver's licenses and a vision of themselves as low-riders, petty hoods, macho goons who would cruise the late-night strips of downtown San Jose, drinking beer, smoking cigarettes, cracking gum like Chicano toughs, the grimy piratical elite of high school. They wanted florid tattoos for their biceps, wanted to carry switchblades and swear in two languages. That both were Anglos, upper-middle-class children of professionals with every chance of attending the colleges of their choice, was as irrelevant as their not having a car between them unless Andy borrowed his mother's Country Squire. In fact they were outlaws without going out of their way: Andy played the violin, Jerry painted.

On summer weekends they climbed on their bikes and rode a few miles out of town to an orchard owned by a friend of Andy's parents. In baskets above the whirring front wheels they carried Andy's instrument, Jerry's drawing supplies, a picnic lunch. Lifting the bicycles over the ditch on the verge of the road, then over the low fence, they pushed through tall, brittle weeds among slender almond trees until only the crushed path of their passage indicated a world beyond the orchard. Parched grass smelled of dust and chaff, crackled in the spokes of their wheels and under their feet—vibrated, a subliminal ratcheting, with the sawing rasps of little golden grasshoppers. They leaned their bikes against trees. Jerry's was too small for him, although it had been new six months before. He was still growing fast—towered over Andy and nearly everyone else, if still two inches shy of his full growth. He was often out of breath, as though his lungs were still those of a boy six or ten inches shorter, was always hungry, painfully so at times, and ripped open a bag of potato chips immediately. Andy uncased the violin, tucked it under his chin and, humming to himself, tuned up. Shifting

131

his grip on the bow, he pointed it at Jerry. "Don't eat everything, leave some for me. I'm hungry too."

Even in the open, no walls or ceiling to focus the sound, Andy's violin spoke louder than Jerry expected. He thought of violins as being quiet—background music. Squawks and slides of tuning gave way to experimental runs and quavers, then to whatever piece Andy had memorized most recently. "What was that?" he would ask when he finished, grasping the instrument carelessly by the neck, breathing hard, a red blotch on his jaw and his bare chest drenched with sweat.

Jerry couldn't tell him, shrugged amiably, gave the ritual reply: "I'm hopeless. I'm musically illiterate." He opened two bottles of Coke, passed one to his friend. "I like the Beatles."

Returning the violin to its case, lined in blue plush, Andy nodded gravely. "I do too."

They talked about music, about art, about books, about cars and school and travel, the future and the past. They did not talk about girls, which Jerry recognized as a lack. He suspected that real low-riders talked about nothing else unless it were cars. Talking about girls would be as theoretical as their formulations of the perfect set of wheels— although Andy was taking a hands-on course in basic mechanics at summer school and had his eye on a cousin's VW bug. Neither of them dated or went to school dances. When Jerry went to the movies he identified with the heroine and had little use for the hero; he actually preferred the Supremes to the Beatles because he liked women's voices, speaking or singing, better than men's; his favorite books were by women—Margaret Mitchell and Anne Sexton, an odd pairing—but he didn't like girls and didn't know any women to talk to, except his mother, whom he couldn't talk to. Rosemarie Kent, a modern woman, had told him when he was very small about the physical differences between boys and girls; then, later, had calmly, succinctly, fairly, explained the human reproductive system, sex, desire, and, somewhat mystifyingly, love.

Andy yawned and ate a sandwich. Jerry had finished off his share of lunch but was still hungry. He watched Andy eat, small, careful bites as if he were suspicious of the sandwich, suspected it of being tainted. He chewed each mouthful thoroughly before swallowing, then paused a moment before the next. Andy was heavy. Not fat; but full, soft flesh disguised bone and muscle, formed slopes and curves rather than angles and planes, creased and gently pillowed with the bending of a joint. Jerry, always aware he was too thin, admired his friend's solidity although he found it unappealing—Rubens versus Michelangelo, where Jerry himself might as well have been a Giacometti.

One night a week, Jerry went to a life-drawing class at the college. Mr. Petrucci brought in a different model every session. Jerry wondered where he found them, women and men willing to strip down in front of eleven students who not only remained clothed but ogled the models with an attention between voyeurism and scientific curiosity. Jerry wondered where Mr. Petrucci found the models because few of them were attractive in any sense that Jerry recognized. There had been a man in his forties with thin, wiry limbs and pear-shaped torso who resembled Rodin's nude studies for the Balzac; a young woman more emaciated than Schiele's watercolor of his adolescent sister; a body-builder who bore a relief map of his vascular system over the shaved and oiled surface of his skin. By the second or third session Jerry had satisfied his residual curiosity about superficial anatomy, and concentrated on each model as an individual problem. In any case he found faces more interesting to draw.

This past week the model had been a man who was especially interesting because of the luxuriance and expanse of his body hair, masking and transforming the contours of his frame so that one was forced to delineate not simple volumes or masses so much as the patterns of growth like electrical currents made visible over an armature of magnetized steel. Jerry himself had started growing a crop of hair on chest and belly at thirteen or fourteen, before anyone else he knew, but he hadn't seen anyone with a hairy back before now. Before stripping, the model had seemed an innocuous enough young man, a college student, his hair not quite shaggy enough to brand him a hippie although the beard was suspicious. Mr. Petrucci introduced him as George. Before he stripped, George caught Jerry's eyes with a peculiarly intent gaze and a wink Jerry couldn't interpret, but during the sitting—standing, rather, with an old broomstick as prop, striking attitudes heroic in the abstract, ludicrous in fact—George avoided looking at Jerry. In the parking lot afterward, George approached Jerry as he unlocked the door of his mother's car. Posing nude and burly on a platform George had appeared large; Jerry was surprised to discover the model was considerably shorter than he. "What's your name?" George asked.

"Jerry."

Eyes narrowing, George lit a cigarette. "I couldn't look at you when I was bare-ass, you might've noticed, 'cause I would've gotten an amazing hard-on and old Petrucci'd never hire me again. Had to keep doing differential equations in my head just so's I wouldn't think about it. You're hot, man." George's voice lowered into a conspiratorial moan. "I'm hard now, Jerry, look." George grabbed Jerry's hand, pressed it against his fly.

Jerry pulled his hand away from the thick, constricted lump, stepped back. He thought: This is it, with a bemused clarity that amazed him, as though he were watching himself through a pane of thick glass, an icy, forced distance similar to that he imposed on himself when he masturbated. He had never considered the possibility that his first sexual experience would be with someone he didn't know, had supposed he would, first, fall in love.

"You're not into it, Jerry," said George, "just tell me. I think you're into it."

"No." Jerry's voice cracked into treble.

"Hey, you're just a kid," George said, and coughed. "How old *are* you?"

Jerry shook his head. What did it matter? "Sixteen."

"Geeze. I figured nineteen, twenty. Forget it, man." George dropped his cigarette to the tarmac, ground it out under his foot. "You're a virgin too, aren't you. Just forget it." In the amber glow of the parking lot pole lamps, his face was unreadable—angry, disappointed, disgusted. He turned his head. In an instant Jerry had memorized the profile, small, upturned nose, chin bristling with beard.

"George, no, wait. I'm into it, I've just never—"

George's head pivoted back. "Look, man," he said, a harsh, throaty whisper, "I been screwing around with guys since I was fourteen, two years younger'n you, that's ten years—I don't know what to *do* with cherry. It's been fun, kid. Gimme a call in four or five years."

"George, I've got a hard-on now, too."

"So? Go home and whack off. That's what I'm gonna do."

"What if they'd said that when you were fourteen?"

George looked at him, looked away, hawked, spat. "You got a car. Gimme a ride home. I'll think about it."

When Jerry parked in the lot of an apartment building ten minutes from the campus, George muttered, "Sixteen-year-old cherry. Jesus." He put his hand on Jerry's thigh. "Okay. Kiss me."

Eyes closed, it was hard to find George's mouth in the beard. A thick tongue, harsh with a taste like the smell of cigarette smoke, pushed between Jerry's lips. He pulled back, startled, but George's hands on shoulder and neck wouldn't release him, and George's tongue forced itself between his teeth. "Christ," George said when he finally let go, "you need training wheels. C'mon, before I change my mind."

Jerry had not questioned the necessity of being homosexual— queer, a fruit, a faggot, a fairy. He resigned himself to it the way he re- signed himself to being an artist or being freakishly tall and skinny. Relatively certain that Andy was queer too, he thought that they might be in love with each other in a way, a romantic friendship that did not encompass desire. Sex with George—if it had been sex, necking, frot- tage, mutual masturbation—hadn't been especially illuminating. He felt no strong urge to repeat the experiment, not with George, not with Andy, but in the dry hot shade of the almond orchard he regarded his friend with a tender, veiled curiosity. "Andy," he said, "sit still for a while. I want to draw a picture of you."

~

OR AS IF I could compose for him the entries in a journal he never kept

San Francisco, California: September 1969
FIRST DAY OF school—registration, all that. A life class. After, talked to this girl—woman, Ruth Goldman. His age. Tea in the student union. She said, all the signals he's putting out indicate he's gay, yes? Just to clear the air.

Not yet eighteen years old, coming from a huge suburban high school with more cliques than you'd want to count, none you'd want to join, never having had a close friendship with a woman nor with more than two or three men, he had never been asked that question. Not in those words. Bright fluorescent light on the floor, the shiny tables, happy get-to-know-you conversations all around: the heart thuds.

As soon as he escaped from high school, Jerry started growing a mustache—he knows what kind of man he wants. He wants a Levi Strauss man, a San Francisco man. Men who take you home to their small or large, calculatingly designed or indifferently thrown-together apartments. How could you count them? The men he's brought home to *his own* apartment—already. He's young, he isn't beautiful but attractive enough. Men like tall, men like gawky. They like eager. He's eager. He gripped his cup of tea, stared across the table at his new friend, nodded. Good, she said briskly, me too.

San Francisco, California: October 1969
EVERYONE EXCEPT RUTH, even his parents, even his grandparents, calls him Jerry. She said, nickname for what? Gerald, Gerard, Jerome, Geronimo. Do you mind if I call you Jeremy, she said. I hate nicknames. Maybe because you can't do anything with Ruth—Ruthie? I had a teacher in grade school who tried to call me Ruthanne. I said, Can't you read, Mrs. Whoozy, there's a space between Ruth and Anne, my name is Ruth, the Anne's just there so I'll have a middle initial. I was a snotty kid.

Please call me Jeremy, he said, I'd like that.

San Francisco, California: May 1971
AFTER THE OPENING of the student/faculty show they went walking, Ruth and he, heading for an all-night coffee shop. Arguing—nobody argues better than Ruth. She's so tall that he doesn't even need to bend to hear her voice, fast, low, uninflected; she's so long-legged and concentrated that he has to speed up his tall-man's amble to keep in step. Cool, fog-thick street, the fog glowing in fluorescent nimbus around incandescent street lamps, the wind cold, damp, salty, pungent with the sewery smell of the city late at night. She said: I can make better coffee than we'd find anywhere at this hour.

Year and a half he'd known her and he'd never seen her place. Had been wondering how to ask, when the time came, if she'd like him to see her home.

These are things he likes about her: She couldn't be bothered to wait for a bus. Walked the whole way from Russian Hill. Street lights at long intervals and the post-midnight traffic. The wide street unreeled like a bright thread through the fabric of the city. Sheets of newspaper lifted by a passing truck or the wind, flapping like ghostly birds. A distant honk or siren or the shriek of tires. The city! He still can't get over it.

His apartment was closer but he didn't think of it. Did he have coffee, in any case—would it meet her standards.

Things he likes about her: Not simply tall, she wore elegant boots with high heels clipping along the sidewalk. She wore (this for the opening) vibrant colors dulled by the night but flaring up when they passed beneath a lamp, purples, deep greens, scintillant blues, a dress of so many layers and components that it seemed calculated for an air of perpetual dishevelment—her long bones and milk-pale skin harassed by her own clothing. Students wear paint-stained jeans and sneakers: he knows this, it's what he wears. So you look at her like she's got on a costume, and you have to admire that, her clothes and her wild hair. In certain lights, auburn looks like magenta.

More: he admires her paintings, admires her fierce, paralytically intellectual approach to the work—admires her for an avidity, a kind of greediness, a basic opportunism that is in effect unselfish. Admires her vividness, a stridency he has not previously encountered in a woman; appreciates a certain inability to function that nonetheless doesn't interfere with her functioning.

This is like kind of a love letter—like saying, Ruth, I'm looking for a man just like you.

The apartment was on the lower slopes of Twin Peaks, where Market began to twist and swerve—a long walk. Not even winded. She made espresso. He said: I'm a rube, I'm from San Jose—I've never had espresso except in an Italian restaurant. She said: You have to grow up sometime, Jeremy.

Where do you live, Jeremy? she asked, real late, down near school, right? I don't think you should think about going home by yourself. It's all right, he tried to say, but she cut in: Look, when I moved out my mother said never go anywhere without a man to make sure you're safe so you did her a big favor walking me home. Least I can do is let you sleep here. Do you ever listen to your mother, he wanted to ask.

San Francisco, California: August 1972
SEEING ANY MAN in his underwear or seeing a man take off his t-shirt on the dance floor, the crossed forearms and the stretchy fabric lifted off a belly bowed by the arch of his back, over a wide chest with dark small nipples and the sternum molten with sweat, the shake of the head, could inspire a thick fast lump of desire, a catch in the pulse that caused him to bite his lip and look away.

Desire for Ruth a response that must be learned anew each time.

Not the first or second occasion he slept in her bed (although they might hold each other through the night, gingerly, a tenderness at arms' length, she in her x-large t-shirt, he in boxer shorts and a t-shirt only large because it must hug biceps and chest, reveal the nipples and show off the hard, flat belly...) but the sixth time, or the tenth, he woke with his hand tucked between her thighs and she showed him what to do.

Have you ever, she asked, ever made love with a woman? No. Have you—with a man, I mean. I knew from the start you were gay, Jeremy, you know why? Remember that first life class we took together—every man you drew, even two drawings of the same model, each one was distinct, but the women were all the same and sort of out of focus.

Here (she said), look, drawing her shirt over her head (the same motion as a man's, the same shake of the head to settle her hair, but the effect different), these are my breasts, they like to be touched, watch, the nipples, they're like little penises, they get hard, and yes, that's nice, this is my cunt. She said: You make love like a woman, a lesbian. I've never made love with a man, no, but I've had sex with men. Didn't enjoy it much. She claims to be fond of his penis, gives it pet names, little roger, vanilla orchid, here's your little bird, he wants to sing; she likes to fall asleep cradling his genitals in her hands, but for a long time, a year or more, they didn't fuck. It hurt the first time (she said), hurt a lot, and even afterward it wasn't much of a thrill, it feels, oh, it doesn't feel like a person's making love to you, it could be a cucumber, bang bang and it's over as far as the zucchini's concerned. I like your mouth, Jeremy, I like your hands.

Wasn't sure he wanted to, after all. He liked fucking a man (liked being fucked, the slow penetration and then the hard fullness like a fist or, yes, a zucchini in your gut) but was that making love or wasn't it simply sex. It hardly seems like sex with Ruth, the lips, the hands, you're so smooth and soft, he might say, or she, it's like you've got pubic hair all over, it's nice, I like it, you're a fuzzy toy, it's something different.

He'll go with men if they look at him in a certain way, even now, because their beauty makes your heart stop for an instant, because in a dark corner they reach for your crotch to find out how big you are, if you're hard, because their mustaches graze your cheek like the stiff bristles of certain paintbrushes, their stubble raises a faint hot rash, because they say in thick, glottal voices, I want that hot meat or I'll fuck your eyes out or Suck it till it hurts, because you know what they

want and what you want. He might know their names or he might
not, he might never see them again.

Sees Ruth every day at school, they eat lunch, go out for coffee, to
movies, galleries, museum exhibits—he might cook for her or she for
him, he learned to bake certain hard, dry, sweet cookies she favored.
They go places in her car: Stinson Beach, Mount Tamalpais,
Mendocino.

Are we having a love affair? she asked last night. I don't know
about the affair part.

San Francisco, California: January 1973
So LATE AT night it's early morning. Pressed against her buzzer a long
time, until she came running to the door and through the space between jamb and chained door, Oh, Jeremy, her face pale, you scared me,
her hair all squashed on one side, flailing on the other, you woke me,
closing the door a little to release the chain, opening it, I thought it was a
fire or the cops or something, oh, Jeremy, it's *four o'clock in the morning!*

Root', couldn't get his tongue around the *th*, I am very drunk, but
his voice was steady, I had to come see you, I couldn't go home, make
me some coffee please, I have to use your bathroom. Had vomited
thoroughly, had sat on the stool for ten minutes straining until his
colon cramped, a hot shower, very hot, then cool, hot again, cold. His
hair damp, his skin damp, bundled in her terry robe, her antique quilt
in the middle of her big bed, a mug of coffee his hands won't hold lifting to his lips for a small sip, another, and she sips, and he again. Oh,
Jeremy, she murmurs, what happened to you.

I'll tell you, the coffee sweet and milky and hot and bitter as his
stomach, but first.

You're hot, you're shaking, you're burning, are you sick.

I'm flying, I don't know what all, I'm drunk, I'm sad, I'm afraid,
Ruth—shakes his head, lowers his chin to the mug of coffee, but first,
Ruth, Ruth, she's pulled all the curtains wide, the windows coming
alight in the dawn, Ruth, will you marry me? Please? Ruth?

Very flatly she says, Can you hold the cup now.

The cup warm in his hands, warming his hands. I don't have a
ring, I'm going to buy a ring, I can't afford a ring, Ruth!

Take the cup, Jeremy.

Ruth wears a large white t-shirt to bed, the sleeves rolled up to her shoulders. While he was in the bathroom she must have brushed her hair. Turning, a turning-away he recognizes, pulling her hair back from her temples, twisting her neck, Why? Seeing her face, the small pronounced bones, the fine pale skin mottled with pink—tiredness, and, perhaps, surprise—seeing the turn of her nose and the tilt of her eyelids, he cannot imagine that she doesn't know the answer to her own question. Bundling her hair into a clump on her neck, Why should I marry you? Kneeling back on her heels, arms raised, elbows high, You're gay, Jeremy, I'm gay, why should we get married, it'd never work. Where were you tonight, what happened?

The coffee, the coffee cup is a solid object in one's hands, something to hold onto. I love you. Loves the coffee, the coffee she's made for him at five in the morning, her paintings, loves Ruth, Ruth saying, You too, boyface, I love you too but I don't think you can make a man of me or me a woman of you so let's just go to sleep for a little while, Jeremy, taking the cup from his hands, Just a little while, stroking his brow, Sweet boy, lie down just a while, her lips against his eyelids and her hands pushing him down onto the mattress, head into the pillow, That's right, it's okay, I'm here.

∾

BUT THE FACT remains that although he *has* told me stories, stories vivid and sordid as diary entries, I can't always make sense of them. Motivations remain obscure. Quirks of personality are opaque, unexplained. As unlikely as it is that Jeremy asked, it seems still more unlikely that she accepted, that they were married in the garden of Ruth's father's Hillsborough estate. I've never even been to Hillsborough—these are not circles I move in. The white-kid wedding album reveals that the entire party, bride, groom, groomsmen, bridesmaids, wore identical black tuxedoes, white pleated-front wing-collared shirts, onyx studs. Dark madder-paisley bow ties and cummerbunds. ("I don't know how to tie a bow tie," muttered Jeremy, and Ruth replied, "None of the other men do either, but not to worry—I do.") Narrow black patent pumps with grosgrain ribbons, deep scarlet silk hose. Dark crimson rosebud boutonnieres. ("We know how many of us the groom's slept with," said the best man, "now how many of the bridesmaids do you suppose *she*'s had?") In the first photograph it is Ruth and Jeremy alone, on the lawn before the rose garden, looking like twins, tall and slim and handsome, holding the big bouquet of crimson roses between them; in the second the whole party poses in a grand arch in the portico of Ruth's father's mansion, mothers in pale springtime dresses, fathers in dark business suits; in the third, Ruth raises her chin, Jeremy lowers his, they have either just kissed or are just about to kiss, one whispers, "Are we fabulous?" and the other replies, "We're fabulous."

I know for a fact that they kept their courage up by inhaling healthy amounts of very good cocaine at half-hour intervals throughout the day, yet I have never known Jeremy to do drugs. While I have known him. I will be forgiven for not having the date engraved on my heart—I hadn't met the people—it was a Sunday in late March of 1973: Ruth was five months older than Jeremy but both were only twenty-one. Myself, I was a few weeks shy of fifteen.

AND THE FACT remains that, fond as I am of Ruth (at least as fond as resentful), as grateful to her as I am—and, with some evidence, I believe her to be fond of and grateful to me—she's not much of a character in any story of mine. She would, I think, indignantly deny she was of any especial importance to Jeremy, as well. "I was a bad mistake," she might say; "now I'm a good friend. For God's sake, Allen," she might say, "I'm your friend as much as his by now—we're all old friends. And as for the kid—well! Who've been his parents, after all, Allen?"

I DON'T BELIEVE it for a minute. Much as I'd like to.

AND HERE'S ANOTHER sad fact: without much encouragement at all, I could sit down at the computer in our study and type out eighty pages about the year they lived in Mexico. Their extended honeymoon. I know the exact page count because I did it once, just that: eighty pages. The Book of Jeremy. I was depressed that weekend—clinically? Who knows. He was away. But I knew his stories, her stories, and what I didn't know I imagined with perfect confidence: this was how it must have been. Finished, I knew every episode to be true—it is a document I could never show to Jeremy—and yet I believed none of it. Because I wasn't there.

I wasn't there by the lakeside where the breeze was cool because of the altitude, the sun warm because of the latitude, and the lake smelled

sedgy and damp, of cattails and water hyacinth. I wasn't there in the little concrete-block house with its blue-and-white check curtains and
window boxes of scarlet geraniums. I never saw the view from the little
balcony of their bedroom, down the hill with its scatter of red tile roofs
and corrugated tin roofs to the church on the square and the hotel on
the lake. I never went to the hotel for Saturday night dinner nor, afterward, did I ever box-step in anyone's arms across the terrace above the
dark water where the reflections of paper Chinese lanterns bobbed and
flickered, tiny colored moons, while a mariachi band played and a
young man in a sombrero sang in aching falsetto of the Revolution. I
never sat up in bed next to Jeremy to comfort him after a nightmare—
a nightmare in which he could not speak English, could not remember
how to pronounce his own name.

Spanish lacks the *j*-sound. The letter, *jota* in Spanish, represents a
breathy *h*, something like a clearing of the throat, a surprisingly
Germanic noise. Jeremy—it was an inept joke, which proved more apt
than he expected—tacked a masculine ending onto his initial and
called himself Joto. I would have advised him against it because,
although all the Spanish I have I picked up from him, I have 20/20
hindsight.

They had engaged a local youth to teach Jeremy Spanish. It was a
mistake—not on Ruth's part. With the discerning eye of a lesbian married to a gay man, she knew handsome, charming, simpatico Rodrigo
Jaramillo to be, at the least, questioning. I hate this about her, hate
knowing it about her. Naturally enough, as if she'd planned it, they fell
in love, Joto and Roddy; naturally enough—and this, I think, she didn't
plan—each was desperately afraid to admit it to the other.

At the end of the summer, Roddy left Mexico, went north to New
Haven, Connecticut, to enroll in the graduate school of architecture
at Yale.

Joto, as it happens, is one of the Spanish idioms for *queer*.

For nine of the thirteen months Ruth and Jeremy lived in Mexico,
I was a prep-school junior happily infatuated with Matthew. Matthew
later attended Yale. I don't know whether he ever encountered Rodrigo
in New Haven. But by then, Jeremy and Ruth had returned to San
Francisco and Toby had been born.

I HAVE NEVER ventured beyond the borders of the contiguous forty-eight states. Does this bother me, cause me to feel inadequate, uneducated, inexperienced? Damn right.

~

IMAGINE THAT: he was born six months before I graduated from high school. Gives one to think.

San Francisco, California: November 1974
THE BLUE AND white Queen Anne row cottage Ruth found for them in Noe Valley was ideal: in the back, a small room with a bay window overlooked the little garden. The alterations were completed and they moved in a month before Ruth was due. While she painted in the attic studio under new skylights, Jeremy painted the nursery. He couldn't remember his own infancy, couldn't imagine how to be sure of creating a happy room for his child—a chamber replete with light and joy like the interior of a tangerine, clean and warm as a snail's shell. On the inner wall he painted the view down the hill from the room in Mexico where the child had been conceived, down over the choppy roofs of the town to the lake blue and gold as lapis lazuli and mica, a scene bright with red roof tiles and pink and blue and yellow stucco walls, scraps of flying curtains in open windows crowded with geraniums, the parasols on the hotel terrace, the bowed fishing nets on the lake.

San Francisco, California: December 1974
RUTH WAS LATE, bulbous as a fat clam or a melon, glad for the first time, she said, of a brassiere's support for breasts like heavy pears, late, a week overdue, climbing the stairs four or five times a day in a superstitious attempt to induce labor. The doctor, who ought to have known better, suggested intercourse—sympathetic magic, as if the tremors of orgasm might inspire the real earthquake, or as if Daddy's penis might act as guide: Here, baby, this way out. Squeamish and innocent, they found the logistics insurmountable, either painful or ludicrous, so Jeremy simply held her in bed, among the sheets, admired the cathedral of Ruth's belly, the fine glowing translucent dome with its lantern the inverted navel. Jeremy held her belly in his hands like

a gilded fruit or a coffer of gold and said, Boy or girl? More to the point, said Ruth, dyke or queen?

San Francisco, California: December 1974

WATCHING, HE HELD her hand, marked his breath to hers, stroked her brow and bore down with her, bore down, a heavy stool that would not pass. Her face glowing with sweat, her hair ragged with damp. Occasionally she whimpered, tight on the pain, but mostly was silent, breath raspy and hard but even, on the count, and her face was ugly as a blubbering child's, as lovely and heartbreaking, while he gathered her tears in his palm.

The doctor said it was an easy birth.

San Francisco, California: December 1974

HE BROUGHT THEM home from the hospital in Ruth's car, fearful that his own noisy MG would frighten the baby. Toby lay in Ruth's arms silent and benevolent as an infant saint. On the crest of a hill below Twin Peaks, waiting on a stoplight, she held him up to see his city, the downtown skyline. He gurgled, then uttered a tiny vertiginous wail, and Ruth clasped him back to her breast.

She allowed Jeremy to carry him up the stairs and over the threshold of their blue and white house, upstairs to the second floor and down the hall to the nursery. Light oiled the floor like butter. Toby was hungry, crowed with hunger. Ruth settled into the chair in the bay window, opened her dress. Jeremy stood back and watched—couldn't watch. He was jealous, of which one?

∽

ONE MORE STORY

San Francisco, California: July 1979

JEREMY HAD BEEN freelancing for Grace & Fenton six months; the agency was pleased enough with his work to guarantee a certain number of commissions for the year. He put the little blue house on the market and bought a three-flat building in the upper Fillmore. Between Grace & Fenton and the income from two rentals he'd make out okay. Ruth advanced most of the down payment and co-signed the mortgage, in addition to providing a child-support allowance he thought ridiculously large, but she wasn't to be argued with. She had long since moved out, moved into Candace's house in Santa Cruz, yet kept herself involved in Jeremy's life in ways he found comforting and disorienting by turns. For a flat-warming present, she gave him a coffee service she'd thrown herself and fired in Candace's kiln, glazed cinnabar red and midnight blue.

He would hear Toby waking in the morning in his room across the hall, stumbling to the bathroom, and every morning would worry for a moment, hearing the step-stool dragged first to the toilet, then to stand before the basin. Wanting Toby to be self-sufficient, he was frightened by his son's real independence, the innumerable occasions for injury Toby put himself in the way of simply by being able to use the bathroom unaccompanied. A minute or two after the taps shut off, the bedroom door, already ajar, was pushed open. Toby was hardly as tall as the doorknob. "Daddy?" he said.

Jeremy kept quiet, that being the game. He lay on his side; even without another person to hold onto or to hold him he occupied only half the bed, pillows bundled around his head and blankets over his shoulders. "Daddy?" The bed rocked when Toby climbed aboard, an unstable raft. Little hands grabbed at the coverings and Toby hauled himself upright. "Daddy being a sleepyhead!" The pronouncement was invariable, between accusation and exhortation, uttered in a piercing treble sharp as a needle.

"No, I'm not," Jeremy would grunt, equally invariable, rolling over to trap his son in his arms. "You're up too early." Paralyzed and light-headed, he would hold the struggling child, swallowing Toby's yelps and snorfs and gobbles as if they were choice delicacies, a pre-breakfast breakfast, the breath of life. He couldn't get over it, couldn't get over his black-haired, grey-eyed son, plump as a puppy dog, writhing and yapping like a puppy dog. He wanted to chew Toby's toenails when they grew too long.

"If I say I don't want him," Ruth had said, "you'll think I'm cold and unfeeling, no kind of mother, but the truth is I don't want him. I'm fond of him, sure, I love the little bugger, but I'm not interested in him and he gets in my way. And I know how much *you* want him."

But it wasn't a matter of wanting Toby, the way one might covet a Persian rug or a handmade coffee service, a cinnamon-colored chow or vivid macaw—Jeremy wanted to be near Toby, to be of use. They had an agreement between them: each to find the other wonderful. It wasn't difficult, not for Jeremy who, when Toby was littler, could watch the baby play with his toes for hours, the two of them as sublimely content as a scented bath and a good book or an arrowroot teething biscuit and a warm bottle, clean diaper and powdered bottom. One night a year or so before, before they moved from the house in Noe Valley, a night when Ruth had driven to Santa Cruz, Toby had wandered into the bedroom, dragging his bunny by one ear. The bunny's face was vapidly, buck-toothedly good-natured but Toby looked preoccupied. He cuddled into his father's lap and Jeremy asked what was on his mind.

"My looking for where my is," said Toby, and Jeremy didn't know how to reply. It had been hot all afternoon while the two of them mucked about in the garden; after Toby's bath and dinner Jeremy had showered himself, not bothered to dress again, put on the thin silk robe Ruth had given him for his last birthday. Through the cool fabric he felt the nappy flannel and plump flesh of his son but couldn't say, Here is where you are—because who knew, after all, here in the pale gold light of the bedroom of a small blue and white house, here in the arms of your father—a man who ought, by rights, never have married at all, never engendered a child—here where the absence of your mother fills the whole house like the last, failing thrum of a plucked string. Toby pushed one hand under the lapel of his father's robe; after a while he fell asleep.

His command of the personal pronoun was more secure and he could conjugate the verb *to be*, now. After he'd got his slugabed daddy out of bed in the morning, he oversaw the preparation of breakfasts, drank his milk without spilling. He might prefer blue jeans and a t-shirt like Daddy's over red corduroy overalls but would be good-humored about the exigencies of laundry. He wasn't very efficient about going *down*stairs yet so, after unlatching the gate at the top, Jeremy would carry him, three flights to the front door lit by a stained-glass panel, the flat-number worked into a design of coiled blue morning glory, 2170, and Toby would repeat the address as his father opened the door, twenty-one seventy Sutter, my name is Toby Kent and I live at twenty-one seventy Sutter. He even remembered the zip code, which was better than Jeremy could do some days, foggy with sleep, opening the door to the foggy street.

Toby would ask to be let down, at four and more than a half too sure of his dignity to be happy seen in his father's arms more often than necessary. Six stone steps to the sidewalk, the risers as high as his knees —he let Jeremy hold his hand. Past the tub of scraggly geraniums and chrysanthemums. Mica flashed in the sidewalk despite there being no sun, the upper stories of buildings bundled in a cottony fog that threatened either to rise or descend, in any case to leave prospects for the day uncertain. Toby and his father turned the corner on Fillmore, headed uphill past the laundromat, crossing Bush Street and Pine, to California. At the intersection, Toby looked through the glass doors of the doughnut shop where a policeman might be drinking a cup of coffee, where a young woman in peaked paper cap slid a tray of twisted crullers with glinting sugar skins into the display case. Then he tugged his father to the curb, to wait for the light to change so they could cross safely. If he saw the bus on its way toward them down the street he shouted, "Here it comes, Daddy," and bounced up and down, intent on its not making the light and getting away without them—although if so another would be along in ten or fifteen minutes.

The day-care center opened at seven. Toby and Jeremy seldom arrived that early since Jeremy wasn't tied to corporate working hours —eight, eight-thirty, nine: they got there when they got there, Jeremy pushed the gate, they went in. This early, still damp and cool, no-one was playing outside. It had been Ruth's idea to put Toby in day care. "Look at it this way, boyface," she said, "he's going to school eventually —this'll give you a chance to get used to it. Anyway, I know you, you'll spend all your time with him and neither of you will ever see anyone else. He's having a weird enough childhood as it is; give him a couple of hours a day to be someone other than Jeremy's son."

Jeremy's reason for being, she might have said, Jeremy's sense of direction, but restrained herself. For her part, the notion of devoting all her attention to any one person—be it Jeremy, Candace, or the extraordinary creature her son—appalled her by its overwhelming attraction, an attraction she was determined no-one would ever discover. Jeremy had no such defense: this was perhaps the first thing she understood about him, one of the reasons she had married him as much as being one of the causes of their divorce. She knew not to tell Jeremy he needed time to himself every so often. He wouldn't believe it, nor was she certain that she did. Knowing essentially nothing about his childhood—he didn't talk about it, was distant to his family, discouraged her becoming close to them—she thought it must have been so claustrophobic he had not developed a proper sense of separateness; either that, or he had beat so hard against the multiple carapaces of his parents, sister, brothers as to cripple his own, open it permanently to influences he could not restrain. She pictured him as something like a sea anemone in a deep tide pool, grasping after current and flow, whereas she was more like a hard-shelled mussel that must close itself off against alien air when the tide fell.

In fact Ruth's diagnosis was overly dramatic, as is Ruth herself. In fact Jeremy had early, as early as memory, discovered himself to be a changeling, a dark Celtic elf-child in a family of fair Saxon skeptics too unimaginative to understand he wasn't one of their own, too accepting not to care for him. This is not to say he consciously thought he had been adopted, although the possibility intrigued him during adolescence. There were sufficient Mediterranean and Celtic strains in his parents' ancestries to account for Jeremy's being black-haired, slender, tall, dizzy with romance, while the rest of the Kents were blond and stocky, solid and stolid. It was more as if he were a reversion to a type his family had evolved beyond, a genetic anachronism, an atavistic throwback, dispossessed heir of wave-drowned Ys or Avalon, Middle Earth or Narnia. Little brothers Jamie and Jonny read Tom Swift and grew up to be a computer programmer and a perpetual Ph.D. candidate in particle physics; older sister Jenny, disdaining fiction, pored over *The National Geographic*, became a doctor, a lawyer's wife. While Jerry's most decisive action, so far as his family was concerned, appeared to be the repudiation of his childhood nickname, reclaiming his birthright as if it were the crown jewel of Faerie, and becoming someone the Kents didn't know.

Just inside the door of the day-care center stood a row of white-enameled cubbyholes, each marked with the name of one of the children. Two Tobys were enrolled in the center—the other was a girl a year younger than Toby Kent. Jeremy helped his son off with his jacket, hung it on the hook in Toby K.'s cubby, checked the slot above for messages. There were none. Then the two of them turned right, past the cabinet, to the four and five year olds' classroom. Opening the door released the high-pitched cacophony of fifteen children cooped up inside with three adults considerably less alert than they. Toby's friend

Sacha rushed over. "Toby, come and look!" Toby let go of his father's hand, followed Sacha without looking back.

"Good morning, Jeremy," said one of the teachers.

"Hello, Paul." Across the room, Toby helped Sacha place another block of oversized Lego, the red of Toby's overalls and as large as his hand, in the correct position. "How's it going?"

Paul shook his head. "It's too early in the morning and there's too many kids in this room." He shook his head again, bent down to a desk scaled for someone a quarter his size for the sign-in list. "That's not true. Just say I had a really great weekend and it's Monday again." He handed the list to Jeremy.

Holding the clipboard against his belly, Jeremy printed his name and the time. "What makes a great weekend?" he asked, handing the list back.

"I got completely ripped and went dancing and, you know, like that." A small blond man whose clavicle showed at the neckline of his t-shirt like a wishbone sucked clean of flesh, Paul slapped the clipboard against his thigh as though it were a tambourine. Small teeth bit into his lower lip, crowded behind a bushy mustache. He tugged at the neck of his shirt. "I don't get tired of the kids, you know, but sometimes I have to be with people who don't . . . talk." Turning, he set the sign-in list back on the desk. His spine creased white fabric. It pulled up from the waistband of his jeans to reveal a hand's breadth of pale skin. "What'd you do this weekend, Jeremy?" Paul straightened and, turning, tucked the shirt back into his trousers, a motion that bowed his chest the way a stretching cat arches its back. "Did you have fun?"

Men, women, children flirted with Jeremy. Perhaps it was the lock of thick hair that fell into his right eye, making him appear always on the edge of winking. Perhaps it was because his mustache, through some quirk of growth, descended a quarter inch further around the left side of his mouth than the right, as though it concealed a wry dimple. "Are you seeing anyone, boyface?" asked Ruth when she called—before inquiring about Toby's health. In the supermarket, on the bus, walking in the park, he was approached by handsome older women, distinguished middle-aged men in suits, coveys of sweating joggers and Frisbee throwers of both genders needing advice, direction, or simply to inform him of what a lovely day it was. Maybe it was because he was so tall, that and Toby's being small, a piquant contrast. In the park dogs lolloped over to say hello. When he stopped in at Grace & Fenton to deliver a portfolio, pick up an assignment, meet with one or another account executive, the receptionist went into a flurry of attentiveness, offering coffee, apologizing for a delay that was Jeremy's own fault since he made a point of arriving fifteen minutes early—but he ascribed Michael D.'s fluttering to the awkwardness of a twenty-one year old on his first job and the novelty of seeing a man without a tie in Grace & Fenton's stylish offices. It was odd (when he thought about it, not often, he found it odd) that he had no attention to spare for these attentions, insinuations, invitations. Paul was an attractive little man who reminded Jeremy, a bit, of Roddy Jaramillo. It was equally telling—although Jeremy didn't stop to consider this until some years later, after the fact—that in fact he noticed the approaches, the feints, the dares. "I fixed a toilet for one of my tenants," he told Paul; "I took Toby to Macy's for new clothes."

"Thrills," said Paul with an expressive flatness.

"It was okay." Looking across the room, Jeremy saw that Toby and Sacha were still involved. "Well, I'm off. I'll be back to get the kid around three."

"All right, Jeremy. See you later."

On the bus, Jeremy said to himself in Ruth's voice, a trick of mental ventriloquism: Have you never heard of baby-sitters, boyface? The fog had lifted after all, it was turning into a pretty day. If it held, he'd take Toby to the beach in the afternoon.

WALLS

Blood

TOBY WAVED TO me as he boarded the bus, one of those enthusiastic whole-body waves that boys seem to forget how to give somewhere between eleven and twelve. He was eight and a half then. Anywhere else, my having kissed him and his father good-bye would be provocative, a subversive act—something to make an eleven year old cringe—but in the San Francisco Greyhound terminal everyone had seen it all before. Jeremy waved too, with a little more restraint, and climbed aboard, and I turned away, went back through the station, out onto the street. By this time I knew every possible permutation of the bus lines that could get me to S.F. General from anywhere in the city. The best time, from the Greyhound terminal, was forty-five minutes. I should have said good-bye to Jeremy and Toby at the house, gone directly to the hospital. Sean had been in particularly bad shape the night before. I hailed a cab.

All the ward staff knew me by now, Sean had been in and out so many times. Eli, the nurse who had taken particular charge of Sean, waved me down as I passed his station. "Allen! I tried to call you." Many of the nurses on the ward tended to look ill themselves, a function of sympathetic magic as much as exhaustion. Eli's complexion was sallow, a little green around the wings of his nostrils and the rims of his ears and whitish where bone pressed against the skin: his chin, the bridge of the nose, the crowns of his cheekbones. He didn't seem to have shaved for a day or two. "I tried to call you," he said again, blinked eyelids that were puffy and raw-looking, and spread his hands out on the white counter between us.

"I was at the bus station, seeing Jere and Toby off." I knew what he was going to tell me, essentially, as much from the fine tremor in his hands as the tone of his voice. "They went to Santa Cruz for the week, to see Toby's mother."

Eli was watching me with a peculiar blinded attention. "Sean's gone, Allen." When he said my name his left hand formed a fist, which he raised, toward his chest but as though he were preparing to strike out. "He was in and out all morning, a series of little seizures like he did yesterday, only longer, and then about an hour ago he went under. That was when I called."

"Is he still in his room?"

Eli's hand moved in such a way that for an instant I thought it was going to tell me something, but anything he had to say was already evident. "They can't turn off the respirator without authorization. The body's still breathing, but nobody's home, the brain-activity curve has been flat since he went into coma."

"I guess I'll need to sign papers, then." Sean had given me power of attorney several months before, along with all the other things you do or have to do when you're dying, the sorts of business that are harder, I think, for the designated survivor. Eli was trying to look into my eyes. "Let me go see him first," I said.

Since getting back in touch with me, on New Year's Day in fact, Sean had gone through the ward five times. I can't keep straight in my mind the rooms he had, can't remember the colors or patterns of the curtains, which room faced north, which east—not even in the case of the last one. He was attended by vigilant machines like electronic godmothers. Transparent plastic tubing hung around him in wreaths carrying essential gases and liquids; grey-green glass screens displayed slow pulses and traces of light and emitted preoccupied pings and drones.

Sean was the first man I knew I loved. There had been others before I'd been pretty sure of, but certainty was never in question with Sean, a brilliant, sleek, hard man, hard as diamonds, so beautiful it hurt to look at him, so beautiful in the precise alignments and relations of his features that any expression at all was superfluous. There was no flesh around the bones of his skull and the skin hugged so tightly it forced the jaw open; tight and discolored, not as by bruising but the way parchment changes color with age as the membranes dry out in incremental layers, and the way rot proceeds inward through the concentric skins of an onion. A dictionary will tell you that a carbuncle is both *a bright red gem cut in a knoblike shape* and *a severe abscess in the skin.* Sores like jewels clustered in the corners of Sean's mouth. Even when I was in love with him I wasn't sure that I liked Sean. This was a question I had endeavored not to answer. His hands lay flat at his sides, the inner parts of the elbows turned up so that tubes could enter the veins where a small pulse beat. The hands, curled a little, looked very large at the ends of the arms. All the nights I spent in the same bed with Sean, he never slept on his back. We nestled spoon-fashion, his chest warm against my back, or faced each other, knees touching, breathing each other's breath, or I lay on my back and he beside me on his belly threw an arm over my chest, a leg over my thigh, and dug his chin into my shoulder. His eyes were shut but he wasn't asleep.

Before I signed the papers I called Ruth in Santa Cruz so Jeremy wouldn't come back to the city in a week not knowing, and so I wouldn't have to tell him when he called that night. Typically, Sean had asked that his ashes be scattered over Donegal Bay—Sean, least Irish of Irish Americans. "I've never been there," he told me, "why not?" As if I were to instruct my heirs to dump my mortal remains in the Danube, the Duna, between Buda and Pest. I signed the papers, I gave verbal authorization to the doctors, I thanked Eli. Eli hugged me. His eyes were red.

It took two buses to get from the hospital back to Pacific Heights—the edge of Pacific Heights, really, where it butts up against Japantown and the Fillmore. I took both buses, the 47 Van Ness and the 2 Clement, but got off a couple of blocks early. It was one of those anomalous summer evenings when the sky is clear of cloud, clear translucent blue, and the breeze only makes you aware how warm it is. All around me people wore summery clothes, vivid t-shirts, pastel cotton dresses, and sunlight gleamed on clean skin and shiny hair. I walked past the fish market with its plate glass windows full of gaudy packaging and displays of plastic food, and went into a sushi bar where the dimness and the Japanese pop played at low volume were a relief. For three hours I drank green tea and ate sashimi, pointing through the glass at different slabs of fish, which the chef would cut for me, a distinct slice and shape for each variety—gorged myself on raw protein and the raw fire of wasabi.

Then I went home. The flat was deserted. The next day I would have to go to Sean's place and get to work. My week off had been planned for months. Jeremy and Toby and I would all go down to Santa Cruz and have a pleasant, quiet visit with Ruth, play on the beach; we were going to rent a car and take Toby further down the coast, Moss Landing, Carmel, Big Sur. Then Jeremy and I would return to the city, leaving Toby to spend a week alone with his mother (Candace was in New York for a show at her gallery) until she couldn't stand having him around anymore and Jeremy couldn't stand not having him. That had been the plan. I wandered through the flat, which often seemed too small. I found Jeremy's cache of peanut brittle in the kitchen and ate it all, standing over the counter, breaking the chunks into small pieces, stuffing each into my mouth before I'd finished chewing the previous one. I watched my hands breaking the candy, but did not wonder until afterward why. It was eight o'clock. Jeremy had probably already called. I turned off the bell on the phone and went to Toby's room.

Toby's room—Toby himself—was peculiarly tidy. He arranged his books in graduated order by size. He made his bed every morning, shoved dirty clothes out of sight. This was not something new, or anything he's grown out of since. When I'm in a cooking frenzy it's Toby who cleans up after me, not Jeremy. It's a matter of watching the surface details and wanting them right. Something I taught him, perhaps. When I'm in a funk he notices, often, before his father does, and comes to me, and gives me a hug, and asks what's wrong. I sat down on Toby's bed, got up to look out the window, to look at the photograph of the three of us on his desk, sat down again, lay back.

It was dark when I woke up, and I was ravenous. I wanted hot, bitter black coffee. I wanted rare beef and baked potatoes, foods I never eat, and I wanted whiskey. In the shower, under water almost as hot as the coffee I desired, I decided to do without the beef, the potatoes, to go to a bar. I hadn't been to a bar by myself for years, not since I moved in with Jeremy, not, really, since I met him. Not too long before, Sean had expressed a certain derisive astonishment that I had never checked out my neighborhood gay bar. I hadn't known there was such a place—we were some distance from the Castro. I didn't know how to carry myself in a bar, how to push the door open and walk in, walk through the smoky darkness and the stares, to the bar to order my drink. The bartender, a fine young man, raised his eyebrows with theatrical precision as he poured Old Bushmills into a shot glass for me. "DIY Irish Coffee?" he asked, pushing the glass and the mug of black coffee across the bar. Just as I don't eat steak or baked potatoes, I don't drink whiskey. Even Sean didn't drink Irish. It was smooth and fine. I drank it in two hard swallows and asked for another.

The bartender placed his hands on the polished oak with a sureness very different from Eli's similar gesture. His hands were big and brown and strong, good hands. With a precise California-blond implacability he said, "Not if you're going to drink it that fast." He shrugged and grinned. "It's the eighties. People don't get drunk anymore."

"I don't drive."

It was quieter than I remembered bars being, but perhaps that was partly because I only went out on Fridays and Saturdays, back when I went out. Loud enough to be noticeable without being oppressive, synthesized dance music pulsed from speakers above the oak Deco swag surrounding the mirror behind the bar, not loud enough to dull the conversations among couples and groups of friends. With a paranoia more to be expected in a man five years younger than I, I assumed none of them had never been in here before. I sipped my coffee but only inhaled the harsh metallic smell of the second shot of Irish. Spotlights trained narrow cones of illumination on the calm, civil, restrained scene within the mirror. Near me, three men sat together in one of those beams, talking together with animated hands and quick glances of peripheral vision. Reversed in the glass, their phrases and exclamations were as meaningless as a tape played backward. One of them I recognized, almost recognized, but couldn't place. I turned on the stool to look at him and he recognized me, and after a moment sketched my name in the air between us.

Hardly anyone in the city knew my real name. I have never gone out of my way to place myself in the community to which my first language entitles me—a two-eyed man in the land of the cyclopes. My mother always resented my, and my sister's, being able to interpret for her, as if the act confirmed the hearing world's view of her as handicapped; she went to great lengths to avoid the occasions of necessity. My father's gratitude, on the other hand, was even more crippling. When I was ten and he thirty-seven I helped him buy his first car. Remembering the phobic caution with which he drove, his hands mute and white-knuckled on the wheel in precisely the position mandated by his driver-training text, I am paralyzed with the same sort of horror, I think, that leads first-generation Americans to disinherit themselves of their parents' culture. But still, I look at hands before faces.

The hands of the man at the table were long and narrow, attenuated, acrobatic, and I remembered both his names now, the real one and the one he signed on documents and checks: Eusebio Gonzalez. I had met him at the hospital, where his trilingual lover Alejandro could no longer speak for him, being dead. Bilingual Jeremy had barged in

first, negotiating between Alejandro's Mexican family and Anglo doctors, before discovering that the problem lay elsewhere. As sympathetic
as both sides were, neither knew what to do with—or for—the be-
reaved widower who stood between them, perfectly mute, terrifying in
his calm resignation. Jeremy called me over. A professional interpreter
is enjoined to remain aloof, but afterward I told Eusebio I had a TDD,
for my parents, and he should call me, but he never did.

Now he repeated my name, and invited me to join him and his
friends. The tall one gestured with the purity of accent and inflection
that marks the nonnative speaker, and introduced himself three times
over, with the name Eusebio knew him by, the finger-spelled transliter-
ation of the name his parents gave him, and aloud: Marc. The other, a
solid black man who would have been tall if he hadn't been next to
Marc and whose fingers darted in vivid colloquial negative before his
white shirt front, ignored me for several minutes, then told me his
name and told me I could call him Willie. A moment later he pulled a
twenty from his pocket and asked me to buy a round. If he went, he
said, the bartender would give him beer, what he always drank, and that
wasn't what he wanted.

What did he want, I asked.

There was something, not so much in the way Willie's entire body
entered into the discourse of his hands as in his manner of looking at
me through half-shut eyes that watched my face so carefully it seemed
they couldn't possibly grasp what I said. A rum and Coke would do him
for now, he said. His eyes were a startling cat's-eye yellow.

Eusebio touched Willie's cheek, to attract his attention, and glared
at him archly. I had not noticed, I think because at the hospital he was
numb and because I had never before met a deaf nellie queen, that his
hands spoke with a boneless fluidity as affected as lisp or falsetto. I had
a *boyfriend,* he told Willie, underscoring the statement with a flourish.

So did he, said Willie. His was working. Where was mine?

I took Willie's twenty to the blond bartender. He looked at me, ex-
pectant, professionally friendly, and I remembered that to him I'd have
to speak aloud. What would Sean do? I asked myself, if Sean weren't
dead. I carried the drinks back to the table and told Willie my lover was
out of town for a week.

Marc stared at me over the heads of the other two. With a sort of
lurid nervousness, a nervous leer, and aloud, he said, "Willie's not inter-

ested in a week. Willie's not even interested in a night. Willie doesn't sleep with anyone but his boyfriend." He blinked and, I think, blushed, and said very fast, "He doesn't fuck anyone but his boyfriend, either, if that's what interests you, if you're interested in being fucked by a big black stud. He's interested in you fucking him, that's what interests Willie."

Eusebio slapped him lightly on the chest and told him it was rude to speak in a language we couldn't all follow. Marc ducked his head and apologized. Willie sipped his drink and watched me with his pale, narrow eyes. Was I ready to go, he wanted to know. He put his large hand on my shoulder, then moved it to cup the back of my neck. His palm was very heavy, very warm, but dry.

Eusebio glanced at me sharply and asked about my friend, not my *boy*friend, the one in the hospital.

He died, I said, and swallowed the last of the whiskey, and stood up.

Near the door, Willie grabbed me, grabbed my face with his big dry hands, and kissed me. His tongue tasted sweet, of Coca-Cola and dark rum. Then he moved into the light to ask me where we were going, we couldn't go to his place.

I stared at Willie—a man more beautiful in his way than Jeremy, more demanding and intent, a competent man, a man who needn't understand. I took Willie to Sean's apartment, and after he left I slept in Sean's bed.

Expatriation

"I REMEMBER YOU," Toby had said—"I think. Didn't you visit us once, a long time ago? Before Dad met Allen?" And Rodrigo with a grim smile said, "Yes."

Now Toby pushed his chair back from the dining room table. Before he took my plate he rested one hand on my shoulder as if he, far more than his father, apprehended and understood my feelings. "Want me to get dessert?" he asked.

"All right," said Jeremy, although Toby had asked me. "Thank you, kid." He glanced at Rodrigo beside him, a look full of uneasy tenderness. "I made flan for you, Rodriguito."

"I thought you didn't cook for men." A smile fluttered for a moment on Rodrigo's thin face, a moth on a flickering light bulb.

"I cooked the whole dinner. No soy un macho."

Rodrigo smiled again. "You never were. You didn't fool me." He seemed sometimes to have trouble breathing, his breath whistled in his lungs, but still the voice was musical, a reed organ with leaky bellows. It was a voice that still sounded foreign, as long as he'd been in this country, still hesitated over the accentuation, intonation, pronunciation of English—there was a suggestion of a *y* to the double-*l* of my own first name, for instance, the one time he'd used it. "I knew you from the start."

And this was another thing that worried me. But mostly I watched them, Jeremy and Rodrigo, inspected them as carefully as an archaeologist might unearth the sherds of an antique past, and tried to see them as Joto and Roddy—relics. But Jeremy was Jeremy, the man I loved, the father of his son, whom I loved as well, and Rodrigo was someone else. The hand lifting his wine glass had so little flesh on it that one saw not only the tendons fanned across the back but the bones beneath them, and the padding at the fingertips was so meager that the nails seemed to grow directly from the bone and it seemed that it must be painful to touch anything at all, to pick anything up. And I wondered again how we must appear to him, Toby and Jeremy and I.

What I knew about him was this: he had lived in New York for nearly ten years, attached to one of those architecture firms whose names you know without knowing why—that is, he was a person of a certain consequence. Had been. A design magazine had published photographs of his SoHo loft; this I knew not because I'd come across the article but because he'd told us. He would refer to people you had heard of, Manhattan people, or he would refer to someone and then say with a sly shrug, "Well, you know, he was one of my boyfriends." The operative words here were *one of* and *was*. I counted my boyfriends and they were too few to count; Jeremy had had tricks, and Ruth, and me. Rodrigo came to dinner in our home and here he was, *dressed*. His suit I would swear was Italian and must have been new because it fit him. His tie was so beautiful you could have strangled yourself with it, and his small feet were impeccably shod: this was a man from New York.

He had regarded his dinner with apparent unease, yet ate with a gleeful greediness, sucking at his teeth as if they ached, smacking his lips, mumbling indistinct compliments. When Toby brought in the flan, each hemisphere of custard unmolded in the exact center of its glass plate, veiled with caramel and quiveringly perfect as a young man's buttocks, Rodrigo sighed the sigh of a small child offered a treat by his mother, and the expression on his drawn face inspired in me a terror I found sickening, precisely, a horror that made my stomach flutter and the beating of my heart loud, sudden, irregular. He reminded me of Sean. "Later," he said, staring with clear eyes at Jeremy, "we might go out?"

"Out?"

Forestalling protest, Toby said, "I'll be okay—I know how to dial 911."

I looked up to the plaster medallion in the ceiling, which must once have supported a chandelier. Many coats of paint had obscured its detail, making of fronds and fruits lumpy frets and blobs. I had a certain difficulty, often (and when had that happened?), seeing Toby as quite a young child still, but even looking across the table, seeing his plumpish, unformed cheeks below the hard lenses of his glasses, his sweetly curved lips and tiny chin, I felt less fear for him than for Jeremy. Or myself. "The guys downstairs will keep an ear open," I said, "if we ask them. They'd probably be relieved to know we know how to have fun. We never go out, Jere."

Toby smiled for me, pleased; lowered his eyes and raised his spoon.

Placing his hands in his lap, Jeremy regarded his flan. "I wouldn't know where to go." He looked up, but at me, not at Rodrigo. "I might as well live in the suburbs—in a split-level with a dog. We never go out." What kind of gay men were we, he was asking, what kind of residents of San Francisco. "Do you?"

Jeremy was looking at me and he meant did I know where to go, but as if every remark this evening were addressed to somebody else, Rodrigo replied. "Do I go out? ¿Sabes qué?—I never went home."

Toby had broken into his flan, eaten half of it already. His spoon halfway to his mouth, he paused. "Sacha says that her mom and stepfather and her dad and his boyfriend like to go out dancing, all four of them together." His lips formed a private smile. "They go to places where they play the kind of music Sacha won't listen to." He beamed at us.

"Sacha's a hipster monster," Jeremy said. "I wouldn't want to go anyplace that played her kind of music." It was decided, then. "You're sure you'll be all right alone, kid? Where should we go?"

"Sacha says they like the I-Beam."

"I've heard of the I-Beam," said Rodrigo with a nod—as close as he'd come, really, to acknowledging anyone's presence but Jeremy's.

"And I know where it is." I wanted to like him, in fact, not because I believed him to have been important to Jeremy, but because I knew he still was. Still, I was scared to death.

"It's settled, then."

I had not yet raised my spoon. I stared at the custard on my plate for a moment, then rose to my feet. "I'll make coffee."

"I don't drink coffee anymore." Rodrigo glanced up at me. "I'm sorry, Allen." There was the *y*-sound again, making my name sound like a cry of pain, rising, falling, and then cut off: Aɪʏ-*ayn*. "Do you have herbal tea?"

"I think so. How's chamomile?"

"Lovely, thank you."

I didn't want to leave the room—I wished nothing more. I didn't want to leave Jeremy with this man he had once loved, whom he had known before me, before Toby. This man who was ill.

THIS WAS IN December, two weeks before Toby's birthday. Sean had died in July, the third man I knew; in August, it was Mick, the young Irishman who had worked with me briefly at Grace & Fenton; in September, an acquaintance from the university where I worked now, Luke. Rodrigo might be next, or it might be Marco or Gary. I had *known*—you couldn't not be aware, in that city—but now it was happening, now it was happening around me, now I saw it happening. Five men in less than a year, five men I knew, young men all, and more to come. You went on, you had no choice.

It was a year, too, for visitations from the past: Rodrigo. Sean. Ghosts, in a way, horribly. When my prep-school roommate, the first boy I ever slept with, confident, charming, aggressive, whom you would take for a WASP to the manner born, so well-adjusted was he, though only two generations removed from Basilicata—when Matthew graduated from Yale, he had moved to San Francisco. Not on my account, although we had remained in touch and had nothing but good to say, one about the other. And notwithstanding our brief, delirious, hilarious rediscovery of adolescent passion, we were simply—although not *merely*—friends.

He came to San Francisco with four college friends, two of whom had family in the Bay Area. They were a band. They called themselves the Sleep of Reason, and composed and played a kind of fast, brittle, highly inflected rock that you could dance to. A certain segment of rock was becoming dance music again, even if you wouldn't know it from the playlists of discotheque deejays. (The Sleep of Reason played music, I suspect, that Toby's friend Sacha would have approved.) I went to a few of their early gigs, ate lunch once or twice at the restaurant where Matthew and another member of the band, June, the bassist, waited tables. But while Matthew had embraced the vivid, marginal life of a musician, I held a full-time job, and soon enough was going home in the evening to Jeremy and Toby—in the same city we lived in different cities, Matthew and I. We seldom saw each other.

The Sleep of Reason landed a recording contract. They released a single that became popular on college radio stations and in Britain, an album, went on tour. On the back cover of the album (the front reproduced the Goya capricho from which they'd taken their name) were individual portraits of the five band members, Matthew, singer/

lyricist/frontman, in the center. He looked scruffy and handsome. If you wrote to a certain San Francisco P.O. box, you'd receive by return mail a lyric sheet. Reading it, you found that the love songs were gender-neutral or addressed to men. This wasn't always apparent, on the recording, the way Matthew sang. When they returned to the city, Matthew called and asked me to come to their homecoming concert. "I can't comp you," he said, "because it's a benefit."

A benefit? I asked. For the volunteer organization that was just setting itself up, in the absence of a rational response from municipal, state, or federal government, to provide care for the ill and the dying, all those youths who had planned to live forever.

Jeremy and Toby and I went to the concert, went backstage after. Matthew hugged me. Sebastian, the drummer and Matthew's lover, hugged me and thanked me for coming. "It means a lot to Matt, you two go back so far." I had never called Matthew Matt. Sebastian drew me aside, and asked me not to say anything, and told me Matthew, too, was ill. That was September.

IN THE KITCHEN I set the kettle to boil for Rodrigo's tea. I ground coffee beans and filled the espresso maker, placed it on the burner. I heard Rodrigo laugh in the dining room; a moment later, Jeremy laughed. After setting up a tray, I leaned back against the counter, waiting, and closed my eyes.

It seemed only a minute, maybe two, before someone said, "You're thinking about Sean. Stop it."

"I can't bear to watch it happen again," I said before opening my eyes, before I'd quite realized I was speaking to Toby.

"Just stop it, Allen." The clarity of his expression was something that made my breath and my heart catch, so that I felt for a moment as if it were all my fault, as if I should have been able somehow to prevent it, to protect him. Behind the small round lenses of his glasses his grey eyes gleamed. I shifted my weight, but he stepped back. "Anyway," Toby muttered, "he's going back to New York."

After a moment he relented, came to me, wrapped his arms around my waist, laid his head against my chest. We stood like this for some little time. He said, "You didn't eat your dessert. It's good."

"I will," I said. A little later I said, as if I had just figured it out, "I don't want to go dancing, Toby."

Letting go of me, he stepped away. "Don't, then. Stay here with me." He cocked his head to the side. "Tell 'em I do need a baby-sitter. He's Dad's friend, not yours."

"Is it that easy?"

"Dad!" Toby called over his shoulder. "Can you come here for a minute?"

Flustered, I turned to the stove, where the water for Rodrigo's tea was on the edge of boiling. I heard Jeremy come in, I heard him ask, "What?"

"Tell him, Allen."

"What is it, Allen?"

Lifting the kettle from the flame, I turned again. "Jeremy." He was peering at me, puzzled. I thought: I love you. "Jeremy, I think I'll stay in tonight."

"He's not dealing, Dad."

"You and Rodrigo—you need to catch up. I'd be in the way."

As Jeremy looked from me to his son and back to me, I thought: Toby understands me better than you do.

"Allen," he asked, "do you want me to stay?"

I turned away, poured water into the cup, over the tea bag. A faint yellow stain seeped through the clear water. "That's not what I'm saying."

"You're being stupid, Dad."

I didn't need to look to know Toby had punched his father in the arm. "No, he's not. It's just . . ." Toby had recognized what it was before I had, but still I didn't want to say anything in front of him. I returned the kettle to the stove. "Toby, could you take the tea to Rodrigo? See if he wants sugar or anything?"

Taking the cup from my hand, Toby gave me a grin that was half not a grin. "Don't fight in front of the kid," he muttered, and went out.

"Allen—"

"Come here. Give me a hug. Please." I couldn't bear to look into Jeremy's face. There were times when he thought Toby and I ganged up on him. "He's not my friend, I don't know him." In Jeremy's embrace I was as small as Toby in mine. "I don't want to know him, because—"

"Because he's going to die." Jeremy's voice was harsh, his hands clenched in my back as hard as stones.

"Toby came in, said, You're thinking about Sean." I was whispering. "Matthew's sick too, I didn't tell you. Jeremy, Rodrigo doesn't care about me. It's you he came to see."

"Allen, what's wrong?"

"I can't bear to care about him."

And then Jeremy broke away. "But what about me?" Fists clenched at his hips, he went to the kitchen window to peer through the darkness three stories down into our neighbors' scruffy yard. "You know what Roddy meant to me," he said. "I don't know that man in there."

"Because he's ill? Or because he's lived in New York for ten years?" Could I go to him, could I say anything at all?

"I don't know, boy. I just don't. If he needs me—" Jeremy raised his fist and tapped it against the glass, then turned to face me but stared at the floor near his feet, the vinyl patterned like Moorish tiles. "I saw how Sean needed you."

Moving to the stove, I turned off the flame under the espresso maker. The coffee smelled bitter and rich, a smell like life itself. "I'll help if I can," I said, exhaling my words into the steam. "If it's what he wants. But it's not what he wants—what he needs tonight." I fumbled for the hot pad. "He needs to find out who you are now, and you to find out who he is. It's something you have to resolve."

"It's not something that's going to be resolved in an evening at the disco."

Still avoiding looking at him, I decanted the coffee into the pot Ruth had made, on the tray beside two of her cups and saucers, the sugar bowl, the little jug of cream. Jeremy pollutes even espresso, a habit I deplore and depend on. "Do you really think he wants me to come with you tonight?" I lifted the tray. "Come on. We've left him there too long. I'll ask if he minds me bowing out."

"Allen." His voice sounded faint, weak. "All those people at the I-Beam...." When I glanced over I saw him blink and shake his head. "I'm sorry to hear about Matthew, boy."

"Come along, sweetheart."

In the dining room, Toby, never a genius at small talk, appeared relieved to see us. Rodrigo's eyes went directly to Jeremy, but he said, "Thank you for the tea, Allen."

"You're welcome."

"Say, De nada," offered Toby.

Setting the tray down beside my place, I watched how Rodrigo watched Jeremy. The expression was hungry, but he watched as though from very far away, as if observing events and personages he could not hope to affect. "Rodrigo," I said, "I've been thinking I don't really feel up to going out tonight. I've got some work to do. Would you mind if I stayed here?"

For a moment it seemed he didn't hear me, so intense his concentration on Jeremy. Then his eyes moved in their hollow sockets, his thin, bladed nose turned. "De vero." One long hand came up in a vague, inarticulate gesture, first touching his cheek, then stroking one eyebrow, and then sweeping back through his hair. "In truth," he said, "I'm realizing that I've overextended myself a little today. My clock says it's three hours later than for you, you know, and my body says six." His eyes caught mine, black as though they were all pupil, and held. "My health isn't especially good right now. I think perhaps I should just go back to the hotel, call it a night well spent."

I wondered if he had heard Jeremy and me in the kitchen. His face was hard to read. Like dark aged vellum, his skin was crazed with tiny lines like those on a glazed pot or below the glaze of an old oil painting. I couldn't be sure of anything beyond fatigue and a kind of sad, resigned nostalgia.

"Don't you feel well?" asked Jeremy.

"I feel *tired*, Joto. Cansado. No más que cansado, ahorita." With a small, prim smile, Rodrigo turned his attention away from me. "Toby," he said, "you seem to be the expert, do you know if there's anyplace one can go to dance in the afternoon? Tea dance? I'm much more myself in the afternoons." His eyes moved again. "I'd like to dance with you, Joto, while I'm here. That's something we never did."

AFTER THE TAXI took Rodrigo away, back to his hotel, Jeremy and I washed the dishes, and after that I went into my study to look over some papers. I was scheduled to make a recruiting trip north, Mendocino, Humboldt, Siskiyou counties, early in the new year, and wanted to check the itinerary. There were bits and pieces of mail connected with my work scattered over the desk as well, things I'd brought home to look at before they got buried in files. In a departmental envelope I found a second- or third-generation photocopy of a flyer being circulated to every member of the admissions team—a job announcement.

. . . *seeks applicants for the position of Admissions Director*. . . . I recognized the name of the school, a private, non-sectarian primary/secondary institution in Providence, Rhode Island. My prep school swim team had bused down to Rhode Island for a league semifinals once; I remembered that we had won, despite my placing third in the hundred-meter freestyle—it was the highest point the team achieved while I was on it. I remembered Providence—that part of Providence, at least—as a handsome, prosperous New England town where tall deciduous trees rose at even intervals from the brick sidewalks lining broad avenues, where the houses had lawns and gardens. The school itself was set in a residential district, its substantial acreage bounded by a fence of iron palings. Within, foursquare Georgian buildings were set about as deliberately as specimen trees in a city park.

My desk sat in the bay window of the study, overlooking the neighbors' yard. Our own house—Jeremy's house—filled its lot front to back, had no yard. I reread the flyer, sitting at the desk, and then regarded my reflection in the glass of the windows, remembering. I had first felt a distinct person, integral in myself, separate from my family, at prep school in New England. At prep school I was simply Allen Pasztory, one boy among many, an asset to history and English departments and to the swim team. I was a son my parents were proud of, but, six or seven hundred miles away from them, I need not acknowledge all the reasons they were proud of me. For months at a time I could forget how to talk with my hands, how to perform the delicate trick of translating from one set of symbols to another. And at the same time the fact that I could do these things set me apart from the other boys in a way more comfortable than my being on scholarship, or than the subversive desires I was beginning to recognize in myself.

Matthew and I had been lovers for two years at prep school in New England. But Matthew lived in San Francisco now, where he was writing songs for the Sleep of Reason's second album, which I hoped with all my heart he would live to complete. I knew no-one at all in New England anymore.

Pushing the chair back from the desk, I covered my eyes with my hands, then lowered them. I turned toward the open door and called, "Jeremy, come here for a minute?" He was in the bedroom, just down the hall: he'd hear.

Requiescant

OLIVER WHITE
November 1959, Birmingham, Alabama
May 1983, San Francisco, California

SEAN FORESTAL
August 1954, Boston, Massachusetts
July 1983, San Francisco, California

MICHAEL O'MALLEY
September 1960, Dublin, Ireland
August 1983, San Francisco, California

Luke Johansen
June 1960, Cloquet, Minnesota
September 1983, San Francisco, California

Rodrigo Jaramillo León
August 1954, Puebla, Mexico
December 1983, San Francisco, California

MARCO BALLESTERI
October 1950, Palermo, Italy
December 1983, San Francisco, California

GARY ELLSWORTH
January 1957, Savannah, Georgia
January 1984, San Francisco, California

Matthew Sanremo
March 1958, Greenwich, Connecticut
February 1984, San Francisco, California

Passage

I HAD FORGOTTEN about spring in the Northeast—it was nine years since I'd been in New England. The lawn in front of the administration building was brown and beaten down, banks of dingy snow still lay behind the trees along the fence, but the trees, magnolias, were in bloom, lifting large blossoms, purplish outside, whitey-pink at the heart, that looked like artifacts of heavy glazed paper wired to bare branches. Daffodils and jonquils crowded the magnolias' roots, every imaginable shade of yellow from a pale buttery cream to the most vivid lemon. The wide beds on either side of the stairway were massed with orange-belled narcissi; I could smell their fragrance as I descended, and I could see the pine green needles of crocus leaves, each bisected by a white spine, and the sodden, spent blossoms like clumps of wet tissue paper, still jewel bright, orangey gold, white, a dense, inky purple. Furled shoots of tulip and hyacinth pushed up from the damp black earth. The chill air felt no colder than back home, and had a glassy, bell-like quality that the air in San Francisco, turbulent with Pacific fog, never achieves.

"Mr. Pasztory!" called a voice behind me.

I have never heard a native Hungarian pronounce my surname so I don't know where the stress should fall, but it always sounds wrong the first time. Myself, I accent the second syllable and make no attempt at the slight burring of the sibilant that those who have seen it first on paper inevitably try. "Please," I said, "Allen."

The man hurrying down the granite steps shifted his trench coat from one arm to the other and smiled. "Allen, then. Don't call me Jacob. I'm Jake." He held out his hand and I shook it. Jacob Touro, dean of the Lower School.

Before the interview I was afraid I'd forget someone's name, I never remember names for more than a minute or two, but somehow I managed not to screw up. It helped that all four were physically dissimilar. The assistant headmaster was a woman, Marilyn Pereira, dark, sultry looking despite the severe grey shirtwaist and navy blazer. That she was a woman pleased me. When I was trying to decide whether to accept the interview offer, Jeremy had said, "They'll all be straight white male bigots. You don't want to leave Berkeley for that." He was right about my qualms, as far as they went, but I pointed out the signature on the letter of invitation—the personnel director's name was George Takagawa. "Token," said Jeremy. Jake Touro was Jewish, I assumed, not that that meant much. The lone inarguable WASP male on the committee, Upper School dean Ben Romney, was only a year or two older than I. Jeremy would get a stern talking-to that night. I did want to leave Berkeley, but more than that I wanted to leave San Francisco.

Jake Touro said, "You've seen the grounds?"

"I was given an exhaustive tour this morning."

"But I'll bet no-one thought to offer you lunch." He was steering me around the corner of the building, either toward the dining hall or the parking lot. "I'm heading that way myself. May I ask you to join me?" He peered at me through the thick lenses of his glasses and laughed, a quick, short sound. "No fear—not the cafeteria. The food isn't bad, but I can't bring myself to eat on campus more than twice a week."

"I'd enjoy that—thank you, Jake."

"Good man." Jake clapped me on the shoulder. How would Jeremy square this amiability with his assumptions about New England reserve? "Now, lunch is on me," Jake said, "so I'll let you drive."

I led him toward my rental. "If you want to trust me. I don't know my way around, and I hardly ever drive."

"I thought all Californians were grafted to their cars?" said Jake as I unlocked the passenger door.

"That's L.A. Southern and Northern California are different states." I closed his door on him and walked around to the other side, where he had already unlocked my door. "San Francisco has good public transit. I don't need a car there—BART takes me right to the campus in Berkeley. Parking's impossible in the city, anyway." I put the key in the ignition. "Where are we going?"

"You'd need a car here. And you'll find that Rhode Island drivers are the worst in the country. Boston, Mass, possibly excepted." He clasped his hands on his knees. "But I won't put you through traffic— we'll stay here on the East Side." He directed me down Hope Street, a broad, attractive avenue lined with brick mansions, large clapboard

and gingerbread Victorian houses with mansard roofs, and more magnolias, saying nothing except to ask me to take a right turn and then,
two blocks later, a left, onto Thayer. "This is where the university students shop," he said, "so it's trendy and ephemeral, but there're a couple
of good restaurants."

I parked the car where he told me. I saw two young men on the
sidewalk, pausing at the entrance to a record store; below their bulky
sweaters they wore shorts. Jake saw them too. "College students," he
muttered.

"Two for lunch," Jake told the waitress. "Can we sit out here?"

She nodded, and led us to a table in the corner of the glassed-in
sun porch. The restaurant seemed once to have been a residence.
Seated, Jake looked over the menu and recommended a few dishes.
After we had ordered and the waitress had provided us each with a glass
of white wine, Jake said, "What do you think of Providence so far,
Allen? Do you think you'd want to live here?"

The interview was still on, then. I supposed that the members of
the committee rotated among themselves taking candidates out to
lunch. "I haven't seen enough to judge, but it's very attractive around
here." What did they say about job interviews, that you should repeat
your interlocutor's name as often as possible? I drew my finger down
the stem of my wine glass. "It doesn't really feel like a city, and I like
that." I looked across the table at Jake, buttering a piece of bread, then
over his shoulder and out the window. Across the street stood another
converted dwelling, High Victorian. Cozily so—not overpowering like
Jeremy's building in San Francisco, which could be borne only because
equally grandiose buildings stood on either side and because, even
from the far side of the street, you couldn't take it all in, it was so big.
The house across from the restaurant displayed snazzy neon sculpture
in the casements of its bay window, announcing a hair salon. "You
know, Jake," I said, "I went to prep school out here, one of your competitors, up in New Hampshire, and New England still feels like home.
I swam against your team once, here in Providence."

"Out here?" Jake was smiling. "That sounds like a Californian." It
was a good smile, cheery but reserved. "And I've been to San Francisco
—I have a cousin *out there*—so I know what you'd be leaving." Still
smiling, the skin creased around his large eyes, larger behind the
glasses, and the two lines on either side of his nose deeper, Jake tucked

a piece of bread into his mouth and chewed thoughtfully for a moment. "Providence isn't in the same league, not as stimulating."

The waitress brought our salads. I poked at the pale lettuce, stirring it into the dressing. "In a way I'm looking to get away from stimulation," I muttered, regretting it even as I spoke. "I mean, doesn't there come a point when living in a big city interferes with what you want to be? There's so much going on and it seems such a shame to miss any of it that you can't concentrate on yourself, on what you ought to be doing." These were rationalizations. I didn't wish to tell Jacob Touro why I was desperate to leave San Francisco.

He smiled again, even more broadly, into a grin. "You don't need to tell me. I came here from Manhattan ten years ago—I can't imagine going back. Still," he said, "San Francisco isn't a big city in quite the same way as New York. I thought it was extremely humane, very livable. Great weather too."

"If you like fog."

Jake waved my objection away. "My wife and I didn't want to raise our kids in New York, but I don't know, if it had been San Francisco . . ."

This was an opening I wasn't ready to take. My quarrel with San Francisco wasn't with its being a bad or good place to raise a child who was not, after all, my son. Toby attended a good school and the city treated him well, offering him the opportunity, among others, to refer to his father's boyfriend without the reference's being remarkable or especially controversial. Even two years before I couldn't have imagined leaving and still could hardly imagine, could only entertain the notion. Jeremy was being uncharacteristically evasive, as well. I said, "Will you come with me?" He said, "I can work anywhere." If I pressed he said, "You don't have a place for us to go to, yet," or, still worse, "We'll build that bridge when we get there." Or had he said *burn*? I came home from work one afternoon to find him painting the stairwell, a task he had been putting off for two years. Another time, returning from visiting Matthew, I found a new Oriental carpet on the living room floor. We called it the living room but—except in the sense that a significant portion of our income, our living, derived from the hours Jeremy spent at the drawing table in the bay window—we didn't live there. Toby practiced his flute in the living room because it had good acoustics but we lived in the kitchen, the dining room, the room across the hall that was called my study, all three of them in the back of the flat. Our bedroom. The carpet looked odd, isolated, like an installation in a minimalist art gallery, without a couch, an armchair, a coffee table to place it in context.

"Another thing I'm wondering about," Jake was saying as he pierced a slice of hothouse cucumber with the tines of his fork, "is why you'd consider leaving a major university for us. Booster though I am, it seems a poor trade."

I contemplated the bread basket. A stiff pink napkin enveloped the thick slices of baguette, which compared well with the bread of San Francisco, city of sourdough and French. The crust flaked and crunched nicely, the white flesh, a soft honeycomb more air than gluten, evaporated on the tongue. "The people at Berkeley asked me the same question," I said, "when I left advertising." I lifted my glass, sipped the dry, slightly resinous wine. It combined pleasantly with aftertastes of oil, vinegar, and pepper from the salad dressing, the simple, plain flavor of the bread. "And that meant a fairly substantial salary cut."

"This wouldn't?"

I shook my head a little. "I can give you several reasons of varying plausibility. I'm not sure that any of them is valid—more than another, or at all. In college I used to admire people who were majoring in computer science or engineering because they appeared to know what they were doing, what they wanted to do. I left advertising—well, I think a lot of people leave advertising after a belated moral epiphany." I sipped the wine again, clinked my lower teeth against the glass. "It occurred to me that I was educating people, and I didn't feel competent."

"That's an odd idea." Jake looked puzzled and amused. The waitress returned, removed the salad plates and replaced them with our entrées, a complicated pasta dish for Jake, for me a grilled salmon steak with a peculiar and, I decided, extraneous and distracting sauce drizzled over it.

"Not really. People who read read everything—menus, cereal boxes, ads. There's more advertising around than literature, it's more available. If you read enough package labeling and advertising you could decide *light* was spelled L-I-T-E. I was mostly involved with fairly text-heavy ads and—say, something like a split infinitive or a misplaced modifier...? I think any kind of writer has to feel a responsibility to the language, an advertising copywriter maybe more than a novelist or a

journalist because he has a bigger audience and usually a less sophisti-
cated one. Remember the old cigarette that tasted good like a cigarette
should?"

Jake nodded and, I think, understood where I was going.

"Thousands, maybe millions of people misuse *like* because that
slogan's part of their heritage by now. Someone—" my father, actually—
"pointed out to me that in one paragraph, printed in the millions over
a very attractive photo, I had placed a modifying phrase in such a way
that a liqueur was enjoying its own bouquet. I was a history major—
what did I know? Worse than that, the client didn't see it either.
Wouldn't have cared."

"You're too much a purist." Jake rested his fork on the edge of his
plate. He was beaming. "Dialect enriches the living language."

"Maybe."

"How's your lunch, Allen?" Jake asked.

I used the tine of my fork to separate a fine, dangerous bone from
a flake of salmon. "Very good, thanks."

On the first leg of my flight east, between San Francisco and
Chicago, I had a window seat and the seats beside me were occupied by
a very young, very handsome couple. They were college seniors, I discovered, heading back to school after a long weekend visiting her parents and, for him, two interviews. When they learned that I was myself
going for an interview, first in several years, he gave me a number of
naïve tips on how to carry myself through the process. Over lunch it
transpired that she was interested in advertising and planned on approaching Grace & Fenton and several competitors, including the
agency where I served my apprenticeship, so I was able to return the
boy's favor. All along I had found something about them vaguely irri-
tating, like an eyelash caught under the lid. Eventually, as he napped in
the aisle seat and she leafed through a copy of *Vogue* and paused over a
highly erotic two-page fragrance spread complete with sealed scratch-
n-sniff flap, I realized that they were wearing, respectively, the men's
and women's versions of the same cologne. The two scents combined
into an olfactory mélange, not unpleasant, the exact effect, I imagined,
the manufacturer had had in mind. I couldn't decide how to remark on
their artfulness, and decided, finally, they wouldn't appreciate my
bringing it up.

On recruiting trips from the university, to high schools and prep schools throughout California, I encountered young women with stiff, hysterical hairstyles and logos all over their clothing who had sprayed themselves with baroque drugstore perfumes that competed with the scent of their hairsprays; spoke to painfully serious young men who stank of nervous sweat, pimple cream, and cheap, ugly aftershave. Before or after their campus tours other young people stopped by my office in the admissions building, polite boys in blazers and ties and girls in pretty frocks, if they were visiting with their parents; young hoodlums with gelled hair, silver skull earstuds, and leather jackets, or tanned blond beachboys who wore fluorescent trunks revealing a yard of skinny thigh and an inch of white boxer short; young women with flat, bobbed hair, whose rumpled pastel oxford-cloth shirts and men's blue jeans set off pearl earrings, or women with shaved heads, ten loops of gold wire stitched through the helix of one shell-like ear, army surplus fatigue trousers, and dingy t-shirts. These are wicked generalizations. They were idealistic, articulate, pragmatic, naïve by turns, and alarmingly bright.

Reaching home in the evenings, after twenty-five minutes on BART under the bay and another twenty on a Muni bus, I would take a long, hot shower with Castile soap to wash off the adolescent, hormones-in-riot miasma of my job, put on clean clothes, and find Toby. He might be working on his homework or reading in his bedroom or practicing his flute or pestering his father. Jeremy would look across the room at me, raise his eyebrows and smile, say, "Hello, boy. Back from the big world and all clean and shiny, eh?" Toby grinned, openmouthed, shouted, barreled into my arms like a frisky, affectionate puppy, and smelled like himself, his own uncomplicated sweat, smelled, somehow, clear and fine, tomato, basil.

There were reasons above and beyond the obvious, behind my lurking, toxic fear, for wishing to leave the Bay Area. It seemed to me, watching Jake across the table as he twirled his fork in what looked like a pile of innocent pastel ribbons, that here one could—Jeremy and Toby and I could—find a kind of security, as if within the limitations of a walled garden. But more: that we might admit as strangers only the young and simple. *Simple* a word that smelled as fresh, as refreshing, as tomatoes and basil—as grace. The main north-south avenue on the East Side was Hope; another was called Benefit. *Providence* itself was a word that made a promise.

AFTER LUNCH AND a cup of coffee, Jake Touro suggested we walk off the meal. "I know a good place," he said, "though some people think I'm morbid for liking it." I asked if he didn't need to go back to work, but he'd told them not to expect him. We found my rented car on the street —for a moment I'd forgotten what it looked like. I heard the chime of a dull, loud bell, and in a moment there were more college students on the sidewalks, in the street, ducking obliviously through traffic, rushing to or from classes with their bookpacks and sloppy clothes and plastic-lidded paper cups of coffee. Jake directed me away from the central enclave of the university. We headed east, toward Massachusetts, and then north, paralleling the Seekonk River, wide, deep, gunmetal grey. The raised span of a derelict railroad drawbridge pointed off at an angle into the sky, immense gnomon of a titanic sundial.

The street peeled away from the river bank, climbed a smooth, looping curve around a water meadow under unidentifiable bare trees. We drove through a district of large, prosperous houses with gardens, with lawns, with trees of their own. A wide grassy median divided the two lanes of traffic, a footpath down the center punctuated by runners in Lycra leggings or, despite the chill, shorts and bare legs. Jake directed me to pull off and park on the side of the road just before an impressive driveway that passed through a dry-stone wall under trees. A sign indicated that this was the Swan Point Cemetery.

"All the good people are buried here," Jake said over the top of the car. "At least, all the good Christian people."

I followed him through the gates. On one side of the drive stood a small, ugly chapel; on the other, a flat meadow was pocked with small stones set into the grass. Several of the graves were ornamented with military decorations, tattered miniature flags above round, bronze-wreathed plaques. Before us, where the drive split, rose a low hillock crowned by an obelisk, the Gothic spires of a mausoleum, and the largest magnolia I had seen, beyond being an ornamental shrub, a true tree. So many blossoms freighted its boughs that they resembled a vast exodus of passenger pigeons, temporarily lighted, which would momentarily take wing with a deafening, sky-blackening whirr, the thunder of their pinions drowning out the hollow canticle of their song, an orchestra of wooden recorders, bass, tenor, soprano, cooing and lowing, which for a moment I seemed to hear. "That's where the good stuff starts," said Jake.

As we strolled up the path he said, "I mentioned my cousin in San Francisco? He's the rabbi for a small congregation there—you might have heard of it."

He told me the name. I knew of it: one of two gay synagogues in the city. I looked at Jake, expecting some ambiguous expression, a smirk, a faint liberal's blush, some sign of complicity or confidence, but he was clear-eyed and already breathless. Taller than I, older, heavier, he carried his gut with distinction. "I've heard good things," I said.

"I'm glad to know it." Stopping under the magnolia, he took out a handkerchief and cleaned his glasses, then removed a slim panatela from the inside breast pocket of his jacket. "You don't mind?" he asked, then, as I shook my head, lit it with a steel lighter. The smoke was rich, fragrant. "Now, Allen," he said, puffing the cigar alight, "I won't say we'd dismiss consideration of your application if we knew you were gay. I like to think we're broadminded. That's a poor choice of words, isn't it? I must admit I was shocked when David, my cousin, let me know what he was up to, but I hope that was only because I hadn't thought about it."

"Am I obvious?" My voice was thin, cold. The cemetery stretched onward, a rippled, romantically landscaped topography marked by monuments, until it dipped and through a screen of trees I could see the flat river.

"You're from San Francisco." Jake shrugged, brandished the cigar. "You're single."

"Actually," I said, "I'm not. At least yesterday morning I wasn't. If you offer me the job and I move here, I don't know." I took two steps away from him, toward the mausoleum. "I've been with the man for three years. If he said no I probably wouldn't take the job."

One hand in his trouser pocket, the other holding the cigar, with his dark suit and greying beard Jake looked like a pillar of society. Sunlight glinted on his glasses. "You'd better find out, Allen," he said. "I'd say you're our prime candidate." Smiling benevolently, he puffed on the panatela, billows of grey smoke rising around his face like incense. "Also, I have some seniority, and I haven't been able to talk to any of the other applicants." Another puff. "Let's keep walking."

Dark conifers shadowed the path. I remembered a graveyard near my prep school, a much smaller proposition, its thin, eroded slate headstones arranged in straight aisles across a flat meadow with a kind of defiant, tedious rectitude. Those stones were so worn you could only infrequently puzzle out a name, a date. This cemetery, vast, involved, of a Victorian amplitude and, in an odd way, a Victorian whimsy and domesticity, seemed to house no-one who had died before 1850; many of the more attractive stones, granite, marble, were in fact quite recent, the 1960s and '70s. We passed a colony of Armenian surnames, and came to a small pond.

"Your friend," Jake said. "Would he have trouble finding work here?"

"He's an illustrator, freelance. He works at home." We had paused again. Jake tapped a fat, solid cylinder of ash from his cigar. It hit the water, broke up, decomposed, but did not sink. Jake had said he had children. He worked with children in the lower school. "Children's books. He's written a few, too. You might have heard of him." He glanced at me quickly. "Jeremy Kent."

"Yes." Jake pulled on his cigar. "Yes, I have."

I was hardly watching him, was staring across the syrupy brown pond to where a pair of boulders seemed to have been placed in such a way as to represent the majesty of nature. A slender tree that I couldn't identify grew from the cleft between them, its trunk silver and scaled, its stripped branches spindly, upreaching. Gravel turned under Jake's feet and he said in a sort of hoarse, voiced whisper, "I was reading one of his books to my youngest just last week." He walked a few steps, then returned. "Allen, I don't understand why I find this very disturbing." He removed his glasses, taking his face out of focus for a moment so that it looked as peculiar as his surroundings must have appeared to him without the lenses' mediation.

"More disturbing than your cousin the gay rabbi?" I felt for a moment that I wanted to embrace Jake, a reaction I wouldn't have expected. Usually the scruples of straight people leave me impatient and hostile. "More than the prospect of hiring a gay admissions director?"

"I thought—" He raised his hands, palms up, the cigar between two fingers of the left hand, the earpiece of his spectacles crooked over the right palm. "The book I was reading—it was dedicated to his son. Jeremy Kent has a son."

"He does," I said, "we do. Toby turned nine a few months ago. I'd like him to come to school here."

LOCKS

Bone, Sinew, Flesh

OUR HOUSE HAS two doors; usually we go in through the back. Partly this is because the back is more convenient to the driveway, partly it has to do with Lena, who rents the first floor. The front door opens right into her living room, essentially, and although she's assured us she doesn't mind, I mind. It's an old house, and I've never been sure whether it was always meant to be a two-household affair—both kitchens, for example, seem to be original. Perhaps the builder, Nathaniel Hart, 1856, had a son who lived downstairs with his young family. When we had the attic done over, before we moved in, we could have taken the opportunity to create a neutral entryway. Perhaps our idea, Jeremy's and mine, was that Toby would live there when he grows up. The mortgage might be paid off by then. Of course it is all too likely that by then Jeremy and I won't be living upstairs.

When I use the front door Lena's two cats come running from wherever they spend their days, sure that I'm here to feed them. The back way, through the yard, I have to deal with her dog, a grand lolloping Great Pyrenees, but I'm temperamentally more attuned to dogs, and Herodias and I get along famously. I held the door wide for Jeremy and shooed the cats back. Their names are Judith and Salome but despite one's being tabby and the other calico and therefore quite distinct I don't know which is which. They mewled and hollered at me.

I was watching Jeremy. He's bigger and stronger than I, but not that much stronger, and an eleven-year-old boy makes an awkward, heavy load. Toby's face against Jeremy's shoulder was lost, drawn and pallid, in a great mass of hair that had been scheduled for a cut later in the week. He looked especially defenseless without the spectacles that I carried in my breast pocket, their frames bent, one lens shattered. My bathrobe bundled around him like a blanket, although I am not a large man. By the time I was eleven I'd broken one leg twice, an arm, a collarbone. Toby, however, a healthy, sturdy, careful child, went to the doctor on a regular schedule and had never needed more immediate care than the school nurse could provide—skinned knees, strained tendons, twisted ankles, a nosebleed or two. An orderly had washed the blood from his face, only making the opulent bruise more obvious. When Jeremy started up the stairs he had to turn sideways and proceed crab-fashion to avoid knocking Toby's cast against wall or balustrade. The back stairs would have been too narrow for the maneuver.

I closed and locked the door. The glass pane let in a stream of light that illuminated the pattern of Lena's Turkish carpet, through the arch under the stairs, cream, rust, dull crimson, faded blue. I followed Jeremy up the stairs; the cats followed me, then rushed past to riot around Jeremy's ankles where he waited on the landing. Light from the narrow window picked out the wide jade and narrow grey blue stripes in the bronze-colored silk robe. "We're home, kid," Jeremy whispered, leaning over Toby, as I unlocked the door. The cats dashed downstairs. Jeremy smiled at me a little, tiredly, as he carried his son past me through our front door.

CERTAIN SENTENCES YOU can finish after hearing the first word, just from the tone of the voice. Similarly, I didn't have to ask who was in question when Jeremy called me at work and said, "I'm at the hospital. Emergency. How soon can you get here?" Hospital waiting rooms are always too bright, the plastic seats too hard, and the coffee that spurts then trickles from vending machine nozzles into paper cups pure poison. Jeremy ruins his coffee with cream and two spoons of sugar, but even fake milk couldn't make the liquid in the cup I held worse than it was. He'd asked me to get it for him, but now he sat on the edge of one of the orange plastic chairs, knees wide, hands clasped between them, leaning forward at such an angle that the line between chin and clavicle didn't curve at all and the back of his skull rested on tense shoulders. A year or so before, when every American gay man between the ages of twenty-one and forty shaved off his mustache and got a precise razor-edged new-wave haircut, Jeremy started letting his hair grow and grew a natty beard. This was about the time we moved to Rhode Island. By now I've known Jeremy bearded longer than not, but when I see him sometimes, in obscure light, from an unusual perspective, I don't recognize the man. I blew on the curdled surface of the coffee but couldn't bring myself to drink. "What happened, Jere?"

He kept looking past me, out into the corridor lit with fluorescents as bright as those in the waiting room, where doctors and nurses and orderlies, gurneys, wheelchairs, all the mechanisms of industrialized medicine rattled past. The PA wheezed and bellowed. "I want to murder five prepubescent boys," Jeremy said. His voice was as drained of color as the walls around us, matte, unreflective. "Two of them are in there with him. What kind of argument would put three boys in the hospital? No-one will tell me what it was about."

"I'll find out." The parents of the other boys must have been somewhere nearby as well, but I couldn't focus on anyone but Jeremy.

"They broke his arm. Toby's never broken anything. He hasn't been in a hospital since he was born." The voice still came flatly from between lips that hardly moved, below eyes that never wavered. The wings of Jeremy's nostrils looked pinched and whitish. "They broke Toby's arm. I haven't seen him. They won't tell me anything." Now he glanced over at me with opaque eyes. "Not even which arm."

In our family hands are of supreme importance, the integrity of hands, their mobility and ability. Jeremy is right-handed. So is Toby. I looked at my right hand. It prompted me, and I said again, "I'll find out."

Before I left the office I'd asked Annie to call the school nurse and find out why she hadn't called me. My name is on Toby's file as the emergency contact, since I'm on the campus anyway and Jeremy frequently turns off the extension in his studio when he's working. On the phone Annie sounded flustered, which was odd, and angry, which was odder. "That woman!" Since she was hired I have felt lucky that Annie is in my outer office. I have worked with secretaries who pointedly misremembered Jeremy's and Toby's names, secretaries to whom my family was anathema. Annie kept a supply of saltines in her file drawer for Toby. "She didn't call you because you're not related to Toby. Under the circumstances, she said, it would have been inappropriate. What's appropriate when you're talking an injured child? I wanted to bash her. What were the circumstances, I said. The boy is not to blame for his unfortunate home life, she said, and hung up on me."

"What does that mean?" I couldn't see Jeremy from the phone booth, but he couldn't see me either.

"That's not the half of it, Allen. Then Jake Touro called. He wouldn't tell me anything but I'm morally certain they're going to try to blame it on you. Not Jake himself, you know he's on our side, but the rest of them."

An empty gurney rolled by the booth; the IV bottle on its pole swayed. Someone must have been pushing but I didn't notice. "I don't even know what happened." I hate hospitals. The last several years I've spent too much time in them.

"You'd better talk to Jake," Annie said gently. "How's Toby?"

"I haven't seen him yet. He's got a broken arm; I don't know what else."

"I'm going to buy a big box of saltines on my way home tonight. Tell him that."

"Okay, Annie. Thanks."

"Love to Jeremy. Don't come in tomorrow, Allen."

I hung up. I fished out more coins. Jake invites Jeremy and me to his Hanukkah open house every year. He and his wife have eaten in my home. Bread and salt. I dialed his office. "Jake. This is Allen. What's going on?"

"Allen? Where are you?"

"I'm at the hospital. Toby's in surgery. Remember Toby? I'm upset, Jake. What's going on?" I didn't especially wish to get on Jake's bad side. The hierarchy is such that I have more power and influence but he's more important. I like him. "Annie seems to think somebody's threatening me."

"She's blowing it out of all proportion, Allen. Everyone is." I heard him suck in his breath. "I'm sorry. I don't mean that—it's terrible, about Toby. . . and the other kids. How is he?"

Weary of not knowing, of saying I didn't know, I said, "He'll survive. He'll be okay." When I looked up Jeremy was standing across the hall watching me.

"It's sticky, Allen, you know. There are certain people who will take any opportunity—"

"Jake," I said, "just tell me why five boys beat Toby up."

His throat forced a noise similar to the sound a telephone makes before it cuts you off. "Because his father's gay. Because you work here."

I waited a moment. "One thing, Jake," I said. "They're lower school, those five, your bailiwick? I want them suspended—not ex-pelled unless you have to—and I want to talk to them." I stared across the corridor at Jeremy. He leaned against the wall, head back, eyes lid-ded, watching me over the wide planes of his cheekbones. I couldn't see the color of his irises although reflected light made them gleam. "I've got to go, Jake. I'll talk to you tomorrow."

"Allen!—okay. Look, Allen, I'm behind you. Remember that."

"I will not speak to those people," Jeremy said when I stood before him.

"Who, Jeremy?" I wanted to take him in my arms.

"Mr. Kent?" The woman in the white lab coat looked at her clip-board, glanced at Jeremy, at me. "Jeremy Kent?"

Jeremy stared at her. "Yes?"

"I'm Dr. Palumbo, Jeremy. Your son is going to be fine." Her lab coat was immaculate, the hair drawn back from her temples tight and shining: she might have been a prop, a reassuringly aseptic symbol behind which the blood and trauma of the emergency room was disguised. "There was a severe fracture of the left forearm but we had no trouble setting it. Otherwise, a lot of contusions and minor lacera-tions but nothing a little time and a lot of rest won't heal. Is Mrs. Kent here?"

Jeremy snorted through his nose. I had winced, although there was no reason the doctor should make the correct assumption. Dressed as I was, I might more easily be taken for Jeremy's lawyer. He brushed his hand down my arm. "Why?" he asked.

Dr. Palumbo looked from one to the other, her glaze slipping. "Well, I'd like to outline the care Toby will need while he recuperates." She touched the eraser of her pencil to her lips.

"Toby's mother," Jeremy said, "always hated being called Mrs. Kent, which is one reason she no longer is Mrs. Kent. She lives in California, Dr. Palumbo. I'm sure she'll be concerned about Toby but there's not a lot she can do, is there. Mr. Pasztory and I will be happy to listen to you."

He was glaring at her. Her eyes moved away, avoided mine.

"Allen Pasztory, Dr. Palumbo," I said calmly. Because Toby is not my son he doesn't get free tuition, unlike the children of every other employee of the school. At the time, he wasn't covered by my health plan, either, any more than Jeremy was, although they were the beneficiaries of the life insurance policy that was also part of my contract. "You could call me Toby's stepmother. When can we take him home?"

JEREMY CARRIED TOBY through to the kitchen, the room where we always end up, while I locked the door. It was still light, but fading, the house filling with the shadows of an evening in early fall when the leaves are bleached and frayed but before they begin to turn. Dust furred the floor beneath low chairs, grime streaked the panes of open windows with sooty sills. The red light blinked on the answering machine. I ignored it.

Toby's bedroom is behind the kitchen, but Jeremy had settled him down on the little sofa before the fireplace, too short for either of us to stretch out full-length; Toby was still small enough to fit. Pillows and cushions supported shoulders and neck. The sash of the robe loosened, its lapels fell open over his pale, narrow chest. The exhaustion of shock glazed half-closed eyes and his mouth hung open as though he were only remembering how to breathe. Unable to look at him, unwilling not to, I watched Jeremy, beyond the camelback of the sofa, pouring out a glass of milk, arranging cookies on a plate. Dr. Palumbo had doped Toby with so many painkillers he wouldn't be able to taste. He was still staring dully at the floor near my feet when Jeremy placed the tray at his side. Jeremy glanced up at me. His eyes, the same color, gleamed as palely, as half-alive, as his son's.

It's hard, sometimes. After so long I can't help but think of Toby as my child, neither he nor his father has ever given me any reason to believe I shouldn't, but at certain moments I hesitate, the lack of any kind of sanctioned bond makes me wonder if I oughtn't step back a little, acknowledge the rationale, the rationalization of his not being my son. There are questions, perhaps, it sometimes seems, that only Jeremy should ask. I crouched down on the hearth. "What hurts, Toby?" I asked.

He didn't answer for a moment. His right hand moved to stroke the cast, adjust the sling. His eyes seemed to focus hard on the motion of fingers protruding from frayed white plaster and gauze. "I'm thinking," he said at last. The fingers wiggled, spasmodically at first, like frog's legs to which an electric current is applied, as though autonomically, then with more purpose and control. The bruises on his cheek

and neck resembled the petals of a purple bronze iris from the garden—
the afternoon before the blossom crumples up like wet tissue paper—
adhered to his skin like grafts. "Will you get my other glasses and my
book for me, Allen?" Toby asked.

As I rose from my crouch, Jeremy clasped his hands together, laced
the fingers. "Chicken curry for dinner, okay?"

Breath

THE CAT'S NAME was Providence. My nephew Kit named her; he liked the sound of the word, of the city where his uncle lived. She looked up with yellow eyes, then stood up off her haunches and placed one paw, as tentative as a benediction, on my thigh. "She likes you," said Kit. Her other paw touched, drew back, touched again, and all the while she stared into my face.

"Nonsense," Kit's mother said. "That cat doesn't like anyone. She likes laps."

In any case Providence lost interest. She sat on the floor beside me for a moment, paws together, perfectly composed, before a shudder passed over her back and she leapt away with a little grunting cry.

"You must be tired, Allen," Steph said. "Why didn't you fly down? Can I get you anything? I bought some good coffee, just for you."

"That would be lovely, Steph."

My sister smiled her loving-big-sister smile, which is quite distinct from the loving-wife and loving-mother smiles, older and because of that younger, less practiced. "Of course, I'm not sure I can do it justice." Her left hand moved just a little before she stood up from the long blond-wood deal table and turned to the counter. The only thing I envied about her big, comfortable, bright house was the size of its kitchen, but her kitchen didn't have a brick hearth and a small camel-back sofa before it where Toby sprawled to do his homework while I cooked dinner. It had lots of pale wood and wide windows and a vinyl floor that must have been easy to keep clean.

"Uncle Allen?" Kit was concentrating on the handheld space aliens game I'd brought him. "How old do I have to be to go to your school?"

My nephew, my elder nephew, was ten, two years younger than Toby, who is as close to a cousin as he'll ever get on his mother's side. I spread my hands out flat on the table, feeling its soft, perceptibly fuzzy, unfinished finish, the grain as clear against my palms as a fingerprint. "You could come now, if your parents wanted. Toby started when he was your age."

Kit's eyes narrowed. His upper lip tightened against his teeth. Short and pointed like his father's, it gave rise to an odd reflectiveness between them so that Kit occasionally looked thirty-five and Derek more frequently ten.

"Allen."

I glanced at Steph. Her hand sliced through the air on a diagonal. I nodded.

Kit looked back at the device in his hand, fired a flurry of LCD missiles at an LCD spaceship. "Uncle Allen?"

"Nephew Christopher?"

Kit's large head twisted on his long neck, glossy black hair shifted, he squinted and sucked his teeth. "Don't call me that."

"Nephew?"

"Christopher. My teacher calls me that. *Christ*opher." Frowning, he straightened his shoulders. "*Christ*opher *Sheri*dan, just like that, *Christ*opher, what is the *an*swer?"

"Nephew Kit, I apologize. I could call you Kitten but you're much too big for my lap."

Steph's hand cut the air again. Kit was grinning, but it was an indulgent, baffled, dim smile. Derek, an admirable man in many ways, smiles like that in my presence, and this is something I do not admire. "Call me Kit," my nephew said.

When I started school it took me several weeks before I learned to answer to my name. Allen. What was Allen? My name was an economical little gesture of the left hand—it doesn't translate. My sister, five years older, had similar difficulty but she never thought to warn me. Even when we spoke English together, our private language, so our parents wouldn't hear, we used our real names. In twenty-five years I've grown into Allen, I know who he is, but a persistent sense of unreality remains. Jeremy tells me that when he first came back from Mexico, after a year of being called Joto by people who spoke a different language, when people he'd known all his life whose language was his own called him Jeremy (or worse, Jerry), he felt like Alice on the other side of the looking glass, as though he were an interloper, a doppelgänger for Jeremy—whoever that might be. His ex-wife still calls him Joto when she's in a mood; so do I sometimes, although Joto's no-one I ever knew; and my name is one sign Jeremy's mastered.

"Uncle Allen, why didn't Toby come with you?"

Every time Kit asked, every time I visited, he'd get a cowed, whipped, pleading expression along the bowed line of his lip and the pink rims of his ears that made me want to slap him, to say unkind things to his mother, because there was nothing at all I could say to his father.

Steph rescued me, set a mug before me. "Son Kit," she said, "it's time for bed. You can ask your uncle all the questions you want tomorrow."

The computer game fell to the table with a click that made me worry it might break. "Mom!"

"It's nine-thirty." She was pouring coffee into my mug. "Your sister and brother are already asleep." She served herself. "It's time, Kit. Give Allen a hug and go to bed."

He was too old, really, to hug his uncle good-night, in his mother's presence at any rate—he sort of bumped into me, clumsily put his arm around my shoulders. I pushed my nose into his hair, for just a moment. He smelled a little sour, of child sweat and sleepiness. "Good night, Kit. Sweet dreams."

"I don't dream," he said with great dignity.

"Good night, Kit," his mother said, closing her hands around the top rung of the chair opposite mine. "Brush your teeth and go to bed." The white gold ring on her left hand gleamed between hard white knuckles.

Kit stumbled around the table to embrace his mother, and lurched out of the kitchen. His voice came around the door frame in a slurred but audible mumble: "Good night, Uncle Allen. 'Night, Mom."

Steph's grip on the chair loosened. Pulling it out from the table, she sat down, ran her fingers through her hair. "My children are pests. My husband is a jerk." She smiled a little, an uneven crooking and twisting of her lips. "Hello, Allen. How are you? Derek won't be back till late next week—you could have brought Toby. And Jeremy, of course. Not that you couldn't bring them if he was here. He'd never admit it, but Derek prefers my family to his. Even though his is as conventional as chopped beef and mine—isn't. How are you, Allen, really?"

"Toby had to go to school this morning. I've got a letter for Kit, I'll give it to him tomorrow." I raised the mug to my lips. An iridescent slick fluttered under my breath. It smelled of coffee. My sister never uses my real name anymore, except when we're with our parents, as seldom as possible. "Oh, and Jere sent a copy of his new book for Ricky and Jess."

"My children are *spoiled* pests. That's awfully kind of Jeremy. And of Toby especially. I would like to see them again. Soon."

I sipped coffee. In the three years since moving back East I'd come down to visit her at least every six months. After the first time it was clear Jeremy and Toby weren't welcome, our version of the nuclear family too close to the real thing for Derek's peace of mind, a precedent he didn't want his children exposed to. I suppose it might have been different if Jeremy didn't have custody, if Toby spent most of the year with his mother, or if Toby weren't such a good example. Derek didn't seem to have much trouble, after all, no more than any basically liberal heterosexual man, with the idea that a gay man, that Jeremy, should have a child; and if his brother-in-law must be gay, Derek seemed to say, at least I wasn't obtrusive about it, at least I wasn't radical, anarchic, promiscuous like the ones he saw on TV. And Jeremy and I had been together almost as long as he and Steph, a living monument to stability—good Lord, we'd bought a house together. Even so, I must be careful of my hands around my sister, who understands when I speak to myself. Especially on this visit: I hadn't seen Derek since making the phone call that placed me in a new category. "Did I tell you I'd started smoking again?" I asked her, holding the mug near my lips.

"Oh, Allen, no."

"It only lasted a week," I said. "It didn't help. The coffee's very good. How's Derek? He's traveling?"

"He's traveling a lot." Steph twirled a strand of hair around her forefinger. "It's a pain. But he's piling up mileage. We're thinking about England this summer. Just the two of us."

I put my cup down on the table. "What about the kids?"

My sister stared at her cup, at my cup, at my hands. My hands did not move, held silence as tensely as my throat. "Derek—" she began, "Derek made me promise to give you white sheets and towels so I can bleach them after you leave. Every dish or utensil you use goes into the dishwasher on the sterile cycle. I shouldn't have let any of the kids touch you. I'm sorry, Allen. They'll stay with their grandparents."

"Not my parents."

"No. It's not possible. They can't talk to each other. Mother can barely handle a half-hour visit when I'm along to translate."

"Your husband is a jerk—"

"He's scared, Allen." Her eyes had narrowed, not in concentration but as if the muscles of her eyelids had lost their elasticity and gone slack.

"Your husband is a jerk and his wife's family is too interesting to be believed. I'm surprised he had the courage to marry you."

"He knew about my family."

"I know that." When people around you regard you as suspiciously as a tainted shellfish, I quickly discovered, when you must put more effort into reassuring them than you can spare for yourself, it is very difficult to concentrate on being well. Selfishness, the maintenance of self, is paramount. Family is a desperate luxury. "I'm very tired, Steph. I need to go to bed." I am more aware than most people, I think, of the tones of my own voice, for obvious reasons, and I heard a tenuous childish whine that I knew would alert Steph. We seemed to be separate persons, my sister and I, with scarcely anything between us but old affection, not even loyalty, yet I could depend on her to ask gentle searching questions about my health, in general and at this specific instant, to excuse my crankiness and to give me a big hug that would make it all better. The responsibility for being her little brother was more than I could bear. "Thanks for the coffee, Steph." I stood up. "Good night." She wanted to hear the answers to her unspoken questions less than I wanted to tell her.

Steph followed me upstairs, up the wide, ostentatiously curved staircase with its polished banister and plush runner. The second door down the hall stood open, lit with the glow of a night-light. I leaned against the door frame. "Okay?" I asked.

In the dimness Steph looked like our mother, a resemblance I had not noticed before, the flesh around her eyes and along her jaw drawn but somehow puffy, the eyes themselves heated. She stepped toward me, put her hand on the jamb. When her ring hit the light I stared at it, mesmerized. The ring that Jeremy gave me, that hangs on a chain against my chest because I can't wear it on my hand, is gold as well, yellow gold, and old, its band worn thin, and supports a thin plaque of polished black onyx. When he found it in a San Francisco junk store the filigree monogram fastened to the stone was bent and broken; he had a jeweler replace it with the initials of our first names, and presented it to me the night I moved into his flat. I didn't want to remind Steph that Toby lives with me. There are advantages one shouldn't take. My weight settled and the door moved in a bit further. "Okay," she said.

The night-light was set low in the wall opposite the bed. Its light glinted on a train of Matchbox cars arrayed on the windowsill, on a fantastic spired edifice built of some kind of plastic construction toy, super Lego, atop the dresser. The room was larger than the one Steph and I shared through most of our childhood, larger than Toby's room in our small old house four hundred miles away. But Kit's bed was the same size as Toby's, narrow, framed in varnished pine.

At first as I approached I thought he looked like Toby, his back turned toward me, the wings of his shoulder blades caught in the creased fabric of pajamas, but Toby, veering into adolescence, was all reach and grasp, tendon and bone strung together by elastic wires that might let loose at any moment, even asleep. Kit was solid, a substantial little boy, his head settled securely between his shoulders and into the pillow. His fine pale skin glowed where light hit the cheek, his hair, already snarled into elf-locks, gleamed india-ink black across his brow. I bent over him, thinking there was no reason in this world why I should feel for him as much as I did, and saw that the cat lay on the pillow by him, nose to nose so that they breathed each other's air. Curled up like a snail in its shell, Providence was smaller than Kit's head, a sleek glossy muscular coil whose wedge-shaped head stirred and, with a motion as swift as a snake's strike, lifted. She yawned, displaying long wet canines, and looked into my eyes for a moment before shrugging her entire body back into sleep. I cupped my hand over Kit's ear, close enough that he might have felt the warmth of my palm if not its flesh. "Who's sucking whose breath?" I asked, and turned, and went away.

Meanwhile

IN THE EMPTY living room the phone rang, once, twice, three times. The bell cut off on the fourth ring and the answering machine started talking, "I'm sorry, we can't come to the phone right now. Please wait for the tone and leave a message for Toby, Allen, or Jeremy. Thanks for calling."

"Where in hell are you, Joto? Don't tell me you were dim enough to go to the airport without confirming the flight first. It's one-thirty and we're stuck in Chicago, there's a blizzard on or something. Give me an earthquake any day. I'm sorry, I know you're having a tough time. They say *for sure* we'll get off the ground tomorrow. Meanwhile they stuck us in this ridiculous Sheraton or whatever it is. You'll like this story, boyface, so will Allen: The fellow at the desk gave us a real look when I said we wanted one room with a double bed so I said, Sweetheart, when you go to Key West in the spring to get away from this wretched weather they give you and your boyfriend a double bed, don't they? Dykes like to snuggle too. He got very friendly all of a sudden. Anyway, as Candace says, we're saving the airline some money.

"Damn. This is so sad, Jeremy. I'll call again later."

and then as if I kept a journal as if my dreams were evidence as if I were an angel
of the lord omniscient and removed

JEREMY STARED BLINDLY at the computer screen, at the frozen record
of a conversation he couldn't have borne to reread, let alone to repeat.

>Allen is in the hospital. It's pneumonia. It's bad.<

And then, turning away, he imagined my father, so many hundreds of miles distant, himself turning away from the same series of
messages, emotionless black type on the glowing white-blue screen.

>Will he live?<

An inexpert typist, Jeremy had entered his side of the colloquy
clumsily, letter by letter, but Janos's responses came fast, chasing after
the cursor as it raced from one side of the screen to the other like the
shuttle of a power loom. Jeremy wasn't sure whether this was because
of Janos's skill, his rapid hands, or the way messages were downloaded
from the BBS in yet another city. He was wary of computers, didn't understand them, didn't wish to understand them. He had left a message
for my father on the board within an hour of being sent home from
the hospital, bereft. (The doctor said, "You're not helping anyone by
being here. Go home, Jeremy. Try to get some rest. Eat something.")
Afraid of the machine, afraid of his own terror and of my father's reaction to an unexpected message, he had simply asked Janos to get on
the board at ten o'clock, three hours later, and then waited. Waiting,
he called Jake Touro to check on Toby; called the hospital again; called
Ruth—got the machine. Called my sister. A small mercy, my brother-
in-law wasn't home—at least, didn't answer the phone. Though Derek
was never impolite, would have made the appropriate noises, uncomfortable, before passing the phone to his wife. Stephanie would hear
no argument; without being invited said she was coming to Providence
right away, as soon as she could get a flight, Allen needed his family
now. Her voice rising, nearly a scream.

>You know we'll come if you think we should.<

Jeremy pictured my father turning away from the computer,
which stood in a corner of the living room before a blank wall. Above

it hung a formal, posed portrait of me, acrylic on canvas. Jeremy had given it to my parents on the occasion of their thirty-fifth wedding anniversary, only the year before, when it seemed that nothing could ever go wrong. Beside it, the printer chattered away unheard, making hard copy for the files, while my father turned to my mother. Jeremy could see it perfectly, a tableau vivant, the elderly couple in their silent house, but though he could set the scene in motion, too, he could not read the language of their hands.

Angry, he shut down the other computer, in our study, turned it off. Across the room, another blank screen stared at him: the television. Whether or not he could talk to them, he'd rather have my parents than my sister. He was scared of my mother (really), but he couldn't conceive of her becoming maudlin. Enraged, perhaps, hysterical, but never maudlin. And somehow he imagined my father as always perfectly calm, composed, unconditionally loving—except when playing with Toby, something that would be even more a gift. He should have asked Jake to bring Toby home.

Leaving the study, he closed the door quietly. Wandering, he went into the bedroom, but the empty, unmade bed was too horrible to contemplate, set up against the mind's-eye sight of a hospital bed, occupied. A nurse would look in from hour to hour, all the frightening machines would be watching, ready to give the alarm, but I needed someone at my side, holding my hand. He shouldn't have allowed the doctor to send him away. I'd be lonely.

Marit says, We must go to him, and Janos points out that not only can't Jeremy talk to them, but the doctor can't and I, in my condition, can't either. And if I could, it would be a debilitating strain.

He's our son! He's dying!

No, he's not. Hopeful, making it a statement of fact, Janos repeats the assurance: He's not dying. He's very ill but he's not dying. Jeremy will keep us posted, he promised.

He needs his family near him! (But no, it was Stephanie who said that, in just that aggrieved, petulant tone, hysterical, wielding her relationship to me as if it were a knife—bleeding liberally all over Jeremy without seeing how much she wounded him, how he was hemorrhaging.)

Who's his family now, Marit? my father asks. Who can help him?

Weeping with gratitude, Jeremy felt the car keys digging their teeth into his palm. He ran down the back stairs into the snow, slamming the door behind him. Sitting behind the wheel of his sporty little car, waiting while the engine warmed up, he wiped his eyes. Let that bastard of a reasonable, realistic, unfeeling doctor just try to keep him away from me.

HE WOKE WITH a pair of narrow, flannel-covered shoulders wedged against his chest, a fragile rib cage under his arm, and his mouth full of Toby's hair. Toby doesn't have nightmares. This is a given. Even as a baby he slept through most of the night without a whimper—confounding all the books and authorities his father and mother had consulted. In his own bed, set against the wall, Toby sleeps with his back to the room, one arm thrust under the pillow and his cheek, mouth open, and, more often than not, a thread of spittle dangling from his lip. (He'd be mortified if I ever told him this detail.) "Toby," Jeremy said, "what are you doing in my bed?"

Toby never wakes up on the first try, stubborn as any child. I sometimes think he's happier unconscious; I sometimes don't blame but envy him. Jeremy sat up against the headboard, waiting. Tousled and rumpled, he knuckled his eyes, dug all ten fingers into his hair, dragging it forward over the brow and then pushing it back behind his ears until it caught in a clump at the nape. He scratched at his shoulder. He was wearing one of my old t-shirts from the glory days when I liked to wear my politics on my chest: it was purple, faded, and with a hole in the shoulder seam that his finger found and took advantage of. The slogan screened in white print was still legible: *So Many Men So Little Time*. The afternoon a lifetime ago that I started unpacking my clothes into the bureau in Jeremy's bedroom, he said, "I used to have all the same shirts—I got rid of them when Toby was born, they seemed inappropriate." Then he held one of mine up against his chest and asked why a man who looked small in a small t-shirt bought extra-large.

Toby grumbled to himself and pulled a pillow over his head. Cold air raised bumps on Jeremy's arms but there were no blemishes on the skin, and when he checked the glands in neck and armpits they were not swollen. It was six-thirty. He'd awakened in time to get me up for work, despite not setting the alarm, despite its being school vacation so Toby could sleep in and bathroom shifts need not be argued.

Despite my not being there. He had forgotten to ask Toby about the night before, how he'd got on at Jake's. He had forgotten, yesterday, to call Jake and Melissa to thank them for taking Toby in. Closing his eyes for a moment, Jeremy lifted his chin and pressed the back of his skull against the headboard.

Toby was mumbling to himself in anticipation of waking. Jeremy stroked his son's shoulder gently, then pushed his own legs out from under the sheet and the comforter. The wood floor was cold in the bedroom and living room, the tile in the bathroom colder. It had snowed during the night, again. Winter was early. The window over the toilet wore a lace border of frost and the garden below lay smothered under a white quilt in dawning half-light. Pruned canes of dormant rosebushes stuck through humped snow, fingers clawing for air. Finished pissing, Jeremy washed his face and hands with water hot enough to break ice. The bathrooms would need to be cleaned before everyone arrived, the convertible bed in the study converted, the sheets in the guest room changed. Ruth and Candace upstairs, Stephanie in the study—where would Kit sleep? In our exclusively masculine household we lived in the open, never shut doors: remind Toby. Jeremy brushed his hair, combed his beard, noting that the right temple showed more white than the left, then tucked the hem of the t-shirt into his shorts. Remind Toby not to wander about the house in his underwear. Remind himself. Looking out the window again he noted that Ray's car stood in the back drive, behind Lena's, both of them frosted like wedding cakes. Toby could shovel everyone out, if he ever woke up.

In the living room, Jeremy turned up the thermostat. He pulled the drapes open. He heard a little froggy voice call, "Allen? Dad?" Toby didn't sound awake yet.

Nor was he, when Jeremy crouched beside the bed and gripped his son's hand. But then Toby opened eyes that showed his startlement through a haze and Jeremy said again, "What are you doing in my bed, Toby?"

"Allen?" Toby blinked and saw his father and looked away. "I was lonely, Dad," he muttered, tactful and kind and protective.

but who is breathing for me who beats my heart who pumps my blood

THE BACK DOOR slammed, rattling the pictures on the hall wall. How
often we have asked Toby not to slam the door. "Dad! I'm done." His
snow boots coming off, thumping on the mat by the door. "What time
is it?" Toby won't wear a watch. "When are we leaving? I need to take
a shower first." Jacket slung over his arm, Toby came into the living
room. "Dad?" The cuffs of Toby's blue jeans rode two inches above his
ankles, showing off the crumpled tops of his bulky orange socks, less
out of a sense for adolescent fashion statements than because he was
growing too fast to be kept in clothes. Only a few months before, when
I took him to the malls to fit him out for the new school year, when
I stood before the rack of boys' underwear in J. C. Penney, he said,
"Allen, no-one wears white Jockeys anymore." "You want colors?" I
asked, bemused. "I don't think they make them in decent colors for
boys." "No, Allen, boxer shorts." I stared at him. He'd just started shaving, didn't really need to because his mustache was still fine as the hair
on a baby's head, but it had darkened, that and his downy sideburns,
and, he said, he didn't want to look like Michael Jackson. I remembered two things: that when I was in prep school the boys who seemed
to be part of the system wore boxers; and I recalled how surprised I
was the first time I watched Jeremy undress because, in my experience,
in the late seventies, men either made a fetish of white Jockey shorts,
emblem and essence of youthful sexuality, or wore tight, colorful, fly-
less bikini briefs as if a limber swimmer's body, even shrouded in a
business suit, demanded underpants that served as a mnemonic for
Speedo Knitting Mills Pty, Ltd, and the beaches of Australia or Fire
Island. "Okay," I said, but boys' boxer shorts were all polyester-cotton
blends so we went to the men's department and finally to a classier
department store where I picked up some flashy shorts for Jeremy, too.

"Dad?" He hung the scarlet jacket on the rack by the front door.
An edge of its lining swung out, hunter green. Gloves protruded from
its pockets like the crushed fingers of someone's hands. Toby un-
wound the muffler from his neck and draped it over the collar of my

winter overcoat, black and green buffalo checks against mustard
brown tweed. Scratching his chest, he looked in the bedroom door:
no-one home. "Where are you, Dad?" His t-shirt was a flat French
blue. He pulled it up in front and scratched his side. Long arms tight
around his chest, long and slender, pale and as lacking in muscle or
flesh as a gibbon's, elbows protruding, he did a little sock-footed shuffle, turning in a circle. "Where is he? Stupid time for a game of hide-
and-seek." Feet still, he shuddered, lifting his elbows so that the
shoulder blades lifted the fabric of his shirt, then stamped, hard
enough that Herodias, downstairs, barked. "*Dad!*" As if shocked by
his own voice, he covered his ears with his hands and took two steps
toward the hall. "Jeremy David Kent," he called quietly, then ran into
the corridor, grabbed the baluster and vaulted up the stairs to
the third floor. "Daddy?" he said outside the door, pushed it open.

He went to his father's drawing table under the skylight. A sheet
of watercolor paper was taped to the surface, an even, pale, chalk blue
wash brushed over it, obscuring the pencil strokes beneath. Removing
his glasses, Toby bent low over it. The paint smelled fresh, the clean
watery scent of much-diluted acrylic; he touched it lightly with one
fingertip—still damp. The penciling was faint but deft, assured, fast,
but Toby couldn't make the drawing out, not with his glasses off or on.
Straightening up, he looked around at the carefully arranged clutter of
Jeremy's studio. Hadn't his father said something about cleaning the
guest room? The door beyond the kitchen alcove was closed.

Toby turned the knob and pushed the door inward. The first he
saw was the light, a harsh white light from the two windows under the
tilted eaves, reflecting sun off a plane of thick snow on the flat roof
outside, bleaching the peaked ceiling. The electric broom lay on the
floor next to a pile of sheets. The bed under the window was covered
by its blue and white patchwork quilt. His father lay on the quilt in his
purple t-shirt and pink shorts, fast asleep. "Dad?" quietly, approaching. "Dad?"

Toby stood over his father, gazed down at him. Jeremy lay
sprawled on his back, one arm bent and the hand resting lightly on his
sternum, the other arm cast off to the side, but his hips were turned in
profile, the legs loosely bent, and his head turned into the quilt-cov-
ered pillow—an Egyptian hieroglyph for sleep except that no ancient
Egyptian would have a neatly clipped beard compromised by stubble

on cheeks and neck, no Egyptian's shoulder-length hair would straggle into his mouth. "Dad?" hardly a breath, "you okay?" Jeremy slept on. Toby brushed his father's hair back from the cheek, over the ear, and ran his knuckle along the jaw, furrowing the coarse beard, but Jeremy didn't wake. "I'm going to take a shower," Toby murmured, "I'll be downstairs. Sleep well," he said, pressed his finger to his lips and touched his father's brow, "sleep well, Daddy." Turning to leave, Toby pulled his shirt over his head in one movement, closed the door behind him.

LENA'S DOORBELL RANG and Herodias barked. Who could it be on a day like today? Lena saved her document—second draft of part one of the dissertation—and started toward the door as the bell rang again. She kept forgetting to ask Jeremy if it couldn't be changed for a chime that sounded less like an angel of the apocalypse. Salome pounced on Lena's foot; Lena pushed her away. Through the glass of the front door she saw a dark figure—oh, he was wearing a black watch cap, pulled low, and a big black jacket with the collar turned up. He lifted up a long, narrow white box so she could see it.

"I'm sorry," the boy said when she opened the door, "no-one answered on the second floor. Can you accept these for—" he glanced at the slip of paper in his other hand—"for Mr. Jeremy Kent?" A florist's van was parked at the sidewalk.

"Sure," Lena said, and signed the claim list, took the box from his arm. It was light. "He's my landlord."

"Thanks a lot," he said. "Rotten day, isn't it?"

"Yeah. I wouldn't want to be out driving in it."

"It's my job." He shrugged. "Thanks again."

Lena carried the box into her living room. Herodias rubbed against her shin when she sat down. She wouldn't open the envelope taped to the box, but she could look inside—a dozen long-stemmed white roses nestled in green tissue paper. "Jesus, I could eat for a month on this."

"Wuzzat?"

Lena looked up. Ray, naked and disreputable, stood in the bedroom doorway scratching his belly.

"Oh, go back to bed. Someone's sending Jeremy roses."

Ray yawned. "The man works fast. Boyfriend's only in the hospital two days and he's already screwing around."

Lena settled the lid carefully onto the box. "Ray," she said, "Allen and Jeremy are my friends."

"Christ, Linnie," yawning, stretching, "it was a joke."

"I don't find it humorous. It wouldn't be funny at the best of times. Now—"

"Sorry, Linnie." He came to her, squatted down, rested his head against her knee as though he were a dog as big as Herodias. "I'm sorry. Look, I'm upset about Allen too, okay? He's a fine guy."

"They're not *boyfriends*." She pushed him away. "They're more married than my parents. Go back to bed."

(FOR THE RECORD, Eamon had wired an identical dozen white roses to me in the hospital.)

hold the pencil as if I knew how in my right hand as if it knew how as if it were
somebody's hand as though I knew what to do with it and could form letters
plot out points on the graph draw a picture a portrait whose portrait whose face
whose face can tell me whose hand hold mine as if it were a pencil in the hand
of an artist illustrating someone's story

HIS FATHER WAS upstairs, working, or so he said. Greg had called earlier to ask if Toby wanted to go to a movie. Toby hadn't wanted to go
to a movie. His dad's lover was in the hospital, maybe dying, no, he
didn't want to go to a movie. "Mr. Pasztory?" said Greg. "Gee, I'm
sorry." Toby fiddled a new disc out of its case and inserted it in the
machine. The first shipment from the music club had arrived that afternoon, worst timing in the world, eight new CDs for a dollar. Turned
up the volume, closed the bedroom door, switched off all the lamps
but the one in the walk-in closet, which, with the door ajar, made the
room glow dimly, a room in another country, on another planet, a
place where nothing ever happened.

The shades were up on both windows. Warmth came out of the
radiator, as pervasive as the orchestral accompaniment to a piano
concerto, desiccating the air so that you could hardly breathe. After
dinner every night I would go through the house with a watering can,
topping up the shallow bowls of spiced water atop each radiator, but
Toby couldn't be expected to remember and the bowl on his own
radiator was dry. He was still wearing a sweater but suddenly felt hot
and stripped it off, threw it on the bed, then the shirt underneath.
After a moment he folded the sweater and took it into the closet,
placed it neatly on the shelf. He sniffed under the arms of the blue
shirt, decided it would do for another wearing, and hung it up.

Turning to leave the closet, he saw himself in the mirror inside
the door, and pulled off his trousers, draped them over a hanger. His
undershorts were white with a pattern of black and white Holstein
cows, each the size of the last joint of his thumb. Their tiny tongues
were red. One of the cows, on his right leg, was positioned so that it
seemed to be lapping at a faint yellow stain. His father ironed his own
boxers after every washing, a silly habit Toby could remember as far
back as he could remember anything, but Toby's laundry was his own
affair. A strikingly neat boy he is, but tidiness only extends so far,
might hide a seething, incomprehensible mess. Open, his underwear

drawer revealed that he didn't even fold his shorts, only smashed them in in a mush with unpartnered socks. He pulled out a pair ornamented with large slices of watermelon on a dark green ground, wondered for a moment why people hid these neat patterns under their clothes and why I got such a kick out of buying amusing boxer shorts for him (those he chose for himself had more dignity, stripes or tartans), and stuffed the watermelons back in the drawer, stuffed the cows into the laundry hamper beside the bureau.

Naked, he felt cold, but never mind. He pushed the sash of the closet window up, unfastened the catches of the storm window and pushed it up too. The breeze that rushed in was clear and clean and damp, and he felt his skin pebble all over, instantaneously, felt his scrotum contract, and leaned out. Snow covered the lawn below; the black branches of the Norway maple in the corner were edged with phosphorescent white; windows in the houses behind and to the side gleamed yellow or flickeringly blue where unconcerned people were watching television. Overhead there were more stars than anyone could number, fiery in a sky closer to black than blue. The sky was more than he could handle so he stared at the snow and uttered a small noise. Cold air burned in his nostrils, lacerated his lungs. He made a larger noise, then inhaled sharply and yelled. The cry tailed up on the last of his breath, going higher than he thought possible now that his voice seemed to have settled on a permanent register. Coughing, he pulled down the windows, closed the catch, drew the shade. Shivering, he came out of the closet and, after a moment's indecision, pulled back the comforter and climbed into bed.

Three days before he'd asked an acquaintance of his, a student at the university, to buy him a copy of *Playboy* at Store 24, but then he came home from his aimless afternoon to find his father and me gone and Mr. and Mrs. Touro waiting for him in the living room. He hadn't wanted to cry in front of them, people he hardly knew, but of course he cried, and after he'd packed his knapsack for overnight, on the way to the Touros' car, he pushed the paper bag with the magazine in it into the garbage, and cried again in the car. Two of the Touro kids were too young to talk to, the other three too old, he hated them, and although he liked Mr. Touro well enough he couldn't talk to him either. *Playgirl* would have been different. He and Allen could have had a laugh over *Playgirl.* Couldn't they.

Not likely.

And then last night, back in his own bed, for a moment he forgot, and remembered and regretted discarding the magazine, but then he fell asleep. He hadn't been able to sleep on the sofa in the Touros' den the night before. Waking suddenly after midnight in his own room he was overcome by a wave of shuddering cold even though he was too warm in flannel pajamas under a down quilt. Getting out of bed, he went through the kitchen, down the hall, through the living room to the open door of Jeremy's bedroom—my bedroom, ours. If he pushed the door quietly enough, I would be lying on the bed just inside the door, next to his father, and neither of us would wake.

Toby's father, the largest figure in his life, had looked small alone in the bed. They didn't make beds long enough for Jeremy's height but still he looked small. Experimentally, Toby said, "Dad? Dad, I woke up and I was scared." Dad didn't wake, didn't stir. "Dad, I'm scared about Allen." Long ago, he remembered, when he was a kid, if he wasn't feeling well Jeremy and I would let him sleep with us. He couldn't recall when or why this had stopped. Was it before we moved to Providence? Once, Jeremy in New York or Boston on business, Toby complained of feeling headachy and asked if he could sleep with me, but I told him I didn't think it was a good idea. After he'd thought about it he agreed. But that was a different occasion.

The comforter had accumulated enough of his body heat that he felt warm now, and had stopped shivering. Turning on the light by the bed, he looked at the pile of books on the bedside table. Two novels, a biography, a history—he'd been going to read a lot of stuff for spring classes before school started. The earpieces of his glasses were cold and uncomfortable so he took them off and as he did so realized that the music from the stereo had stopped—how long ago? More than half blind, he got out of bed, fumbled another new CD out of its box, didn't matter which one, all he wanted was noise.

Through the thumping bass and swooping strings Toby recognized the selection he'd chosen because he thought his father and I might get a kick out of it: disco classics of the seventies. A woman with a large voice started to sing. Crouching before the stereo, he listened. Turned up the volume. He didn't care, damn it, didn't care at all if he disturbed Lena and Ray downstairs. He turned it up some more, and stood. The woman with the big voice kept on singing, something about how there was always another man around the corner. He'd read several novels about New York or San Francisco in the seventies, and in all of them men partied all night to music like this, danced forever, took wild drugs, drank vodka tonics, made love to beautiful boys they'd never seen before, never would again, but all of that was over. In the bottom of his underwear drawer was a little plastic bag of pot and a twist of paper wrapped around two tabs of Ecstasy, but that was over too. Naked and weeping, Toby began to dance.

MASKING TAPE SECURED paper to drawing board, framed its implac-
able whiteness. It ought to be easy enough to start. He had a sheaf of
sketches to work from, had read the text three times. He knew the scene
he wanted—had it visualized in such detail he could have touched it:
the boy's windblown hair, the great-uncle's scored and twisted hand,
the blood black rose it held. But he couldn't touch it—it couldn't touch
him, or it touched too closely. What was the point? What was the point
of another jacket painting for another young-adult fantasy novel to add
to the five-foot shelf? He got down from his stool. Silence disturbed
the house. He poured a cup of coffee, then held the cup in both hands
and watched its single creamy brown eye wink.

Switching the radio on, he scanned the channels for something he
could bear to listen to, then turned it off. He had a deadline. Eamon
would understand—Eamon had sent roses—but still he had a deadline. Returning to the drawing table, he took up the pencil again. He
had figured the boy as Toby, as always, sorcerer's apprentice as always,
a little clumsy, ready to be surprised, ready to marvel.

In the story the boy, Pete, a city child, an orphan, discovers that
the old man who has raised him, whom he has always thought to be
his dead mother's uncle, is someone quite different while still being
Pete's great-uncle Gamaliel who, Pete learns while going through
newspaper microfilms in the library, researching a school project, died
the very day Pete was born, fourteen years before. He was not meant to
discover this yet, Uncle Gamaliel tells him, Uncle Gamaliel a frail,
white-haired old man walking through the park who, from one glance
to the next, seems to grow straighter, stronger. Pete would have been
told on his eighteenth birthday, when he was ready to work with the
knowledge, to accept his destiny, his quest. For, Pete, there is another
world, edgewise to this one where we live, and in that world the
Shadow, rising, has exiled the princely family. My uncle, Gamaliel says,
was king; I was the prince, but a prince in exile, a prince without a
country, and still the Shadow sought us, it poisoned my sister, your

grandmother, and at last it found me. But your mother, when she learned that the Shadow had discovered her, called me back from the land of the dead to nurture the new prince. The story, inevitably, was the first volume of a trilogy.

Great-Uncle Gamaliel, in the sketches, resembled my father Janos Kossuth Pasztory, another exile, from the country of his ancestry and from his own world, my father aged by many years and then by magic resurrected with the strength of young manhood—still white-haired, still wrinkled, still with the massive, bony hands of old age, but an old man who moved with the vigor and grace of a young prince. The feral-eyed boy who took form under the pencil, as if graphite simply revealed what was already implicit in the paper's grain, a small, thin boy with pointed chin and high cheekbones, the boy whose coarse black hair falls into intent, hazel eyes, the boy, the haunted, destined prince, the boy has my face.

RUTH'S PLANE, SCHEDULED to arrive half an hour before Steph's, was stuck at O'Hare. Ruth would have been grimly patient, her ex-husband supposed, while the delay still seemed temporary, although she might have snapped at her companion when Candace returned from the newsstand with a copy of *Vogue*. When the young woman at the desk announced that the flight was postponed indefinitely due to weather conditions and the airline would put the incommoded passengers up in a hotel for the night, she would have gone up to the desk and said, "My husband is in the hospital in Providence," not above lying, not that it would get her anywhere. My husband, Jeremy said to himself, is in the hospital.

Soon enough, three days, four days, he found himself settling into a routine despite himself, two or three hours in the studio in the morning, four or five hours in the afternoon at the hospital. It was December, cold and ugly, there were too many people in his house. When he and Toby went to pick Stephanie up at the airport, day four, a woman and a boy came through the gate, she slender, well-dressed, pale, he looking so much a younger version of his uncle that Jeremy bit his tongue. "Kit!" said Toby.

Jeremy approached my sister wondering if he should offer to embrace her. "Stephanie. I won't ask about your flight. It's good of you to come."

She stared at him. "He's my brother."

Thinking: We can't talk to each other, but Allen's father at least knows the language, Jeremy stifled his grimace. Why is it this relative who comes running? "Would you like me to take your bag?" he asked. "Is there more luggage coming?" He's *my* husband, he wanted to say, as it were. He's *Toby*'s father. Who are you? Who, he amended, who *t he fuck* are you.

Luckily Candace and Ruth kept her off his hands most of the time, a terrible, conventional woman whose helpless love for her brother enforced a retreat into suburban conventionality, the image of her husband's wife, her children's mother, so that she wouldn't return to the hospital after the first visit. "He's so sick, he's going to die, there's nothing I can do, I can't—" And, guilty, she bought things for the patient, useless reminders of his illness if I'd been lucid enough to recognize them, potted flowers in the dead of winter, fancy boxes of candy I wasn't allowed to eat if I'd wanted to, new pajamas, an ugly terry cloth robe, a teddy bear of all things, and guiltily cooked bland, nourishing meals for the household, heavy four-course dinners no-one wanted: why didn't she just go home. Surely her own family needed her, more than mine did. But keeping Kit occupied kept Toby occupied, allowed Jeremy's son the occasional moment, like grace, of

cheer. He would turn thirteen in a matter of days, what kind of cele-
bration could anyone muster, but Ruth and Candace and Jeremy, in
shifts, in hidden conspiracy, made their preparations.

Jeremy pulled his car in behind mine. A drift of snow crested
across the forest green trunk of my Volvo and broke on the rear window. He should give it a run, before it forgot why it existed. They'd
been using his car the whole time, or Ruth's rental, a wagon. He didn't
like driving my car. It didn't sort with his image either of himself or
of me. A four-door sedan, it was a year old when I bought it, and entirely appropriate to the new position and the new city that required
my owning a car. He liked it when I drove him. The heater always
worked, cushioned us against the cold jabs and spikes of the world
outside. Warm leather upholstery cradled him more safely than would
my arms (he glared at the vehicle, eyes burning), if I were there to hold
him—the passenger seat was as comfortable as an easy chair before a
roaring hearth, so long as someone else was driving.

Jeremy is a safe driver only because he hates to drive. The fingers
of his left hand clutched the steering wheel as tightly as if his glove
were a frozen metal gauntlet. Jeremy hates to drive. He held out for six
months after we moved here before buying a car. The extremes of
climate defeated him, so unlike northern California; a public transit
system erratic and unwise; the ignominy of having to ask me to chauf-
feur him to the supermarket or the train station or the malls. Even
then, defiant, he bought an impractical, temperamental machine: a
thirty-year-old rag-top Triumph two-seater—as if to insist, before
the fact, he didn't need it. (Toby loves the Triumph, lives for the day he
can drive it.) The door stuck when he tried to open it. The isinglass
sidescreen rattled, almost came unseated. It was no colder outside
than in the car. Clumsily, hating the finicky necessity of it, he ran his
fingers along the overhanging flap of the top, ensuring its seal with
the sidescreen, before he locked the door, and fetched the parcels from
the trunk.

If we hadn't moved—if I hadn't found a job that offered me the
excuse to leave San Francisco, if Jeremy hadn't agreed to uproot
Toby and come with me, we wouldn't have had to buy our cars. If we
hadn't moved, snow and ice would be something we went out of our
way to see. He pushed gloved hands into his pockets, started toward
the back door. Snow creaked under his boots. Why hadn't Toby shov-

eled the driveway yet? If we hadn't moved he could have continued to do all his business by phone and mail, wouldn't need to drive to Boston or New York to talk to his publishers, wouldn't have to shrug Toby off onto friends' families, wouldn't leave his own family so dangerously far behind.

Opening the gate to the back garden, he headed toward the back door of a house with too many people in it. Too many people, and none of them welcome, not even, actually, his own son. (Jeremy was finding it occasionally difficult not to become annoyed with Toby, when the boy posed some reasonable but irrelevant puzzle, or when, busy with Kit, he forgot to shovel the drive.) If we hadn't moved, Jeremy said to himself, if we hadn't moved, Allen . . . would still have gotten sick.

THEY PUT ON heavy sweaters, coats, mufflers, gloves. At the front door they pushed their feet into boots. Toby checked for his keys, opened the door. Halfway down the stairs they were met by Lena's cats. "Hello, Judith," said Toby. "Hi there, Salome," Kit said, kneeling to pet them. "You know, I miss Providence a little."

"You're in Providence."

"My cat, stupid."

Outside, the door closed and locked behind them, Kit pulled his cap down over his ears and said, "It's cold."

"It's winter. Cold and winter go together." Toby snorted. "Come on."

If the sidewalks hadn't been shoveled it would have been easier. An icy crust made walking treacherous so Kit said nothing, watching his own feet and holding his hands out for balance, followed Toby down the block, around the corner at the church. Toby walked slowly, his shoulders hunched and his hands in his pockets. The air felt nearly solid with a damp chill. "Where are we going?"

"I told you, it's not far." Quickly, Toby bent to the heaped dike of snow along the curb, scooped a handful into a ball and tossed it at Kit. "Just to the park, okay?" The snowball missed Kit by a mile—striking the pavement, it shattered with a thump.

"What's wrong with you, Toby? Are you mad at me?"

"Don't be stupid." He waited for the smaller boy to catch up and they walked on together. "What's with your mom, she's acting real weird."

"Is she? I don't know." Kit stared up into Toby's face, wondering whether he'd ever be as tall. He couldn't really remember a time before he knew Toby although it was recent enough—before he had known Toby and admired him and wanted to be like him although Toby was someone he hardly knew, certainly less than any of his school buddies back home. Toby was only two years older (a year and nine months, if he worked it out right—only a year right now if you looked at it one way because he was already eleven and Toby hadn't turned thirteen yet) but it seemed much more. "I guess she's worried about Uncle Allen, maybe."

Toby's expression twisted and he looked away. "Aren't you?"

What amazed Kit the most, made him feel a hard knot of jealousy and despair, was that Toby and his father were friends. Toby and Uncle Allen were friends, too, he remembered, when he remembered the time they came to Annapolis for a visit (he couldn't allow himself to connect the person in the hospital with his uncle, the person with tubes coming out of his nose whose breathing was so loud, who looked a hundred years old, the person who said, "Hi, Kit," in a little croaking voice but didn't seem to see him; his mother hadn't let him come nearer to me than the foot of the bed) or the time Jeremy and I rented a place at the beach for a month and persuaded Steph and Derek to send Kit up.

But everything was different now, no-one's face looked the same. "Yes," he said. Kit knew all his mother's smiles, the whole variety of them, except the one she'd worn almost continuously since telling him I was ill, did he want to go with her to Providence to help out? This smile pinched her eyes and trembled at the corners of her mouth. "Mom," he had told her, "Toby and I are going out for a little while."

"Out?" The smile turned even more false. "Going to make snow-men in the backyard?"

"I thought we'd take a walk down to the park at India Point, Mrs. Sheridan."

"Oh, Toby, please don't call me that. You know my name. Is it far?"

Toby had turned away from her. "Just a few blocks." He scowled blackly. "We won't be long."

"Okay," said Kit's mother. "Sounds like fun. But bundle up before you go out." She had turned back to the onions on the chopping board. She had done nothing but cook and clean and go shopping since the second day. "Wear your cap, Kit."

"He's really sick, isn't he?" Kit ventured now. "But he'll get better soon, won't he?"

Toby didn't answer but kept walking, shuffling along the crust of ice and snow too fast for Kit to keep up. On either side of the street stood houses and other buildings but they all looked empty and there

were no cars driving by; you'd think everyone had gone away except
for the tire tracks on the street, you'd think the neighborhood had
been evacuated. Toby's bulky scarlet jacket was the only spot of real
color anywhere and the way it rode above his hips and swelled over
his shoulders made him look deformed, spliced together, the pillowy
torso of a fat man grafted onto the slender legs of a boy.

The next cross street formed a T-intersection. Rather than turning
left or right, Toby crossed the street and waited for Kit on the far sidewalk, then led him onto the narrow footbridge. Below, the highway
rushed past—here were cars, here were people, but all dashing away in
one direction or the other. Halfway across, Toby stooped for another
handful of snow. "If I throw this," he said, "it might hit someone's
windshield and he'd be so startled he'd lose control and skid all over
the place—would that be fun?"

"What's wrong with you, Toby?"

"The same thing that's wrong with your mom." He stared for a
moment at the snowball in his gloved hand, then threw it a few steps
ahead of him where it smashed on the pavement.

"Uncle Allen's going to get better, isn't he?"

"Quit asking me!"

"Why?"

Toby wheeled away, his arms flying like the vanes of a windmill,
until he fetched up against the railing of the footbridge and pressed
his face against the wire-link fence. "Because I asked you to." He
pushed his fingers through the links, grabbing, as though he meant
to climb it. "Because I don't know the answer." Whirling again to face
Kit, he crossed his arms over his chest and leaned back. "Because
I'm scared shitless, Kit, okay?"

Below, the cars rushed past going and coming, so fast they made
Kit giddy. Above, the sky was pale and clear and cold, a sheet of sil-
vered glass so high you couldn't see your reflection but you knew it
was there, somewhere, far overhead, so small you'd need a microscope.
He didn't need a microscope to see Toby's face or the tiny white reflections of his own in Toby's glasses.

I know you're there, I said, I wish you were here, I can't find my way around the bed without you, can't tell north from south without a landmark, without the reef of your spine to orient me. I need the coves and fjords and deep harbors your body impresses on the sheets of an ice-locked sea, need to make landfall. I want to scale the peak of your hip, to climb hand-to-hand the ribbed rock slope of your side, stretch flat out, gasping, fingers tingling, calves aching, on the upland meadows of your chest. How long can I continue wallowing in this surf of chill cambric? How long go on without human warmth? I will eat my own flesh.

Coals guttered and snapped and hissed on the brick hearth, like newborn kittens nestled in a soft fur of warm ash. Toby sprawled across the couch, breathing through his mouth with an occasional honk or snort—Jeremy's pragmatic son was reading *One Hundred Years of Solitude* and he had awakened that morning with a cold. Huddled in the other arm of the sofa, hunched in on himself more than he needed to be, being small and with Toby's legs leaving plenty of room, Kit was reading something else, a slender paperback.

Jeremy's son, who has a powerful sense of the fitness of things and would choose a more appropriate time for his ascension into grace than while hanging sheets out to dry, looked up, finally. The lenses of his glasses flamed; his hands, their bones as fragile as lances, fought little skirmishes with shadows on the page. Jeremy wanted to touch him. Jeremy wanted to tell him things he already knew. Jeremy wanted to tell him lies. "I'm going now, Toby," Jeremy said.

Startled, Kit shut his book and glanced up—at Toby, though, not Jeremy, of whom he was shy.

Jeremy smiled at my nephew, as far as he was able. "Kit's mom should be back soon. Will you two be okay?"

"Sure, I guess. Won't we, Kit? I wish I could come with you, Dad."

"You know why you can't."

"I know—" Toby closed his book and took off his glasses and blinked his small, pale eyes. "I hope—"

"Don't worry about it, kid, you wore your mask yesterday, the day before, we just don't want to take any chances."

"I hope you didn't catch it too. Will you give Allen a hug for me?"

"You know it. But I won't kiss him, just in case. You two stay warm, okay, stay by the fire. There's orange juice in the fridge, tuna salad if you get hungry. Kit, keep Toby out of trouble."

My nephew nodded solemnly, accepting the responsibility as if it meant something. "Will you tell my uncle," he ventured, "that I love him and I miss him?"

"I'll do that, Kit. Thanks." He took a step toward the boys on the couch.

"No hugs, Dad." Toby had put his glasses back on. "Just in case."

"You're right. Okay. 'Bye, then. I'll send your mother and Candace home. Watch the fire. I think Lena's downstairs if anything happens."

"Dad?"

"Yes, Toby."

"We'll be all right. Go."

Watch me as carefully, as gingerly as if I were crystal, something transparent
and breakable, so fragile that if your glances fell too hard I'd shatter. This love.
This pity. I want to tell you to go running, to run until your breath breathes
through you, till your blood is clean and chill as air. Why don't you fly away?
I want to ask you this: why don't you run from, away, into? Don't stay with me.
Please don't.

"It's cold," he said.

"Grumble, grumble," said his father, "snarl. Time to get up." Toby squunched his face at Jeremy and pulled the duvet tighter. "Toby," Jeremy said (he was exhausted, hadn't slept for weeks, it seemed), "I would really appreciate your cooperation this morning. It's going to be a tough day."

Toby opened his eyes. They were bright and cruel, pale as glass, like a husky's. "You're not sick, are you, Dad?"

"Maybe a bit, but mostly tired. Not so tired I can't get you out of bed, though. Not bad."

Toby pulled his knees up and propped himself on his elbows but still kept the warm down around his chest. "Breakfast?" he said. "You want I should make breakfast? When are Kit and Steph leaving?"

Jeremy nodded. "I've got pancakes ready to go; you can cook 'em if you want."

"Sure," he said. "Dad, why's Steph leaving? She thinks Allen's gonna die. I don't understand why she's not sticking around to be sure. He's not—" Toby leaned forward, clasped his arms around his legs.

Jeremy looked away. The frost on the windows melted suddenly and he sat down on the bed, pushing his son's feet out of the way. "Everyone's going to die," he said. "Sooner or later." But not yet, please God, he said to himself: not just yet. He looked across the room at Toby's desk. Schoolbooks in their brown paper covers were stacked neatly on the surface, obscuring the threefold standing frame under the lamp. Jeremy knew the pictures by heart. Toby's mother and father, arms around each other's shoulders, flushed and happy and grinning with relief: the night of their divorce party. Toby in bed (the boy spends an unconscionable amount of time in bed) the year we moved to Providence, and I reclining on the pillows beside him with a book open across my lap— *The Secret Garden*, Toby's favorite book that year; we're both staring into the camera with red eyes and considerable alarm. (A second after the flash went, I stuck my tongue out and bulged my eyes.) Jeremy and Toby and me at the beach, at Toby's mother's house in California when we visited last summer (Ruth took the picture): we're standing against the water with waves curling around our calves, Toby between Jeremy and me with his arms about our waists, and we're grinning, grinning, grinning like crazy. Please God, Jeremy said: not in the snow. Allen hates winter.

He heard a movement behind him, and then Toby's arms wrapped around his neck in an affectionate stranglehold. Those skinny, healthy little arms, cool as clover. "Hey, Dad," he said, "it's not that cold. I'm going to get up now. Go get dressed. I'll take care of it."

CANDACE ANNOUNCED THAT she was taking them all out to dinner, now that that appalling woman was gone, her and the mopey kid. "Kit's okay," Toby protested, "he's my friend."

"Well, considering—" Ruth said, putting her arm around her son's shoulders. "The best thing Mrs. Sheridan could do for all of us, most especially for Allen, is not to stick around here getting in our way and emanating doom like it was her favorite perfume—I really don't like straight women. The husband's probably worse. Just think, Toby—" expansive, good-humored—"just think if your parents were like the Sheridans."

"Kit's okay," Toby said again. "*He* wanted to go see Allen."

"Let's drop it," said Jeremy, "they're gone." Ruth and Candace were easier to deal with, but not much. "It would be nice to get out for a few hours but—"

"Jeremy," Candace said firmly, "I know what I'm doing, remember I've done this before, back home. I left explicit instructions. If anything happens, they call here; if they get the machine they call the restaurant, I left the number. We'll take both cars. It's all set. Eight-thirty reservation. Now," she said. "My honey here and I are going upstairs to make ourselves beautiful, the very epitome, hah, of bountiful womanhood, and in an hour, make it an hour and a half, when we come back down I want you two looking like gentlemen. Don't stare at me, Jeremy. I'm not butch by nature, I just do it to amuse Ruth. Right? Just wait. Meanwhile—" She shook her head, a woman who seemed to know him better than he knew her, stepped forward and placed her hands on his shoulders, a woman far more beautiful than his ex-wife. "Meanwhile, boyfriend," staring into his eyes, "make yourself a little drink and take a shower."

Jeremy did what he was told, a half inch of dark rum, staring out the window over the kitchen sink where snow was drifting onto the neighbor's floodlit yard, flurrying and settling, but it was warm inside, warm and safe, and only—. He swallowed half the rum on one swallow and went to the bathroom.

"Dad," turning from the mirror, "sorry, I'm almost done," Jeremy's not-quite-thirteen son in candy-striped boxers and damp, tousled hair, half his face lathered, the other scraped clean, "I thought I'd cut myself but it's just a pimple," his son thin as a rail, pale as stripped bark after two months indoors, scrawny and growing, "it's tough shaving when I can't see but my glasses get foggy," growing too fast, all long bones and tendons, no meat on him, a chest as small as his waist, a waist you could put two hands around. "Dad? Are you okay?"

Leaning against the jamb, his eyes watering unaccountably, Jeremy blinked and stared. "Kid, you're thirteen, you've got more hair on your chest than Allen, when did that happen?"

It is true that I have hairy legs, the kind that Jeremy likes best; it is also true that I can count the hairs on my chest and that my beard is sparse and patchy, my mustache, back when I had a mustache, a feeble gesture maintained only because you couldn't be a gay man without one and abandoned with some relief when that truism suddenly became false, although for something like eighteen months my face disappeared every time I looked at it and I still tend not to notice men who lack facial hair.

"This?" Toby placed one hand over his heart and peered down at his torso, hairy only in the same sense that he needed to shave, a down, really, across his chest and on his belly, like the downy head hair of some newborns, which falls out in a day or two. "I guess I got your gorilla genes, Dad, I guess I'm really your kid. Anyway, I'm not thirteen yet—two more days."

"My son—" staring at him—"yeah, I guess you are, kid, my kid."

"Oh, Dad—" Toby dropped the razor into the sink with a splash and a clatter, and embraced his father, pressed his soapy face against his father's chest. "Don't cry, Dad, please, it's okay, I know he'll be home soon."

Safe as houses. Through the kitchen, repeating it: safe as houses. Avoid the floorboard at the entrance to Toby's room, which creaks, and bash into the wall instead, quietly, quietly. Safe as houses. My house is very safe. Stand at the open door, in the dark. His uncurtained windows, south-facing and westward-leaning, leak a slow pallid glow, unctuous as one of those cream liqueurs, and as sickening. The hand on the door frame just as pale. Toby asleep, mercifully asleep, his shoulders and back humping the comforter. Turn around, too fast, too hard this, back fully into the kitchen. The little camelback sofa before the hearth sensibly turning its back on the kitchen table and four ladderback chairs huddled guiltily, interrupted in a conversation about the great unspeakable. Echoes of their rich plummy voices envelop me in an odor of stale sweet sherry and Madeira. Check the windows, why not, even on the second floor, best to be sure. Is the back door locked? Are we secure, are we safe? The corridor, the living room. Inspect the plants in the bay window—no infestations of mites or whitefly. Outside under the sterile light of street lamps the houses across the way wear their windows like eye-patches. The front door: secure. Herodias downstairs, faithful watchdog, and Ray, a man likely to own a gun. Safe as houses. My house secure against all incursion. And now. And now. The next door over, the bedroom door, Jeremy's room, my room, the room where we sleep and where we make love, where we fuck when making love isn't the issue, our room, a room with a door that doesn't lock. A door that won't open. Who has locked me out. What am I locking out?

JEREMY WAS CUTTING out Christmas cookies; Toby, in striped Brooks Brothers silk pajamas, birthday gift from Mom, read his book in front of the fireplace; Ruth and Candace, at the kitchen table, used red-hots and currants and hundreds-and-thousands and small tubes of colored icing to give faces, personalities, and wardrobes to a tray of gingerbread people: a cozy picture, domestic tranquility, precarious comfort, happy birthday, nearly Christmas. I hated to interrupt.

Jeremy waved his floury hands. "Can someone else get the phone?"

The kitchen smelled warm, of spices and molasses and chocolate, vanilla, yeast. Jeremy had been baking since seven, long before anyone else got up, the gingerbread the third project of the morning, after pannetone and Toby's birthday cake. The smell had probably awakened Toby; not long after, the girls—call us that, that's what we are—lumbered down from the third floor wanting coffee and company. The windows were fogged over so that the room made its own self-enclosed world, but outside a brittle freeze had clasped the city in its spiky, comfortless embrace. Jeremy tore off a short ribbon of cookie dough and put it in his mouth, where it dissolved into a soft, pungent, sensuous slush.

"Allen!" Toby yelped.

A hard fist knocked in my chest, I swallowed hard and blinked, and held the phone away from my face for just a moment. "Happy birthday, kid," I said. "Can I talk to your father?"

Jeremy discovered himself washing his hands at the sink. He grabbed the phone from his son. "Allen?"

"Heyyuh, Jere. How's my main man?"

He leaned against the refrigerator. His calves cramped. When I'm especially tired or sick or cheerful my accent and the idioms of my childhood come back, lay a soft, thick glaze over my voice, something Jeremy likes a lot. Something to know.

"I couldn't wait to wish Toby a happy birthday," I said. "How're you holding up, Jere? Festivities in hand, movable feast in motion?"

"I can't wait to see you, boy."

Candace poked Ruth in the upper arm. Ruth nodded. A nod to Toby, a wave to Jeremy, they picked up their trays of unbaked cookies, armloads of decorating supplies, their coffee—how could they carry so much? superwomen with four arms each—and retreated down the corridor to the living room.

"That's part of why I called." My voice was thin, even I could hear, but firmer, I was sure, than the day before. "Listen, can you come an hour early, two instead of three? Oh, and haul along the mink for me."

"Are we going for a walk? There's nowhere to walk. It's been snowing for two weeks, Allen."

"I said to Dr. Ribeiro," I said as though picking up an anecdote, a delaying tactic, a strategy, "I said, Look, today's my lover's kid's thirteenth birthday. Some kind of milestone, hey? Can I go home? Did you get the heater in the Triumph fixed yet, sweetheart?"

The refrigerator thrummed and froze Jeremy's shoulder blades. He swallowed. "Not yet. We've been using Ruth's rental mostly."

"You're helpless without me, aren't you, Jeremy? Use my car, okay?"

"Yes," he said. He said, "Allen, are you really coming home?"

Toby turned, so fast he almost fell over, from the counter where he'd been poking raisins and red-hots into the faces of more gingerbread people, another delaying tactic.

"They were planning on letting me out next week anyway, you know, be kind to the prisoners at Christmas—" (this was hard, so hard, my hand on the telephone hurt from how tightly I held it, and José, sitting by my bed, perfect image of a happy doctor, grinned like a fool), "and José said seeing as I've been such a good boy he thought he could advance my parole date. I have to go in on Friday so he can look me over, make sure I'm not overdoing it, but that's just an office visit. He figures the stress of being here pretty much cancels out the benefits and I'd be better off at home. For now."

Jeremy's heart was pounding. "Oh, Allen, that's so fine." He grinned helplessly at his son, at his blurry, glistening face.

"Two o'clock," I said briskly. "Don't forget. My car. The warmest clothes you can find. Don't bring anyone with you, okay, Jere, just yourself? If I'm going to relapse from happiness I'd rather do it with no-one but you watching. Now let me talk to the kid again."

Jeremy handed the phone to Toby, turned, pressed forehead and the palms of his hands against the cool enamel of the refrigerator. It breathed as loudly, as raggedly as he. A tear ran into his mouth. It tasted sweet, like gingerbread.

"'Bye, Allen," said Toby indistinctly. Jeremy heard him hang up the phone. Then he felt Toby's hands on his upper arms. "Allen said to give you a big—a major hug," said Toby.

FURNISHINGS

Their Children at Play

EARLY THE NEXT spring Kit wrote me a letter. Short, carefully composed sentences in a stiff hand: he wished to be considered for admission into the lower school in the fall. Would I send his mother the application forms. Love to Toby and Uncle Jeremy, and to me. He had never called Jeremy *uncle* before. Jeremy said, "Your brother-in-law must have undergone a miraculous transformation. The whole family. *My* nephews don't call me uncle."

We were in the kitchen. Jeremy was fooling around with the pastry for an apple pie before I made dinner, I'd been looking through the mail; Toby, in his bedroom with the door open and the stereo going, leaned over a pictorial map of Rhode Island he was creating for one of his classes, marking and annotating the birth sites of the Industrial Revolution in America. I reread Kit's letter. "It's very strange." There wasn't anything in the letter to work with. "Toby," I said, raising my voice over synthesizers, guitars, drum machines, then went to his door and looked in. "Do you know anything about this?"

"What?" He set down his pencil. The light of the desk lamp formed an aura around his head, tangling in hair that had been fine and limp and flyaway a few months before, a child's hair, but was now suddenly, overnight, full, wavy, capricious, prone to cowlicks and to standing off his skull. His jaw had been planed down too, to the bone, sometime when I wasn't watching, so that it fit more aptly his big, handsome nose. The jewel in his earlobe glinted. His glasses shone.

"This letter from Kit." I waved it at him. "He wants an application from the school."

Toby pushed his chair back. "Hey! That's great. Would he stay with us?" He took the sheet of paper from my hand.

I leaned over his shoulder as he read the letter, not easy now that he was so tall. "He'd have to, I guess. He's still too young to board."

"Keen." Toby's vocabulary startles me on occasion, studded with slang that was already obsolete when I was his age. "Well, he's been talking about it for ages, you know that, but he didn't say anything specific the last time." He grinned, a little unsurely I thought. "I guess he must've finally talked his dad around."

"Don't be naïve, kid," Jeremy said. He put his hands on my shoulders so that the three of us were lined up like the choo-choo train in a children's game.

"Your father's right—Derek isn't somebody who can be talked around. Not by an eleven year old, anyway."

"Why don't we call them and find out?" Toby had pulled away from me, looked at me with a curiously blank stare of reflective lenses that gave my face back to me, doubled, Jeremy's face perched on my shoulder in one lens but not the other.

"Bet on it—" said Jeremy, "Derek's got some kind of angle." Ordinarily Jeremy is the least judgmental of men, who listens to insults as if they were the most banal of conversational gambits, but in certain cases—his own family, some politicians and public figures, the doctor who told me, when I first became ill, that I'd brought it on myself—after sufficient provocation, he is the least forgiving.

Toby nodded. "That's easy." Tactful, he turned away from us. "Kit's part of your real family, Allen, so he'd get free tuition. If he stays with us everything's free, right? Derek knows you'd never ask for room and board. Kit goes to a good school and his dad doesn't have to pay for it. Derek can buy that sailboat he wants. Anyway—" now Toby handed Kit's letter back to me, and the lines of his face were set into a hardness that made him resemble his mother—"Kit and his dad don't get along. Kit isn't normal enough. I didn't tell you this, Dad, Allen." For a moment he said nothing, sat back down and stared at his map.

"What?" Jeremy sounded as angry as, suddenly, I felt myself, my heart thumping. I was close to guessing what Toby would say.

"One of his letters, Kit said—I was so mad, Allen." Toby spread both his hands flat on the surface of the desk. "He heard his mom and dad fighting. Derek said Kit was turning into a fag like his uncle."

Jeremy's forearm pressed against my throat. "The kid's only eleven!"

Looking at Toby, I couldn't tell whether he was angry or sad.

"He wanted to know why it would be a bad thing if he *was* gay. He said you two are the only grown-ups he likes and maybe he wants to be like you." Toby picked up his pencil and stared at it, an unaccountable object, an implement whose purpose he couldn't guess.

Later Jeremy said to me, "Your brother-in-law is an evil man," but this was later that night, in bed, when I began without provocation to cry, silently, the tears bubbling out of my eyes with so little mercy I felt sick. Both of us staring at his son, Jeremy only held me closer, more tightly, and said in a small, hard voice, "What did you tell him, kid?"

Toby set the pencil down, carefully. He took his glasses off, then put them back on again. Suddenly he stood up, and suddenly his arms were around both of us and he had ducked his chin, pressed his cheek against my chest. "I didn't know what to say," he mumbled.

"What did you tell him, Toby?" I asked, holding him against my chest as if he were a child, feeling the sharp bones in his back. I cannot, after all, protect him from much of anything.

"He's just a kid, he doesn't know what's going on." A sigh shuddered down Toby's back. "I mean, I don't think he could handle it. Sometimes—oh, fuck it. Sometimes I just get so mad, you know? Derek isn't any worse than most of the people I know. And I like Kit a lot, it'd be great having him here, but maybe he's better off . . ." Wrenching himself away from me, Toby threw himself on the bed. "Can we just not talk about it right now?"

His father pushed me forward. "I think we'd better." Pulling out Toby's desk chair, he sat down in it, legs straddled, leaning forward and crossing his arms across the back. I crouched down to pick Kit's letter up from the floor. "It's not going to go away," Jeremy said.

Toby punched his pillow and sat up. None of us is particularly shy of our bodies. Returning home from school, he'd taken a shower and not gone further toward getting dressed than pulling on clean undershorts and a t-shirt. As he wrestled his legs around, like stilts he couldn't control, I caught a glimpse of his genitals—hairy, no longer a child's but not yet a man's. For some reason this evidence that he was growing up made me catch my breath, and was more affecting than the redness of his eyes. It had been a while since I'd seen Toby cry. Helpless, I sat on the floor.

He stared at me. His voice a wretched snarl, he said, "I know two kids at school whose parents are getting divorced. Eric's father just went bankrupt, he'll probably have to pull Eric out and put him in public school. I know another guy whose dad beats him sometimes. Jamie's mom just had a mastectomy. Look, that's life. I don't have to worry about things like that. I got it just fine." He drew in a honking, snotty

breath. "All I've got to worry about is—" And now he simply looked at
me, blinking hard, the tears dribbling from the corners of his eyes
ceaselessly as a spring.

"Toby," I muttered, standing.

Toby glared at his father. "I told Kit his father was narrow-minded
and prejudiced." He showed his teeth in an expression nothing like
a grin. "I told him fag was a word only stupid bigots used, and he
shouldn't. I told him he was too young to know if he was gay or
straight, and anyway it wasn't something you could choose, either you
are or you aren't." He hiccuped, a little laugh. "Then I said he was a neat
kid and I'd still like him even if he was straight. But—Dad, Allen—"

A sneeze buckled his shoulders, and when he sat up straight again
there was snot on his upper lip. I stepped toward him but he wiped his
face with his shirt and waved me away. "He said he wished he could live
with us, Allen. He loves you, he respects you, he wishes you were his
dad instead of Derek."

Jeremy hummed judiciously and said, "From what you're saying,
Toby, he'd maybe be better off if Allen were."

Turning on him, Toby yelled, "Don't be stupid, Dad! You're the
one who's naïve!"

Now I understood. "Toby," I said, and sat beside him on his bed.
"Toby," I said, and placed my palm between his shoulder blades. "Toby,
it's all right."

"It's not all right!" First he shrugged my hand off and then winced,
then, quietly, said, "It's not okay. I don't want you to die, Allen." He bent
forward, over his knees; with a twist of his spine, abruptly, his head was
in my lap and he was sobbing, deep choking sobs louder than any I'd
heard from him since he was a small boy.

I have always tried to be honest with Toby—the least I could do.
He knew about those of our friends who had died—he visited them
when they were ill. When it began to seem plausible that his father or I
might become ill we told him—told him about it, told him how it
might have happened. This may have been unkind, he was only eight or
nine, but then I did become ill. Nearly a year later, when I went into the
hospital, Toby was the rock of fortitude and good sense in whose lee we
sheltered ourselves during those terrible weeks—more terrible, I believe, for Jeremy and Toby than for me—and I nearly forgot that he
was, still and after all, a child. Now I nearly wished that I had lied or

could lie to him now, could make him promises I wished to keep. His shoulders heaved. I slid one hand under his shirt, up his cool back to rub uselessly at his neck, and I leaned over him. Amidst his sobs, he grunted and honked, said, "I love you, Allen"—a declaration he makes often enough but never casually. Never offhandedly, the way any child might. My eyes stinging, I leaned over him, pressing on him a comfort as false as it was meant.

TOBY PICKED UP his opponent's serve and slammed it across the net, then grabbed the return on his backhand and lobbed it into the empty forecourt. Outmaneuvered, the other boy called, "Your serve!"

I sat on the bench and pulled a file out of my briefcase, something to do while I waited, although I never opened it. Tennis is nearly as uninteresting a game as golf. If Toby had chosen water polo as his spring sport I might have been more enthusiastic about doing the father thing and could have given him useless pointers left over from my own prepschool career; I was even able to get excited over his prowess on the soccer field. The scoring of tennis baffles me, for one thing, the action isn't continuous enough, and I've never been comfortable with one-on-one combat. Nevertheless, I watched them. Toby and Greg were fairly evenly matched, it seemed, neither one good enough for the team but giving it their all anyway. The little ball jumped from one side of the net to the other and back, thumping on concrete and snapping against racquet strings, the boys grunted and yelped until Toby lifted his glasses off his nose to wipe his eyes and Greg, poised, yelled, "Service!"

Tense, Toby hunkered down and nodded. The ball flew at him. His return was clumsy though he recovered enough to catch the next two volleys. The third, a sneaky, artistic shot, whizzed past him to land just within the line. "Your game," Toby admitted, dangling his racquet, then twirling it into the air and catching it by the handle. Sportsman to the end, he met Greg at the net and shook his hand.

They gathered up their balls and I slipped the file back into my briefcase and stood up. "Afternoon, Mr. Pasztory," Greg said as they came out of the gate.

"Good game, Greg."

"See you tomorrow, Tobe." He slapped Toby on the shoulder and headed off to the locker room.

"See ya," Toby said, wiping his face with the end of the towel hung around his neck and peering at me. "Hi, Allen. Anything wrong?" For sports he had a pair of spectacles with shatterproof lenses, flexible wire stems that wrapped all the way around his ears, and a loop of cord around the neck for added security. As he fit them back on I noticed a small, red pimple on his chin.

"I thought you might like a ride home."

Like a colt bothered by a fly he shook his head. "Not especially." He nudged at the gravel walk with the head of his racquet. "I was going to run. Tennis isn't the right kind of workout."

"You looked good on the court." He didn't pull this type of adolescent backing-off on me very often, and I wasn't sure how to handle it. "What about your books and stuff?"

"Allen." This was dismissive, a snort. He half-turned away.

"Sorry, Toby. Just asking." Hardly a rebellion, little more than irritation. "Am I being tiresome?"

"I did my homework in study hall. Yeah, you are." He recovered, grinned. "At least I'm honest, right?"

"Right. Okay, I'll see you at home." Nodding, I turned and started away.

I'd only gone a few steps when he called after me. "Allen! It's not like I have to beat them up anymore, but the other guys give me grief sometimes, okay? That's all." Coming up behind me he placed his hand between my shoulder blades. "Want to wait while I take a shower and change?" he asked. He was still a kid but his sweat smelled as rank as a man's.

"Fine. I'll wait in the car." Inhaling deeply, I said, "Do they?"

He swatted at the air with his racquet. "Oh, sure," he said, "it'd be weird if they didn't. You know—" he grunted, roughened his voice, "betcher daddy looks real nice in a dress, eh, Tobes?" He laughed, once. "Like that. I can handle it." Another laugh. "I tell 'em Dad doesn't look half as nice as I do. Shuts them up."

"Oh."

"Allen, like I said, I can handle it, okay? Quit worrying. At least they don't know about Mom." Changing his voice again, he said, "If they're both bent, how'd they get you?" A beat. Another, uglier voice. "His real daddy's a foot-long dildo, that's what!" He bit his cheek, blushing. "Shit. Wash my mouth out with soap."

"Toby," I said, "go take your shower. I'll be in the car."

It was only recently, since we moved from San Francisco where Toby had six or seven school friends whose fathers or mothers were gay—since Jeremy made that commitment to me—since, really, it became some kind of issue—since, no doubt, I became ill, that I had felt a need to question the wisdom of our raising him together, Jeremy and I. I didn't regret it for myself, certainly—any vision of myself without Toby and Jeremy at my side, of the man I would be without them, was bleak and cheerless, inconceivable. And Jeremy, when he met me, seemed well on the way toward becoming someone who divided his life on a sharp blade between who he was and what he felt, either Toby's father or no-one at all. Any number multiplied by zero equals out to nothing.

Nor was it that I felt we'd shown—or would show—Toby a bad example. I used to ask myself what I would feel if he grew up to be heterosexual, a man with no social problems except embarrassing parents, a man who might be pressured to repudiate us; or if he turned out to be homosexual and wondered if that were our fault—my fault specifically, I suppose. But the parallels were too plain to miss: had my parents worried, before our births, that Steph and I would be deaf like them? Or, still more unsettling, *not* deaf. You loved your children regardless, if you were any kind of decent person, anyone I wanted to know: you loved your parents, wanted the best for them. And noting that imperfect parallel forced me to distrust another. That being homosexual was a profound social disability could not be denied, but it could be avoided —there were ways, none I cared to take, none that would not destroy my sense of self, but ways. Deafness, however, was a disability both social and physical: inescapable. If I could not see my mother and father as cripples but rather as heroes and admirably everyday people, how could I demean their everydayness and heroism by not living up to it? To be alive, a thinking being, is to be handicapped, unless one is a god. Who would choose not to be human?

And when I thought about it I realized that ever since I met him Toby had seemed to me a boy who knew his own mind—who consulted his own judgment before he looked to others; and his sexual persuasion not subject to influence, only his attitude toward it. So, after all, I suppose it wasn't Jeremy's or my wisdom I questioned, choices we made that were no choices, but if there couldn't have been some way to protect Toby from having to make jokes about his family.

Most of the administrative staff had already left for the day so there were only four or five cars besides mine in the lot. Emerging from the back door, Ben Romney gave me a genial wave but didn't come over or say anything, only climbed into his car and drove off. I put my briefcase on the back seat, loosened my tie, and leaned against the side of the car. On the baseball field practice was winding up, coaches shouting, boys roughhousing.

Toby's life wouldn't be any less complex if he had grown up in his mother's household. This wasn't something I believed only because it was a comfort—in fact, I suspected it would be that much more difficult. In any case, Ruth and Candace wouldn't have him. But there was still the question of my nephew.

"Okay, Allen." Slinging his gym bag into the back seat, Toby bumped against me in a way that might have seemed accidental. "Ready to go?" His hair gleamed, wet and slick against his skull, and he smelled of institutional soap. "Want me to drive?"

"Two more years."

"One and a quarter, then I can get a learner's permit." He grinned and went around to the passenger door.

Getting in, I unlocked his door. "I dread the day. Will we have to get you a car?"

"Not for me. Might be helpful if you got one for Dad, though, since I'll be driving the Triumph."

"You wish."

I pushed the key into the ignition, put the car into neutral. Toby's hand grazed mine on the stick, then clasped it. "Sorry," he said.

"For what? I should apologize. Put your seat belt on."

"Yes, Daddy," he said and, when I glanced at him, grinned like a fool.

Pulling out of the parking lot, I said, "I called my sister today."

"Steph? About Kit?"

"Yeah." She was surprised when she figured out, after a moment, who it was on the phone, worried that something had happened. Something had happened, I told her, and told her about Kit's letter. Had he written with her knowledge, her permission, I wanted to know —what was going on down there in Annapolis? I tried to be quiet about it, not inflammatory, but Steph is a genius at reading the tones of my voice. "She told me I ought to talk to Derek, so I called him too."

"That must have been tough," said Toby. He was staring out the window, studiously avoiding my eyes as we drove down Hope.

"Derek was well trained as a child, he's never impolite except behind your back."

"Allen, remember," Toby said, his voice quiet, "remember when I wanted to get my ear pierced? You said I shouldn't rock the boat."

"You did it anyway."

"That boat sank a long time ago." He made a little noise. "If it ever floated. What's Derek's story?"

KIT CAME TO stay with us for the summer, a kind of dry run. I had disqualified myself from pronouncing on his application, but the committee that evaluated staff members' children for admission approved him handily, so if Jeremy and I and Toby could handle him for three months, were willing to handle him, he would stay on. I could not believe, when I picked him up at the airport and after he'd been with us for a few days, that he needed any *handling*. He was my nephew, a shy, bright, funny boy who carried the groggy Providence's traveling case as though it were the most precious thing in the world, something to hold onto—hardly the punk delinquent, shoplifter, pothead his father accused him of being. I was more concerned about the cat.

We had set up the small study next to our bedroom for Kit. The first night I looked in the door and he said, "Uncle Allen?"

"Are you comfortable, Kit? Do you think you'll be able to sleep?"

"Oh, yeah, I'm fine." He sat up as I came toward him, moving his face into the cone of light from the lamp beside the extended sofabed. Providence, a notably complacent animal, yawned and went back to sleep. Seeing Kit's face in that light I wondered, if I compared it to a photo of myself at the same age, would the faces be the same? "Uncle Allen," he said, "you were very sick last winter. Are you still sick?"

"I'm not very sick." If he were Toby I would have sat on the bed. I stood and gazed down at him. "I'm okay most of the time. Why?"

"Will you get sick again? I need to know." He was so serious.

"I'd like to know that myself, Kit." This was turning into a conversation I had avoided having with my sister, my parents—with anybody except my doctor. "My doctor says I'm doing well, but there aren't any promises, you have to understand that. I could become very ill again almost any time." I stared at the cat, an alien in our midst, aloof and uncomprehending of our lives. "Are you worrying that you might get sick too, Kit?"

He shook his head brusquely, as if I were missing the obvious. "I know about that." He was silent, not looking at me, watching his hands on the blanket. His hands were inarticulate. I wanted to teach him to talk.

"What's bugging you, Kit?" I asked at last.

Still staring at his hands he said, matter-of-factly, "I hate my father." A moment later he said, "And he hates me."

This conversation I had expected, was more or less prepared for. "I don't think he hates you." Now I sat down beside him. "He doesn't understand you right now, and when he doesn't understand something he gets irritable. I mean, look, Kit, I make him nervous because I'm not the brother-in-law he thinks he should have but he doesn't hate me. Really, I think he really loves you a lot, but you're both confused and angry so it looks like something different."

Kit's mahogany brown eyes looked black. "But he does hate you, Uncle Allen." His small, pretty face was fierce, and I wanted to tell him I didn't need defending. I wanted to tell him a bedtime story, soothe him to sleep. "I hate him," Kit said. "I wish he was sick instead of you."

"Kit." I placed my hand on his knee. "I wish you wouldn't say that. Not because he's your father, not because if you really thought about it you'd find out you don't hate him that much. Only because—Kit, the way I'm sick, you shouldn't want anyone to be like this, not the worst person in the world."

"He says you're gonna die and then I'll learn something."

"Did he say that?" I stared at Kit, cruelly perhaps because he shifted under my gaze and his nod was uncertain. "Kit, may I ask you a favor?" He nodded again, more surely. "You can say no, but I'd like it if you gave me a hug."

"Uncle Allen?" He leaned forward over his knees. The top two buttons of his pajamas, hand-me-downs from Toby, had come unfastened, revealing a pale child's chest striated by the shadows of ribs. "My dad doesn't like Ricky or me to hug him."

I extended my hand to him. He grasped it with a hand that seemed much smaller than Toby's but which surprised me with its strength. "I'm not your dad," I said.

He nodded a third time. His chin was small and sharp, his cheeks broad and high, still a little plump so that he looked younger than he was, his head not quite proportionate to neck or shoulders. Under his pointed upper lip the teeth gleamed; one of the upper front teeth slightly overlapped the other and he had an overbite that Toby's orthodontist, I was sure, would love to get her hands on. His weight leaning into my arm, I pulled him forward until he knelt at my side, nearly in my lap. Moving out of our way, Providence nevertheless began to purr.

There is something about holding a child in your arms, whether the child is five or fifteen, that is nothing at all like holding another man, however fraternal or chaste or comradely that embrace may be. It's a little like hugging my father, there's that element of helpless, happy embarrassment and nostalgia about it, the feeling that you can't draw close enough to make up for your being separate persons, and the adult stoicism that says a grown man can't blubber against his father's chest, burble snot and tears and spit on the spot that, only a few years ago, was dedicated to those sticky fluids. When the child is a boy of Kit's or Toby's age there's an awareness too that, while both of you are sacrificing your dignity, his is more integral than yours, more breakable. And although you're aware of being older, of being responsible if in the most abstract way for his safety, you can't help feeling that he is stronger, that it is he holding you down rather than you holding him up. I had been fond of my nephew, in the unpremeditated way one is fond of nephews and nieces, but with Toby at hearthside Kit had not been invited past the front parlor. "Kit," I whispered. Holding him around the shoulders with one arm, I placed the other hand against the side of his skull, thumb behind his ear, a warm, porcelain shell, fingers cupping the tendon of his neck. I leaned my cheek against his brow so that bone slid against bone. There is one act more frightening than being a father, I think, and that is to teeter on the line between taking a father's place and resolving not to.

"Your father's right, I'm afraid, Kit," I said. He moved, perhaps in protest. "I probably am going to die, and you probably will learn something. I wish I could make a deal with you—I used to try to bargain with my mother; I'd say, If I get straight A's will you stop smoking? You wouldn't have to get straight A's to satisfy me, Kit, but it doesn't work that way."

"I know that," he said, but he said it in such a way that I knew he didn't accept it.

"The way it works is that I take good care of myself, my doctor takes care of me, Jeremy and Toby take care of me, and we all hold out as long as we can. Do you understand? We aren't fighting anybody, there isn't anybody to hate. Nobody." His hair was fine and soft under my fingertips, his skull as delicate and hard as the bowl of a crystal goblet.

"Can't you get well?" This as though he'd just thought of it, twisting his neck so that he could look into my face.

Drawing him back against my chest, I said, "I'm working on it."

We were quiet. He was warm and solid. I lifted my chin, as if it would help me breathe. The ceiling of the study is dropped, lower than the ceilings in the rest of the house, I don't know why, and there is only one window, which opens on the blank, grey clapboard wall of the house next door, only a yard away. The room can seem either cozy or claustrophobic, or, sometimes, disorientingly, both. We had moved the television into the living room, where it might be turned on more often, and moved the computer to the guest room on the third floor. It all seemed very provisional, impermanent. We had discussed Toby's moving to the third floor, leaving his room for Kit; Toby had even, without much hesitation, suggested sharing his room with Kit, it wouldn't be too tight a fit with another bed. (Perhaps he hoped Providence would sleep with him. He seemed as pleased with her presence as with Kit's.) But the arrangement was provisional.

Deep in Kit's suitcase, when he unpacked, cushioned by t-shirts and socks and underpants, lay a gift Jeremy and I had given him a few years before. The original of one of Jeremy's jacket designs, it was a watercolor portrait of the young hero of the story, a prince who believes himself to be the son of an evil wizard. The prince is pushing through a tangled thorny thicket whose branches have a more than vegetative vitality—they are branches, but also arms that hold him back. Glowing beyond the thicket, the prince's goal, is a clear spring. Its water, colder than ice, so cold it cannot be contained in any vessel but a hollowed-out diamond, has magic properties which the wizard requires for the spell to seal his dominion. What the boy doesn't know is that the spring is the source of his real family's power and legitimacy, that only members of the royal family can draw water from the well. Nor does the boy know that his unknown elder brother, the crown prince, is pent within the waters the way the soul is imprisoned in the body. Questing prince, clever younger son, possessor of unsuspected

magic powers—hero of any fairy tale: within the book, a story for children older than Kit was when we gave him the painting, this is who the
boy is. A grotesquely huge raven perches on a branch watching, the
wizard's familiar and spy. The boy is Toby. At Kit's request, I had hung
the painting on the wall opposite his pillows. If he was to live with us, I
wanted him to feel he lived with us, not that he was a guest.

"Uncle Allen," Kit asked, "do you think I'm gay?"

I stroked his hair. "I don't know, Kit. I don't think we can be sure
for a few more years."

"I think I am," he said, sounding sure, "and I'm glad."

"Just be your own self, okay?"

A light knock sounded on the door. As we turned, the door
opened and Jeremy came through. "How're we doing in here?"

WHEN WE DROVE into town from the airport, Toby rode in back with
the cat but leaned forward between the seats—he and Kit had to catch
up in a way that their once-a-month correspondence couldn't cover,
had to plan the summer, trips to the beach and Newport and Boston—
and California! Kit would go with us to visit Toby's mother, wouldn't
he? Kit had never been to California. But he had been, I reminded
them, long ago when he was a baby, and this entailed a whole story.

"Toby," Kit asked as I took the Gano Street exit, looping around
above the waters of the Seekonk, "do you think your dad will mind if I
call him Uncle Jeremy?" Kit glanced at me, too, his eyes as wide and
hopeful as a puppy's.

"I think he'd like that, Kit."

WE ARE IN bed, Jeremy and I, his weight warm and solid in my arms.
Every night, at last, we lie like this, front to back, as close as the leaves
in a closed book, mantled, in winter, by flannel sheets and the airy
warmth of down and our own breath, dry as the air heated by the radiator despite the shallow bowl of water balanced on its coils, redolent
with crushed cinnamon and cardamom; in high summer mantled by
our sweat. Last week, an annual rite, we dragged the bed away from
the interior wall and placed its head between the two windows above
the street, open now, the new foliage of the tree outside brushing
against the screens with a fragrance like cut grass. Against my cheek,
his shoulder, broad and strong, and he smells of a perfume that is only

his own. He breathes. Under my arm his chest moves and settles, my fingertips, grazing the soft hair of his breast, grazing his nipple, sense the slow beat of his heart while his own arm, crooked over mine, slides down my flank, the hand brushing my hip. My belly inflates against the small of his back then draws away, allowing a moment of warm air to separate us. Pressed to his buttocks, my penis stiffens with the reflex of desire, relaxes, stiffens again, an irregular meter marking, faultily, a rhythm that does not change.

If I disengage myself, get up and out of bed to pad, naked, across the bedroom and the living room to the bathroom to piss, he will groan and shift in his sleep; when I return I'll find him sprawled on his back snoring lightly. I will draw the sheet off him and kneel beside him, this man, this man of thirty-six with his long hair tangled around his head in the white puddle of the pillows, hair that is still mostly black but whose texture has changed over the last few years so that it reflects more light; the neat beard with its thin white stroke, like the stroke of a paintbrush, at the left corner of his mouth, the stubble rising on his cheeks and on the neck; his chest, so broad and deep, so hairy, that beside him I appear an adolescent; his taut, expansive belly. He has thickened since I've known him, solidified, become more substantial; underneath the beard his jaw is softer, the hard wedge of bone masked by flesh as well as beard; he buys trousers a size larger now. He is a man, fully a man, a man who says hello whenever he notices me as though I were still a surprise to him, says Hello, Allen, with a kind of savor and delight and astonishment, or, sweetly, Hello, boy.

I will stretch out beside him, and this time, in his sleep, he will gather me with his arm, press chest and belly to my back, push one knee between my thighs. By morning we will have drawn apart, back to back, backs glued together by a night's sweat, only so that we can turn into each other's arms, breathe morning breath into each other's faces, kiss with stale mouths and tongues, and, always surprised, compare morning erections.

But now it is night, still night, a night which though it stretch across eight years and from one coast of the North American con-tinent to the other, from San Francisco Bay to Narragansett Bay, seems short, too slow to arrive, too swift to end.

The Small Conversations of Our Hands

MY PARENTS PLANNED a visit, something they had never done before, wherever I lived. It felt like an irrevocable act, final, fateful. For one thing, it would be their first time on an airplane, flying into Boston. The message on my computer said:

>You know, Allen, these computers are useful things. I found a most
pleasant and helpful travel agent on the BBS. You don't even have
to leave the house. I had been going to ask you to buy the tickets. Your mother still thinks we should drive. I told her—When
you learn to drive.<

Suspecting my mother would find it annoying rather than charming, still I asked Kit if he wanted to learn how to say Hello, Grandmama.

He glanced up from the kitchen table where he was writing a letter to his own mother. "I already know how, Uncle Allen," he said, and demonstrated that he did, in fact, and Grandpapa too. It was strange, watching his small, brown hands form the signs, with fair fluency—I hardly ever see children talking with their hands. "Toby taught me."

I showed him how to refine his articulation a little. What else had Toby taught him, I asked, and then asked again, aloud.

He showed me that he knew my name and the name signs I had given Toby and Jeremy—Jeremy's a kind of pun on the verb *to draw*; Toby's a portmanteau of December, for his birthday, and October, for the month I met him: Dectober, perhaps, Octember. Not the kinds of names real people have, but how often would I use them. "But I don't know what they call me," he said, a little fretful, "Toby couldn't remember."

For a few minutes I couldn't remember either. I hadn't spent more than a week at a time with my parents for so many years, and when I was with them we seldom talked of Steph's family. I remembered the summer after Kit was born, when he was referred to as the baby or the grandchild or, in another kind of portmanteau that doesn't translate, Stephanie's son. Pulling out the chair opposite my nephew, sitting

259

down, I stared at him and talked to myself. Kit had somehow learned the first lesson, he watched my face rather than my hands although I could tell from his blank, annoyed expression that he'd hoped to understand more than he did. His face, with its high cheekbones and dark eyes, his black hair, which we were letting grow out longer than his father had allowed—I stared at his face, and remembered his name. "This is it," I said, and showed him.

"But that's *your* name, Uncle Allen," he said.

"Not quite. See?" As though it were a physical object, a tiny token, I prized out the diminutive bound into the sign and showed him. "When you were little, your mother always said you looked just like me. And then, because you're not left-handed, we turned it kind of backwards, look, like this, so it's all yours."

Tiny Little {Left-handed [reversed (Right-handed)]} One—in English it reads clumsily, impossible, but Kit got it on one try. He beamed at me. "That's my name!" he said, and made the sign again. "But I don't know if I want to be" {tiny}, pulling the diminutive particle out again.

"Okay." I leaned forward. "Let's work on this." It was a kind of problem I'm not good at, partly, I think, because my mind was shuttling back and forth between English and sign and I was, I realized with a surprised pleasure, speaking and talking simultaneously. As if the language were agglutinative, we took Kit's name apart, deconstructed and reconstructed it, analyzed each component. "We can't mess it up too badly, Kit, or your grandparents won't recognize it. But look—this is my name, and this is what your grandfather calls me, we could do something like that—" Something like the transformation of Christopher into Kit.

"I wish my mom had taught me sign," Kit said at last.

A month before he would have blamed his father. I reached across the table and gathered his hands into mine. He liked to be touched, frequently, the way a much younger child does, or a cat, his cat at least— I'd see him hug Toby, impulsively, and was glad that Toby could hug him back. Kit would be fine. "We'll have you talking like a native, Kit. Watch this."

He concentrated. "You want me to help you—to go to the supermarket with you?"

"You got it. Let's go!"

A SIGNAL ADVANTAGE of the BBS over the TDD—or a conventional tele-phone, if that were applicable—is that my father and I can have real-time conversations when we're both on the computer at the same time, but I can also leave him messages, as short as

>access me at 11:00 so we can talk<

or as long as necessary when I have something delicate to tell him but don't wish to witness his response. Inviting Kit to live with us had been one of the occasions when I had to explain myself to myself, first. The next day, this was my father's reply:

>Allen, you're a grown man now, I'm surprised you still need my
   approval. I won't say it doesn't flatter me that you do. I don't
   think you're asking for advice?

>Your mother and I don't see much of how Stephanie and Derek are
   raising their children. You know how your mother feels about
   Derek. I'm sorry to say my opinion isn't much better. Nor yours
   either, apparently. I don't know the children well, obviously,
   and wouldn't if they came to visit more often since they can't
   talk to me. Unlike your mother I've never felt this was a tragedy.
   They are hearing children growing up in a hearing world, their
   grandparents a distraction. These days anyone's grandparents
   are a distraction, even in so-called normal families. I believe
   this wasn't always so, but wouldn't know since I don't even
   have parents. I'm not indulging in self-pity. You and your sister
   didn't have grandparents. I am pleased that Ricky and Jess
   seem to have a good relationship with Derek's parents. And
   pleased in somewhat the same way by my friendship with Toby,
   although I understand he has no contact with Jeremy's family
   nor much more with his mother's.

>I don't know whether it's because I'm an orphan or because I'm
   deaf, or because I spent all of my childhood in an extreme
   environment, but I find the conventional definition of family—
   the kind of emblematic American family on which politicians
   predicate their campaigns—beside the point when it's not
   pernicious. (Take a look at that sentence! A trifle bookish, perhaps. All those dictionary words.) I suspect your mother would-
   n't agree with me, but we disagree often enough. A family is
   what you make of it. I mean you, Allen.

>There was a subtext to your message that I'm not sure you were aware of. Perhaps it's simply that I see more clearly than you the parallels between your and Jeremy's lives and mine. There is also the fact that you thought your being gay was a surprise to me. I think children frequently believe their parents are naïve. Did you know, I read somewhere, the proportion of homosexuality among the deaf is something like twice what it is in the population at large.

>Your mother would agree with me, I think, that you and Jeremy between you have created a more stable structure than have your sister and her husband. I would be more inclined to call yours a marriage. (A conventional woman against all odds, your mother wouldn't.) Toby is a fine young man, a credit to his families. I am grateful that he allows me to call myself his grandfather. I will be glad if Kit, my real grandson after all, will one day allow me to do the same.

>In my own long-winded way, Allen, I'm telling you that I approve. (Interesting turn of phrase that, long-winded. I wonder how I'd translate it. Slow-fingered?) It appears that Derek is making Kit's growing-up untenable. Not the first time a father has wrecked his son's life. I trust that both of my sons will be of use in helping Kit make sense of his life, and live it. If I have never said this before, please tell Jeremy that I do think of him as my son. And, after some resistance, your mother thinks of him as her son-in-law. I just asked her.

>I know that you are also considering your illness. I think, in this one instance, that you should not. Although I understand this to be impossible. I cannot not think about it myself, Allen. But not in terms of how it might affect Kit. And I think that you also must not consider those terms. No parent is not mortal, any more than a child isn't. That last clause was one of the most difficult I have ever had to type.

>There is no trade-off between a bad father who is mortal and a good father who may be more mortal. (I write may be not so much in blind optimism as with the consideration that Derek is a prime candidate for a mid-life heart attack. I wish I could be blindly optimistic.) In this case, also, Kit is gaining two good fathers, in addition to one who may be salvageable and a mother of

occasional distinction. How many children can boast so much?
>It is probably not cricket of me (where do I pick up these idioms?
    I read more than ever since I retired, but still, you'd think I
    were educated, or spoke English) to reveal that Toby had al-
    ready apprised me of the situation, so I have had time to think
    about it. You and Jeremy, and Toby, have made the choice I
    hoped, and expected, you would. I must admit to being a little
    surprised Derek went along with it, as I'm sure you must be as
    well, but I gather he had already washed his hands of Kit. He
    was seriously considering one of those appalling pseudo-
    military-academy reform schools that advertise in the back
    of the <u>National Geographic</u>? I respect my daughter, now,
    more than I have for some years.
>When Kit arrives, give him his grandfather's love. Meanwhile, I send
    my love to you and your family. Please call me, real-time, soon.
>JKP<

AFTER HERODIAS HAD offered her customary all-out welcome, I asked
Lena to keep her indoors, or tie her up or something, in the belief that
my parents would find the dog's enthusiasm too much to handle.
Providence was distraction enough. They had never owned any kind
of pet, least of all a huge white beast who outweighed me by a service-
able number of pounds and who had not yet understood that she was
no longer a puppy. My mother surprised me, wondering where
Herodias had hidden herself and then chastising me when I confessed.
Herodias was a good dog, my mother said, less trouble than either of
her children had been, a dear. I should go fetch her at once. While I was
at it, why didn't I invite Lena and her young man to join us. They
seemed to be bright young people who could handle there being a language barrier.

What's got into her? I asked my father.

Your mother? He glanced across the lawn to where she sat with her
drink and her ashtray under the big Norway maple. Something wrong?

Toby had seen. He touched my father's arm. She's nice, he said,
emphatically. Kit agreed with him.

Well, of course, my father said, looking back and forth from my
face to Toby's and Kit's. Then he laughed, that wonderful raucous
laugh. Oh, you mean she's nicer than usual. I think it was the plane.

With the boys watching, and Jeremy, standing over the grill, looking puzzled, I worked on the simultaneous-translation trick. "She wants the dog. She told me to ask Lena and Ray to join us. She complimented Toby and Kit on their signing. She hugged Jeremy at the airport. This isn't nice, it's uncanny."

My father spoke rapidly, seriously, and I caught on quickly enough not to attempt interpreting. After my last visit, he told me, she had said with a kind of horrifying dignity and stoicism, We'll never see him again. I have been a bad mother, she said. My daughter is a terrible woman I no longer wish to know, my son is dying. I have been a bad mother. She's trying to make up for it, Allen. That's why we're here.

Please tell my mother, I said, the movements of my hands constricted by fury as I breathed hard and felt my eyes burn, that I am working diligently on not dying. I am not yet in need of Mother Teresa. I would rather have my real mother. My father raised both his hands. I waved them away. You may also tell her that this kind of flabby thinking and fake courage is what I'd expect from my sister. Or my brother-in-law.

Turning, I saw that she was peering inquiringly in our direction, a small, grey-haired woman sitting at a green-enameled metal café table in late-afternoon summer sunlight. Her white blouse glowed, making her arms and face appear tanned. Behind her a bank of fulvous daylilies flourished against the fence, pale green leaves and waxy blossoms, and the trunk of the maple, massive, muscular, climbed into the air. She took off her sunglasses, placed them on the table next to her drink, formed the sign for my name in the air. I walked across the lawn, away from her, to the back door.

Upstairs, I went from kitchen to living room, dim now, the sun having settled behind the house next door, and dimmer for my eyes' being accustomed to the glare outside. Downstairs, Jeremy, Toby, and Kit wore shorts and t-shirts, each of them physically very different from the others though all with hair as dark as my own—Jeremy tall and massive and solid, his forearms and his long legs thick with fine, glossy black hair, his beard mussed and his hair wild, blowing around face and shoulders; Toby still a foot shorter, though not for long, gawky, elbows, wrists, and hands too big for his arms, his bare feet massive and clumsy, his recent haircut bristling, avant garde and short; and Kit, smallest of all, compact and wiry but still a child with a child's flyaway hair. My father, too, wore shorts, an elderly man's Bermudas, and had rolled the sleeves of his chambray shirt up strong tanned forearms; my mother's blouse, sleeveless, revealed sharp, bony shoulders. The adults wore pale, summery colors, the boys neon-bright fluorescents.

The leaves of the plants in the bay window gleamed waxily, Ficus benjamina and Ficus lyrata tall and lush, pothos and jasmine cascading from hanging pots. Standing in the window, I saw a small, black bird perched on the telephone wire outside. Its plumage looked wet or oily, bedraggled around the head and neck, and the feathers were iridescent, green around the eyes, purple on breast and back. The bird's sharp, lemon yellow beak opened and closed, its throat pulsed, but I couldn't hear anything. I moved, or it saw me, and it cocked its head rapidly from side to side, then fell into the air below the window, out of sight.

I pulled the left sleeve of my black pullover up to the elbow. The latest lesions, a cluster of five, gleamed like stains of blueberry syrup on the inside of the forearm, between two blue veins. The hairless skin glowed palely in the dusk. After the first four lesions, on my left ankle, nothing happened for nearly a year, my test results remained stable and blood work revealed no imminent danger. Dr. Ribeiro and I were becoming complacent—he didn't want me on any kind of drug therapy as long as I was doing so well. Then two new blemishes bloomed on the left calf, and a month later I was in the hospital with pneumonia, and José (by now we were on a first-name basis) began deploying his battery of medical acronyms, weapons as secret, unproved, and expensive as the stealth bomber.

Well for the last six months, as far as it went, functional, I could pass, now—wearing long trousers, socks, shoes, sleeves close around my wrists and a collar that opened no further than the clavicle. I went into the bedroom and sat on Jeremy's side of the bed.

AT WORK MY father had three particular friends, deaf men, whom he sometimes invited home for supper and a game of dominoes. They were younger than my parents, rough, strong, good-natured bachelors when I first knew them, Desmond and Hap and Rory, who might tickle a four-year-old boy until he screeched, not that they could hear him, or, holding him by the ankles, whirl around the backyard like a drunken helicopter until we tumbled in a heap. They seldom came all three together—too much of an invasion for my mother's preference—and

soon enough Hap was bringing his fiancée Saralyn, an unnervingly
beautiful young woman who appeared to have stepped from the pages
of a Hans Christian Andersen fairy tale—a mirror-bright changeling
sea creature who told Steph and me wonderful stories of her childhood
in Charleston. She had been hearing until the age of nine and could still
speak aloud, but without ever knowing that her voice was ugly, harsh,
loud, and inflectionless, so that she seemed even more a figure of en-
chantment. I imagined that one of the old gullah wise women of her
stories had magicked away her hearing, jealous of the child's beauty,
and condemned her to this croaking, froggy voice instead of the clear
contralto she ought to have possessed, which the sorceress kept for herself. It was in the person of Saralyn, I believe, that I first understood
deafness as a loss.

Desmond, too, married, a few years later, but I never met his wife,
she never joined us for supper or sat fourth at dominoes. You only
knew he was married by the gold ring on his left hand that flashed in
lamplight when he talked, and because he stopped drinking.

Of the three, I remember Rory best. He liked to have me sit on his
lap at the domino table—his luck, he called me, although he usually
lost, neither of us having a head for strategy, and Steph refused to part-
ner him. Rory, when he came to visit, brought flowers for my mother,
who called him a gentleman, bourbon for my father and beer for himself, candy or ice cream for Steph and me. He always smelled clean, of
Ivory soap and faintly of lavender or rosewater, never of sweat or printers' ink, although the crescents under his fingernails were indelibly
stained. Something of a dandy, he wore starched and pressed shirts,
which felt cool to me, on his lap, on even the warmest evenings. The
fabric rustled, almost crackled, when he stretched or threw out a tile or
when I shifted position. His chin and cheeks and upper lip were stained
as dark as his fingernails by the blue shadow of his beard, which felt like
coarse sandpaper against my palm, a sensation I enjoyed and which
was enhanced by the contrast between this roughness and the smooth,
fine, translucent skin of his brow. Most astonishing to me were the
curls of black hair that sprouted at the open neck of his shirt. It was as
though he were part beast, a creature as magical in his way as Saralyn.

But Rory never brought a fiancée to visit, nor did he ever turn up
displaying a gold ring on his left hand. He always came alone, and it
seemed to me he was as much my friend as my father's.

A SETTLING OF the mattress and a warm pressure against my side. Jeremy leaned into me but, tactful, didn't place his arm around my waist as he might have, as I might have wished. "You okay?"

"Yeah. Thinking."

"Good thoughts?"

I moved a little. I could have leaned my head against his upper arm but not against his shoulder, which was too high. "Maybe." The light around us was thin and green, an arboreal light, as if we sat in a boys' tree fort in the canopy of a forest with the summer afternoon settling into a dusk that would last for hours, for miles and miles. But we sat on our bed, in our bedroom, on the second floor of our house. Leaves brushed against the window screens. A car drove by, not by the house but on one of the cross streets, its stereo tuned too loud so that the passengers must be muddled and deafened, not hearing the music but something else. "I was remembering a friend of Dad's. Rory must have been the first gay man I ever knew."

"My parents didn't have any gay friends," Jeremy said. "Probably still don't."

"My mother is waiting for me to die," I told him.

"I thought it might be something like that. Allen? She's wrong."

"Rory died." I stood and gazed out the window, into the crown of the tree. "Sean died. Luke and Marco and Gary died. Matthew died. Matthew was the first boy I ever slept with. He died. Jeremy, Rodrigo died. Remember Rodrigo?"

He was staring at me. He nodded.

"Rodrigo died. Rodrigo was sick when I met him. I would have liked to know him. It's a miracle no-one we know here has died. Jeremy." My throat hurt. "Jeremy, I'm sick."

He stood up. He held a scrap of paper in one hand. I saw a line of my father's handwriting. He moved closer, raising his hand mutely.

"Please don't touch me."

"Allen."

I spoke to the tree beyond the window. "I am thirty years old. I have a job. I have a car. I have a house. I have a handsome lover who loves me. I have everything I ever wanted—better, I have Toby and Kit. My mother is waiting for me to die."

"Boy."

"You can't call a thirty-year-old man with a mortal illness *boy*, Jeremy. It's not seemly."

His hands were rough on my shoulders. "I can slap him when he acts childish and hysterical and morbid." He was never rough with me, unless we both wanted it. "Allen." His hands closed around my throat. "You're going to die. Okay. I know that. But not yet." My hands are big for my size, but not big enough to go around Jeremy's neck. His hands had grasp to spare. "We're all going to die. Are you forgetting that it's got me too? But *not yet.*" One set of fingers released my neck. Those that remained were sufficient. Outside, the leaves of the tree moved but its branches did not. "Allen." The free hand cupped itself over my left ear. I am left-handed. All of the lesions, so far, were on the left side of my body. "Boy." Jeremy's right hand moved from my throat to my shoulder and the tips of four fingers dug into the hollow below the clavicle. "Allen, I don't want to fight with you." Pressing himself against me, my shoulder blades like barbs snagged on his ribs, Jeremy bound me with his arms. The hair on his forearm swept over his wrist onto the back of his hand. "There's too much to do." His scent enveloped me. "When Ruth was pregnant, I told her I thought it was time I took care of her. She wouldn't let me, either. Just because you're grown up, boy—" He pressed his mouth to the crown of my skull. "Your father asked me to take care of you, Allen. I can't do that if you won't let me."

"What about them?" I felt fine, in fact, able to breathe despite the constriction of his arms, able to distinguish among his sweat, the nearly effaced traces of soap and shampoo, and the smells, identical, theoretically, of deodorant and the cologne dabbed on the insides of his wrists, the hollow of his throat. "Who's going to take care of everyone else? What about dinner?"

"The coals aren't ready yet," he said. "Toby's watching. Your father's helping. Kit and your mother are playing with the dog. Everything's all right for a little while, Allen. Tell me about Rory."

I WAS FOURTEEN, home for the summer. Every fourteen-year-old boy in the world becomes impatient with his family but I had no friends of my own age at home. My friends were scattered over New England, the Middle Atlantic, a few in the upper Midwest, one or two out west. You could write only so many letters telling your friends how boring it was to be home, and even as you wrote you suspected that your friends' homes weren't dull. You could only read so many books, take the bus downtown so many times. My sister had found a job and stayed in

Baltimore for the summer. I could have looked for a job of my own, I suppose, slinging burgers at McDonald's, pumping gas, shelving books at the library where I spent so much time anyway. My father suggested I do something with the backyard, make a garden of it.

I sat on the back step early in the morning, sipping coffee. It was already hot, a damp, unappealing heat, the earth exhaling and the sky breathing in. Our small backyard was bounded by a tall wooden fence, its boards warped and weathered a fuzzy, silvery grey. In the far corner stood a stunted magnolia—not the variety that blooms in the northern spring, before the leaves, but with glossy dark foliage and a few creamy white blossoms like hands cupped in prayer or like white doves tucked in among the leaves high in the crown. In the other corner a thicket of camellias displayed round, compact flowers of an unattractive, strawberry ice cream pink, stained with brown. The rosebushes were out of bounds, attenuated canes muscling up from the crowns and then trailing all about in an inextricable tangle. So much effort went into their flowering that the leafage seemed a poor afterthought, yellowed and sclerotic, but roses couldn't be pruned while blooming. The center of the yard was a lawn of sorts, an oblong of grass already wilting as the day's heat rose, more from the ground, it seemed, than the air. Little as I knew about gardens, I knew it wasn't the season.

My mother emerged from the house. So early, she was already smoking, holding the cigarette between two fingers of her left hand, using it as punctuation. I was too young to be drinking coffee, she told me, and thanked me for making it. She walked out into the center of the lawn. Well? What did I think? What was I planning?

My mother made many of her own clothes. She wore a shift of pale green, so pale it was almost white, with a sprigged print. In a gesture at style, she had edged neckline, placket, and armholes with moss-green ribbon; a length of the same ribbon bound her hair at the nape. A lace of white webbed the smooth chestnut of her hair. Squinting, she inhaled on her cigarette, an unattractive action that caused her to look old, and asked me again.

I'd mow the lawn, I said. There wasn't much more I could do. If I cut back the roses now they wouldn't bloom again this year, and it might kill them.

She turned about, looking young again, my mother. I could tie them up at least, so they wouldn't always be snagging on people. I could clear out the weeds—including, she said pointedly, that annoying as-paragus. Or whatever it was. Returning to the step where I sat, she suggested it might be nice to have a little brick path around the lawn, and a border of flowers. What did I think about petunias.

Where was I going to get the bricks, I asked impatiently. The only place was miles away, and what did she expect, I'd carry them home two at a time?

Perhaps they delivered. She dropped the butt of her cigarette, rubbed it out underfoot. She stared down at it for a moment, then crouched and plucked it from the grass. More coffee, dear? Or—Rory's friend, the man he lived with, had a truck; we could ask.

That evening, a Thursday, she told my father to invite Rory for supper. I noticed she didn't mention his friend. At intervals during the day—as I mowed the lawn; when I bicycled to the community rec center to swim; in the afternoon, after lunch, when, back in my swimsuit, I lay out on the lawn with a book and a Coke—at odd moments I remembered Rory. Since growing too big for his lap I hadn't thought much about him, Dad's friend, a good guy after all, but maybe not too bright. Not a man who'd go out of his way to make up for the defects in his education the way my father had—my father the measure for every man, an impossible burden.

But, though my mute father was my yardstick, I was, around then, as intoxicated with the spoken language, as fascinatedly ignorant about it, as I was by the capricious urges and leanings of my adolescent penis, as likely to flare up in chapel or English class, listening to Mr. Grigorevich recite Emily Dickinson in his reedy quaver, as at swimming practice or in the showers. I listened for accents, hearing the different deformations of vowels, apocopation of or emphasis on certain consonants, the stresses and rhythms of speech and the sonorities and timbres of voice, without knowing how to classify or place them. Mr. Grigorevich, for instance, lisped slightly and molded every phrase into iambic pentameter, but whether this was personal or regional I couldn't tell. Back home, I heard the accent of interior North Carolina, adored it —the distinction between the speech of Miss Abernathy at my local library and that of the school librarian, Mrs. Smithfield—but couldn't characterize the difference. What kind of accent did I have? I read Shakespeare soliloquies aloud, and couldn't tell. I had never seen deaf people talking in New England but even if I had the regional accents of

sign wouldn't have enthralled me as much as those of English; you notice your second language more than the first.

Wandering off on a tangent again: I had been thinking about Rory.

Rory was still Rory in his starched white shirt. He shook my hand
firmly, fondly, this first sight of me since last winter, then asked with a
silent laugh if I remembered how to talk. Hey, Allen, he said, welcome
back, and handed me a half-pound Hershey bar.

Hey, thanks! even though I was leery of chocolate's effect on my
skin, how are you? I grinned, unable to help myself, and hugged him. I
had sat on his lap as a child, after all. His shirt-front crumpled as satis-
fyingly as it had then, but when had he started wearing tight Levi's?
When had I started noticing the way a man wore his clothes, not just
the clothes he wore? Rory had a mustache now. He was thirty-five. His
shirt was unbuttoned three buttons, his sleeves rolled up his forearms.

Over dominoes, my mother brought up the bricks, the truck, the
necessity of something to occupy my summer. Not breaking stride, Sure,
Rory offered, why didn't he and Danny come by tomorrow morning.

He hadn't said Danny, of course, but the designation was a slurred,
rapid elision of D-A-N, spelled with his fingers, not a proper sign, not
the kind of name real people have. I had never even heard of the man
before, what did I know.

Danny was a black man, first, surprising enough, who didn't climb
down from the cab of his pickup when it pulled up in front of the
house the next day, and who only nodded when I climbed in after Rory
and Rory introduced us. I had to forgive Dan, Rory said, grinning, he
had a bitch of a hangover. So did Rory, for that matter.

"Don't you go listening to his slanders," said Danny, the second
surprise, his voice a velvety tenor that—after a moment when soundtrack was out of synch with picture so that I saw his mouth move before I heard him—seemed inextricable from the chocolaty sheen of his
skin, darker than a Hershey bar, or the shiny pink of his lips, like satin.
"My hands don't talk so good this early in the morning any day of the
week. Whether I got a hangover or not. So," he said, "what'm I gonna
call you, hey? Alls I know is this—" and, lifting his left hand from the
steering wheel, he sketched my name.

"Allen," I said, "my name's Allen."

"You call me Danny."

Rory grinned hugely, looking from one of us to the other, gauging my reaction to Danny's speaking aloud, Danny's subtle pleasure at my surprise. What had Danny said? he asked.

"Go on tell him. He hates it I can't talk when I'm driving."

Danny helped move the bricks from the bed of his truck to the backyard, but when my mother offered him a glass of lemonade he shook his head, said, I'll be going on home now, Mrs. Pasztory. Coming, Rory? Watching the play of his hands with their two colors, dry pink and glossy brown, I hardly noticed the hesitations in his sign but it was clear it wasn't native. He wasn't like me, then—sign was a language he'd had to learn.

Rory slapped my back. He'd help the kid for a couple hours. Danny would fetch him later?

Sure thing. Good-bye then, he said, and, "'Bye, Allen," to me. "Work hard."

Helping me mark out the paths with twine tied to stakes, then to excavate a bed for the bricks, Rory asked, Would I like to take in a movie with him and Danny some night? How about tonight? There was a Fellini double-bill downtown.

I stared at him. It was Saturday: Rory hadn't shaved and his beard had grown beyond shadow. Drops of sweat glinted in his mustache—it was hot, and Saturday: he wore shorts and a t-shirt. It was summer, but he wasn't tan, and the black hair on his white legs, the black stubble on his pale face in the terrible light of a late June afternoon were beautiful. I caught myself wishing he'd take off his shirt. Well? he asked.

A movie, I said stupidly.

Fellini—subtitles.

In a theater I could sit next to him. Sure, Rory, that'd be great.

When Danny came to pick Rory up I had taken a shower, and I climbed back into the cab of the pickup, between them this time. While Rory explained—quick dinner downtown and then the movies—I leaned back against the hot vinyl seat. Danny kept glancing at me as he drove, his brows creased, eyes speculative. But first, Rory said, he wanted a shower too. His thighs were flattened out slightly, fleshy, on the seat. Even his knees were hairy, even his elbows.

"Dad!" Toby yelled from the back door, circumspect as always, "we're getting hungry."

"Ya! Espéranse momentito, ¿okay?" Jeremy called without moving, his belly beating beneath my ear, echoing. He had taken to speaking Spanish to his son in self defense, everyone else in the household going bilingual on him. "Diez minutos, te digo, no más."

"Ten minutes. I'm counting!" The door slammed.

Leaning against the headboard, Jeremy drew me up beside him. With a surprising delicacy which is never a surprise he smoothed my hair, then, with one finger, ruffled an eyebrow, traced the descent of my nose, the line of my lower lip. "So," he murmured, "did you make it with them, boy? Was Rory's chest as good as you hoped? Did he have *hairy shoulders?*"

I pressed my lips against his palm, warm, sweaty. "You're in the wrong story, sweetheart. I've told you—Matthew was the first boy I slept with, a year later." I sat up. "Let's go. I have to talk to my parents. You have to grill salmon."

"They weren't boys," he muttered, poor grace in action as he wrestled me back down. "You wouldn't have to have *slept* with them." With his hands on either side of my head he bent down to kiss me. "So?"

I pulled him down. "Rory had hairy shoulders, I saw that when he came out of the shower." Jeremy's bulk lay heavy on my chest. He outweighed me by more than Herodias. "I didn't make it with them. I want to make it with you but there isn't time. Okay? And his chest?—well, you know those hunky blue-collar types. His chest was better than yours."

Two Pictures

MY CAR WAS in the shop so for the week I drove Jeremy's. You're so much closer to the ground in his little Triumph than in my Volvo sedan that you notice things you'd never see. Pulling into the driveway, I saw that the hyacinths we'd planted in the narrow bed along the side of the house were in bloom—must have been going for some time. I'm not especially fond of hyacinths, which seem to me too rococo for their size; I think of them as kitsch flowers, looking more like injection-molded plastic, especially the pink ones, than many well-made artificial blossoms. In masses of blue and white, though, from a distance, they have a sort of Delft charm and look less fussy than a similar border of paperwhite narcissi would. Supposing paperwhites could survive a New England winter, something I wouldn't gamble on. Forced paper-whites indoors, in shifts, through the winter, daffodils and jonquils in April, in the real garden behind the house. Then tulips, and then it's summer again, a whole different set of problems.

It was chilly inside, on the second floor where we live. We'd turned off the furnace the week before, but I would have expected Jeremy to have a fire going in the kitchen. And perhaps a pot of tea waiting. I'm predictable—he knows my schedule. But he was nowhere around and there was no sign the boys had come home yet. The cat yelled for her dinner but I ignored her—she was Kit's pet, after all, his responsibility. On the kitchen table a small vase held a stem of white hyacinth.

Jeremy seldom works past four-thirty. Just because he works at home, he says, is no reason he shouldn't keep to a routine. Every morning after Toby and Kit and I leave he goes up to his studio and shuts the phone off; every afternoon, just as regularly, when I get home he's waiting, gardening maybe, or cooking, or sprawled on the couch in the living room with a book, Providence purring on his belly, the radio tuned to the classical station out of Boston or to one of the local rock stations, depending. He hadn't been in the garden, he wasn't in the kitchen, the radio was silent. I checked Toby's bedroom, which, in the back of the house, is quieter than ours over the street, and preferable for afternoon naps. The bed was narrowly, fussily made, as usual, obviously un-touched. Toby and Kit might not get back for hours yet.

I started upstairs. Jeremy's studio is in the attic, with two windows facing north—although during the summer they don't let in much light, obscured by the crown of the big tree on the sidewalk. We put in a big skylight when we bought the house and made over the attic. I knocked on the door. "Jere?" I pushed the door open.

Swiveling around on his stool, Jeremy looked somehow startled and sleepy at the same time—something to do with how deeply set his eyes are under heavy brows, one of them, the left, tilting up at the outside corner, and the way his upper lip was hidden by his mustache. "Allen!" He glanced up at the skylight. "Am I late or are you early?" He leaned forward a little, characteristically, and clasped his hands together between his knees.

"We're both late. It's almost five." I closed the door and went to him.

He butted his head against my chest, then looked up. A faint red stain colored the corner of his mouth and a few mustache hairs, where he sucks on his sable watercolor brushes after rinsing them out, to re-shape their points. "I felt a little peaky this morning," he said with the confidential, dismissive tone he adopts when referring to his health, "so I went back to bed after you left. Lost most of the morning."

Holding the volume of his skull in my palms, I warmed my fingers in his thick soft hair, dark but threaded with white. We had an unspo-ken agreement not to dwell on our illnesses, mine definite, Jeremy's provisional, so long as nothing much changed. "Do you want to keep working? I'll do dinner."

"Nah." Sighing, Jeremy pressed his cheek against my belly. "I'm fairly sick of it. How was your day, boy?"

"Okay," I said. "Standard issue." He'd called me boy since we first met, almost ten years before—partly to distinguish me from the real boy in the family, Toby, who's called kid. (Somehow this is never con-fused with my nephew's name.) Toby calls me Allen and I call him Toby; he calls his father Dad and I call him Jere or Jeremy, occasionally Kent, infrequently, on special occasions, sir. I looked over his back, at the surface of the drafting table where a lozenge of light from the sky-light was obscured by the illumination of the lamp. "What are you working on, Mr. Kent?"

He let go of my thigh and pushed me away a little. "You look so nice all dressed for work, boy," he said, then offered a silly grin. "Good-looking suit. Handsome tie. Anyone'd think you were all grown up." Standing, he pulled me back to his chest, laid his lips against my eyelid. Jeremy is ten inches taller than I. He had bought the tie I wore. I would be thirty-one in three weeks. "Hello, Allen. Good to see you."

"What are you working on?" I asked again, after I'd kissed him.

"Did I tell you Eamon called last week? He thinks it's time I graduated from kiddie books, so he wants me to do the jacket for a grown-up novel they're bringing out in the fall." Jeremy butted my shoulder, as if he didn't want me to see the drawings on his desk. "Silly idea, I told him. You want a cup of tea?"

"That'd be nice."

The front half of the attic is Jeremy's studio, the rear our guest room, Kit's room for now; between them there's a bathroom, and an alcove with a little refrigerator, an electric kettle, so that guests can have their first cups of coffee before having to face us in the morning, and so Jeremy can make tea while he's working. He went into the bathroom to fill the kettle. I loosened my tie and took off the suit jacket, then found the phone and turned it back on.

On top of the flat files where Jeremy keeps papers and completed work, among the jars of pencils, pens, brushes, beside the plastic palette with its wrinkled worms of drying watercolor, stood another glass vase, another stem of white hyacinth. Taped taut to the drawing table was a sheet of fine-grained watercolor paper: the hyacinth in its vase stood in a shaft of light, before a mirror that reflected the blossom and the glass, and a dim bedroom where a dark figure leaned over another figure who lay against white pillows on the bed. Even in its reflected image the hyacinth looked more substantial, more real than the scene behind it in the depths of the mirror. Each individual floret on the stem, each trumpet of curved ivory petals, had a waxy, palpable sheen as if it were painted in a different medium than the translucent watercolor of the background.

Scattered over the surface of the table around the painting were pencil studies of the flower in its vase, sketches that blocked out the various elements of the composition, doodles and notes. Jeremy puts a lot of preliminary effort into his work. Although the final illustration may take only a couple of hours to put together, it's preceded by intensive, detailed thinking-on-paper—an inefficient way to go about it, he says, but there it is.

Under the window stood a low table, beside the chair where Jeremy sits when he needs to think, next to the tape deck for thinking-music. I turned on the radio; it was tuned to the classical station and started playing something lugubrious and slow, thick with strings. Turning down the volume, I stared out the window. The boughs of the tree bore hard green buds that wouldn't begin to unfurl into flowers, then leaves for another week or two. Across the street, in the narrow fenced yard of the opposite house, the handsome cinnamon colored chow whose owners I've never tried to meet reclined on a patch of grass. "Tell me about it," I said over my shoulder.

A spoon clinked against the rim of the teapot. "Eamon gave me a synopsis over the phone," Jeremy said. "I almost wish I'd remembered to turn it off that day. If he'd gotten the machine maybe he would've offered the commission to someone else." Our friend Eamon, the art director of Jeremy's New York publisher—a house so small it doesn't support separate design staffs for juvenile and adult divisions —detests answering machines, won't talk to them, hangs up when he realizes he's listening to a tape. "He sent me a copy of the manuscript. I read it yesterday. I don't like it. Eamon should have known I wouldn't like it."

On the table lay another sheaf of pencil studies. The top one showed several different arrangements of two faceless male figures— embracing, wrestling perhaps, one supporting the other, one bent over the other lying in a limp mournful sprawl. I lifted the first sheet to look at the next.

"Not that dislike will stop me from doing the job," said Jeremy. "I'm a professional. But Eamon's insensitivity is appalling."

"He sent us flowers when I was in the hospital," I said. The second drawing, surprising me, was a scrupulous portrait of Jeremy himself, his long face with its classic bone structure, the dark beard and thick shoulder-length hair that make such a dramatic contrast with translucent, easily bruised skin, pale eyes. The next had several studies of the same head from different angles, bearing different expressions, and without the beard, the hair cropped close to the fine skull.

"It's a short, sensitive, *poetic* first novel," Jeremy continued, "by some kid who must have read too much mythology in college, and thinks he can apply it as a metaphor to a situation he doesn't know anything about. He's probably only read about that too."

"What's it called? What's it about?" I was ready for the following drawing: a serene portrait of me, from Jeremy's eidetic memory, which made no attempt to flatter the tightness of skin against my bones, the general look of pervasive ill health that no régime of rest, sensible exercise, and diet, nor my doctor's carefully chosen and deployed battery of medications do much to alleviate, three years on.

Right behind me, Jeremy said, "It's called *The Death of Hyacinthus.* It's about the epidemic."

"I figured." I turned around.

He held the teapot in both hands, cradling it, an object of great worth, and it was only the old floral pattern porcelain teapot we picked up in an excess of anglophilia at a San Francisco junk shop years ago. "I couldn't carry the cups too." His eyes were bleak and hard.

"I'll get them."

Jeremy had brought the cups out and left them on the counter. They too were English bone china, but didn't match the teapot or, for that matter, each other or the saucers. All were decorated with flowers, although not hyacinths. Since neither of us puts anything in our tea he hadn't got the milk jug or the sugar bowl, which don't match either, but he had arranged some of his famous lemon-ginger cookies on a porcelain plate. Even though these days he's nearly as likely as I to feel unwell, Jeremy still takes care of me. I carried the cups out to the front room, then went back for the cookies while Jeremy poured the tea.

When I returned he was looking at the portrait of me. "Good likeness," I said.

He turned from the drawing to me, then back. "I guess." He sat down before his desk, sipped his tea.

In general I prefer not to look at images of myself, if only to avoid one more opportunity for self-pity. (This can be difficult in that I am, after his son, Jeremy's favorite model.) In fact, what I take to be the aspect of illness may be no more than no longer being twenty-five or whatever age I was when I last enjoyed looking at myself. In fact, my doctor congratulates me on how well I look, saying that no-one who didn't know would guess—but then, I am the only one of his cases to survive more than eighteen months and so, I suppose, am an object of some wonder for him. In fact, the most obvious marks no-one but he and his staff, Jeremy and the boys have ever seen. I can count myself lucky that, so far, no lesion has occurred where it can't be covered by my clothes, that all the things going wrong are going wrong inside. I opened my collar further, rolled up my shirtsleeves, and sat down. "Tell me about this novel," I said. I could guess what the writer had tried to do. It was a tempting idea, as, I guess, many suspect metaphors must be.

"I guess it's well written, well made," Jeremy said. "You can read it if you want. The protagonist dares to love the god, to sport with the god, to aspire to godhead himself, so he dies. The god, of course, is the first and only man he ever fucks with."

"Like the virgin who gets pregnant the first time she has sex."

Jeremy glanced at me over the rim of his cup. "I hadn't thought of that. Yeah."

"He probably isn't as young as you think, Jere, he's probably only a couple of years younger than me. Just old enough to know what he missed. And read a lot of Victorian novels in college." I put my cup down. "Those are the kids I worry about, the twenty-seven, twenty-eight year olds who're phobic about sex instead of the disease. The ones who can't separate the two, can't convince themselves it's a virus that's killing us, not sex by itself." I could feel a flush building on my chest and shoulders. I wonder sometimes if it isn't my anger that keeps me as healthy as I am. That, but more my concern for Toby's, and now Kit's, future. "The younger ones aren't sex-phobic—they take precautions the same way sane straight people take precautions against pregnancy, and get on with it."

If the phone hadn't rung just then I would have told him about the little talk his fourteen-year-old son and I had had a few months before, when Jeremy was last in New York—visiting Eamon, for a fact. Toby I don't have to worry about. Not that I had, not in this household.

But the phone did ring, and Jeremy answered it, and I watched his face develop the complex, tender, exasperated expression it generally does when he talks to Toby on the phone. I sipped tea, ate a cookie, and looked beneath the portrait of me on the table.

When Jeremy is working from a text not of his own composition, he frequently makes several assays at the subject. This final drawing must have been an alternate design for the cover of *The Death of Hyacinthus*. It was done in colored pencil, a medium with which Jeremy achieves more subtlety than one might expect. In the foreground two men have just turned away from the canvas hung behind them, have bent their heads together. The arm of the taller is around the shoulders of the other. The taller, of course, is Jeremy, his eyes shadowed with pain, and the shorter, younger one, whose lips are parted as though he were about to speak or as though he had trouble breathing, is Allen. The canvas that fills most of the background is framed in baroquely carved and gilded wood. It is a romantic, nineteenth-century, Alma-Tadema-esque painting, with the sort of soft-porn realism that passed for classicism—the two figures are naked, burnished athletes whose genitals are hidden by carefully careless wisps of drapery. The god holds his fallen, mortal, mortally wounded comrade in his arms in a pose reminiscent of a Renaissance pietà. The boy's limp hand has just loosed his discus, which lies in the millefiori meadow beside the fatal, bloodstained discus of the god. Oddly, perhaps, Apollo's grief-struck face is mine, some years younger, while the pale bloodied face of Hyacinthus is what Jeremy's must have looked like when he was an adolescent.

"Toby and Kit won't be home for dinner," Jeremy said, hanging up the phone. "He said they'd be late. I said they'd better not be." He bent forward, stared at his hands. "They're growing up, boy."

"Mr. Kent," I said, holding up his drawing, "this is vile."

For a moment, only a moment, he looked confused, grim, a little sick. Then he grinned broadly. "Isn't it awful?" When he smiles like that, despite the beard and the grey in his hair I see the strapping stud I first became infatuated with and then, an instant later, the man with whom I fell in love. "Perfect for the book, though."

"Eamon will love it." I got up and went to him and crouched down near his feet, took his hands in mine. "He has a fine appreciation of kitsch." Jeremy's hands are large, long-fingered, bony, and each has a sweep of fine dark hair across its back, a small thing, something I find profoundly beautiful.

"You don't mind?"

"What's to mind? Sort of flattering, actually, being mythologized."

He lifted his hands to hold my jaw.

"Jeremy," I said, "can I have a cookie?"

OUTDOORS

Head over Heels

THE BOY'S FATHER was named Neil DeVincenzo and when I pronounced his surname as if it were Italian he corrected me; his son Jimmy was a sulky twelve-year-old brigand who I suspected would be a real asset to the jayvee lacrosse team—a prediction that pleased them both. I had known, as if by clairvoyance, as soon as Neil DeVincenzo shook my hand when I met them in the outer office before their campus tour, who he was. Having read Jimmy's application, I knew mother and father were divorced and she remarried, but not whether Jimmy didn't get along with his stepfather nor if he knew of his father's homosexuality—which of these might inspire his callous rudeness and show of stupidity; he also had a two-year-old half-sister and that might have been enough cause. Having read the application I knew he was not stupid—knew that his mother was a real estate broker in Newport, her husband a career Navy man, and Jimmy's father, Neil, a department store executive in Boston. I knew there was enough money among them that they wouldn't be looking for financial aid, but I would have known this anyway, simply from the sharp double-breasted suit Neil wore: all he needed was a diamond pinkie ring and a fedora to appear the stereotype mafioso. In fact he was powerfully attractive and his son held promise of becoming a real beauty. I liked the way Neil DeVincenzo looked at me and it was this, his manner of sizing me up, that made me know he knew as much about me, without reading any applications, as I did about him.

With the various parts of Jimmy's completed application spread over the desk before me, I took notes on a conversation I could have repeated in my sleep, word for word, and attempted to have neither question nor response appear rote. Both Neil and Jimmy had the usual queries and comments, and Jimmy became less surlily withdrawn as we continued. I am, in the end, good at my job. On the face of it, the only aspect of the interview at all peculiar was that the single parent present was noncustodial. In any case, an interview carries very little weight in my decision making—although I suppose the parents could find it more useful or crucial. I think of the interview as a service to the applicants, which is why I like to provide lunch or some kind of refreshment, and why I offer two different tours of the campus, the first, which I lead, being the official tour, for applicant and parents together.

By now we had reached the point where I would begin to speak of tuition charges, fees, payment options, parental involvement and responsibilities—matters best discussed in Jimmy's absence. I buzzed Annie on the intercom and asked her to summon the guide for the second tour, one of a cadre of upperclass volunteers who realized that this kind of experience looked good on their college applications. I offered Jimmy cookies and a soda while we waited, coffee for his father. When I came back from fetching them, Neil DeVincenzo was peering at the four pen-and-ink drawings of houses on the wall. "These are nice," he said.

"Thanks." I gave Jimmy his Coke and placed the plate of cookies and Neil's coffee on the table between the two chairs.

"This one's New England." Neil was inspecting the portrait of our Federal Revival in Fox Point. "Not the other three, though."

The other three being two San Francisco Victorians—an Italianate three-decker and a Queen Anne row cottage—and a concrete and stucco box in a Mexican hill town. "We're transplants," I said.

"We?" Neil turned. He looked at the floor for a moment, or at his shoes, checking that the cuffs of his trousers broke properly, then lifted his face and presented me with a knowing smile.

Taking my own coffee, I returned to the chair behind the desk. "My lover's an artist." I glanced at Jimmy, flipping through a copy of the school catalogue. "They're houses he's lived in, one in Mexico, two in California, one here."

Annie knocked on the door and ushered in Jimmy's guide, Vik, one of our scholarship boys. "Mr. Pasztory," said Vik with a flash of startlingly white teeth.

"Vik, good afternoon." I waved him forward. "Vik is a junior here," I told the DeVincenzi. "He knows his way around, right?" Nodding, with another smile, Vik flipped his thick, straight, shiny black hair out of his eyes. "This is Jim, and his father, Mr. DeVincenzo." Jimmy had stood up, and the three of them shook hands, making polite noises. "You're a lacrosse player, aren't you, Vik? So's Jim."

They had something to talk about—as much as adolescents with three or four years between them could converse—so I sent the two boys off. Annie, whose family is Italian, shook her head sympathetically and shut the door behind her.

"I wish I had a tan like that." Neil gestured toward the closed door. "That's one astonishingly beautiful boy." The look he turned on me was charming and calculated, venal but somehow innocent.

"Vik's parents immigrated from Bombay—the tan's built-in. I brought you some coffee." Sipping from my own cup, I regarded Neil DeVincenzo with a similar attention to what he was giving me, feeling the nervous little thrill flirtation always inspires, whether I intend to carry through or not, a prickling in the palms of my hands and in my armpits as though I were sweating. "You've got good color yourself."

"Mine's from Sicily, couple generations back." Neil DeVincenzo laughed, his teeth as white as Vik's. "Not the same." He came over for his coffee, but instead of sitting again in the chair, which made him into a supplicant or an interview subject, he propped his hip on the edge of my desk and picked up one of the photographs, holding the Lucite frame at the rim the way one used to remove a record from its sleeve. "Is this your lover?" he asked, and tilted the picture so that I could confirm his guess.

The snapshot, one of my favorites, was taken at the beach house we rented one summer, on Sakonnet Point across the channel from Aquidneck Island. The little house was set on a half acre of lawn, and the picture shows Jeremy sprawled out on the grass, on his back. It was a cool, foggy afternoon, so Jeremy wears a cotton sweater over his swim trunks, but the sweater is rucked up over his belly, and his hand lies flat on the naked skin, fingertips furrowing the hair. His head turned toward the camera, he smiles, squinting, and his hair trails out among the stems of grass, the white clover and daisies, like another form of vegetation. "That's Jeremy."

"And these other people?" Neil asked, indicating the remaining pictures.

"My parents," I said, and, "My nephew, Kit. He's living with us for a while, while he's in school here. And the last one—that's Toby, Jeremy's son."

Replacing Jeremy's, Neil picked up the photo of Toby. He regarded it carefully, and in the steadiness, the intentness of his gaze I seemed to recognize his wish to be a good father to Jimmy. "Does Toby live with you too? While he's in school?"

"He's always lived with us," I said, shocked, and leaned forward to see the picture in Neil's hand. "I mean, he's always lived with Jeremy, and I've been part of the picture since he was six."

"Oh." Returning the photograph to the desk, where he placed it in precisely the same position, Neil blinked several times, his lips thinned against his teeth. Taking up his cup, he walked away from the desk, then turned back with a small, wistful smile. "Would you mind if I smoke? I only really like coffee if I'm smoking. How old is Toby now?"

"Let me find you an ashtray." The odd fact is that Jeremy and I didn't spend much time with other gay men, even when we lived in San Francisco, and so I have never become accustomed to the variety of re-actions our raising Toby inspires. Nearly always there is a certain kind of fascinated horror involved. You can't help but wonder if it's horror at the thought of being tied down by a child's needs, one's life compro-mised by having to be responsible for someone else, or if it isn't a form of naïve envy. Annie kept an ashtray in the cupboard in the outer office, a heavy, ugly saucer of pressed amber glass; I fetched it for Neil and told him that Toby was fifteen, Kit thirteen. Not going behind my desk again, I sat in Jimmy's chair.

"You already know that I'm gay too," Neil said, lighting his ciga-rette, and then he sat down as well, crossing one leg over the other and leaning forward. "Funny how you can tell, isn't it?" Gazing at me with an intentness that made me uncomfortable, he said, "See, I'd like Jimmy to be in boarding school because I don't much like his step-father, but it wouldn't have occurred to me to try to get custody. Rhode Island Italian Catholics—Mamma takes care of the babies and Pop goes out to make a living. My ex-wife, Jimmy's mother—I thought we were happy together. Just three years ago." Neil DeVincenzo closed his eyes for a long moment. His face had that combination of a brutal boniness of feature and weathered sensualism of the flesh that seems to me particular to men of southern Italian descent. When he opened his eyes again, they were the soulful, uncomprehending russet brown of a dog's eyes. Taking a drag on his cigarette, he leaned back in his chair, uncrossed his legs and set them wide apart. "Sometimes I still think we ought to be happy together," he said, offering to the space in front of him, but not to me, a thin, pained smile.

WHEN VIK BROUGHT Jimmy back to my office, I noticed that the younger boy had had his hair cut within the last week or so. I wanted to lay my palm against the back of his neck where the coarse black hair had been clipped to a prickly stubble through which his olive oil–clear skin gleamed. Shaking my hand, his father asked if I ever got up to Boston and whether we could have lunch together sometime. I wanted to make no promises but at the same time it is also true that at times I find myself acting the sounding-board or counselor for an unhappy, worried schoolboy who knows nowhere else to turn, and Neil and I made a date.

CREDIT CARD READY, I drove the fifty miles to Boston and left the car in a parking garage a few blocks from the department store where Neil DeVincenzo worked. We had agreed to meet at the store, a landmark for the out-of-towner, even though Neil didn't work on Saturday, and although Toby's and Jeremy's birthdays were both a few months past and Kit's half a year in the future. My own was a week away, but what could I buy for myself that I both needed and wanted and which would not also prove an occasion for self-pity?

We had agreed to meet in Housewares at eleven-thirty. Meanwhile, carrying a slip of paper on which I'd written all of Toby's and Kit's sizes, I prowled the Boys Department without finding anything I could trust myself to buy. I tried Men's Furnishings where, out of desperation more than because he needed them, I bought four pairs of jazzy boxer shorts for Jeremy; detoured through Toiletries, avoiding the come-ons of stylish young men pushing a new fragrance, and picked up a four-ounce flask of his cologne, something I knew he didn't need since he wasn't halfway through the last one; bought myself a fifty-dollar tie because it was marked down to nineteen, and found that it was only a quarter past ten. When I'd asked the boys if they wanted anything from Boston, Toby said no, not really. Kit gave me a look that meant his father wasn't paying his prep-school tuition, after all, while Jeremy and I provided room and board and saw nothing of the allowance his mother sent every month, unless he bought us a gift. Jeremy I told—because his son and my nephew were in the kitchen with us—that I just wanted to get away alone for the day. I walked out onto the street again and considered going into the record store across the way but assumed that any CD I found would be something Toby already owned or by a group he didn't like.

It was cool and windy, and there were hundreds of people about. I went into a crowded drugstore and bought a small container of orange juice and a pack of cigarettes. It would not be the first time I'd smoked since the bout of pneumonia, but nearly. Smelling Neil's cigarette in my office, I had almost asked him for one. Standing on the sidewalk again, I drank the juice and smoked half of two cigarettes, then returned to the department store, which in my mind on that day was called DeVincenzo's but which I pronounced according to the rules of Italian: Day-Vin-chent-so. Later on, I had told Jeremy that I was going to lunch with someone he didn't know and he had said, "Whatever," and then, I remembered, "Allen, have you noticed that these sheets are getting frayed around the edges?" I took the escalators to Bed and Bath on the fourth floor.

At a certain point in telling me the story of his marriage and its end, Neil DeVincenzo had said—and I am not sure whether he even heard himself saying it, whether he meant it to be taken as a truism or a truth —"Every Italian husband cheats on his wife." He had been married for sixteen years when he was transferred from the branch store in the mall outside Providence to the flagship in Boston and took a pied-à-terre there so he wouldn't have to drive back to Newport every night. He told me, and I believed him, that it had been by then more than a decade since the three times he had cheated on his wife, once with a woman and twice with men. Some months later she asked him for a divorce because she had fallen in love with a Navy lieutenant to whom she'd sold a waterfront condo.

Even then, whether out of relief or despair, Neil did not start going out to bars, several within easy walking of his apartment. His wife and son moved into the lieutenant's condo, and Neil asked her to sell the house, commission and half the closing price to be her settlement. He refashioned the Back Bay studio into a place he could live full-time, and one weekend every month drove down to Newport to be Jimmy's Dad. Meeting the lieutenant for the first time on one of these expeditions, Neil saw a man no better looking than any other but one he wanted, suddenly and inexplicably, to make love to.

There are supermarket-tabloid stories, sad tell-all memoirs, and volumes of pop sociology, and always the deceived wife discovers her husband's secret life or the unhappy husband decides he can no longer live a lie.

I BOUGHT ONLY one set of sheets because I didn't like to choose patterns without Jeremy's agreement, and in any case those sheets, all cotton, a slate-blue-and-white pinstripe, were not on sale, and it was eleven-fifteen. After consolidating my purchases in one bag, I went to Housewares, on the same floor. It was no trouble to convince myself that we didn't need a microwave oven, but sleek, stylish toasters, cappuccino machines, electric pasta makers, a set of attractive mixing bowls—these I found harder to pass by. An enamel-red coffee grinder, which would sort oddly with the colors in our kitchen, had caught my eye when I heard my name.

"I found you." Today Neil DeVincenzo was not wearing a suit; in wool jacket, bulky sweater, and snug cords he looked younger and, paradoxically, more serious. "Hi, Allen. I'm glad you made it." He gave me the same charming, corrupt grin and took my hand.

"I said I'd be here, Neil."

In fact he looked sexy, and knew it. He held my hand for a moment, then moved his grasp to my biceps. "I came in on the subway—I was afraid I'd be late." Steering me toward the down escalator, he said, "Are you hungry? I made a twelve-thirty reservation. You drove up? We'll need the whole hour to find parking."

We reached the ground floor and he paused long enough for me to say, "Are you nervous, Neil?"

First he stepped a little away from me, and then he smiled again, and then he said, "Yeah."

"Why?"

The escalator had let us off in the middle of Menswear, Better Slacks on one side, dress shirts on the other. Directly in front of us, the headless torso of a mannequin wore a crisply pressed white shirt and a pine green necktie patterned with pale orchids. One arm of the shirt, bent before the mannequin's belly, was draped with more ties, and, overlapped like the apple slices in a tart, folded ties rayed out over the surface of the table on which the mannequin sat. Moving forward, Neil stroked the array of silks with the tips of his fingers. With his head bent, his admirable nose appeared larger and the flesh under his chin creased into three distinct folds piled up atop the Adam's apple. He lifted the tip of one of the hanging ties. "I'm so glad the day of the power tie is over. We do have good buyers." Turning, he headed toward the exit. I had to hurry to catch up.

Outside, we paused a moment to breathe in the cool tasteless air. He pulled a pair of gloves from his pocket and put them on, watching his hands as he eased each finger down. "Yeah, I'm nervous. I mean, I don't know how serious I am." He spoke slowly, his mild tenor voice thoughtful and quiet. "I can't figure out if I'm looking for a friend or if I want to seduce you, Allen."

I placed my hand on his shoulder. "Let's leave it up in the air for a bit. Let's get the car. Where are we eating?"

In the cold, damp, concrete parking garage, he said, "Thanks, Allen," and then, playful, "What did you find to buy?"

It seemed to me that if I were going to allow him to seduce me I shouldn't tell him but at the same time that my purchases reflected my intentions and position as well as if I'd planned them. "Sheets," I said, reaching the car and unlocking the doors, "cologne, underwear. You know where we're going, Neil, do you want to drive?"

He stood near me. An April morning, it shouldn't have been cold enough for our breath to steam. "Are you sure?" he asked, staring at the oil-stained concrete floor. A moment later he lifted his gloved hands as if to take the keys from me, but closed the palms around my hand, the leather of the gloves chill on my skin. He raised his chin, proud, and I noticed for the first time that he hadn't shaved—his chin and upper lip were stiff with blue-black bristles a fraction of an inch long which, sprouting from his fine, dense skin, seemed to make clear his solidity, his being carved out of three dimensions and his being there: standing before me, Neil gazed into my eyes.

"I'm sure."

NEIL DeVINCENZO's APARTMENT, a first-floor studio in a brick row house on a narrow back street, was chiefly notable for a massive marble fireplace. Taking my jacket, he hung it on a peg by the door, then, first thing, called the restaurant to cancel the twelve-thirty reservation. He knelt by the hearth and wadded together a few sheets of newspaper, piled them on the grate, and asked if I would like a cup of coffee or something to eat. Kneeling, he appeared to be intent and sure, but his expression, peering back at me, belied this decisiveness.

I had taken a seat in one of the two chairs facing the fireplace. The raised platform of Neil's bed was covered with industrial-grey carpeting and constructed with a bench-high shelf along one length, perpen-

dicular to the fireplace wall and padded with a pallet made from a russet Oriental rug. I felt tired and dazed, somehow, depleted, as if we had
already made love, and for a moment could not reply with more than a
nod, but when he began to rise I said, "Do you have an incomprehensible coffee maker? I know how to boil water."

Apparently relieved, he told me I could find the coffee in the
freezer and where to look for filters, and turned back to the fireplace. In
the kitchen, a cramped, narrow affair hidden behind a folding screen, I
measured coffee into the machine, filled the reservoir with water. A
beefcake calendar hung from a pair of magnetized clips on the refrigerator door. Saturated with hyperreal color, the photograph for April displayed a tanned, muscular, hairless torso, cropped at the neck.
Emerging from a swimming pool whose glittering blue surface, scalloped with sunlight, formed the backdrop, the model balanced on
hands that grasped the coping of the pool, his thighs pressed against it
so that his genitals, slung in a minuscule bikini only a little darker than
the water behind him but equally shiny, were presented to you as if they
were a gift. My name was written in green ink on the square for today's
date. Under that, in the space for the following Friday, the notation
read *Newport* PM—*Jimmy*, and a green line was drawn through
Saturday and Sunday.

Behind another screen, folded into itself like a concertina, a wide
bay window looked out on a dank, mossy yard shaded by a magnolia
laden with blooms. Shed petals littered brick pavement. The window's
embrasure formed another padded bench, long enough and wide
enough for a boy the size of Neil's son Jimmy to sleep on; a dusty plastic model of a fighter plane hung from a length of nylon line above this
narrow bed where a pillow lay at one end and a folded blanket and
sheets at the other. Piled atop the blanket were two pairs of laundered,
folded dungarees, a couple of t-shirts, and several pairs of white cotton
underpants too small for Neil to wear.

"Did you find everything?" He had come up behind me, and now,
placing his hands on my shoulders, leaned in to lick my neck between
the two rising tendons. I turned and—this was what I wanted—I kissed
him.

For an instant Neil pulled away and I caught a glint of something
in his eyes, a flicker, but then he embraced me and lowered his face so
that I wouldn't have to stretch. His mouth, or perhaps it was my own,

tasted of old cigarette smoke and faintly, stalely of breakfast; he touched his tongue to mine—our mouths were both open—then drew back, a thread of saliva joining us together like a rope. Under the heavy masking of his sweater I felt his shoulder blades flex as he placed both hands on my hips and held me against him. I was used to a man much taller than I—to Jeremy, against whose broad chest I could rest my head, both of us standing—but neither Neil nor I had to strain, there was no awkwardness in our embrace, no hesitation as we kissed again, and I felt, in addition to the pressure of his lips and the exploratory probing of his tongue, the sandpaper rasping of his chin against my cheek.

Releasing me again, Neil pushed me down onto the window seat. He stood above me, his arms hanging loose at his sides, his mouth slightly open and the lips already chafed and inflamed. Above my head the model plane turned slowly in the air. I wondered if it was Jimmy's or a relic of Neil's own childhood. Grown up, Neil gazed at me for a moment, his eyes warm, perplexed, then smiled. "You're a very pretty man, Allen," he said. Moving decisively, he pulled his sweater over his head, dropped it on the floor, and sat down beside me. "All the guys must tell you that." He took one of my hands in both of his. The flesh of his palms was warm, warmer than mine, dry, confident. He wore a sage green t-shirt that, while not tight, revealed the solid bulk of his chest and shoulders and showed damp patches under the arms.

"You're not nervous anymore," I said. "Does that mean you made a decision?"

Lifting my hand, he gave the palm a dry kiss, then drew the tip of his tongue up the lifeline and along the index finger, which for a moment he inserted between his lips. "I made mine," he said, quiet, serious, "but I think the important decision is the one you have to make. And I'll abide by it. Do you think the coffee's ready?"

"No doubt." Removing my hand from his grasp, I touched his cheek, traced the curve of his ear, the line of his jaw. He had a short, flash haircut and a high forehead, his beard and mustache were no more than a day old: Jeremy's hair fell past his shoulders, thick and soft, and his beard was an ornament I was accustomed to and fond of. "Do you have a boyfriend, Neil?" I asked him.

"No." He ruffled my hair, then stood up. When he stretched, the fabric of his t-shirt stretched upward, taut below the flaring rib cage, and when he crooked his arms the biceps swelled. "How do you like your coffee?"

I touched my fist to his belly. "Black and unadorned."

IN FACT, I had nearly ten years of history to deal with, either to justify or to condemn the action I meant to take—ten years I could not imagine ever ending. Jeremy had been unfaithful to me at least once that I knew of, enough years before that it should not have provided a precedent; the whole matter of keeping score was as invidious and hateful as the concept of sexual fidelity seemed untenable. The truth being that there might be moments when each found the other physically repulsive or, although we never fought, days when we could not bear to be in the same room together or days when our desires intersected rather than coincided so that we both desperately wanted the same beautiful stranger browsing the frozen foods bins in the supermarket or, his profile turned in a fashion that seemed provoking and deliberate, reading the descriptive paragraph on the back of a cassette box at the video store.

Six years before, scared out of my wits, I had flown east from San Francisco to be interviewed for the job in Providence, and then to visit my sister and her family in Maryland and my parents in North Carolina. I left behind a house that was clearly mine although Jeremy's was the name on the deed, a city where all of my life that wasn't a fairy tale or a story for adolescents had been spent. Determined somehow not to return unless with sufficient reason not to stay, I left behind my lover, and a boy who might as well have been my son. I carried with me a burden of too many names, each incised into granite with its dates, and in particular the memory of two cadaverous faces whose bony structures alone could be reconciled with the faces of the first boy I ever slept with and of the first man I ever loved. Jeremy knew what was in my mind but we couldn't speak of it. I hoped to outrun death.

While I was gone Toby spent a few nights at the house of Sacha, his best buddy from school, leaving Jeremy by himself to rattle around the huge flat alone. I called in the early evening, his time, to check in, and he said, "You know, boy, I don't think I've spent a night all by myself, no-one else in the house, since you moved in."

I had moved in three years before that call, and in this period—so it seemed to me—Jeremy had hardly left the house. I said, "Well, enjoy it," but what I meant was, Remember all the recruiting trips I've taken and the nights I've spent alone in ugly motel rooms in southern California and the interior valley, or tonight, for example, in a city where I don't know anyone at all, trying to make a decision.

He had been working late when I called, polishing the text and putting together the dummy for his next picture book. After saying good night and hanging up, Jeremy cleaned up his drawing table, then went to the kitchen where he spent two hours preparing and then eating dinner. Dishes washed and put away, it was still not quite nine o'clock. Walking from one end of the flat to the other and then back, he decided he'd go out and rent a movie. The video place was around the corner and a few blocks up Fillmore. Because it would be cool outside, he put on a sweater and his leather jacket, then trotted down the stairs to the front door. One of his tenants had pushed a note under the door, saying her doorbell was out and should she call an electrician or would Jeremy take care of it. He left the note on the stairs, and went out.

Across the street the illuminated sign of the Macedonia Baptist Church glowed through a thick fog but the building itself was hardly there, hardly more than a charcoal sketch smudged by translucent watercolor wash. He walked down to the corner of Fillmore and turned to go up the hill.

When Jeremy reached the video store he went first to the new releases. We hardly went to the movies, unless it were something Toby wanted to see, and cable hadn't yet reached our block, so he didn't recognize many of the titles. One would look interesting, he would pull the case out of the rack to read the plot précis on the back, and, disappointed, return it to its slot. There was no telling what he wanted to watch—comedy, drama, science fiction, a thriller, something arty and enigmatic. Seeing the box for a movie based on a novel he remembered enjoying, Jeremy plucked it out, irresolute, but he might as well.

At the front of the store, between the cash registers and the section of children's films, a man who had just come in paused before a display for the latest Hollywood mega-release. Every resident of the neighborhood who didn't have anything else to do was in choosing movies. Shaking his head in disgust, the man passed up the cardboard silhouette of the brawny star. The aisles were narrow, and when he came to where Jeremy stood he couldn't get by without saying, "Excuse me."

Jeremy moved out of his way. The man nodded his thanks with a small, polite smile. Taller than most Asians, though not as tall as Jeremy, he wore metal-framed glasses balanced on the shallow bridge of his nose, and his hair was cropped so short it stood out from his scalp and gleamed with gel or pomade. Twin loops of thin gold wire pierced his left earlobe. Passing Jeremy, he headed toward the back of the shop where a clerk posted at another cash register watched to ensure no-one younger than eighteen entered the alcove of X-rated videos. Showing the clerk his membership card, the man went in.

Jeremy had never been back there, but when he was much younger, a horny art student, once or twice a month he might go to the porno theater a few blocks from his apartment. It was easier and faster than taking several buses to a bar or a discotheque. And, he remembered, though the point of the exercise was to meet an older man, not too ugly or too old, who would take him home, still, the hugely inflated images on the screen had excited him. He recalled the tone of my voice when I told him to enjoy himself, magnified it into a hateful sarcasm, and thought how desperate I was to move away from this city—so eager he wasn't sure I wouldn't leave without him, wouldn't pick myself up and move to New England only because it wasn't San Francisco. But he had lived in San Francisco a third of his life and all of his son's life: he loved me and was sure of my love for him, but this love was new, hardly four years old, and twice before he had allowed someone he loved to expel him from the home he'd made. It was my home too, he thought, angry, the most home I'd had since going off to boarding school at thirteen—how could I wish to leave?

For both of us knew this about the other: home was more than an idea or an ideal, and it consisted in far more than the physical space itself, or than affection, love, or desire. When Ruth had taken him away from the house in Mexico, and when he had taken Toby from the blue and white cottage in the hills below Twin Peaks, he was leaving each home to make a better one, ultimately, a home more real and definite, even if it hadn't seemed so at the time, but he didn't know that he could do it again. How many chances did you get to perform a miracle? The flat on Sutter had been his and Toby's home before the first time I climbed the stairs from the street, but how could he tell that it would be still if I left. And how could he know that I wouldn't be helpless at making my own home for myself, by myself—I had never had to try—or that I wouldn't manage the trick right off, in a city named for God's grace.

Glancing down at the empty cassette box he held, Jeremy knew that he didn't want to watch the movie. What he wanted to do was get me on the phone and shout at me and, when his anger was expended, tell me exactly how he wanted to punish me. It was past midnight in Rhode Island, though, and if I weren't asleep I would be tense, nervous, unhappy, asking myself the same questions perhaps, and our anger might become mutual and dangerous. Instead he would place the box back on the rack, go to the rear of the store, and ask the attractive Asian man if he could recommend a steamy hot video for someone who'd just as soon not be alone tonight. It had been ten years, give or take, but Jeremy thought he would still know how to pick a man up.

Feet First

I

IT MIGHT BE suggested that I am attracted most to men who are fathers, and it is true that my own father is the measure for all men. My father has the most beautiful hands imaginable, hands like razor blades or chisels, fine tools–or like gold-nibbed fountain pens that scribe his meaning in pristine calligraphy across the air. Jeremy's are an artist's hands, intent and sure, but with the sinuous flexibility of sable or camel hair brushes; while Neil DeVincenzo has businesslike, economical hands that do what they intend to do, no less. My first lover, Sean, beautiful in every other respect, had ugly, grabby hands. They were broad and stubby, with short spatulate fingers and tufts of wiry hair between the knuckles—hair of a brassy color that seemed inevitable and right on his chest but inappropriate on his hands. Sean's, however, is not a memory I wish to pursue further, except to confirm that he was never a father. And of course I had already fallen for Jeremy before I knew that he had a son.

Something I noticed early about Neil was that he was one of those people for whom walking appeared to be a conscious act, a decision, made with some unease but which must be carried through. He made the action appear uncomfortable, as though his body had been designed for another method of locomotion—although one couldn't imagine what that might be. There was something about how he walked that made you feel sympathetic aches in hip, knee, ankle: the transparent ineptitude in the movements of his joints, jerky, about to dislocate themselves; the sudden, unconscious hesitation, infinitely repeated, before each foot touched ground; a pathetic stiffness in his ankles, hips, and, oddly enough, shoulders. You couldn't call it clumsiness —he got where he needed to get without tripping or stumbling, and when he reached his destination he knew what to do, and did it.

Naked, I had shivered in the cool air of his apartment where it was dim with closed curtains and the warmth from the fireplace was a solid rather than an atmospheric presence, and gently he stroked the rosette of blemishes on my ankle before he stood up. "We'll just have to be especially careful, then, won't we, Allen?" He took me into his arms and held me against his chest. The smell of his cologne and his sweat filled my nostrils; I rested my cheek against his shoulder as his hands moved up and down my back, raising trails of gooseflesh. Then he took off his own clothes, revealing a certain early-middle-aged solidity that was very comforting, and then he took me to bed and showed me what his hands could do.

Naturally, I told Jeremy about Neil, and naturally, though he admired the sheets and undershorts I had bought in Neil's store, Jeremy was hurt. He said, "Are you going to see him again?" and I said I didn't know—the same answer I had given Neil. How often, after all, did I have occasion to drive to Boston?

WE TALKED FREQUENTLY on the phone, nevertheless, Neil and I, nearly every weekend. If anyone else picked up the phone, he simply said, "This is Neil. Is Allen there?" Often when I spoke to him I caught myself imagining him naked or, more exciting still, clothed but ready to remove his clothing. Yet we hardly spoke of sex—our project and our object appeared to be friendship. We talked about his son and about Toby and Kit; we talked about my wish, unrealizable and before hardly articulated, to adopt a child of my own. Was this because I felt my nephew or Jeremy's son could be taken from me at any time? We determined that I was envious of him, and of Jeremy, of my brother-in-law even—envious of their having known their sons as infants. Because Neil's blood had been tested and shown to run clean, we spoke of my illness.

"I'M GOING TO keep bringing it up," Jeremy said, another day. "Does he make you feel desirable?"

"Yes, he did. That once."

"Don't I?"

It was one of those chilly, cheery spring mornings when you begin to believe that winter has actually ended although the lawn in the backyard is still soggy and dense, resembling moss more than grass. The magnolia in our neighbor's yard, over the fence, preserved only a few blossoms among the newly breaking leaves, but our daffodils were in bloom. Jeremy had told me not to help him. Wearing a heavy sweater and wool trousers, with Lena's great white dog asleep by my chair, I sat and watched Jeremy where he knelt on a green vinyl cushion, pulling weeds from the daffodil bed. I sipped my coffee. I nodded, though he couldn't see. "Don't I?" Jeremy asked again, looking over his shoulder.

"But I expect you to. You always have."

When Jeremy stood up and came to stand before me, I had to crane my neck to see more of him than his presence alone. From this angle I could not interpret his expression. He bent a little to tousle my hair. "May I meet him?" he asked, and then, closing the subject for the moment, he said, "Ruth called about the California trip. She thinks we should go for all of August, and use a week of it to take Toby to Mexico. He's never been. Nor you, either."

"What about Kit?"

"Kit's been to Mexico? I didn't know."

"I meant," I said, lifting my hand to his leg, "is Ruth expecting him, too?"

Jeremy knelt down beside my chair. "I know what you meant."

"Do you think it's a good idea? Mexico?" I touched his cheek. "What if—this sounds stupid, we've been so lucky. Jeremy, what if I . . ."

Lifting his hand to cover mine, Jeremy lowered his eyes. "What if you had an episode? I don't think we can worry about that, boy, can we? Realistically. What if I had one?" Then he lifted his head, and the smile he wore was wicked, enticing, deeply sad. "For myself, if you're going to have an episode at all, I want it to be me visiting you in the hospital, not Neil DeVincenzo."

I wanted to be angry. "If I were in the hospital I hope he would visit. He's my friend." I tried to make my voice hard. "Do you want me to make promises, Jeremy?"

"Allen. Allen." He stood up and returned to the flower bed, turning his back. "I want you not to leave me, Allen."

"He's not that good. I like your kid a whole lot better than his. They'll carry me out of here feet first."

"I'm afraid of that too."

Looking at him, I saw that Jeremy's shoulders were shuddering. "Are you crying?"

"Of course I'm crying, damn it." He pushed his fists hard into the soil but didn't turn to look at me. "What the fuck do you expect me to do? Go to the bars downtown? Find myself some hot *boy*? Sometimes,

Allen, sometimes I think you love Toby more than you love me. That you only stay with me because of him."

Moving in my chair, I startled Herodias. She barked in her sleep, then woke and leapt to her feet and stared around the yard, wild. I held my hand out to her. "Sometimes I think so too, Jeremy, sweetheart," I said slowly, "but it's not true. I love him *differently*. I love Kit, too. I don't love Neil at all." Hardly thinking, I knew it would be a bad thing to get up and go to him.

Herodias slopped her big tongue over my hand; sure of me, she swaggered over to Jeremy and butted her brow against his side. Jeremy uttered a little cry, and pushed her away, but when she came back he threw his arms around her shoulders and buried his face in her neck.

Now that it was safe to move, I rose to my feet and took a few steps toward them, the man and the dog, a few steps away. "Jeremy," I said, and I felt frightened, and could hear the fear in my voice, "Jeremy." I stared down at his dark hair mingled with Herodias's cream-colored fur. "Jeremy."

Without lifting his head, his voice muffled, he said, "I don't think I can talk to you right now."

I stumbled a little farther away, but then I turned back. "Jeremy? You *have* to."

His face when he turned it up was blotched, streaked, twisted, a tuft of the dog's white fur caught in his beard. "No, I don't," he said, his voice an ugly croak. He shoved Herodias away again. "Why?"

"Because it's important! Because you're important. You and me." I was shaking my head, dizzy.

Sure that it was a game we were playing, the three of us, Herodias barked hoarsely, feinting at Jeremy, and then she turned and threw herself at me. Stumbling, startled, I went down under her paws.

"Herodias! Get off!" I had never heard Jeremy's voice quite so harsh. "Bad dog!" Certainly never when speaking to an animal. He lifted my head from the grass, then helped me up. "Are you okay, boy?"

"She was just playing." My hand was muddy; when I brushed the tear from under his eye it left a streak. "I'm just trying to stay alive, Jeremy."

He held me. "Do you have to hurt me to do it?"

Circling us, Herodias whined, begging forgiveness.

"I guess maybe I do, a little bit. Sometimes."

"But you won't leave me?"

"How could I ever do that?"

"Are you sure?" He was serious, but he was smiling a little. "I really need to know, boy."

"Did I leave you when you sprang Toby on me? Scariest trick anyone's ever pulled. Did I let you push me away when you were trying so hard?"

He shook his head and shrugged and held me tighter. "That was a long, long time ago."

"It sure was, sweetheart. That says something, doesn't it? Let's go inside, Jeremy."

"No, not yet." Shifting his grip so that we could both walk, he steered me over the lawn, around the back of the house. "We were inside all winter. I came to Providence for you, Allen."

"I know you did." I couldn't look at him as I said this. "Do you wish you hadn't?"

"I'd go further for you. You know. I'll go as far as I can, but you have to promise to meet me along the way."

I made him stop. I lifted my muddy hands to his jaw. "I'll call Neil this evening."

"No." He tried to shake his head in the cradle of my hands, then ducked his chin and nibbled at my fingers for a moment, then said again, "No. Don't do that. Do what you have to, for yourself. Just call me first. Call me a little more often. Okay? And Allen, don't play around with Herodias if I'm not there to rescue you. She's bigger than you are."

Hearing her name, Herodias barked, and barked again.

∾

II

THE NEXT TIME I had occasion to go to Boston was two months later, in early June, but this was to be a family expedition and I told Neil I wouldn't be able to see him privately. He was, I thought, at once as relieved and as disappointed as I. Still, I invited him to the reception, and Neil didn't say he wouldn't be there.

Getting Jeremy's work onto a gallery's walls was Eamon's idea, his project. Jeremy's New York art director, distressed that he had no commissions to offer, had contacted an old friend from art school, a woman of vast taste and distinction but little talent who therefore ran a gallery

on Newbury Street in Boston. The logistics seemed excessively complicated: Eamon came up to Providence on the train, needing to be met at
the station; his friend Eliza drove down from Boston, needing clear directions; while Jeremy was as excited as if they went to all this trouble
for him and therefore lunch had to be perfect. The boys were banished
for the day. Meanwhile I had a violent headache and the night before
Jeremy had spoken for two hours long distance with Ruth, not an
action calculated to endear—although, given Neil, I could hardly complain. Not that I didn't. I found myself often querulous and unreasonable, a bad sign.

Wheels of friendship revolve, networks of relations draw tight—
Jeremy was not famous but his work was known, and if Eliza found
him more interesting as a personality than as an artist she nevertheless
offered to represent him. "Do you only illustrate?" she asked—the
phrase *children's books* remaining unspoken. Jeremy showed her the
work hanging on our walls, then led them upstairs to his studio, as to a
private view. Staring at the strip of discolored lemon peel on the bottom of my demitasse, I remained at the dining table, feeling happy,
hopeful, and ill; and who's to say Eliza wasn't motivated by pity.

IT WAS EAMON's idea, also, that we spend the weekend of the opening
in Boston—a break from routine, he called it, a vacation. For himself as
well. He made reservations at an inn for all of us, and we promised to
pick him up at the airport. Then it was Thursday evening after dinner,
and I went upstairs to check on Kit. I still worried a little about Kit,
even after two years with us. Day to day he seemed fine, as sweet a boy
as you could ask for, and he and Toby got along like no tomorrow. But
then a moment would come—you couldn't predict it—when he closed
up, walled himself off, and you found yourself dealing with a thirteen
year old who acted more as though he were five. A stunted five. He
clung to me then—gratifying but scary.

Sprawled out asleep at the foot of my nephew's bed, his cat looked
like a discarded toy. Toby was helping Kit choose what to pack. "Why
don't I have clothes like this?" he asked, turning from the closet to show
me Kit's suit, still shrouded in the dry cleaner's plastic in which it had
come from Annapolis.

I took it from his hand, checked the label—Brooks Brothers, naturally—and gave it back. "Your father isn't a businessman." I sat down on
the bed next to Providence; she shifted and muttered in her sleep.

"My mother bought that for me." Kit looked distressed. "I don't really want to wear it, it makes me look like a dweeb."

Toby held the suit up again, shook his head, hung it from the doorknob. "You have to, Kit, it's an occasion." He shook his head again, grinning, and threw his arm around Kit's shoulders. "Besides, you are a dweeb—name like Kit, you can't help it." The two of them stood before me, posing as if for publicity stills for a sitcom called "Brothers" or maybe "Cousins" (though they were neither), perhaps simply "Best Friends," which was the truth of the matter and something that made me very happy when I stopped to think about it. The small, compact one twisted out of the grasp of the other and threw an easy punch at his jaw.

"*Toby's* just as geeky," my nephew said fondly.

"What's a dweeb?" It was already warm; the man next door had mowed his lawn that afternoon and the smell of cut grass rose through the open windows. Leaning back on the support of my elbows, I regarded the two of them. "What's geeky? Your mother bought that suit over a year ago, Kit—probably it won't fit anymore."

"Have I grown?" The possibility appeared to thrill him.

"Try it on," I said. "We'll find out."

Shy, Kit went into the bathroom to change. While he was gone, Toby sat down on the bed and nestled up against me as though he were a puppy or a little boy. No little boy, he was a quarter inch taller than I and if he weren't growing so fast his enormous appetite couldn't keep up he would have outweighed me as well—big bones. "Allen," he said, putting his arm around my waist, "can I get new clothes in Boston, nice clothes? I mean, I've got nice clothes, but like Kit's? Will you help me?"

"Sure. You want to be a dweeb? It's sort of a waste, the way you're shooting up, but your father doesn't have a first gallery opening every day."

"It's sure made him easier to live with, since he met Eliza." Toby cocked his head, regarded me quizzically. "I know all about it, Allen. You think I'm dumb? Dad's the stupid one, if he's worried you'd leave us for the Italian stallion."

Grinning with shock, I pushed his shoulders down into Kit's pillow. "If you're trying to embarrass me, you've succeeded, kid." With a squeak of alarm, the cat leapt off the bed and ran out the door.

"Don't tickle me!" He wrestled with me, but held back. "Hey, I seen the guy. He's studly! The son's sort of pretty, too, but he doesn't have half the personality I do."

"Studly? *Pretty?*" I was winning, because he held back. "What's this, big het boy changing his tune? Coming to your senses?"

"Nah." Easily he pushed me off, then embraced me and kissed me on the lips. "Where could I ever find a man like you? But I'm still a virgin, what do I know. Maybe I'm bi."

I held him away by the shoulders. "Careful, Toby."

"Yeah." But he was grinning still. "Anyway, with my two dads, I'd have to have worse eyes than I got not to have figured out what a handsome man looks like." He shook his head. His glasses flashed. "Tell you what, let's go to Neil's store to get my clothes." Ducking his head, he turned away, gulping with laughter. "I'll behave."

"You're an odious child."

"Yeah. That's why you love me." Then he laughed again, and jumped to his feet. "No, what am I saying?" Standing before me, legs spread, he pounded his fists against his chest. "Me mighty big heterosexual he-man! Me ravish nubile maidens in a single gulp!"

"Jesus, I hope not. Or your little pansy stepfather'll have to beat you senseless."

He fell to his knees before me. "Can I let a distinguished older lady seduce me, if I'm very quiet about it?"

"Get up off the floor. *Very* quiet and *very* careful. I don't want to hear about it till you're eighteen."

"You're no fun." He pulled himself up and pushed his hands through his hair, adjusted his glasses. The little garnet in his earlobe winked. Turning toward the bathroom door, he said loudly, "What's taking the little geek so long? You put one leg in one side of your pants, Kit, and then the other in the other. It's easy." Then he fell back on the bed beside me. "Actually," he muttered, "that's not true, that you're no fun. I sort of forget sometimes, since I've gotten so good at interacting with my own age group, making sure I'm properly acculturated."

"Big words!" I leaned over him to ruffle his hair. It was coarse and shaggy, for the moment. He had a habit of getting it clipped very short, without warning, and then letting it grow for six or eight months.

"That's what they teach me in school. Allen, we don't play around together as much as we used to. And when we do—" he grinned, milking the suspense, "I get crazy out of control! 'Cause I need it so much!"

I ran my fingertip along the curved rims of his glasses. "Your father says he sometimes thinks I love you more than him."

"Dear old Dad. Goes without saying, doesn't it?"

When I flinched and drew back, he sat up immediately but wisely kept his hands down. "I didn't mean it. You know me, big old joker, whatever comes into my head. What a jerk. Allen?"

"Yeah, you're a jerk all right." I let him put his arm around my shoulder, and I allowed myself to lean against him. "Hell of it is—I'll never do it, but I can think about leaving him. I can't even think about leaving you. How'd you get to be so important, Toby? You're just another pimply kid breeder-wannabe. What'll I do when you go to college?"

He had a snide retort all ready, but held it back. After a moment's silence, he said, "Speaking of jerks, what's with the dweeb in the john? Kit! Are you beating off in there?"

As Toby started off the bed, I pulled him down. "No, let me. I'm the nurturing authority figure around here." I went to the bathroom door and knocked. "Kit? Are you all right in there?" The only reply was a muffled little noise. Toby was breathing on my neck, but holding back. I pulled the door open.

Wearing the khaki Brooks Brothers suit, perched on the lid of the toilet, Kit looked tiny and miserable. "It's too small, Uncle Allen," he said in a sad little voice, and looked up at me, warping his lips into a smile enough to make one weep.

Going to him, I lifted him to his feet—he was small enough still to be manhandled. "Why didn't you come out and show us?"

He looked past me to where Toby lounged in the doorway and shook his head. "You two were having so much fun." With another glance to Toby, he moved closer to me. "I didn't want to interrupt." Suddenly he canted over against me, head on my chest. It wasn't a hug, his hands hung limp at his sides. I had Toby in my sight and saw him blink, his mouth twist. I lifted one hand to the center of Kit's back.

"Hey," Toby said, "you should have come out, Kitster. It would've been even more fun. We could've ganged up on Allen."

"I don't want to do that."

Glaring at Toby, I motioned him out of the door. "Come on out, Kit. Let's see how awful this is. How much have you grown?" I drew him through to the bedroom. "Two inches?" Positioning him as though he were a mannequin, I stepped back.

The suit was classic Brooks boys' department—if it had been the right size it would have fit badly: boxy in the torso, spindly in the leg, but very well made. The sleeves were half an inch short, exposing his bony wrists, the trousers an inch; not as much as I thought he'd grown, but Steph had probably bought it large. I asked him to turn around. He had fastened both buttons on the jacket. "You're right," I said, judicious, as he peered hopefully at me, "it's too small. And on top of that—don't ever tell her I said so, but your mother has terrible taste. It's a really ugly suit."

He tried to smile. "Really?"

Quickly, I went to him, unbuttoned the jacket. "It's hideous. I can't bear to look at it. Isn't it awful, Toby?" Pulling the jacket from Kit's shoulders, I tossed it across the room. "If you weren't so handsome it'd make you look like Jerry Lewis. Trousers too—off!" As I reached for his fly, Kit put up his hands to fend me away, then let them fall. I stripped the trousers off him, kicked them aside. Standing for a moment alone in his t-shirt and white briefs and dirty socks, blushing, Kit looked blazingly happy, either completely oblivious or supernally aware of the stiff little erection in his shorts. Placing my hands on his shoulders, I turned him around, pushed him toward the bathroom. "Put on some pants, Kit."

Toby crept up to me and said very quietly, "He had a hard-on."

"Yeah, well, he's infatuated with you or me or both of us. Thanks for not pointing it out."

"Are you kidding, Allen?" He was grinning like a maniac. "It's great. It wouldn't be fair to you and Dad if one of us wasn't queer."

Taking advantage of his good humor, I pushed Toby hard, so that he sprawled back onto the bed, cackling. "There's still hope for *you*, sweetie-pie."

I heard him say, "Not a chance."

Then I went to catch Kit where he stood in the bathroom door, jeans on but watching us now so intently he couldn't get the button at his waist fastened. They were boy's jeans: zipper and a single button. He flushed and smiled and pushed the brass disc through its slit. I said, "Now get lost, Toby. Go pack or play with yourself or pester your father or something. It's Kit's turn for some quality time with pseudo-Dad." When I stroked Kit's shoulder he leaned against me, and together, amiable, we watched Toby stumble through to the studio, still cackling, and then we heard him lope down the stairs.

"Thanks, Uncle Allen," Kit said.

He leaned against me, and I realized that while the physical sensation of his leaning was much the same as if he were Toby, the pressure that I felt was different. I had never really doubted that Toby could stand on his own. I meant to take Kit over to sit by me on the bed, but first I crouched before him, hands on his hips, so that his head was higher than mine. "Are you okay, Kit?"

His upper lip lifted off his teeth and he blinked. "Yeah? I mean, I guess I'm sort of embarrassed—"

So he had noticed. "Hell with that." I shook him gently until he grinned. "Just shows you're all in proper working order. No, I meant before—when I opened the door and saw you sitting there on the john you looked so unhappy."

"That?" He blinked again, willing to try, confused. "Oh. Well. It's just—" Lifting his eyes, he gazed over my head. When he spoke again his voice had a certain hollow tone. "Sometimes my dad plays around like that with my little brother—no, not like that, not like you and Toby, but loud and kind of happy. I mean, I don't want to join in, Ricky's a little snot, Dad'd just tell me to shove off, and how they fool around . . . it's not like they *like* each other. They're scoring points. Ricky can't win unless Dad lets him."

"But you wanted to join us?"

Biting his lip, he nodded.

"Why didn't you?"

Breaking out of my grasp, Kit walked steadily over to the window by his bed. He spoke to the glass. "It was private. You were making fun of Toby's dad and talking about—sex, and I guess you were wrestling? I'm no good at wrestling."

"Me neither. Toby let me beat him. Kit, if it was private we wouldn't have been so loud."

"But you—I heard you, you were talking about that man in Boston."

"It's not much of a secret. It's kind of a mess but it's not a secret." I got to my feet and stood there feeling foolish, staring at my hands. "Toby calls him the Italian stallion."

At the window Kit let out a little noise. "But you love Uncle Jeremy? You wouldn't leave?"

I looked away from the slight figure against the glass. "I love him with all my heart and soul, Kit. If I could just get *him* to believe that—"

"I believe you, Uncle Allen."

"Do you?" In my own ears my voice sounded bleak.

"I *do*." He came running up from behind and grabbed me. "I *do*! And I want to love someone just the same, like you."

Startled, scared, I pivoted in his grasp and put my hands on either side of his face. Wild-eyed, he stared up at me. "You do?" I said, quiet.

The pressure of my hands prevented him from nodding—I felt the movement in my palms. "Yes!"

"When you're grown up?" Moving my hands down to his shoulders, then to cup his shoulder blades, I felt his stare as an influence, calming, hopeful, confident. "Well, Kit, they say you're just like me, so I guess you probably will." Faint with a kind of relief, I urged him toward his bed, but when we reached it, instead of both of us sitting side by side on the edge, he lay down with his head on the pillow and I lay down beside him.

His face was alight with the same joy, so that his eyes seemed to glow. "A man?" he asked.

Careful, I didn't touch him. "Kit, when you're aroused, when you get an erection, what do you think about?"

In a small voice half-pleased, half-private, he said, "I've got one now. A hard-on."

"I kind of thought you might." I sighed, and smiled to show it was all right. "You know we're not going to do anything about it." His face had been changing since he came to live with us, a transformation so gradual as to be imperceptible until you thought about it, a matter both of inevitable physical maturation and of discovering new expressions to replace resentment, humiliation, cowardly sulkiness. How any father in the world, any man, could treat a child as cruelly as Derek had treated Kit I could not comprehend. Kit had never been struck in anger, that I knew. But his father, pleased as could be with hellion younger son and tomboy daughter, took every opportunity to degrade his hapless eldest child, a boy too young to be called a sissy. At the same time I wondered, if Derek was determined on breaking Kit's spirit, how had he brought himself to send the boy to us? Who could be expected to foster the very traits and inclinations Derek disapproved. *Disapproved* too mild a word, but I could find no other.

Kit was still pretty in the way children are pretty, but, although he reached for puberty with less impetuousness than Toby had, his features were sharpening, firming up, assuming a promise of their adult cast. Like me, he would not suffer the adolescent indignity of acne; like me, he would never be hirsute, was unlikely to grow tall, and would preserve a certain air of boyishness at once annoying, to one's self, and, I'm assured, attractive; unlike me, he would have beautiful, even teeth, for I was more prosperous than my father had been and could not begrudge Kit the disfiguring rite of a mouthful of steel and rubber bands. He had learned not to be self-conscious of his braces. His hair, when he stood upright, fell in a thick black comma over his brow, and he had a trick of jerking his head sharply to flip the hair out of his eyes. He carried his small, pointed chin up and flared his nostrils with assurance. I felt certain that as soon as he graduated from the Lower School he would ask permission to pierce his ear, as Toby had done—a different rite of passage.

"I think about kissing someone and—doing other things," he mumbled, then more clearly, "and I jerk off."

"That's good. That's healthy." I remembered my own early fumblings. In a way I wanted to touch him, as I had wanted to be touched. "Someone in particular?"

This succeeded in embarrassing him, in a manner that seemed also to make him proud. "Sometimes."

"You don't have to tell me. I trust you." Now I did touch him, only caressing his cheek before I sat up. "And I trust you—this is important, Kit. I trust you to know that jerking off is one thing and sex with another person is something different, something you probably shouldn't try for a few more years."

He blinked, moved his head a little. His voice was breathy, a thin, child's treble. "I haven't. Only—Uncle Allen, a couple of times, me and another guy, we've watched each other. It's kind of scary." Suddenly, he rolled over, turning his back to me. "He kissed me once, I asked him to, that was scary too, but we never touched each other." He inhaled, and seemed to hold his breath a moment. "Uncle Allen, it was Toby."

"I figured it was." I also figured Toby had not needed to be asked twice to kiss Kit; he would have been eager to try the experience, and it would have been a meant kiss, passionate and sure. At the same time it would have been analytical, thoughtful, as Toby absorbed the event, comparing Kit's childish mouth, marred by his braces, to the lips of the girls whom he made sure I knew he had also kissed. Doubtless there were other boys as well, heedless experiments, whom he wouldn't tell me about. Toby was determined that his father and I should be as convinced as he was of his basic heterosexuality. I stroked Kit's hair. "I bet afterwards he told you he'd rather kiss a girl."

"I wouldn't."

"That's okay. Me neither."

Rolling over onto his back, Kit stared at the ceiling. Heartbreaking and enough to make me feel still more tender, the little fold in the fabric of his jeans was still stiff. "He told me when I grow up to be sure to always use a condom."

"That's a good thing to be told."

Then, as I gazed at him, he choked and began to cry. "That's not what I meant," he cried, and I slid my arm under his shoulders and lifted him up, and pressed my lips to the crown of his head and murmured, "I know, Kit, I know."

~

III

EARLY THE NEXT morning, before we left Providence, Toby caught me alone and, diffident, asked if it could be just the two of us when we went shopping in Boston. "Do you want to talk?" I asked.

He was holding Kit's cat in the crook of his arm, stroking her blunt head. "I just want to *be* with you, Allen." Then he glanced at me sharply. "I know Dad needs you and Kit needs you, but I need you too, to myself, sometimes."

There was nothing I could reply except that I needed him as well. "Yippee," Toby said quietly, with conviction.

WHEN HE CAME out of the dressing room my breath caught. "You look sharp, Toby," I said, "a real clotheshorse." It took no more than a jacket and a striped dress shirt buttoned to the neck to make him appear a man, adult. The broad, padded shoulders of the blazer structured his torso, gave it weight and solidity, went a way toward resolving the contradiction of his growing two inches in six months without gaining twenty pounds. He'll be as big as his father.

He fussed with the pleats of his trousers, curled his toes against the carpet. "I guess I need new shoes too," he mumbled, staring at his feet. "You sure I don't look dumb?"

"You look like a dweeb. You look like a geek. You look as handsome as your father would if I could get him to dress up."

He grinned, and looked younger than the moment before, his own age again, or younger. "To die for?"

"To die for," I agreed. "Any girl would go for a guy like you. Any *guy* would go for you, if he had any sense. But we've got to get you different socks—white tubes don't make it. And after that you can help me choose an outfit for myself."

"Okay." He brushed the hair out of his eyes, his father's eyes, the color of stainless steel, set at a tilt. "Allen," he said with a certain degree of gravity, "will you show me how to tie a tie?"

The tie he'd chosen was conservative, even old-fashioned, a repp stripe in pale blue and violet, heavy twilled silk. It hung around the collar of the navy blazer, as vivid as a victory flag on a coffin. I touched his shoulders, moved him to face the three-fold mirror. As they turned up his shirt collar, positioned the tie, my hands spoke a phrase I couldn't read, reversed in the glass. He smelled of new, expensive fabrics and his father's cologne, and the angles his shoulders and chest forced on my elbows made me clumsy in lopping the silk through its half-windsor. I could see where, shaving, he had missed a patch of fine stubble alongside his ear and grazed a pimple. He was tall enough that we could have gone to the men's department. He watched my hands and I watched his face as I tightened the slipknot around his throat.

After we had him all fitted out, khaki trousers, blazer, the striped shirt and striped tie, oxblood loafers and dark, patterned socks, Toby decided he wanted to wear his new clothes to lunch. The salesclerk snipped off the tags and charged them to my account. "Thank you, Mr. Pasztory," she said as I signed the slip and she folded Toby's shorts, t-shirt, sneakers into a bag. "Your son looks very handsome in his new clothes."

"He's not my son," I said quickly, almost involuntarily. Then, remembering, I looked around. He was riffling through a carousel of ties, safe and sound.

Glancing up at me, she pulled off my copy of the sales slip and tore it nearly in two. "Oh." Her voice was small and she looked hurt, as though she'd offered candy to a child and been rebuffed. "I'm sorry."

"Thank you for your help." Taking the bag, I turned away, touched Toby on the neck, led him toward the escalator. The hard leather soles of his new loafers clattered on marble.

I am weak, not in the physical sense, not often, not yet, but the smallest thing can throw me. In the men's department all the suits seemed to be black. The clerks were each young and very fine and abnormally solicitous. Toby brushed up against me the way he does, touched my hand from time to time, took my measure with practiced, edgy eyes. At last, wool flannels and twills, serges and gabardines aside, he said, "This is stupid. You've got lots of suits, Allen. Dad doesn't want you to look like you just came from the office, not tonight." He held up a sharply tailored pinstripe collapsed around the wooden shoulders of its hanger, grunted, put it back. "Does he?" Toby needed a haircut; that would be another mission, after lunch. His glasses were slipping down his nose. "I don't either. Come on."

The fifteen-year-old son of the man he spoke for, this boy whose contribution to my existence was equally immeasurable, who could be raucous and hilarious or confiding and needful—this boy who from a little distance appeared to be a man led me down aisles of fabric and shiny chrome, over travertine and industrial carpet, through zones of new age music and freakish alternative pop. I let him lead me, watched him move with the suppressed cunning of a soccer player, followed him wondering what he had in mind for me, for this suit-wearing, fearful man he knew more thoroughly than he did his own mother.

He led me to the shoe department, sat me down on a plush banquette that exhaled under my weight. "Feet first," Toby said. His eyes were hard with a sort of urgent solicitude. Despite the eyes, Toby doesn't look like his father—not in the way my nephew resembles me. I'd say Toby too looked like me if there was any chance of it, but he takes after his mother. In their fine bones, the impervious pallor of their skins. The impression he gives of looking over his shoulder, a kind of skittishness that is, in his mother, profoundly disturbing but in Toby, resolute as his father, reassuring: he's looking over his shoulder after me, watching to be sure I'm keeping up. He went along the display of shoes, cordovan, burgundy, tan, black, brown, and I stared at my hands.

My hands knotted in my lap. I have never been big, never worn much flesh on my bones, but it seems to me, now, that my hands used to carry more weight. Large enough to play the piano, although I never have. There was no place for a piano in my parents' silent house. Toby's father gave me a ring, long ago in San Francisco, and if I could wear any ring I would wear that one, but it became quickly distracting, I couldn't think to speak, couldn't concentrate when I was talking to myself, became inarticulate in my native language. Jeremy understood, and he gave me a chain to hang the ring around my neck, wear the pledge against my heart—but my hand looks naked without it, and most of the time, these days, I don't care to see what my hands are saying. They are economical prophets, my hands, speaking in fingers-and-thumbs with a fine disdain for euphemism or false hope. It is only in my second language that I can lie.

"What do you think?" Toby had brought me a single tapered cowboy boot with dangerously pointed toe. It was black. I had never owned a pair of black shoes. I took it from Toby's hand. The leather of the shaft touched my hands, smooth and soft and traced with sprawls of stitching that felt, to my fingers, like scars. It had a certain undeniable weight. The vamp was black snakeskin; a tracery of silver plate ornamented the toe.

"I don't know, Toby."

"Try them on, at least."

"They're more comfortable than they look," the salesman said. He knelt before me, calm, professionally servile, took my foot between his thighs. Without asking if I knew my size, he removed the shoe, measured the foot, and stood again. "I'll be right back."

"Do you have another color?" I asked before he'd gone too far. He said he'd check.

"But black is just right," Toby said, and took the boot back, examined it from the sole upward. An inverted circumflex creased the skin between his heavy brows. "Black's just what I have in mind." He sat down beside me.

"Why?" I reached out for the boot, covered its toe with my hand, covered Toby's fingers. We both, I think, acknowledged and appreciated and remained wary of the ways we could and could not display our affection—he could be flirtatious, outrageous, but I could not. Not out in the world. "I've never worn black shoes," I said softly.

He pulled off his spectacles, balanced them by the bridge on the pad of one finger—an habitual gesture, one that I've come to expect his father to perform for all that Jeremy doesn't wear glasses. The v-shaped wrinkle was there again, pleating the bridge of his nose. "Time for a change." His hand turned over, under mine, the fingers slid between my fingers. "Time for a major change." His small, dismissive frown said as clearly as words or signs that I ought to know he knew what he was doing.

I said, "I'll try them on."

The salesman brought back only one box. "Just black in your size, I'm afraid." He knelt down all in one long movement combining the sinuous and the brisk, opened the box at my feet. Nestled against each other in white tissue paper like long accustomed lovers, somehow the boots looked blacker, more black, elementally and essentially black. He handled them familiarly, as intimately as he grasped my foot and pressed the crimps out of my instep between his palms. "You have a very high arch," he said, slurring the *r*'s in an apparently calculated manner. A connoisseur of feet, he straightened out my toes, holding the fixed, complicit smile of a man whose position excuses liberties, and eased my foot into the boot. It fit as snugly as a narrow glove. Simply, efficiently, he removed my other shoe, slid the second boot over my heel.

"How do they feel?" Toby asked before the salesman could.

"Fine."

"Can you stand?" asked the young man who still held my left foot in his lap, who looked up at me, engaged, amused, his head cocked nearly into his shoulder, an invitation, a sure dare.

I looked down at him. I thought of Neil DeVincenzo. Toby had insisted we come to the store where Neil worked, as if to face the Minotaur in his lair, a kind of bravado I had no intention of following through. I leaned forward. The salesman was more conventionally handsome than Neil, younger. Doubtless Jeremy would feel less threatened by a short, slender, aggressively attractive retail salesclerk than he did by Neil. "We'll see," I said, but before I stood I glanced at Toby again, saw him taking it in, saw something in his eyes that wasn't quite alarm. I widened my eyes. He blinked, and busied himself putting on his glasses.

The salesman nodded, sat back on his heels, stood up, moved out of my way. I set my feet flat on the carpet. They felt strange, encased so closely in this new skin and canted by the heels so that they splayed outward. When I stood, gingerly, it seemed that my hips swayed forward to accommodate a shift in my center of gravity and my shoulders slipped back and down a notch on the spine. I took one step forward. My ankle nearly buckled, but the second step was surer. In the boots I was almost as tall as the salesman, taller, once more, than Toby. Pacing around the carpeted shoe department I felt as though all my bones were realigning themselves, as if I had become a new kind of being, a skeletal, armor-plated machine, impervious, invincible. Ordinarily I walk with short, quick, straight strides that propel me on a steep trajectory; in the boots I ambled on cocked ankles and with long swinging steps, striking the heels against the floor with a jolt. I must have looked unsteady because Toby grasped my elbow. Scarcely anyone I care for can speak intelligibly to me in the language my parents taught me, but there are certain gestures that mean more for their very lack of articulation. "How you doing?" Toby asked. Behind the glittering lenses of his spectacles his eyes seemed to wink and flash, confident again.

"Fine," I said, trying to drawl. "Do I look like an old cowpoke?"

"You look like you'd be happier on a horse." His teeth glittered too. "Don't get them if you don't like them, Allen."

I walked away from him. "I didn't say I didn't like them." At the base of one of the display cases was a mirror angled to show how your new shoes looked afoot, from the front. The pointed toes of the boots turned up slightly to reveal the silver toe guard more clearly; the underside of the soles was still an unmarred pale greyish tan. One trouser leg was crumpled up above the scalloped cuff of the boot. I bent down to work it over the shaft, and my face appeared in the glass at an unaccustomed angle, from an unexpected direction.

I suppose my face is as familiar to me as his is to any man who shaves every day, but you expect to see it at a certain time and in a specific mirror, and if you have shaved routinely for some years the mirror serves only to clarify what hot water and shaving cream have already demonstrated, what the blade of your razor will prove: that you are alive, are there. I am as vain as the next man—which is to say I think I'm better-looking than many of the next men—but I don't check my appearance in every window I pass; I keep my hair short enough that once I've brushed it in the morning I needn't look at it again. If a lesion were to develop on nose or cheek, no doubt I'd become as morbidly curious about it as I had been, at first, about the four purple blots on my left ankle, but this hasn't happened yet, and the drawn gauntness, the pallid crepeyness that surprised me could have been a reflection of the mirror's tilt and the obscure lighting.

Straightening up too fast, I overcompensated and nearly staggered. The jolt took me in knees and ankles. The back of my throat closed and I tasted bile. I turned to the salesman and said I'd buy the boots. After he'd removed them from my feet and replaced my old shoes, placed the boots tenderly in their box, and rung them up, he gave them to me in a large paper bag and said, "You shouldn't wear them more than a couple of hours at a time for a few weeks, until you get used to them."

We were to meet Jeremy and Kit at noon for lunch; it was just past eleven. I let Toby carry my bag as well as his own. "Am I going to buy a black Stetson too?" I asked him.

Toby used his father's credit card to buy me a pair of black jeans and a dark blue silk shirt printed with ornate paisleys and medallions. He wanted to buy a black suede bomber jacket as well, but it was, I reminded him, summer.

"Were you taking notes when you were six?" I asked Jeremy's son. In the mirror I had looked like any stylish young man on the make, even without the jacket.

He shuffled his feet. "Is that how you dressed when I was six?" He moved his chin once, twice. "When you met Dad? I don't remember."

"Not really. But the effect—it's like you're dressing me up for a date."

With a laugh, Toby tossed his head. "Aren't I? You're a handsome guy, Allen, I was just trying to gild the lily." Sobering, he said, "But not for the benefit of the Italian stallion, okay?" And then he looked puzzled, edgy, as though he were grasping after an important memory but not finding it. He shook his head again. "I don't remember. I don't remember when I met you, Allen."

"I don't remember either. Didn't I watch you being born?"

Shifting his parcels to his left hand, Toby put his right arm around my hips. If I'd been wearing the boots I'm sure I would have staggered, have fallen.

∽

IV

A LONG DAY. After our morning's outfitting, Toby and I met Jeremy and Kit at a flashy, crowded joint on Newbury Street for lunch. Jeremy admired his son's new clothes and pouted when I wouldn't show him my own—the bags were in the trunk of the car. Cheerful, affectionately rivalrous, Kit called Toby a preppy nerd, and asked if he could please not have to buy a new suit or wear a tie. "How about a feather boa?" Toby asked.

I saw Jeremy preparing to say something sharp, and saw him see that both boys were grinning, delighted with their repartee, so he satisfied himself with announcing how helpful Kit had been, hanging the show, and asked of the air above the table why his own son, child of two artists, had no eye for design.

"Because Allen raised me," said Toby, in perfect obnoxious teenager form.

After, Jeremy went back to the gallery. We found the salon Eliza had recommended. Leaving Toby in the hands of the stylist, Kit and I prowled Newbury Street until we found a place that sold the kind of bright, simple clothing he had in mind for himself.

In some fashion, after the fact, I concurred with Kit's opinion of Toby's outfit. For the greater part of a decade I had dressed for work every morning, despising the necessity for it on occasion but going ahead anyway, and for nearly as long as I'd suited and tied myself Toby had been a boy in dungarees and t-shirts. As handsome, adult, and appropriate as he looked in navy blazer and khaki twills, it troubled me to see the raucous teenager who had wrestled and insulted me the night before transformed so, suddenly an anachronistic, emblematic prepschooler or Ivy Leaguer. He ought to have felt, I thought, as uncomfortable in his finery as I would have at his age, dressed up for a special event. No hope of that. Instead he reminded me of his mother, amused by her family's useful wealth as often as disgusted, comfortably at home. And I wondered whether he actually had a taste for such appearances, or if it were a kind of joke. Like the outfit he'd chosen for me?

Shopping with Kit was easier: he wanted help in determining his own preferences. His only agenda was to find clothes he liked that would please me as well. It didn't take long. We came out of the store happy with ourselves, Kit carrying his new clothes in a paper bag, and each wearing a bright new cotton baseball cap that Kit had bought with his own money. His was royal blue, matching the stripes in his new shirt, mine the purple of summer plums. In his bag also were a green cap for Toby and an apple red one for Uncle Jeremy.

The spindly trees along Newbury Street were blowsy in leaf, the street brilliant with shiny cars whose windshields mirrored glare, the sidewalks rustling with hordes of summery pedestrians among whom passed, from time to time, preoccupied men and women in business suits, carrying briefcases and with their jackets slung over their arms. I checked my watch and saw we would be early to collect Toby at the salon. Kit was a child of the humid East Coast who thrived in the heat, but I suggested ice cream nonetheless.

"Won't Toby want one too? And Uncle Jeremy?"

"Tough shit," I said, cavalier, and led him into the press.

What I hoped to find was a soda shop, an ice-cream parlor, a little café, someplace where they would have thirty-some homemade flavors chalked onto the board above the marble counter, where clean attractive youths in short-sleeved, open-necked pastel shirts and matching caps would engineer elaborate sundaes for Kit and me, where we could sit at a small table on the sidewalk or inside a broad plate glass window with our ice cream and tall glasses of fresh lemonade, watching the crowds. A false memory from some other man's childhood. What we settled for, after scouting both sides of the street for several blocks, was the freezer case of a small grocery. As we passed under the awning between raked displays of giant strawberries and tiny zucchini, it occurred to me that this was Neil DeVincenzo's neighborhood, that he might shop in this very market. After a long day at work he might stop in to pick up a gourmet frozen dinner for the microwave, or a can of clams, bunches of scallions and Italian parsley, a pound of imported pasta. Or, standing before the glass doors of the freezers, he might waffle between a pint of double-dark-chocolate chunk or one of the more baroque concoctions Häagen-Dazs and Ben & Jerry were currently pushing. Call it clairvoyance, call it coincidence, call it bad luck. I had chosen for myself vanilla ice cream on a stick, dipped in milk chocolate and crushed praline, but Kit couldn't reach a decision.

"Allen," the voice near my shoulder said. "I thought it was you."

I turned to face him, but moved closer to my nephew. "Neil."

"I thought it was you," he said again. He looked good. I was discomfited by how good he looked. His shirt was white, with a narrow ribbon of decorative braid across the chest, broadening it; the dropped yoke of the shirt and the small knot of his brilliant tie between the short points of the collar somehow made his shoulders appear wider. Early in the season, he was tanned—weekends at the beach in Newport with Jimmy. He came to Rhode Island once a month, at least, trading off against Jimmy's weekends in Boston, but he didn't come to see me.

"I like your cap," he said. He gleamed: prosperous, expensive, happy.

"Kit bought it for me. My nephew." I reached for him; he had stepped away. "Kit," I said, "this is Mr. DeVincenzo."

You could tell, from his faint flush and the way the whites of his eyes showed all the way around the irises, that he knew, had known: this was *that man in Boston,* whose existence he feared. And you could tell that he, too, found Neil attractive. For a moment I felt scared, for I wanted him not truly to comprehend desire for a few more years, and then in conspiracy with a boy his own age. A happy conspiracy, I hoped, and with a boy as silly and hilarious as Toby—though not Toby himself, who could break Kit's heart, and knew it. A boy like Neil's son Jimmy, perhaps, a confident roughneck or pirate. I feared that Kit would spend his youth helplessly infatuated with men—Uncle Jeremy, Uncle Allen—and be damaged. Again.

I turned to Neil, casual. "We're getting ice cream. Want some?"

"Sure!" Neil grinned. "Good idea. What're you having?"

I showed Neil the box with my own confection. Above us, in the wall above the freezers, the fan behind a grill pumped into higher gear, blowing chill air over us. In a small voice, Kit said, "I can't decide."

Still grinning, Neil stepped past him to open the next glass door, and removed a small plastic tub that contained, so the label said, authentic Italian-style gelato, all natural ingredients, cantaloupe. "They've got spoons at the register."

Distraught, Kit looked at him and then at me, and then, quick, selected the same bar I had. He glanced at me again. "Can we get some for Toby and Uncle Jeremy too?"

"They might melt before we get back," I pointed out.

"Not if we hurry." His eyes, his lips had the pleading, wincing expression I remembered too well, had hoped never to see again.

"Toby? Jeremy?" Neil asked. "They're here too?"

"Okay, Kit." I took a box of three from the freezer case—Eliza or her assistant might appreciate a break for ice cream—handed it to Kit, and we went to the front of the market, to stand in line at the register. Kit went ahead, keeping me between Neil and himself. "You're not at work, Neil," I said over my shoulder.

"I left early. I had some things to do."

I thought for a moment—we were standing close together—that Neil might touch me, press his hand into the small of my back, or brush it across my shoulder. Distracted, I didn't notice until the moment had passed that Kit was paying for the ice cream, all of it, even Neil's.

Out on the sidewalk again, blinking against the glare, we both thanked Kit, who only shook his head, uncomfortable, and reached into his paper bag for the plastic spoon he had remembered but Neil had not. "Thank you again," Neil said, accepting it, and gave Kit the full force of his smile.

Ducking his head, Kit looked away and concentrated on opening the box and then the inner bag that protected his ice cream.

"I was on my way home," Neil told me. "I saw you down the block and wanted to make sure it was you. What are you doing in Boston, Allen?"

We were walking now, moving through the crowds, ambling back toward the salon where Toby waited, and then to the gallery. "Tonight's Jeremy's opening." We walked three abreast, Neil, myself, Kit, and I was conscious of the odd hesitations in Neil's stride, exaggerated as he tried to walk and eat gelato at the same time. "Remember? I invited you."

"Tonight? Shit. I forgot, Allen." One of those hesitations caught him standing and he had to take two quick steps to catch up. "I've been busy. Tonight? What time?"

Swallowing a too-large bite of cold ice cream too quickly, I felt a sudden ache at the base of my neck, where shoulders met spine. "Starts at six, goes till whenever, nine-thirty, ten. I had them send you an announcement, Neil."

"I know you did, I got it. The picture's lovely—Jeremy's picture. I put it up on the refrigerator. I just—I forgot."

"It's okay," I said, seeing myself clear. "It'd be uncomfortable for everyone, anyway."

"No, I wanted to come." Neil exhaled, hard, a grunt. "I went out and . . . and bought one of his books."

"Neil," I said, surprised, but didn't ask which one.

"He's really good, I'd like to see his pictures. I'd like to meet him. See, Allen—" he said, and in my peripheral vision I saw him stab the white plastic spoon into his gelato, glaring or staring, and then he threw the whole thing into a trash can on the curb. "This is where I turn. You'd better hurry, before Jeremy's ice cream melts." He looked past both of us, down the cross street toward his apartment, a safe haven. "Nice to meet you, Kit," he said.

"Neil."

"The thing is, Allen, I've got a date tonight."

"Oh." Across the street rose a great pseudo-Gothic pile, all rusti-cated brown stone and narrow, pointed windows, a home furnishings store now, though it might once have been a church. Its lowest floor, on the Newbury side of the corner, mostly below street level but lit by a greenhouse lean-to that looked incongruous butted up against the fortress wall, was the restaurant where we'd eaten lunch. The salon was in the next block. "Well, bring him along, if he wouldn't be bored."

"Allen."

The light changed. Pedestrians who had grouped up around us at the corner pushed through to cross the street. For a moment I couldn't see where Kit was, hidden by adults, but then he stood at my side and, although he was thirteen, much too old, he took my hand in his own.

"Maybe." Neil was backing away. "I'll see." He lifted his hand, turned.

I raised my voice, nearly shouting: "Neil."

He waved his hand again, not looking back, and strode off.

Kit didn't say anything until we reached the steps up to the salon, and then only, "I don't think the ice cream melted, Uncle Allen, it's still cold."

∽

V

TOBY AND I went to meet Eamon at the airport late in the afternoon— he had left work early but not overly so. Jeremy and Kit stayed at the gallery, overseeing last details. It seemed to be a day when I would di-vide my attention between the boys, seldom dealing with both at once. Driving through traffic to the airport, I wondered whether Kit would tell Jeremy about our encounter with Neil—whether he would be will-ing to admit to Jeremy that he knew about Neil. I hadn't yet resolved my own reaction to Neil's admitting he was seeing someone else: the fact of it, his not wanting to tell me. My reaction appeared to be a com-plicated collision of dismay and relief that I didn't wish to understand. I tried to listen to Toby's gabble—he was playing *boy* again—to re-spond appropriately, to put Neil out of mind; eventually—the traffic was thick, slow-moving—I succeeded.

It was instructive to see Eamon out of his usual element. He said to

me, "You're looking well, Allen." No irony in his voice—Eamon is a
New Yorker. "Hello, Toby," he said; "you've grown just since the last
time I came up from the city."

Toby and I glanced at each other and laughed.

"What is it?" Eamon had put his bag down. He hooked one finger
in his collar, loosening it, shifting the knot of his tie off-center. He
stared at me. "What did I say?"

"You just cost me twenty bucks." I pulled out my wallet and re-
moved two tens, handed them ceremoniously to Toby, still grinning.
"On the way over here, Toby bet me you'd find an occasion to call New
York *the City* within ten minutes. As if there weren't other cities; as if
Boston weren't a city."

Taking the bills, Toby flattened a crumpled corner before inserting
them in his own wallet. "And that you'd mention how much I've
grown," he said. "Thanks, Eamon."

"Well." Eamon looked at Toby, at me. "It was fairly stupid of you to
take him up on it, Allen, wasn't it."

"It's good to see you, Eamon." I stepped forward to embrace him
but, when he flinched back, satisfied myself with touching his upper
arm, the tweed of his jacket's sleeve prickly under my fingers. "I'm glad
you could make it. How was your flight?"

He had brought only one bag, a carry-on, so we didn't have to
wait around at the baggage claim. In the tunnel beneath the Inner
Harbor, I glanced over at him. His face looked bleached and weathered
in harsh fluorescent light. Just because of his name, unadulterated
Irish, I tended to link Eamon in my memory with Sean, although they
weren't at all alike and I didn't finally meet Eamon until after Sean's
death. I knew Eamon had himself chosen, in high school, to be known
by his middle name in preference to a more standard-English first.
Where Sean inhabits my memory as a twenty-six year old of spectacular, golden beauty, cutting as a sword's blade, because I cannot bear to
recall him as he was in his last months, Eamon hardly comes to mind
at all. A gentleman of a certain age who has survived several changes of
ownership, management, and direction at the publisher where he has
worked longer than Toby's been alive, a New Yorker more likely to fly
to Frankfurt, Milan, or Tokyo than take the subway to Brooklyn,
Eamon is, whenever I see him, small, substantial, tweedy; courtly and

old-fashioned: a child's favorite bachelor uncle remembered for the treats in his jacket pockets rather than any real presence.

I parked near the Common and the Public Garden because Eamon wanted a walk, to stretch his legs after an hour on the plane and remind himself that not only was New York not the only city in the world but that Central Park wasn't the only park. We strolled broad paths under trees fully leafed out in early summer splendor, beside lawns green and splendid, beds of remarkable flowers. Dressed in his new clothes, with his new haircut, less extreme than usual, Toby walked a little ahead of us. How was life in the City, I asked Eamon.

"Same as always," he said—"a life sentence. I love it. Too many funerals, though," he murmured, looking away, looking ahead after Toby. "Two last week. How are you, Allen? How's Jeremy?"

When you are ill, the way I'm ill, no-one is tactful, no-one can ignore it, everyone has to know everything, every symptom, every prognosis—the assumption being, I guess, that a doctor's opinion is the closest you can get to a fact and that facts are the breath of life. I was sick of it. "Jeremy's fine," I said, giving Eamon a hard stare that meant, You won't be the last to know so don't push it. "I'm stable." They always think, too, that you envy them their health, which is true as far as it goes, and resent them for it, which isn't. What did Eamon's health do for him that I should resent? He was a frightened, aging little man who lived alone in an inimical city, in a small apartment with rent higher than my house payments; a man whose life revolved around his job and his annual vacation, a matter of three weeks in some sunny, tropical locale where he would cover himself with sunscreen and envy the youngsters who hadn't heard of skin cancer. In any case, I was willing to wager Eamon was healthy only in the sense that Jeremy was: provisionally.

"Sorry," he said, and looked away, in search of another topic.

I took pity on him. "Once the show's over, Jeremy's going be at loose ends again. Do you have any plans for him?"

"I'm talking to Editorial." He was relieved. "There's a lovely script, but they have the idea Jeremy can only draw boys. I don't know. If they don't come up with a firm name soon I'll send it to him. I think he can do it."

"What's it about?"

He started telling me, and I stopped listening—it was, so it appeared, a picture-book story: that is, not much. It takes a certain amount of story to hold my attention, more than most picture books sustain. My imagination is so much more verbal than visual that I can't see the pictures unless they're in front of me.

The first story Jeremy illustrated, not long after I moved in with him, was as much a surprise to me as Toby had been. Jeremy was satisfied to be a freelance advertising artist, I had thought; the money was good and he had plenty of time to devote to his real career, as Toby's daddy. Of course, at the time I thought I was satisfied to be an advertising copywriter. One evening after dinner he led me out to the nominal living room of the flat on Sutter Street, sat me down at his drawing table, pulled a portfolio from its drawer, and said, "Come tell me what you think when you're done."

What did I think? The text, handwritten in his neat, architect's capitals, was short, no more than three or four lines to a page for eighteen pages, keyed to the ink and watercolor drawings by circled superscripts. A little boy and his daddy climb aboard a Muni bus to go to school, the boy's first day at kindergarten. They travel through the city on a remarkably complex and topographically unlikely route that takes them through the Mission, the Fillmore, Pacific Heights, Chinatown, the Sunset, Japantown—tucked in almost unnoticeably a glimpse of the Castro—and the boy, an imaginative child, asks his daddy whether he will make friends at school. The text was gently didactic, although it became less so before publication, promoting an admirable kind of multiethnic pluralism. But it was in the illustrations that you found a reason to read the book, as San Francisco—a city not much less prosaic than any other—became a carnival of possibilities, a magic-realist extravaganza seen through the windows of the bus, where a Chinese-American child might find herself in one of the cities of pre-Columbian Mexico, a Latino boy at the court of the Round Table, a WASP child on the African veldt—all very naïve if you stopped to think about it, but the beauty and idiosyncratic detail of the paintings suggested you not think but only examine the magnanimous glint in a lion's eye, the eyes on the wings of a tropical butterfly, the wings of a soaring paper kite, or the crayon-bright kindergarten classroom where Daddy leaves his son, vivid with marvel. The book was retitled a number of times before finally being published, but in the meanwhile Jeremy was commissioned to illustrate two picture books by real writers and to provide the jacket painting and frontispiece for a young-adult fantasy novel, Toby moved on from second to third grade, and I left Grace & Fenton, a tiny but inexorable trajectory with the inevitability of fate.

∾

VI

EVENTUALLY WE ALL ended up at the inn, a rather overwrought place Eamon had found in the Vacation/Travel advertising section of a gay magazine. We took showers. We were already exhausted. Jeremy was cranky. When I suggested we bathe together, he shook his head, said he was going to lie down for a bit and I should take as long as I pleased. So I indulged myself, and when I came out I had to wake him.

By the time he emerged from the bathroom, I was long dressed, attired in Toby's new clothes, even to the boots. "Excuse me," Jeremy said, and when I looked over to where he stood in the doorway, damp, a towel hitched around his hips, he blinked and shook his head. "I'm sorry, do I know you? I think you must have the wrong room."

Nonplussed, I stared at him.

"Unless . . . management sent you up? I didn't realize that was one of the amenities. But I don't know if I can afford it. Can you take an out-of-state check?"

Catching on, I grinned, trying to make it an obsequious expression, took one step toward him. "Oh, no, sir, the service is complimentary. We at the Lavender Arms pride ourselves on catering to *all* a gentleman's needs."

"Is that so?" he asked, straight-faced. "Charming."

"Indeed, sir." I had begun to unbutton my shirt. "I notice that you're still a little damp — may I dry you off?" I approached a little closer, servile and accommodating.

"But I should tell you, I have a lover."

I raised my eyebrows, spread my hands. "Oh? Will the other gentleman be joining us? That could be amusing."

Jeremy laughed, delighted, merry, lascivious. "Take off your clothes, Allen." At his crotch the towel had tented out — he pulled it off, coming into the room. His erection bounced engagingly in time with his steps. "You look like a whore."

Dodging back, I frowned. "Jeremy, this is the outfit your son picked out and *you*'ll be paying for."

"I didn't say I didn't like it. I didn't say you looked like a common streetwalker. You look like a very expensive callboy with extremely cultivated tastes." He fell back on the bed, opening his arms expansively. "I could never afford you. Take off your clothes and come here. Then I'll put them back on you."

"We'll be late."

"Screw the reception. Screw fame." Sitting up, he grabbed his cock and shook it at me. "I want to screw *you*."

"You'll have to sell a lot of paintings to pay for this," I said, waving the silk shirt at him. But I locked the door between our room and the boys', and then I sat on the bed to take off the boots and he was all over me, gurgling in the back of his throat, running his hands up and down my flanks, unbuttoning my fly and groping within, and I was laughing, of course. Exhilarated, exasperated, I said, "You're not helping."

"I'm going to give you a hickey!" he announced, and proceeded with great dedication to do so, on my shoulder, while I struggled out of the boots and, with difficulty, jeans and undershorts.

But before I let him do any of the things I wanted him to do, I said, "Jeremy, I like the clothes Toby chose for me. You won't tell him you don't?"

Jeremy grinned wildly. "There's something a little peculiar about that kid. I mean, he says he's straight, but he's got really good taste. You looked fabulous, boy." He shook his head and drew me down on top of his chest. "I fell in lust with you all over again, just seeing you there all cocky and sleazy-elegant—you were beautiful." He kissed me, gently. "You are beautiful. I must remember to thank him." He kissed me again, less gently.

THE RECEPTION WAS an affair of white wine and designer waters, airy little nothings in puffs of pâté à choux, the caterers' personnel a job lot of moonlighting college students. Eliza wanted to take us out to dinner after: she consulted with Toby and me, the powers behind the throne. Then I went looking, and found Jeremy in an alcove of the gallery, neatly pinned between one of his watercolor interiors and the cover painting for a children's fairy tale, speaking to Eamon. Jeremy nodded to me, happy and drunk.

"Toby says sushi," I told them. "Eliza looked at him for a moment, and then said, That's right, you grew up in San Francisco. What if I sent my kids out there for a year, Toby, would they learn how to eat? —He thought she was kidding. Is Japanese okay with you two?"

"Sounds great." Jeremy's face was flushed, a stain on cheeks and nose. He never buttons his collar or puts on a tie. I'd chosen his tie, since I would end up wearing it to work.

Eamon, a good and thoughtful man, placed one hand on my arm. "Should you be eating raw fish?"

"I'm not really hungry. They'll have something else, teriyaki, tempura." I held up my glass. "This is water, Eamon."

I went off in search of Eliza again, to tell her the plan was approved. The gallery was not large, but larger than it appeared when you came up the stairs and through the entrance, broken up into nooks and culs-de-sac by a number of freestanding false walls. The walls, white the first time I saw them, had been repainted in Jeremy's honor, a pale, matte, chalky blue, the baseboard moldings darker. A gratifying number of the white cards posted beside each frame, giving title and date of composition, bore circular red stickers. Most of these were illustrations, a comment of some kind. I saw that one was the final design for the jacket of *The Death of Hyacinthus*, done over at twice the scale from colored pencil to acrylic imitating oil but still grotesque, and wondered who in the world could bear to hang it on their wall.

Coming around a corner, I nearly collided with Toby and Kit, standing shoulder to shoulder, their backs to a wall on which was displayed the portrait of Toby as questing prince that ordinarily hung in Kit's room. Its identifying tag bore the notation, *Collection of Christopher Sheridan*. Startled, we stared at each other for a moment, and then Kit blurted, "He's here, Uncle Allen."

"Who?" I asked, knowing.

With a twist to his lips, Toby said, "Studmuffin. The Italian stallion."

"Mr. DeVincenzo," Kit confirmed.

"Kit told me you ran into him this afternoon."

"I'd better go say hello."

"Allen." There was an edge to Toby's voice and expression that didn't sort with the youthful, romantic image of him hung on the wall. "He's got a *guy* with him."

"Okay," I said, thinking: You ought to be relieved. "Thanks for the warning. We'll be going to eat soon, all right?" And I left them, my paladins, my protectors, princes in waiting.

There had been a fair crowd; now it was thinning out, isolated ones and twos moving from picture to picture. I told Eliza's assistant the dinner plans were fine, and he nodded and went to phone in the reservations. Then I saw them.

In fact, I first saw Neil, from behind, a figure I could not mistake for anyone else, only distinguishing an instant later his companion—the fact that he was accompanied. Recently arrived, they stood three or four paintings in from the entrance and had neither made a trip to the refreshments table nor been caught by one of the caterers' waiters. I picked up two glasses of white wine and went over. "Neil. I'm glad you made it."

Turning, accepting a glass, he made it appear we were old friends, touching my arm, chastely kissing my cheek. "So am I. Allen, this is Will."

Will was slender and fair, unmemorable. "Pleased to meet you," he said, his pale eyes searching my face. Releasing my hand, he gestured at the painting on the wall. "That's you, isn't it?"

Not an illustration for any story, not even the story of our lives: I hardly recognized it—in real life it hung in the living room, a room we used as a corridor, and I must have passed it thirty times a day. It was big, two and a half feet by three, bigger in its wide, simple mat and narrow frame. What I saw, before I saw the painting itself, was the label on the wall: the title, *Safe as Houses*, the date, *1981*, our first full year together, and the uncanny fact that it said neither *Collection of the Artist* nor *of Jeremy Kent–Allen Pasztory*.

"I recognize the house," Neil said. "One of the drawings in your office."

When you first regarded the big watercolor, you saw a portrait of a house, a Queen Anne Victorian cottage, blue grey with white gingerbread. The real house stood on a prototypical San Francisco street, other cottages of the same vintage on either side, similar yet distinct; but in the painting it had no neighbors. Above the broad bay window, the high peaked gable—an equilateral triangle—contained an ornate urn, which itself held a pyramidal arrangement of flowers: tulips, roses, iris, peonies, painted not as if they were an architectural bas-relief but a seventeenth-century Dutch still life. This much was fantasy. I had never lived in the house, never been inside, but had seen it often enough— Jeremy pointed it out every time we passed through the neighborhood.

In most of Jeremy's renderings of houses the panes of the windows are opaque, brilliantly glazed by sunlight. In this house, every window was transparent, every window framed a figure, every figure was myself. The scale was large enough, the detail fine enough, that you could tell. In an upper window—a bedroom or a dressing room—I used the glass as a mirror while I tied my necktie. In another, I sat in profile, gazing at an invisible ceiling. I leaned out over the sill of the small window above the front door, gazing to the side, down toward the bay window. Here, in each of three tall double-hung windows angled to form the mirror image of a haberdasher's glass, you saw a version of the same pose from a different angle. In each, the sill cut me off above the knee. On the left I wore blue jeans and t-shirt, a typical mustached San Francisco clone though too small, too thin. On the right, I had taken off the shirt and held across my arm a sheaf of purple iris. In the central pane, I stood nude, pale, slight, bony, young, and instead of the bunch of iris I clutched a naked infant who reached out with both hands, pressing his tiny palms flat against the glass. Toby, in the painting, was younger than I had ever known him, plump and pink and happy, a baby of about eighteen months, an age when he had in fact lived in this blue and white house.

I offered the second glass of wine to Will. "Back when I was young and pretty." I shook my head. I couldn't figure out why there was no indication the painting wasn't for sale. "Would you like to meet the artist, Will? Neil?"

When we turned away from the painting, I saw Toby and Kit staring at us. Sometime during the evening Toby had pulled down the knot of his tie and loosened his collar. I gave them a warning look, and led Neil and his friend away.

"I already know him," Will was saying in a low, preoccupied voice as we went on, "Jerry Kent. I mean, I knew him, years ago."

Jerry: an antique nickname that antedated not only myself but Toby and Ruth as well. I glanced at Will and revised my estimation of his age sharply upward. "Really? In California?"

"San Francisco. Art school." He wasn't looking at me or at Neil but ahead, scanning the spaces of the gallery, taking in the few people who still stood around, searching. "Actually, I knew Ruth better, we were both fine arts, but I lost track after the wedding. When they went to Mexico. They cut everyone out of their lives." Now he turned his eyes on me. "I gather they're not married anymore. I never thought it would work."

"It worked fine for three or four years, but no, not now." I was taking him in, absorbing him, a relic of the archaeological past for which you'd need carbon dating. "Ruth's in Santa Cruz."

Neil's regard shifted from one of us to the other, his expression fascinated, slightly stupid.

"Yeah. I mean, I've read the articles. But Jerry—I didn't have a clue."

"There he is," I said.

There he was. Alone now, Jeremy stood away from the wall, looking at nothing. Until he saw us. Then a slow smile lifted the corners of his mustache, crinkled the skin under his eyes. I thought for an instant it was a smile of recognition, that he recognized Will from seventeen, eighteen years before. But then I understood he was smiling for me. When he noticed my companions, his expression flattened and he tucked his chin, a hesitant, small interrogative.

"Jere," I said, laying claim with my own nickname for him, drawing close, "I've told you about Neil. You've talked to him on the phone."

Panic bloomed in Jeremy's eyes.

"And his friend Will."

"Remember Prof. Hildesheimer's life class, Jerry?" said Will. He held out his right hand. "We always used to complain because he never brought in a male model. And Ruth would say, Who'd want to draw a man when you can have a girl?"

"Will?" Jeremy's eyes narrowed, he stepped back. "That Will?"

"That Will," he agreed. "Long time no see, Jerry."

"It's Jeremy now. It's been Jeremy for a long time."

"I didn't know." That was Neil's voice, nearer to me than Jeremy or Will.

I was watching the tiny adjustments and readjustments around Jeremy's eyes and mouth, one variety of alarm modulating into another, and an odd sort of happiness, all of it muddied and emphasized by his having drunk more than usual. Wine affects him harder than distilled spirits. He accepted Will's hand, shook it, and hesitated a moment as if he would embrace the man.

Neil and I were left standing side by side in a kind of forced intimacy. "I told him there was this gallery opening I'd been invited to," Neil was saying in my ear, "I'd forgotten, did he want to go, and he said sure, but he didn't say he knew Jeremy."

"Quelle coincidence," I muttered, unhelpful. But then I glanced at Neil, saw that he was upset, and said, "It's got to be almost twenty years —they don't know each other, not really."

Neil moved his head and raised his glass a little, but didn't drink. "It's only our second date." Then he lowered his eyes and said, "That boy with your nephew, that's Toby?"

"Yeah?"

"Handsome kid. He looked at me like he hated me."

Will and Jeremy were talking intently together now, both facing one of the paintings on the wall, and you couldn't tell whether they were catching up on each other's lives and careers, on a fossil friendship, or if Will were offering a harsh critique of the work. When I looked away, I saw Toby and Kit posted like sentries, watching us. "Can you blame him?"

"We can't be lovers, Allen, even if it was what we both wanted." Neil's voice was low, serious, more passionate than when he made love to me.

"I never thought we were." This felt a hideously cruel statement to pronounce—I couldn't look at him.

"I can't let myself fall in love with you."

"You thought you might?"

"I was married for a long time. You can't expect me not to be jealous of you, Allen, you and Jeremy, what you have, what you are. That picture, the one we were looking at—I want to buy it."

Shocked, I stared at him. "It's not for sale."

"Are you sure?" Abruptly, expression set as though he'd donned a porcelain mask, Neil strode away from me, toward the front of the gallery.

Panicking, I stared about wildly. Jeremy and Will had moved to a different picture, still talking, still intent. At a little distance, Toby and Kit watched over us, Toby's eyes cruel, somehow, Kit looking scared and confused. He made a move toward me, but I shook my head, and went after Neil.

At the desk near the entrance, Neil was speaking to Eliza. He gestured at the portrait of the blue and white house. Nodding, she picked up the photocopied catalogue and leafed through it.

The high heels of my new boots carried me across the floor. "It's not for sale," I said, harsh.

Eliza glanced at me, surprised, and smiled, the smile she might offer a cantankerous child. "Yes, it is, Allen. See?" She showed me the entry in the catalogue, neatly typed, *No. 34. "Safe as Houses," 1981. Graphite and watercolor on paper*, which she had already, in the few seconds it had taken me to reach them, marked with her red pen. The price was low—all the prices in the catalogue were low.

"It's not for sale," I said again.

Eliza glanced at Neil, apologetic, a look that said What can you do? "I can check with Jeremy?"

Setting his wineglass down on the desk, Neil smiled too, high-end retail professional, one to another. "It's okay." He put his hand on my shoulder. I flinched. "If it means that much," he murmured, and started to draw me away from Eliza.

Frustrated of her sale, she glanced at her watch, then said in a perfectly normal, accommodating voice, "Allen, Mr.—?"

"DeVincenzo."

"We'll be closing in about five minutes."

"It shouldn't be for sale," I said. "It's mine—Jeremy painted it for me."

"It's okay." Neil patted my shoulder, kind, patronizing. "Look, I'd better find Will, we have to leave. Can I call you next weekend, Allen?"

I broke away from him. In the bay window of the little blue and white house, I stood perfectly at ease, confident, certain, sure of myself and of my future, my life, but it was a house I had never entered.

~

VII

ELIZA MANHANDLED us into taxis: she, Toby, Kit, and her assistant the person she called the Man, capitalized, or My Right Hand, in one, Jeremy, Eamon, and I in the other. "The buildings are so squat," Eamon said, "there are trees," before lapsing into the admiring silence of a single man prone to infatuation with couples. Jeremy pushed his nose into my shoulder and muttered, "Don't let me drink any sake. I'll be sick."

The restaurant was some distance from Eliza's gallery. Although

I go to Boston often enough, I don't have the city down, it doesn't make sense to me, doesn't cohere. I think this is because I'm usually driving. In San Francisco, where I didn't have a car, I had to know the city to get around and even now, years after leaving, I can reel off the names of neighborhoods, bus lines, streets, could place myself blindfolded; but Boston is a great mystery. Every so often I think I ought to come up for a weekend and walk over the whole city. In the same way, I'm always planning to learn Providence, which is, after all, where I live. I know the area around our house, the school where I work, and between them the extended campus of the university; have some familiarity with the gim-crack sector with its toy high-rises that passes for downtown; but most of the city I've only driven through, if that, going somewhere else. It's as though, in Providence, the house is my home and might be anywhere, while in San Francisco, a young man, I had laid claim to the entire territory.

Eliza, the Man, and the boys were waiting for us on the sidewalk in front of the restaurant, an unprepossessing storefront. Heads together, the Man and Toby were laughing. The Man was in fact not a man but a youth of nineteen or twenty, a slight, golden-skinned Thai who called himself Ted because, he said, "My name has approximately eighteen syllables and you Americans can't pronounce it." Toby was trying, as we entered. I counted only ten syllables.

My new cowboy boots had begun to pinch, in addition to throwing me off balance. Following the others into the restaurant, I said to Jeremy, "It's too bad Ruth and Candace couldn't make it." I was thinking about Will, that visitation from Jeremy's past, in part so that I would not think of Neil, a visitation, mirage, a portent. I could not bring myself to ask Jeremy about the painting Neil had tried to buy.

The black-and-white-print banner hung inside the door slapped Jeremy across the face as he ducked, too late. Inside (I hardly needed to incline my head for the fabric to miss me entirely) he nudged against me, biceps against shoulder, shorthand abbreviation for embrace. "I would have liked your parents to come."

We were seated in a large booth at the back of the restaurant. Knowing exactly what he was doing, Toby ordered for all of us — without being told, he made sure that my own meal would be fully cooked. Eamon and Eliza and the Man continued their congratulatory chorus, so that Jeremy was forced to feign modesty. Leaning against my shoulder on one side, Kit yawned and shook himself back into alertness, and Toby, on the other, whispered that he was *very hungry*. Simply enjoying the close presence of my boys, I gazed across the table at my man, feeling my lips slacken into a smile as complacent as his, and for an instant it almost seemed that Ruth and Candace, Janos and Marit, were there, nearby. This is our family, I said to myself, meaning not only Jeremy and the boys and me but all of us, present or absent....

But I was tired—stressed out to the max, Toby would say— maudlin and sentimental, would be better off at home. The waiter brought a flask of sake and four cups. I nudged mine down the table to the Man. Jeremy took one sip, then, watching me, pushed his cup across to Toby's place. I wanted to ask him, abruptly, if home, our house, were as much home to him as the little blue and white house—if that was why he'd been able to put a price on it. This was a stupid question. Toby didn't remember that house, couldn't recall the mural on the wall of his nursery that Jeremy had described to us on any number of occasions, any more than I recall the apartment where I spent my first two years. A small house in a working-class neighborhood of an industrial city; dorm rooms at prep school and university; Sean's apartment; the studio behind the Mint—only six months there, and hardly there at all; the Sutter Street flat; the house in Fox Point. Where is home? Home is where the heart is. Safe as houses. I placed my hand over Toby's and he leaned against me, comfortable as a cat. I lifted the cup of sake to my lips and swallowed.

~

VIII

THE ROOM AT the inn was lavishly overstuffed, a midsummer blossoming of glazed chintzes, crocheted doilies, Victorian wallpapers, pleated lampshades with bobbled fringes, all of it stiflingly coordinated for color—the overall impression one of asthmatic yellowness—but not for pattern or period. If you were prone to hay fever the room by itself could set you off, even without the massive arrangement of peach, strawberry, lemon gladioli set on a paisley shawl on the bureau. Toby and Kit's room next door was similarly upholstered but pine green; Eamon's, down the hall, an inspired blue—the same blue as my new silk shirt.

The room was too warm, as well, as if all the flowers of Anglo-Indian fantasy festooned over curtains, bed linens, wallpapers, two armchairs required a subtropical climate—or as if air-conditioning would be out of period. Groping through three layers of fabric, flowered chintz, yellow velvet, sheer voile, I found the catch for the window, pushed up the sash, then hooked the heavier curtains back. The window was dressed more formally than any of the people who had attended Jeremy's reception. Filmy ivory voile drifted around me on a faint breeze from the street, insubstantial as a petticoat, the sounds of late night traffic. Turning, I saw Jeremy engulfed in the larger of the armchairs.

"Decorators run amok," he said. Flushed all evening, now, reflecting the upholstery, his face looked sallow. "Is it as bad as I think or am I just muddled and drunk?"

"It's worse." Taking off my shirt, I threw it onto the bed where it added another pattern to the cacophony. "The horror vacui of high-concept homosexual taste. Not that you might not be drunk and muddled. Can you help me get these boots off, Jere?" I sat on the bed, higher than I'm accustomed to so that my feet dangled above the carpet, shod in black leather and snakeskin, looking too narrow and severely pointed to be walked on. I couldn't get used to the idea of my wearing black shoes. "I think my feet are all over blisters."

Kneeling, Jeremy still looks tall. He took my left foot between his thighs, cupped his palm around the heel. "They're splendid boots," he murmured, drawing the one off. "It'd be a shame if you couldn't wear them. They make you look so tall and butch." He molded the foot in his hands, then dragged the knuckle of his thumb along the sole from heel to toes, making me flinch and whimper.

I remembered the good-looking young salesman as Jeremy pulled off my other boot. Setting the boots off to the side, he clasped both of my feet between his palms. Wearing the boots I was a reasonable height, still short but not annoyingly so, five-eight or five-nine. In similar boots, the salesman could have passed for being of average height, neither tall nor short—that in-between state when a man is compared neither to jockeys nor basketball players. I needn't suggest to Jeremy that he not consider buying cowboy boots for himself, because he's as conscious of being too tall as I am of my shortness. They say opposites attract. They say women prefer men taller than they. I am clear that his height was one of the factors that first made Jeremy attractive to me, although the men before him had been more my own size. Jeremy peeled my socks off with some deliberation, and inspected my feet for blisters. There were none. He covered my left ankle with his hand. "You're okay," he said, but the last syllable angled up a little. "What now?" He pressed his forehead against my knee.

"Jeremy," I said, "you're drunk. You're very nearly famous. Why don't you take a shower?"

I KNOCKED ON the connecting door between our room and the boys'. "Allen?" Toby's voice asked.

"Yes, it's me."

After a moment he opened the door. He had stopped wearing pajamas six months or so before, slept now in the nude and with his bedroom door closed, as though he were grown up, but tonight, away at an inn, sharing a room with my nephew, he wore pajamas. They were too small, exposing wrists and ankles, his thin white neck rising from the open collar like the stem of a calla lily. "Do you think you'll be comfortable?" I asked. "Able to sleep in this jungle?"

"I'll close my eyes," he said, grinning. "Anyway, I like green better than yellow. Kit's already out flat."

Unthinking, I moved closer to him. The way he does, for which I will always be grateful, he embraced me, unthinking, as if it were only because I was there, as if I might be anyone, but specifically because I was Allen and he loved me. He was taller than I but his narrow back felt very fragile in my arms, hardly protected by cool broadcloth or my arms. "Thank you for buying my clothes," I said into his hair, clean and fresh and fine.

One hand on my hip tightened its grasp. "Well," he said, "I can't get cowboy boots for myself because my feet are growing too fast, they wouldn't last six months." He butted his nose against my neck. "You're welcome, Allen. You looked handsome tonight—" a teenager's snide giggle, "almost as handsome as me."

"No chance of that." I tightened my grasp.

"Dad liked them too. I chose them for him, you know."

I nodded, remembering, smiling a little, though he couldn't see me.

"He's a little drunk, isn't he? He's taking a shower? Maybe that'll sober him up." Toby's voice was tolerant, amused. "He was a success tonight, wasn't he?" He muffled a yawn by pressing his open mouth to my shoulder. "I'm really tired. Will you ask him to come in and say good night? I won't lock the door."

"All right, Toby. Good night. Sleep well." I kissed his forehead and let him go. I don't often need to say it, but I said it: "I love you, Toby."

Surprised by my sentiment, Toby grinned. His glasses glinted with amusement. "Dads always love their kids," he said; "tell me something new." Then he hugged me again, quickly, clumsily. "I love you too, Allen. Good night. Sweet dreams."

Closing the door behind him, I heard the shower shut off and went to stand in the bathroom door. Jeremy pulled back the shower curtain—another Anglo-Indian chintz, printed to look like crewel-work—and stepped out onto the bath mat. I handed him a towel. He was wet and gleaming, drops of water sparkling in his chest hair and beard, he was chunky, a little soft, working on becoming middle-aged, his skin was pale as old ivory and his eyes as pale as steel. When he turned his back to me, his wet hair hung below his shoulder blades. "Your son," I told him, "just called me his dad."

"Well, of course." Jeremy turned around again. "Goes without saying." He held the towel out to me so I could wrap it around him and he could wrap his arms around me. "Or did you think you were his *uncle?*" he said, mischievous, young as his son. "Hello, Allen," he said, and closed his large hands on my hips, pulling us together. "Are you thinking what I'm thinking?"

Probably not, I thought, holding him the same way I would hold Toby or Kit, my sons, marveling at their preciousness. Something so valuable should not be so solid, so large, so real. "Tell me," I said.

The Safe House

WHAT'S WRONG WITH this picture.

Here they are, the family, walking through the garden behind the house: mother, father, son, son's spouse, two grandchildren. The lawn is cleanly mown. Narrow borders along brick paths brim with petunias colored to the stridency of plastic but textured like damp velvet. In the corner of the fence stand camellias decked with pink blossoms that look dyed, among dark leaves that look waxed. Roses like porcelain teacups, glazed and shining, fat and heavy with scent, lift on sturdy stems from shapely bushes. The mother, who believes her son to be barely convalescent, offers her arm for the promenade but he, feeling quite well thank you, prefers to lean against his spouse, who offers the mother a shy smile over the crown of the son's head. They understand each other, finally. Lagging behind, the father and grandchildren chatter happily together, everything to say and no time to say it.

I STARTED OUT of sleep when the door, which we had left unlatched, eased open, but Jeremy only groaned and turned over in the new guest bed. It barely fit in the room, the bedroom of my childhood. My father edged around the door. He grinned as I pulled the sheet up. Carrying a tray with both hands, he couldn't say anything, couldn't have knocked even had it occurred to him. Good morning, I said, leaning up against the headboard. It's early.

He wagged his chin at the tray, prettily set up with morning coffee for two. A single nougat pink camellia blossom floated in a shallow glass bowl. Having set the tray on the bedside table, my father turned to me and shrugged and said, I've seen naked men before, Allen, I've seen you naked.

Momentarily I felt foolish with the sheet drawn over my chest. Not recently, Dad. It's not pretty.

Would you rather I not know? He sat down on the bed beside me. You're my son. I can't be more afraid than I am already. Then he placed his hand on my shrouded knee, his lips bent into a smile but his eyes not smiling.

I held out my left arm, turned up so that he could see the stains like spattered blueberry syrup on the tender flesh inside the elbow, then allowed the sheet to slip down to my waist. Like the negative of a photograph of the night sky, the skin over rib cage and breast, nearly as pale as the cream-colored sheet, was pitted with a constellation of lesions. In the full-length mirror in the walk-in closet back home, when I changed clothes after work, sometimes I would try to connect the dots into a coherent pattern, but never could. Perhaps if I saw them as they were, not inverted in the glass, I might divine the emblematic figure. His hand trembling gently, my father reached out, pulled back, said, You're so thin, Allen! Do they hurt?

His eyes glimmered like moonlight on windblown water. I shook my head.

He reached forward again, his hand forming the paralytic claw of a much older man, and lightly pressed first one finger, then a second and a third against the three small blemishes where the chest hollowed into the left shoulder. The lesions hardly protrude above the surface of the skin, less than a blood blister might, and to the touch are indistinguishable. For my part I felt the pressure of my father's fingertips but as though distantly, through a topical anesthesia, as if the nerves were paralyzed although not yet dead. How many? he asked.

Twenty-seven.

No change, then.

No change. I'm hardly aware of watching the hands of someone who talks to me, any more than one consciously listens to each phoneme when someone speaks, but the eloquent flatness of this gesture struck me, a phrase admitting no development. No change, I began to say again.

My father grabbed my hands out of the air, pressed them together between his own and pressed them against his chest as he leaned forward to kiss my cheek. Bending further, forcing the bones of our forearms against each other so that mine hurt, he had kissed two of the dry sores before I could push him away.

He released my hands but wouldn't look into my eyes. You're my son, Allen, he said, I love you, his hands as firm and sure as ever in my childhood. Don't get up yet, have your coffee first.

Jeremy had slept through it all, nor did he wake when my father latched the door behind him. Jeremy's invariable reaction to a strange bed is to lie wakeful several hours before falling into impermeable, dreamful sleep. The coffee was in a covered pot and would stay warm. I settled down closer to the breathing, living body beside me in the bed. Never before had I seen tears in my father's eyes. I closed my eyes but still felt the light that poured through the sheer, blowing curtains, and still felt the heat of the sun through the window. Not since I was a small child had my father touched my naked skin. Nor could I recall being touched in quite that definite, physical fashion. I placed my hand on Jeremy's shoulder and angled my nose into the back of his neck but he didn't react. His skin smelled of the thick, sour savor of sleep.

Eyes still closed, I pulled him down off his side, onto his back. Even this didn't wake him. I rested my head on his shoulder for a moment, then opened my eyes. His long body stretched out before me, a calm, expansive, thrilling topography, wide golden downs and moors extending to where the sheet covered his angled hips. Sitting up, I stretched, and moved the sheet further down. Jeremy's penis lay flaccid, curled indolently up over his belly, where it rose and fell with the rhythm of his breath. I knelt beside him and took it between my lips. Soft, warm, bulky, it fit in my mouth and lay on my tongue like another tongue, and for a while I was simply content to have it there. We had been so cautious so long that I nearly missed the chemical taste of latex and lubricant, flavors I had been sure, at first, I could never become reconciled to: Jeremy's penis tasted of skin and sweat, slightly of urine, a little salty.

But after a while the dusky smell in my nostrils and the weight on my tongue had its effect, and I began a small sucking motion and to push the second tongue against my palate, to roll my own tongue around it. My arms were outstretched, one hand perched on Jeremy's knee, the other covering the warm slope of his chest. As his penis began to grow in my mouth, to go from being a tongue to a hard, solid object, his cock rather than simply his penis, I drew my hand across his chest, brushing over the hair, brushing the peaks of his nipples, and drew the other hand up first to cup his balls, a fine pair of weights in the palm, then to encircle the span of his cock that no longer fit in my mouth.

Waking slowly, Jeremy moaned, breathed in, exhaled loudly through his nose. His hand fell on the back of my head, he said, "Boy," then "Oh," then "Yes," raised his hips a little and pushed my head down.

He was still half-asleep, groggy, faltering, as, between us, we shifted our positions, he sat up, I half-knelt, half-crouched between his legs. Many homosexual men, I believe, believe the erect penis to be the most beautiful part of a man's anatomy; myself, I'm of two minds—I look at hands, I look at faces, at the overall shape and form of the body, and the phallus by itself I find not so much beautiful as endearing, clumsy and intent as a small child. In my mouth, Jeremy's cock knew what it wanted. "Suck on it," Jeremy muttered, "do it good, give that big prick a wild ride," but his heart wasn't in it because he giggled, but his heart was in it because he held my head firmly between his hands, pushed his thumbs into my ears. "Cocksucker," he said. He said, "Allen." And then, puzzled, he said, "You didn't put a condom on me?"

By now I was suckling blindly, drawing up the length of his penis which by now tasted mainly of my own saliva, palping it with my tongue, pressing down, while with one hand I extended the grasp of my lips, with the other poked and pulled at Jeremy's nipples, as erect and attentive as the flesh in my mouth. He brushed that hand away. "Don't." His voice was uneasy, thin. "Don't, Allen." He moaned, as though I'd done something especially clever. "I'll come, Allen, I don't want to come in your mouth." I pushed him down and concentrated.

A new flavor filled my mouth now, barely perceptible at first, a slimy, fluid saltiness. What I wanted was for his semen to flood my mouth, and what I wanted was to swallow it, but this was only a pre-liminary leakage. I closed my eyes. His hands grasped my ears, pulled me off, and he said, "Allen!"

If I could see my own face I would have seen a slack, open mouth, flushed cheeks, inflamed lips dribbling spit, I would have seen nostrils wide for breath and dopey, bloodshot eyes. Instead I saw Jeremy's face, excited and distraught at once, and I said—as if I might have said, the check's in the mail—"It's what I want, Jeremy, this time."

At last he came, and it was bitterer than I remembered, and I gagged, but I swallowed. "You're out of your mind," he said, more sad than angry, as I sat up between his legs. "You don't know what you're doing." He moved his head on the pillow, glancing away although from his position there wasn't much to look at but me, said sadly, "I won't do it for you." Then, angry, focusing, "You don't even have a hard-on, Allen."

"Jeremy." I lifted my shoulders, stretched out my arms, yawned, then spread myself flat out over him. "Jeremy, that didn't have anything at all to do with my own cock. Okay?" Reflexively, his arms had closed around me. "Dad brought us some coffee. Can I have a kiss?"

"Why didn't it?"

"Please," I said, "can I have a kiss? Then some coffee. Then we can talk about it, if you want."

Glaring, he pressed his lips together in an expression that wrinkled his chin, nearly—bizarrely—a pout, as if to hold back his words or as if his mouth tasted something foul. When he released the pressure, his lips for an instant flared white. "I want to talk now."

"Why? It's done."

He rolled me over until his weight was atop me, crushing me into the mattress, forced a knee between my legs. "Because I'm tired of being good, too—what do you think, I *like* latex? You think I like it to have you come and know I can't have it?"

Despite his anger, despite the bulk of him making it hard for me to breathe, despite his own hot, stale breath on my face, I felt happy. I stroked his shoulder, then along the knobby path of his spine. My arm wasn't long enough and he lay upon me in such a way that I couldn't quite reach his buttocks. In any case, then, he pulled away and sat up. I took in a good, healthy breath, and asked, "Why are you angry, Jere?"

For a moment he only glowered, glaring into my face, then shifting his gaze to my crotch. His hand trembling with suppressed strength, he touched me, gentle, tenderly gathering my genitals into his palm. "Do you think I don't love this?" Then he squeezed, not hurtfully but enough to make me wince. "And I want you to fuck me but I'm not crazy and I can't put a rubber on you if you're not hard. Okay, boyfriend?" His head was lowering, his face, flushed, approaching mine, his voice rising. "Okay, lover? I want you to plow my ass until we both come and you can't do that with just a little dinky thing." He was nearly shouting. "Okay, Allen?"

I put my hands on his shoulders. "Hush."

"Your parents can't hear."

"The boys can."

"When was the last time?"

"What last time?" I peered into his eyes. His face was close to mine, breathing morning staleness into my lungs, so close that I couldn't focus. "The last time I fucked you?" I asked. "The last time I didn't use a condom? The last time we took risks?"

"The last time we fought."

"Jeremy, when was the last time you kissed me? When was the last time we necked like that was all we wanted to do, like teenagers?" It occurred to me that it wasn't—or wasn't only—the meaningless risk of my having swallowed his semen that made him angry, or that he was afraid of doing the same for me (would I allow him to, if he tried?). It was an issue we had wrestled through before, years before, but that couldn't be disposed of: had he (his semen) infected me in the first place? Or, worse, had he not? Irrational, Jeremy never heard if I tried to shoulder blame (the blame, if you could call it that, was too amorphous, ambiguous, for its source to be pinned down), but I couldn't stop him from taking it on himself. "When was the last time I told you how much I love you, Jere?"

He groaned, a sound I had never heard him utter before. He put his mouth on mine, lightly, glancingly. "A long time ago." Licking his lips, he pulled me up against his chest, and kissed me again. "Too long ago." This time he forced his tongue between my lips and licked my teeth. "I'm still angry," he muttered. "What did you think you were doing?"

I felt secure in his arms and I kissed him, and kissed him again, once, twice, and three times more, a sequence of little pecks until I needed to breathe again. If it had been he, if his blood and other fluids had become polluted before mine—if I was ill on his account, as one might total up debts—I couldn't bring myself to care. "At this point I don't think it can do much harm. I couldn't remember what come tasted like." It couldn't matter. There were real debts I couldn't repay, repayment he would accept only in kind.

Holding me away, he looked at me with his brows drawn down, still angry around the eyes. "How did it taste?"

"Nasty."

"Didn't it always?"

"But it felt good, and it wasn't rubber."

"Boy," he said, tender, confused, unhappy, "don't do it again." Lowering his eyes, shy, tentative, he touched my thigh, drew his hand up under my testicles, my soft penis.

"Jeremy," I said, and moved his hand to my chest, "can I have a cup of coffee first?"

"I want you to screw me in your parents' house. Then I'll know we're okay."

"Yes. Of course. Like a porn flick, hey? Like we were teenagers, like it was the first time. But coffee first."

THE MOTHER AND the father wake early, as the sun is rising, and before they can see to talk to each other they have made love: In the leisurely, considerate fashion they've grown used to, they remove their night-clothes, slow, deliberate, with small pats and caresses and silent good humor, pleased with each other. After so many years neither is a sur-prise to the other yet each is surprised, once again, by one's anticipa-tion of the other's desire, by one's vigor and the other's lassitude, tak-ing turns—by a mutual and involving passion, seldom anticipated, which can overmaster the one's arthritic joints, the other's perennial shortness of breath, which encourages both to forget everything but the moment as they cause it to occur. In morning light the man sees the woman athwart him as though for the first and only time and it is as though she felt every sensation he feels, as though they vibrated in perfect sympathy, a pair of notes forming a chord, and as if her or-gasm were his, although he has not yet come nor is ready to. In the dimness of early morning the woman can barely make out the man below her, scarcely distinguish the contour of him against the sheets, still less the expression on his face although it must mirror her own, self-involved yet open, feeling, oh, feeling but uncomprehending. In the small muscles of the face and the groin, in the tendons of forearm and foot a kind of tautness and elasticity signals something, an ap-proach, an advent, a coming, signals with a form of numbness that is the precursor of sensation.

I FEARED LOSING my sight. Perhaps only an artist, like Jeremy, one whose own existence is so defined by the visual, could appreciate how deeply I feared going blind. If I were to become deaf it would be in a way as if I had been given back to my parents but blindness would isolate me en-tirely. Yet this is what I looked toward. Traumatic deafness does not fall within the etiology of the illness. My sign is rusty, I know this, I do not shape my meanings with the grace nor the eloquence of my youth, but my parents understand me, my mother refrains from snide comments, and I understand when I talk to myself. All this is to be lost.

MY MOTHER, AN early riser, sat at the kitchen table, a cup of coffee before her, a cigarette between her fingers, a book open. She knew when I came in, looked up. Good morning, dear. The smoke from her cigarette traced a different ideograph on the air, one I couldn't read. Sleep well? Are you ready for breakfast? The boys up yet?

Where's Dad? I filled my own cup from the carafe on the warmer. New since my last visit, the coffee maker was a nifty solid-state device with a timer that, programmed the night before, had the coffee all ready when one staggered into the kitchen in the morning. What are you reading? I sat down across from her.

Just a book, she said, a novel, and closed it with the back upward so that I couldn't read the title. I recognized it, nevertheless. Your father's out in the garden. He was afraid to mow the lawn in case he woke someone. If you wanted to rouse everyone, I'll make some breakfast.

I don't know that I'm hungry.

You should eat. She lifted her cup to hide her mouth, lest I understand what she meant, lest her hands say anything more. Her hair fell around her face, greyer than the last time I'd seen her, less chestnut in it and the white strands brassy. If she were less vain she'd dye it.

I reached across the table for her book. Sometimes it seemed we had nothing to talk about but books. Why are you reading this?

Your father and I aren't supposed to eat eggs very often but maybe you'd like an omelette? Today isn't every day. Staring away from me, she said she had to go to the supermarket in the afternoon and maybe I'd come with her? Then she stood and walked to the sink, to peer through the window into the garden. How would she attract my father's attention—if that was what she wanted to do?

The novel was a sensationalized account of the epidemic—a book I had refused to read, although I'd enjoyed some of the author's other novels, because I thought she was taking advantage of others' misfortunes (my own, I suppose), profiting from them, taking up a topical theme only because it was topical. As well, several reviews had pointed out how many details she got wrong, and the book—unlike a few others, whose perspective was earned—had been a best-seller. I pushed the thick paperback away. How could I attract my mother's attention?

FIRST TO WAKE is the cat, although she has settled in well, learned her way around the new territory, ceased skulking cowardly near the baseboards and under the furniture. With a little mew she wakes and swivels one ear toward the interior of the house before turning her head and yawning over her shoulder. Extending the claws of one paw, she draws the sheet up, then straightens her front legs, then the rear, rising on a small footprint with her back bowed like a horseshoe, yawns again. She takes one step forward, elongating herself, and follows the line of the boy's back up to the pillow, where she noses his small, whorled ear. Pulling back, she sits and stares for a moment at the ceiling. She barks, a small coughing cry. Now she circles the boy's head and hunkers down by the pillow, staring into his sleeping face until she blinks, then lowers her nose and closes her eyes.

On the other cot, the older boy may have been watching all along, without even knowing he was awake. Now he rolls over with a sigh and stretches out one hand, draws the tips of his fingers down the fine wire mesh of the screen. Farsighted, he could see the cat fairly clearly, five feet away, but when he brings them down before his face his fingers form a handful of blurs, smeared with rust. Near his head, a small table holds a lamp to read by; his spectacles are there, their stems bent around the stem of the lamp, but he doesn't want them yet. He turns over again. The cat moves her head before opening her eyes, slowly, and fixing him with her intent topaz regard. With a crooking of the fingers of his left hand that might as well mean Come here, he signals her, then whispers her name.

Disconcertingly, she yawns, displays wet canines and a pink tongue curled like one petal plucked from a chrysanthemum. Taking this as rejection, the boy lies back and stares at the ceiling where beams painted a flat French blue support the horizontal ribbing of the porch roof. After a moment, though, he hears the neat thump of her leap from cot to floor, then feels the resilient impact of her landing near his foot, and he sits up. The cat, a slinky beast whose pale belly swings between her haunches—not because she's fat but because the muscles were severed when she was spayed—treads paw by paw over the sheet and the boy's legs. Already she's purring as she butts her forehead against the boy's chest, then scrapes her cheek over his ribs. When he strokes her back she stands up on tiptoes and emits a nearly soundless squeak, pushes her head into his palm, a neat fit, one ear poking between the fourth and fifth fingers, the other folded under. The boy leans over her, gathers her into his arms and lifts her to his chest. Although she doesn't like being held, she doesn't struggle but stretches to lick his chin. Her breath is rank.

The boy lowers the cat to his lap and strokes her gently, murmurs to her, tells her secrets that she, purring beatifically, ignores.

Wind on the Water

TOBY WAS DOWN the beach, beyond the reach of my voice, a little black mannequin staggering against the wind. His father's big wool topcoat beat around his legs. Above the turned-up collar dark hair flapped. The rims of ears and nostrils would be pink, cheeks whipped to a flush, lips thin and white. The metal frames of his glasses would surround his squinted eyes with two zones of intense chill, and he would be staring at the sand as he stumbled forward, thin shoulders hunched, gloved fists thrust deep into pockets. I had asked him to bring a hat. At least he was wearing thermal underwear under his worn black jeans and three of my old t-shirts. I knew this for sure, because of the artful rip across the knee of his Levi's and the short sleeves of the t-shirts. The outermost was purple, faded with age and washing; silk-screened in white across the breast was the slogan *So Many Men So Little Time*. I had bought that shirt the summer after my junior year in college, before I met Toby's father. Toby was not yet five when I bought that shirt. Below it he wore a more recent acquisition, black, a pink triangle, *Silence = Death*; and under that royal blue with the insignia of the school where I work, where Toby is a starting member of the varsity soccer team and the only boy in his class with a pierced ear. Now, after all the inches in the last year, he is tall enough that when we go walking near the university, back home, it's hard to distinguish him from college students three or four years older who wear the same clothes, carry their skateboards with the same insouciance, or career down the streets on their expensive ten-speeds, hair flying, jewels glinting in earlobes. But an eighteen-year-old college freshman wouldn't buy me little gifts when we go walking, designer chocolates and muffins, a crystal paperweight for my desk, flowers, a brilliant woven Guatemalan wristband, and wouldn't walk close by, his shoulder brushing mine, in case I stumble.

The Atlantic pounded steep waves against the sand. We were the only people on the beach, and the only car in the parking lot behind the dunes was Toby's father's old two-seater. Driving into the lot where

skeins of sand drifted over the tarmac I had said, "Well, it's not summer." We'd been up to the Cape the summer before, all four of us, Toby
and his father and Kit and I, when the lot was full and parked cars lined
the road almost all the way, it seemed, to Provincetown, and the ocean
was wide and blue and warm, and there were so many healthy brown
bathing-suited people, their long gleaming limbs unmarked, that
Jeremy couldn't persuade me to take off my trousers and long-sleeved
shirt.

Lulled by the engine's heat on his feet and its monotonous roar,
half-asleep, his spectacles halfway down his nose, Toby glanced dimly at
me. "It's January, Allen." With one finger he pushed his glasses up and
looked out the windshield. "Winter people are skiing in Vermont, summer people are huddling around their radiators."

"What kind of people are we, Toby?"

"You're a crazy people. I'm just along for the ride." He had put one
hand over mine on the shift lever. "Let's go look at the beach."

Now I started walking again, following Toby's deep footprints.
The wind was leveling them off, filling them in. The wind was so cold
it had no smell or flavor, so strong I had to lean into it, leaning sideways toward the ocean while the tilt of the beach canted me to the
other side and only my substantial boots, it seemed, kept me on the
beach at all, weighted my feet so I wouldn't fly off up the dunes like a
kite. The boots are as old as the oldest t-shirt, lumberjack, carpenter,
telephone lineman boots I bought to wear to bars and after-hours
dance clubs where the wind that would have blown me away without
them was the emphatic interminable bass line of a hundred discotheque standards, the vivid whirl of acid and MDA and Quaaludes,
the lurid fragrance of sweat and poppers. This was before I discovered
how little I enjoyed going to bars or discos. An old married man now,
stepfather, uncle, a professional, I wear the boots to tromp through
snow when there is snow, as there hadn't been this winter, and to walk
on the beach when it's too cold to go barefoot. Although I hardly ever
go to the beach. I grew up inland and never got into the habit. Only
during the first year of his marriage has Jeremy ever lived more than
an hour's drive from a coastline. He claims that he gets claustrophobic
if there isn't an unlimited horizon within easy reach, but I don't notice
him going to the beach very often, either. Toby, I knew, would far
rather be home by the fire, drinking cocoa, reading his book. If I

wanted to drive across the river, though, across the state line and across southeastern Massachusetts out to the tip of the Cape on a day when the temperature wasn't expected to raise thirty-five, well, he'd come with me. Even in Jeremy's drafty, ill-heated Triumph. Especially in Jeremy's car, which Toby loves as much as I do. I get anxious if Jeremy drives any distance in it, though, alone, in winter, so I make him take mine when he goes to New York. But I can drive anywhere.

I will not die in a car crash. I will not die in the explosion of a plane bombed by terrorists. No madman will strafe the bleachers at a soccer game if I am there, Toby's cheering section. A crazed junkie in a dark city alley will not plunge a knife into my belly, angered that I don't carry enough cash to do him any good. Lena's boyfriend Ray will not fall asleep before the TV with a cigarette between his fingers and the hundred-thirty-year-old frame and clapboard house whose lower floor Lena rents will not blaze up and burn down—because I live upstairs. My flesh is sealed, my fate verified in a purple rich and indelible as blood, twenty-seven dry lesions scattered over my limbs like candle drippings and one on the roof of my mouth. I will die in bed, in a hospital or my home. The newspapers in the tidy Catholic city where I live will commit to print euphemisms about long illnesses and grieving survivors without being able to name the illness or mention that the chief survivors will be my beloved friend, the man who has shared my life for going on ten years, his teenage son, and the nephew we have taken into our home. I can drive anywhere.

Toby had stopped, and now he stood gazing out to sea. His hair blew back off his forehead. In the hard flat light, the lenses of his glasses were round frosted shields as opaque as the grey sky and the frames glittered with the fugitive brightness of the steel grey ocean beyond the surf. Trudging heavily through sand like thick snow, sand that must have creaked like snow if it could be heard over the wind, I approached. Pocketed hands held the unbuttoned coat close around his chest; the tail ends of his plum-colored scarf flapped behind him. He took off his glasses and blinked into the wind, then, turning, put them back on and came toward me.

"What are you thinking?" With clumsy gloved fingers I did up the buttons of his coat.

"Look, Allen," he said, pointing his chin out to sea.

Balancing on the horizon, as on a knife edge, a ship stood poised and immobile. It was too far to determine its profile, what kind of vessel it might be.

"It's going to snow."

"Here?" I leaned against him and we started walking again. "I wouldn't think so."

"Look at the sky." He was taller than I, just two or three inches, just in the last year, and hadn't really got control of his new long legs yet, but he made an effort to keep in step with me and bent his head so I wouldn't feel short. The little garnet in his left ear glowed coldly. "Besides, I heard a report out of Boston this morning."

"Good thing we're not driving back to Providence, then."

"Does Dad know we're here?"

Suddenly a race of gulls appeared from somewhere, from back in the dunes maybe, a raucous choreography just above the crashing waves. We paused to watch, and I put my arm around Toby's waist. "I'll call him tonight, from the inn." When I decided out of nowhere, out of nothing more than missing Jeremy at eight o'clock in the morning, to make this drive, I wasn't confident enough of my strength to try for a round trip so I made reservations at a bed & breakfast in Sandwich. Uncharacteristically, Toby hadn't offered to drive. "I couldn't reach him at Eamon's this morning."

Toby laughed shortly. "Eamon must be the only professional in New York who doesn't have an answering machine."

"We could get him one for his birthday. It's sometime soon."

"He'd never turn it on." Toby walked out of my grasp, started down toward the water, toward the uneven line of demarcation between land and sea where the sand darkened. He called back to me, "You could have tried them at the office."

A wave chased him back. I met him halfway. "I didn't think of it. Is it important?"

With his back to the waves, Toby's hair blew around his face. He stared at me wildly. "I guess not," he said. His glasses were misted over. I barely remember Toby without glasses—he got them when he was seven, great owlish frames that brought his serious little-boy face into an odd kind of focus, pointing his small chin, giving him premature cheekbones. His nose, then, was really too small for a pair of glasses, but Jeremy told me to wait, just wait, he'd have a nose like his mother's before he was twelve. Last spring we'd taken him to be fitted for contacts. Looking at himself in the optometrist's mirror Toby shook his head and said, "My eyes are too small," so we got him new spectacles instead, chic small circular lenses and anodized black metal frames. When his mother saw him, when we flew out to California for the annual summer trip, she had said, "You're much too handsome to be any child of mine." Now Toby's shoulders moved in an exaggerated shudder. "It's cold," he said.

"Keep moving."

"You mean it?"

"Do I mean what?"

"I want to run. Hold my coat?" He pulled it off, grinning, and I took it from him, and he was off, a long staggering lope on legs that seemed to choose their own directions and velocities. He looked clumsy, like any other clunky adolescent growing too fast to catch up with himself. Sometimes Toby is like any other fifteen year old—no, he'd just turned sixteen. Hard to believe. Sometimes, at any rate, but not often—not often enough. We should have brought a Frisbee, but the wind was too fierce. If Kit weren't spending New Year's, under protest, in Annapolis, he could have come with us. We should have brought Lena's dog, but she wouldn't fit in the car. I would have liked to see Toby and Herodias run crazily down the beach. Jeremy and I would follow at our own pace and perhaps Jeremy, who is healthy still, might chase after them for a little, the way young, healthy fathers are supposed to chase after their sons.

Far away, Toby wheeled around, paused a moment, and headed back at an easier trot. As he came near enough for me to see the white plumes of his breath I turned and started following our tracks back the way we'd come. Hearing his hoarse panting close on me I turned again, and feinted at him, chased him a few steps, and threw the coat over his head. Toby roared and rushed at me. I tripped him. Out of breath, I fell to the sand beside him. His glasses had fallen off. I picked them up and cleaned them on the end of my scarf.

He was flushed and breathing hard. I hooked the glasses over his ears. "Put your coat on. You'll get chilled." Pushing his hair around, I said, "I wish you'd brought a hat, Toby."

Instead of putting it on, Toby wrapped the coat around both of us. Taller he might be, but I was still bigger, marginally and temporarily. His shoulders felt small and fragile against my chest, and his cheek was cold, as cold as the garnet in his ear. After a while he began to shiver. "Allen?" he murmured. "You shouldn't get cold." He huddled closer into my embrace. "We should go."

"In a bit."

Waves raced ceaselessly toward us, beating blindly at the sand, again and then again and again, another after another after another. I knew what Toby was thinking, that unconscious, reasonless association of chill with pneumonia, and about that winter, the only time in the almost five years of my illness that I've been really truly sick. Beyond the surf the flat grey ocean stretched out until it merged with a sky just as grey, just as flat, without a true dividing line, a horizon.

"Allen?"

"Toby?" I breathed on his neck, between the scarf and the necklines of his four shirts.

"It's started to snow." He held up the black sleeve of the coat, where little fragments of light glinted for an instant, then melted.

OPEN

Awaken

WHEN JEREMY GOES to New York to see his publishers, I have trouble sleeping. Our bedroom is above the street, on the second floor, but this isn't why. The street, a short two blocks, carries little traffic; far enough from the university that undergraduates don't prowl, the neighborhood is quiet, its worn Federal Revival houses sheltering young families on the verge of making it, mostly, and one or two relicts of Fox Point's old Portuguese population. When Jeremy's away I go to bed early, right after Toby and Kit (sometimes before), with a book, a cup of herb tea cooling on the table beside the bed. The white plastic alarm clock drones to itself, its quartz-regulated ticks running together. In winter the radiator under the side window gurgles and pings. The lamp sheds a low light that gilds the small silver frame beneath it, obscures the glass and the photograph behind the glass. I fall asleep with the light still on, but then I dream, and I wake. When Jeremy's here I usually don't remember dreaming.

I've asked him about his dreams, which he reports as being vivid to the point of tactility, as if in sleep his eyes became another kind of sense organ, more comprehensive, uncovering a broader spectrum. The dreams are ultimately visual, though, colorful with image and event that resist synopsis but might be drawn or painted. No doubt the inexplicable vision of some of Jeremy's illustrations is transcribed from his dreams. Mine, on the contrary, are verbal. I'm not sure whether I hear a voice, a faceless monotone reciting text, or see an interpreter in black turtleneck before a black curtain whose hands and face tell me the story, or whether, in fact, the words themselves print out as though on a sheet of paper or a computer's screen. In any case, my dreams arrive as monologues or snatches of narrative or rhetorical address, the phrases, sentences, paragraphs as distinct as the print in the book that, pages bent and dog-eared, lies beneath my cheek when I wake, making its own impression.

The first summer after we moved to Providence, when it came time for Toby to spend the ritual three weeks with his mother, I saw

Jeremy getting anxious about putting his ten year old on a plane alone, and I told him to go too. It was our first real separation, more than a week and a half or two or three hundred miles. I fell asleep fairly easily around ten, with all the windows in the bedroom wide open, a breeze scraping the screens. A stem of tuberose in a tall glass made the air almost too thick to breathe. When I woke, suddenly, the bed seemed much too large, with too many sheets, too many pillows. The last sentence of my dream was this: I will eat my own flesh. I picked up the phone on the third ring.

"Collect call for anyone from Jeremy Kent," said the operator. "Will you accept the charges?"

It was three hours earlier in California, eight-thirty or nine. "Yes," I said. I didn't turn on the light. The white walls of the bedroom were grey, had shifted position, closer around the head of the bed so that the windows on either side were bent, then farther, the far wall so distant and high that the door had become a white-bordered rectangle no larger than an envelope which seemed to be sealed. I don't ordinarily close the bedroom door.

"Boy?" said Jeremy.

"Hello, Jere. Forgot your calling card? How was the flight?"

"I was asleep, I don't know." His voice moved away from the plastic pressed against my ear to ask Toby, whose reply I didn't hear as more than a staticky mumble. "The kid says boring, stupid movie, but the food was sort of fun. Are you okay, Allen?"

"I was asleep too. Funny dream."

"Already? Oh, I guess it's late there. I should have waited till tomorrow."

"No, I'm glad you called. Just not awake yet."

"Well, okay."

We covered the bases, how were Ruth and Candace, what was it like being back in California—home for Jeremy and Toby, for me too in a way, although I'm no kind of Californian—while I trailed the phone's long cord around the bedroom. It had resumed its proper shape and size, and the door was ajar. I was sweating in the muggy heat, and switched on the ceiling fan, then stood before a window. The tree outside had leafed out fully so I couldn't see anything but the foliage. Ruth and Candace had a new kitten—we had descended to trivia by the time Jeremy put his son on. "Hi, Allen."

"Hey, Toby, shouldn't you be in bed?"

"The sun's still up."

"Not here, kid. I went to bed hours ago."

While Toby worked on that conundrum, I picked up the silver frame. Although the photograph was no more than a blur I knew it by heart, Jeremy's portrait of me on an earlier trip to see Ruth and Candace in Santa Cruz. My back was to the sea and my head turned to the side so that Jeremy had had to tell me he'd snapped the picture. I remembered Jeremy in his leather jacket, a burgundy so deep it was nearly black. His turned-up collar slapped his cheeks in the stiff Pacific wind, raising a flush. He lowered the camera and came over to me. This was California, not Rhode Island, I was young and in that period when infatuation veers giddily into something else: I put my arm around his waist and leaned into his side, smelling the leather smell of the jacket, the musty, physical, sudden smell of his sweat, the salt and kelp smell from the beach below the cliff. I suppose it's odd that I should first realize how much I loved Jeremy while visiting his ex-wife.

"Allen," said Toby on the phone, "can we get a cat? Dad said I had to ask you."

"We'll see." It was as though I'd seen the question coming as soon as Jeremy mentioned Ruth's kitten, another one of her sly, affectionate digs at me. She knew how I felt about cats. "How's your mother?" I said. "How's Candace? Are you having a good time, Toby?" He said he'd only been there a few hours, how should he know. I like talking to Toby on the phone because he won't put up with chatter. "Let me speak to your father again," I said.

"I wish you were here, Allen."

"Me too, Toby." I inhaled sharply. "I wish I was there."

"Here's Dad. I love you."

"I love you too."

"Well, that's encouraging," said Jeremy.

"I was speaking to your son, Mr. Kent," I said, "who ought to be in bed." I replaced the frame on the table. "Me too." It seemed lighter in the bedroom, or my eyes had adjusted. "You too, probably." I hugged my chest with one arm. "I was just remembering the first time you took me to Santa Cruz, Jere."

"Yes?" He was silent for a moment. "I remember too. You told me you loved me. I'd been dreading that, but it wasn't so hard."

"That wasn't what I was remembering, Jeremy." My arm dropped. I stepped over to the window again, leaned against the frame. My breath quickened. "Remember what we did before I said it?"

"I guess we made love."

"I screwed you." Looking down over my chest and belly, I saw my penis stir, not that I needed to see it. "First time. I want to do it again."

"Was that the first time? Really? I waited six months?"

I had slipped down into a crouch, my back against the wall. "You made me wait six months."

"Hold on just a second." He was chewing his mustache, I would lay odds, groping at the corner of his mouth with his tongue, drawing in a hair or two, biting them off. "Did you ever ask?"

"Get real, Mr. Kent." By this time I had the phone crooked between shoulder and ear to free my hands, although I did no more with them than press the length of my cock against the thigh. "A twenty year old who stands five-six in shoes, weighs a hundred twenty sopping wet—how's he going to ask? You were seven years older than me, ten inches taller. Jesus, Jeremy, you had hair on your chest. How was I supposed to ask?"

"You were twenty-two, boy. Almost twenty-three."

"You called me *boy* then, too."

"What on earth are we talking about, Allen?"

"Oh, Jeremy, sweetheart, you're as dense as lead." I laughed, and stood up. "It's midnight, it's at least eighty-five degrees here, I'm stark naked and sweaty and I've got God's own hard-on. That's what we're talking about. This is a collect call, right? I want my money's worth."

"Oh." Silence again for a moment. I imagined his slow grin. "Well, look, lover," he said quietly, "I'm fully dressed and sitting not ten feet away from me are two lesbians who probably wouldn't appreciate it if I hauled out my meat."

"Not to mention a ten-year-old boy."

"He's okay. I could call you back later, Allen."

"Don't you dare. I'm going right back to sleep."

"After you take care of one little matter."

"Maybe. Maybe not."

"I think I'm going to be embarrassed when I turn around," he whispered. "The odd positions you get me into."

"I pride myself on being an inventive lover."

He laughed, and it was good to hear him laugh. "I'll call you to-morrow night, boy. Eleven-thirty your time, okay?"

"I'll be ready. Is there an extension in the guest room?"

"Take good care of yourself, Allen."

"Jeremy," I said.

"Yes?"

"I miss you."

"Strategic parts of you miss me."

"I miss you. 'Bye, Jeremy."

Just as I hung up I remembered what I hadn't told him. It could wait, but I decided I didn't want it to wait. When Jeremy called the next night we'd have other things on our hands. I dialed Ruth's number, which I have memorized—a fact I'm not sure she would appreciate if she knew. The voice that answered the phone was Candace's, though. "Hello, Candace, it's Allen, I was just talking to Jere."

"Oh, hi, Allen." She didn't sound especially pleased to hear from me. "How are you?"

"I'm fine. You? I'll bet your weather's more humane than what I've got here."

"It's cool. We're wearing sweaters. Did you want to talk to Jeremy?"

"Please. Oh, Candace? It's good of you to take both the boys off my hands for a while. Not part of your contract. I appreciate it."

"Allen," she said, severe and kind. "We're the grateful ones. Three weeks as stepmom is my outer limit. It's just too bad you couldn't make it too, but we'll take good care of them for you. Here's Jeremy."

"What's up?" said Jeremy. "Aside from you know what."

"Oh, that. Look, Jere, I forgot to tell you—I talked to Dr. Anderson today."

"What?" He was laughing. I was ridiculous. "What's that got to do with the price of sausage?"

I glanced down at my penis, which had gone limp. "Well, I'm sorry, Mr. Kent, but *someone* has to keep track of your son's health. What is it, optometrist, pediatrician, dentist? Orthodontist any day now, I'd imagine. You told me his glasses were bugging him, remember?"

"Okay, okay, you're right, I'm not a fit parent. But you have to admit it's incongruous, boy."

"No, I don't." I imagined, all across the country, wives and husbands in bed, talking about their children. "Anyway, Dr. Anderson says it's more than likely Toby's prescription needs some fine tuning, it's been six months, so I made an appointment for the week after you get back. Has he complained any more?"

"I'll ask him tomorrow. We're just about to put him to bed."

"Give him a hug for me." That was it, that was what was missing. "Tell him I love him. Tell him—tell him he can get new frames, my treat."

"Allen." His voice dropped. "You still got a hard-on?"

"Actually," I said, "no."

"Well, I do."

"Give that a hug for me too."

"Allen." Jeremy sounded mournful, as if one of those lovely, temporary sadnesses had just hit him, the kind of mournfulness you feel on birthdays and anniversaries. "You're a very strange man."

"I owe it all to you, sweetheart."

"I love you."

"You're a soppy romantic. I'm going back to bed now, Jeremy."

"Allen." One more time. "What we were talking about? I wish you would."

I breathed in. "Just for you, Jere, you and me. Don't forget the hug. Hugs all 'round. Plural hugs. 'Night, Jeremy. Tomorrow."

My libido has no sense of humor, or any sense at all—I went back to sleep as contented as a baby, and I dreamed again. For my birthday that spring Toby had given me a leather-bound manuscript book, the same color as his father's jacket, with lined paper to discipline my scraggly handwriting. I keep it by the bed and sometimes transcribe my dreams if I remember them. Oddly, the more memorable scraps of soliloquy or narrative, little chunks of story, are those in the third person, about somebody else, events I'm not concerned with—or those in which the *I* is someone other than myself.

He's the ugliest little thing I've ever seen. He's beautiful, red as raspberry Jell-O, quivery as a blancmange turbid with tremors, a fauve baby, a wild beast with blind eyes like slate pebbles and lips like a toothless angel's, who fits in my arms like a steamed Christmas pudding wrapped in cheesecloth, dense with candied citron and dates and brandy. He smells like old milk, hardly smells at all, and his hands, like the inner lips of a conch shell, nacreous and pink, with their sharp miniature mother-of-pearl nails, grasp at my finger with an unreasonable, unmistakable ferocity, cling and won't let go, while far away—far away for him—his plump Chinese-bodhisattva face with no eyebrows or eyelids presumes to stare up at me, and spittle bubbles on his tongue. His name is Toby Kent, a small name just the right size for the little creature that he is.

*AT NIGHT HE cries out and I stumble down the hall resentful until I enter
the glow of the night-light and see him thrashing on his back, a squalling
turtle unable to right himself. He's hungry, he wants to be changed. While
the bottle warms I mutter to him close against my chest, Toby, Tobias,
Tobykins, foolish as an indulgent teddy bear, and he rips at my chest hair,
frustrated and furious, gums my unavailing nipple. He lies back, still
angry but patient, as I remove the soiled diaper, clean him, powder him,
then lift him, naked and slippery, into the air. We stand in the window,
the two of us, he entirely intent on his bottle, suckling greedily, noisily, I
inhaling the sweet milk-and-talcum scent of him, still muttering, staring
out over the garden, and he is as warm and heavy in my arms as my
naked heart.*